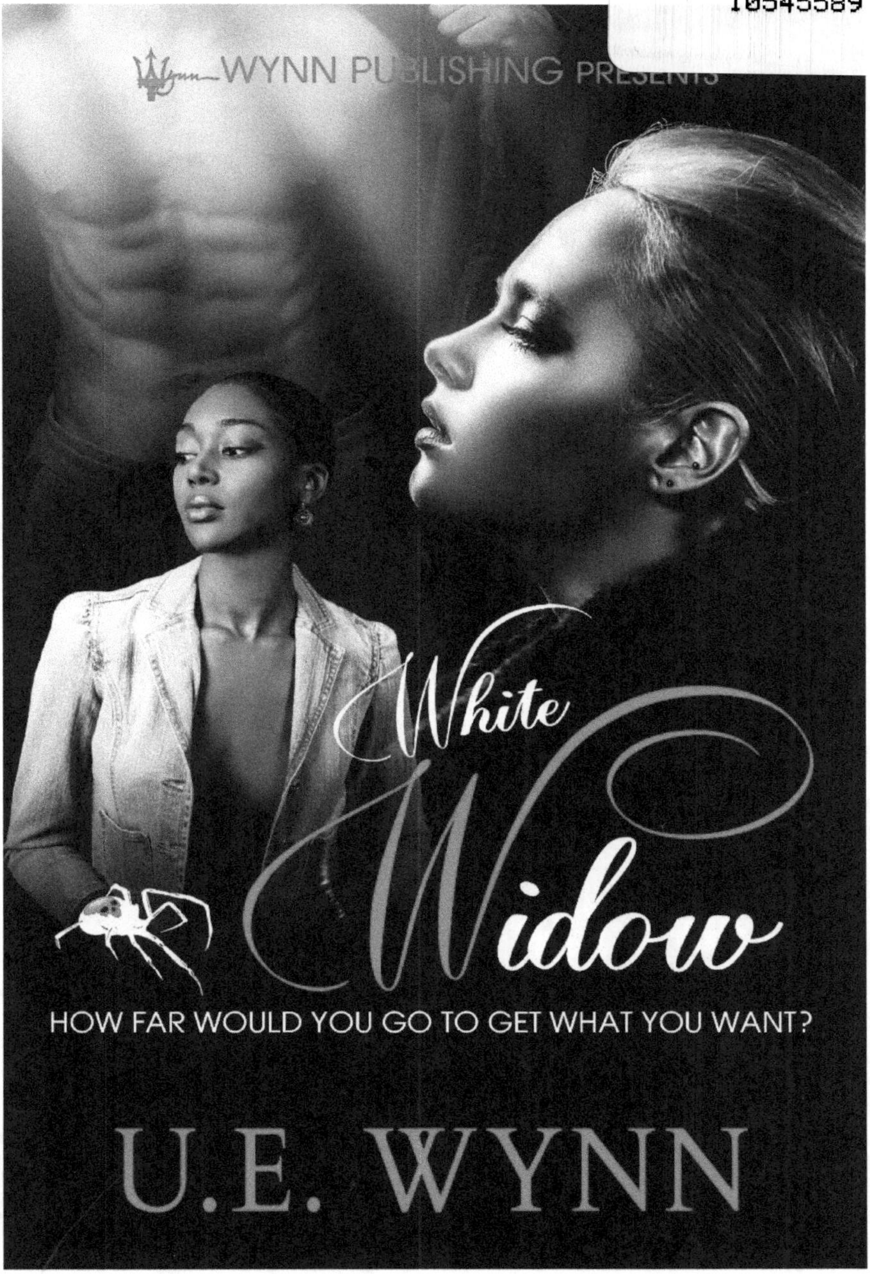

I0545589

WYNN PUBLISHING PRESENTS

White

Widow

HOW FAR WOULD YOU GO TO GET WHAT YOU WANT?

U.E. WYNN

White Widow

U. E. WYNN

Copyright © 2021 U. E. Wynn
ISBN-13: 978-1-7320325-6-9

All rights reserved. No part of this material may be reproduced or altered in any form or by any means, electronic, mechanical, photocopying, recording or otherwise without prior written permission of the writer.

This book is a work of fiction. All of the characters, organizations, and events portrayed in this novel are either products of the author's imagination or are used fictitiously.

All rights reserved. No part of this publication may be reproduced, stored in a retrieval system, or transmitted in any form or by any means, electronic, mechanical, photocopying, recording, or otherwise, without the prior written permission of the publisher.

Cover designed by Dynasty's Visionary Designs
www.facebook.com/dynastys.coverme

DEDICATION

This novel is dedicated to my uncle, Steven Eddie Wynn, and my aunt, Carol Watson. Steven who was more like my little brother, was brutally slain in Virginia early 2020. He left behind a beautiful daughter, Stephanie, who I vow to always look after. This novel proceeds will go towards her college fund.

Shorty Roc, you are loved, missed and will never be forgotten. Triple Ogz! And to my sweet, loving, caring, meticulous, and considerate Aunt Carol, who also met an untimely death early 2020, you will always be embedded in my heart. I know you are an angel that shields me from this wicked world.

U.E. Wynn

ABOUT THE AUTHOR

U.E. Wynn

A self-educated, business savvy, humble entrepreneur was counted out at a young age by his peers, teachers, and family members. After enduring life altering events that would destroy and/or diminish any individual, he chose to overcome and excel. He turned what would be deemed a negative into a positive. He reevaluated himself and reclaimed a positive position within society.

U.E. Wynn is the founder of 501C nonprofit, Save a H.O.M.I.E. Inc. and an active activist within the community. He continues to assist disenfranchised youth, feed and clothe the homeless and bring forth literacy to the illiterate. Wynn also helps in providing a positive, productive and social atmosphere for the youth to unwind and enjoy themselves throughout the Carolinas via events, concerts and parties.

This is Wynn's second novel presenting you with a page turning, nail biting, exotic read.

Chapter 1

"Hype, you It was an early morning for Kalitha. She usually allowed Trevor let his burly monster of a cat in the house. This is the cat that roamed the backwoods and obstacle filled backyards of their neighborhood, but always managed to make it home by breakfast time. It meowed and scratched at its favorite part of the ragged screen door where it had already torn it nearly to shreds. Though they were few and far in between, she relished these kinds of mornings. It was a good thing that Trevor's sleeping eyes wouldn't witness her landing a good ole kick to the cats fat furry backside. She opened the door ready to savor the moment.

As the cat squeezed its big ole brown and black body through the crack in the door, she booted it nice and swiftly. It whined and hurried on past her. As it darted past, she wondered who would name their cat Frankenstein anyway. Was Trevor saying that it was some kind of freak creation? She watched as it scurried around the chipped wooden built-in bar cabinet to its bowl. She always thought it looked like a dirty hubcap from a car out of the 50's. She smiled to herself even though there wasn't much to smile at.

She and Trevor had pretty much struggled ever since they first met. They hadn't been attracted to anything other than the possibility of true love and happiness, and their beautiful black skin. Kalitha had fallen for Trevor long before she found out about the 10 strong inches of manhood he was slinging. That man knew he could rock her world in two different galaxies. The fact that they lived two shades above poverty in a rundown trailer home off of Mason Baro Loop Road didn't matter to her. She loved Trevor, and come hell or high water, she knew that he loved her even more.

She left out taking the usual long walk down the trailer park road to the mailboxes at the end of the street. It was nearly impossible not to notice all of the fine looking double wide and triple wide trailers with their manicured lawns and expensive vehicles in the driveways. She hated to make that trip, but true to her African heritage, she always held her beautiful short haired head high.

At 25 years of age, Kalitha was a true and living bombshell. She was gorgeous by all standards, married to her handsome husband Trevor, and filled with spark and pure sexual energy. She reached the boxes and opened theirs. She pulled out the morning paper that she more often than not complained about. Her argument stood that it was a bill that they could do without, but she always had her nose nearly pressing a hole through the inky, and informative, gray sheets.

Though she would never admit it, she thirsted to know what was going on in Wilmington, N.C. The Port's opening had become her secret hobby. There was once a time when she believed that they would have faired better in a bigger, more industrial city like Charlotte than the Port. Trevor's argument was, if they were struggling to survive and being beat down by bills in smaller more insignificant Wilmington, what would a monster of a city like Charlotte do to them? They would be swallowed alive in the faster and more expensive place they knew as Queen City.

She glanced through the daily articles knowing that he was right as usual, but she would never let him know. Not out of her mouth anyway.

She delved into the local section: *A boy shot and killed in Creek Wood Apts. the day before the Gay Parade and its unwanted problems.* She shivered at that thought and kept on reading: *One Tree Hill, the local T.V. show is going on its 4th season.*

She thought, *Four seasons? WOW! I guess people will watch and like just about anything.*

The sudden outburst of a car horn startled her. She jumped off the road to the side and looked back to see the property owner, Tom Collins, waving.

"Oh. Hi there Mr. Collins, you startled me."

"Hello, Kalitha." He went right into his next sentence without a moment of hesitation. "Is the rent going to be on time this month?" he shouted.

His white country drawl irked Kalitha to her core. The way he seemed to couple it with a condescending manner of speaking, and poorly failing to disguise his contempt, always lit a fire under her pot of attitude. She absolutely loathed his always having a question about the rent. Yet he never had an answer for her about the grass being cut, that raggedy screen door, or that disgusting thing he called a trailer that she and Trevor did what they called living in. He always wanted something, but never did nothing.

Kalitha smiled and did her best to conceal her feelings. "You know we're working on it."

"Okay... well," he looked at her, his old white face, making her think of melting vanilla ice cream with eyes. He wore a dirty ball cap to cover his balding head. He spat, then continued. "Tell Trevor I said hi." He began to pull off in his old style truck.

Kalitha knew that what he really meant was for her to tell Trevor that he asked about the rent. She turned away agitated walking back to their trailer seething about the encounter. She willed herself not to turn back around because she knew she would see his old eyes watching her ass in his side view mirror, but she couldn't stop herself. She spun around and bingo. There he was ogling her with cold, but lustful blue eyes. She took every ounce of sway out of her walk on purpose.

It creeped her out how his old white eyes stayed glued to her young black curves. Even with her watching him, he continued to watch. She shook him out of her thoughts and continued to the trailer. As she reached the screen door and opened it, a black and brown blur darted in between her legs, giving her a good scare and forcing her to drop the paper all over the porch.

"SHIT. FRANKENSTEIN!" she yelled as it skidded around the corner of the trailer. Her hand shook as she held it to her heart. "One day I'm gonna take that dusty little thing to the beach and drop him off. I swear."

She squatted to pick the paper up and an article was sticking out of the top. It reads: *The White Widow*. She continued into the beat up trailer reading the article. The paper told of a recently widowed rich woman named Sara Arania Coli White.

Kalitha noticed immediately that she was an extremely beautiful, creamy complexion 51 year old woman with long flowing white hair, with a slamming body. From the article she didn't look a second older than forty. She sat down at the table and continued to read.

The paper said that she was on her way to bury her 5th husband. He had died of cardiac arrest as did all of her other husbands.

Kalitha chuckled. "WOW. She has to have that killer cat for real."

She continued to read on: *Sara Coli had no children and was worth well over a staggering 860 million dollars.* Kalitha's eyes popped at the number. Sara Coli had a regal mansion sitting on five plus acres of land out in Odgen, N.C. She had everything, even a man made pond with exotic fish in it. Kalitha shook her head in awestruck disbelief.

"Damn," she exclaimed as she read on. The business ventures left to her by her belated husbands made her an easy Forbes candidate. She was rich beyond her means with no chance of ever going broke. According to the newspaper, she was the only person in N.C. on record for having a stretched Bentley limousine.

"Damnnnn," she exclaimed again.

"Damn, what, babe?"

Trevor's manly voice boomed from behind her, causing Kalitha to light up like a firework show. She jumped up to hug him. He wrapped his dark skinned arms around his wife and planted a loving kiss on her soft juicy lips. She caught fire whenever he touched her. Kalitha quickly slipped out of his arms, smiling.

"Are you ready for breakfast?" She sashayed sexily over to the fridge. The mere presence of Trevor made her come to life.

He smiled his big smile at her. "You know it babe."

Trevor stood an even 6ft with chocolate brown skin and a very muscular figure. He stayed in shape due to his job at a manure plant called Complex Constructions. That and the side jobs he worked kept him muscled up. Clean cut with extremely sincere dark brown eyes, people knew, and respected Trevor for being a straight up and honest man.

Even an honest man like Trevor couldn't find but so much opportunity in the Port. During the Spring and Summer months, he worked 6 days a week so he could stack up for the off season when the job opportunities were miniscule, and he needed ways to make ends meet. In the off seasons he worked as a clean up repairman for the trailer park they lived in. It didn't pay cash at all, but it did knock $100-$200 off their $700 a month rent and lot fee.

Trevor was 33 years old and no stranger to hard work, but a total stranger to the other side of the glass ceiling. Whenever it did get around to snowing in Wilmington, which was hardly ever, he would attach a large rectangular shovel to the front of his used Bronco and clear the pathways and the streets near his neighborhood for whatever the inhabitants would toss his way.

Their trailer park only had homes on the left and a ditch on the right, so it was fairly easy to keep their strip snow free. His brown Bronco was the only vehicle they had and he really wished he could afford a car for Kalitha, but it wasn't any money for that. Times were hard for them and the off season was coming upon them like a fog off the shore.

"Eggs and ham sandwich?" she asked, pulling the food out of the fridge.

"Yeah," he said, lifting the paper up. "Have you seen Frank?"

Kalitha turned toward the cheap dinosaur of a stove with the eggs and butter in her hands. "He's around here somewhere with his ugly self."

"You ugly," Trevor jokingly shot back at her.

Her smile was as radiant and as beautiful as a day in heaven. "Don't be ragging on me about no cat."

"That's my buddy girl," he said, sitting and going straight to the sports section. "He's his own person, but I don't expect you to understand."

"Mannn, please." She glanced over her shoulder and laughed aloud. "It's a dog on cat Trev."

"What do you mean dog-on-cat," he joked? "What kind of freak stuff are you into woman?"

"Oh," she laughed hard. "Don't even go there with me."

"You said it, not me," his smile widened.

"Like I said, don't you even go there," she quipped as she went back to cooking.

Trevor smiled, then waved her off. He looked up and zeroed in on her plump and super round booty as it went into a jiggly motion as she stirred the eggs. He slowly peeled his eyes away and went back to the sports section.

The smell of seared ham and scrambled eggs with cheese filtered into his nostrils from the small space of the kitchen. The succulent aroma made his stomach rumble in anticipation. His hunger matched his desire to take Kalitha out of their slum of a place and into a better life. The knowledge of the fact that he couldn't, kept him awake at night. He snapped out of his thoughts as the plate with the two delicious sandwiches hit the wooden table in front of him. He looked up to Kalitha with a loving smile.

Looking down at his handsome face, she asked, "Orange juice?"

"Sure babe," he said, digging into his first sandwich.

She admired his big strong hands swallowing up the bread as he took a hearty bite. *How I love those hands*, she thought. She turned to the cabinet and grabbed a glass, then reached into the fridge and pulled out a carton of Tropicana. She began to pour and stared in despair as the glass only came to half full.

Trevor looked at her and smiled consolingly. "Water is fine babe."

Kalitha suddenly threw the carton on the floor in a fit of

poverty induced rage. Trevor turned away compressing his anger at her outburst, then looked back at her. "Babe," he said, grabbing her attention. "Water is fine."

"That's not it," she yelled. As she attempted to pour the half glass of orange juice into the sink, the glass slipped and shattered against the corner of the white porcelain structure. Orange juice splashed all over her while pieces of broken glass sprayed the sinks interior. The contrast looked like orange blood draining from the life of the sink.

"Shit." she screamed out.

Trevor rushed to her side fearing that she had somehow cut her hand or a finger. She began to clean up the mess as he stood back relieved that she was fine. "Be careful with that Kalitha."

"I know what I'm doing. I can see very well."

He backed away with his hands raised in submission. He turned back to the table as she started trashing the broken glass. She then reached up into the cabinet, grabbed another glass, then opted for a much sturdier cup instead. She pulled the ice tray out of the freezer and began to fill his cup.

"I think..." She dropped the cubes in saying," I think I should look for a job Trevor. We need so much more."

"We'll be fine babe."

Kalitha filled the cup with water. "We could have more if—" she handed the cup to him.

"If we had more, we would need more to have more, and soon we would be in a headlong race to stay ahead of Mr. Needmore," he said cutting her off.

She tried to reason with him. "But Trev, I could really help out if I had a job too."

He drank from the cup, then sat it down. Exasperated, he began to speak tightly. "Okay, find a job then, Kalitha." He bit into his sandwich again and spoke with a mouth full, something he knew she hated. "Start looking for a job that's going to make us millions so I can stop working at a shit plant to support us."

A silence settled between them. He looked up to find her staring intently at him.

"Don't be like that Trevor."

"What?" he asked seriously. "If we had two cars you could, but since we don't..." he shrugged his shoulders and went back to eating.

She walked over to the table and slumped down into the seat. Her back pressed against the chair hard as the realization settled in like dirt at the bottom of a pond. She released a deep breath of defeat. He looked to his beautiful young wife and saw the disappointment in her eyes.

"Come on, babe," he said with a warm smile. "I do all I possibly can and we survive just fine. Orange juice doesn't make or break my breakfast."

Kalitha looked away, then slowly back to the paper and the White Widow article. Lifting it up from the table, she asked, "Did you read this?"

Trevor looked at the article in her hands, then to her, "Nope."

"It's about that rich lady. Her 5th husband just croaked," she said with avid interest.

"Interesting," he replied, keyed in on the sports section.

"Isn't that crazy, baby?"

"Yep," he responded uninterested.

"Yep," she repeated, thrumming her fingertips on the semi-rotted wood of the table. "It says she is worth 860 million and she's single once again."

Kalitha began to entertain the thought of having an abundance of millions. How wonderful it would be to have crispy $100 bills to spend as she very well pleased. She looked over to Trevor. *I wonder how that old chick would view you? You're a very powerful and attractive man. You're very strong in bed with the size and length to turn just about any woman out. I really wonder...*

She only imagined because she knew that Trevor was a dedicated and faithful man. He was all about her and determined to do whatever it took to take care of her. Her devious little mind started to churn, concocting and loosely piecing together ideas and strategies to achieve what she believed was a plan in the making. She knew better than to speak her thoughts prematurely because he was a master at spotting her ideas and picking them apart. She was no more than a sheet of glass to him, and more often than not, he would shatter her plans easily. She continued to watch him make quick work of the second sandwich.

"Trev," she cooed.

"Yeah, babe," he she answered while still absorbing the sports section.

"Can I, uh," she leaned up fingering a chipped piece of the table,"drop you off at work today and keep the truck?"

He looked at her."What are you up to now, babe?"

"Nothing, honey."

"Honey," he repeated while staring her down inquisitively, His dark brown eyes intensely set in his firm, but sharp facial features. His clean shaven face, giving him the young lawyer look. "Don't do that, babe."

"Really. I just want to go to the library to look at a few things." She rubbed her short curly hair nervously, but stopped she knew that act implied guilt. "That's all, Trev."

"Okay. You're rubbing your hair—"

"That don't mean nothing, baby," she shot back quickly with her sunshine smile and beautiful light eyes.

"No," he said, pointing at her. "It means you think you got all the sense. I keep telling you that I have a little bit of sense myself woman."

"Baby," she whined. "I swear."

He took his last bite. "You know, swearing makes you sound really guilty."

"I'm not up to anything," she said as she removed his plate from in front of him. She placed it in the sink.

He stood up. "Whatever you say."

As he walked by her, he popped her on her ass really hard. It jiggled and bounced as she moaned sexily. She watched him walk down the hall to the bathroom. She loved to watch him walk. His stride was always so confident. She thought about the fact that she loved to see him coming or going.

The shower water running brought her out of her dazed like state and she sat back at the table to look over the paper once more. The White Widow article was front and center. She decided that she would take the day and learn all she could about Ms. Sara Coli White. Then, in time, she would introduce her idea to Trevor. She didn't know what he would say to her or how he would even react to such a risky and outlandish idea. She only knew one thing and it was the one thing she could count on in all certainty; Trevor loved her beyond reason and would do just about anything to please her. And if he agreed, then please her it would

Chapter 2

Kalitha dropped Trevor off at his job's front gate and after giving him a big ole juicy kiss to send him off with, she pulled back into the semi-busy traffic and made a beeline for the library in the middle of downtown Wilmington. It was her luck that she found a parking meter with a whole hour left on it. She smiled and gave a silent cheer as she hurried into the crowded library.

There was no surprise that it was packed with community college students and older patrons alike. She stood aside and waited patiently for this very cute Asian boy to finish up. When he did, she hurried into the computer kiosk and logged onto the internet. He smiled at her hastiness as he toted his book bag away. She googled Sara Coli's name and as if the computer was ready to tell all knew about her, a barrage of informative details assaulted her eyes. *Wow. It won't be hard to find out anything about you, she thought smiling.* The wealthy of the wealthiest.com website had all the goods on all the prominent people and anyone worth talking about.

There were columns on Sara Coli White dating back 20 years and better. Kalitha was more than just a little impressed. The site showed her marriages, companies, charity donations, out of country business ventures, and personal properties.

Kalitha delved deeply into the section on her 5 husbands' deaths. Upon pulling up their photos, she immediately noticed all of her late husbands fit very closely to the description of Trevor. They were all handsome, beyond wealthy, and very physically fit for their ages. If any of them were unhealthy, then their bodies with their muscular attributes hid the truth from any suspecting eyes. Cardiac arrest seemed like the furthest from any medical reasons that would have possibly determined their untimely demises. Though their autopsies showed no sign of foul play, Kalitha couldn't help but consider the possibilities. Sara Coli sure hadn't been charged in any cases.

She shook her head and clicked over to a personal file on her. The virtual picture taken of Sara Coli was breathtaking. She used the mouse to rotate the picture on the screen feeling a crazy kind of attraction her. Her body and face was simply amazing. From her silver white hair, to her voluptuous feminine assets, she was a certified dime and this Kalitha knew, since she was a strong nine herself.

She spoke softly to herself reading the same caption from this morning again. "Sara Coli is the sole beneficiary of $860 million. That seems well worth the thoughts I got in mind." Kalitha closely observed Sara, rotating the three dimensional photo again. "Can't say that I've ever considered sharing my man, but for all of that money, I'd happily join in honey."

She looked at her watch and saw she had 30 more minutes remaining on the computer. She quickly read about all of Sara Coli's likes and dislikes. She read about her favorite places to eat, hobbies, and things of that nature. It was enough information on the beautiful widow for any man to get to know her and at least have half a chance. She leaned back, staring at the words on the screen.

In time she could prepare Trevor well if he would go for it. Maybe I might have to do a little matchmaking to spark his interest. She figured that she would at least pitch it at him and see what his response would be. She would have to be subtle about it because Trevor was not the cheating or even the threesome type. But he did desire to give her the world and she would base the idea on that. Besides, if he slung that big black bat to Sara Coli the way he gave it to her, they would have struck pay dirt. Trevor's dick was a gold mine and Sara Coli was a gold mine, so in Kalitha's mind, two gold mines could do nothing else but produce an abundance of wealth.

Kalitha's heart fluttered when she thought about all the things they could afford if they successfully made a sugar momma out of Sara Coli White. She suddenly looked down at her watch and saw that she only had 6 minutes left on the parking meter. She quickly sent the information she had read to the printer and paid for it. Though she didn't have much, the info would be well worth it if Trevor would just hear her out. If he didn't, she would go into overdrive to persuade him. She would suck him off until the morning light came if he would just consider it. She smiled at her thoughts of taking his 10 inches into the back of her throat with purpose.

She hurried out and caught the meter on its last minute. She got in the truck and headed home. She had a little preparing to do before Trevor got off of work. She was determined to lay the game down strong on him. She was going to come at him hard and swift, but as subtle as a prowling cat. She would be ready. She just hoped it would work.

****

The day had flown by uneventfully. Other than her daily scuffles with the monster Trevor called a pet, she had nothing but time to map out her approach and method of execution. She hurried through the busy five o'clock traffic on 23rd street, nearly hitting another car in the rear trying to get to her waiting husband. There he stood as she pulled up. He smiled and walked over to the Bronco. He was smelly as usual and looking more overworked than ever. Yet, he was always smiling.

"Hey babe," he crooned as he waved at a few other workers who shouted and hooted their after work farewells.

"Hey big daddy," Kalitha sung sexily. "How was your day?"

"Shitty," he responded, leaning over to kiss her.

She instantly rejected his notion. "Um umph," she grunted. "You know you stank."

He bellowed out a rumbling bout of laughter. He looked away, then back to her. She pulled out onto 23rd, and as she did, he noticed her watching him and not the road.

"Watch the road woman."

Snapping out of her gaze, she placed her eyes back on the road. "I am watching the road," she protested.

"Yeah," he said, tossing his hard hat on the plastic on the floor of the Bronco. "That's what you said when you rear ended that old fat guy."

"That wasn't my fault." she defended.

He laughed again. "The insurance company sure seemed to think so."

"Oooh," she squinted at him evilly. "Don't you even go there."

"You started woman." Playfully he poked at her, but she avoided his contact.

"Anyway," she said slowly pulling up to a stoplight. "Did you really have a shitty day?"

"Nah, it was good," he returned. "Hard work as usual. Yours?"

"Oh, just another day," she responded simply. Trevor turned toward her with an accusing stare.

"What," she asked guiltily?

"What did you do to Frank?"

"I ain't did nothing to that nasty little creature," she said teasing him.

"You better not have," he warned her playfully.

She rolled her eyes and continued to drive. They were home in no time and were met by Frankenstein on the porch. He bent to pet the cat just before it hurried off after something neither one of them saw. Kalitha shook her head at their strange show of affection before keying the door open. Once inside, Trevor went to the shower and began to wash the smell of manure out of his pores.

Kalitha quickly darted into the bedroom and dressed in her sexy fishnet bodysuit. It was the one with the exposed breast and open crotch area that he adored. She made her way to the kitchen after strapping on her sexy six inch heels and he began to cook dinner. Her mind told her that he would be aroused from the moment she gave him all of her goodies. She looked over her shoulder every couple of minutes trying to time it perfectly for him to see her and take in all her sultriness.

Trevor got out of the shower and dried himself in front of the long mirror on the door. He was glad to be home and even more grateful to have washed the shit smell off of him. He walked out in his favorite house shorts and no shirt. As he turned the corner, he took in Kalitha wearing her fire red outfit and heels, looking over shoulder and resembling a stripper in heat. He had to stop to breathe and admire her beautiful curves and her exposed flesh through the fishnet outfit.

"Whoa," he spoke in a deep growl. "I see you."

She wiggled her eyebrows and walked a model's strut to him. She looked up into his dark brown eyes. "Now I can get my kiss."

She gave him a sensual kiss and quickly broke away. "Relax, Daddy. Let me get you a beer."

As she walked to the fridge, Trevor followed her. He caught her just as she was opening the fridge and pressed her soft body against the door closing it again. Kalitha moaned and he cuffed her half exposed ass cheeks tenderly. She arched her back, pressing her ass into his hands, pushing it out even further for him to enjoy. He smelled her neck, taking in the intoxicating scent of her perfume. Her golden brown skin seemed to glow under the 70 watt light bulb in their kitchen. Kalitha loved every second of the foreplay. She turned around facing him again. After a small kiss on the lips, she pushed him on his chest. He backed up under her spell. He loved when she was frisky early in the evening. It always made for great sex later in the night.

"Relax, big boy," she said, nodding over to the recliner. "Dinner will be ready at seven. Have a seat and I'll bring you a beer."

He backed away like an animal hunting his prey, but deciding not to eat it until later. He smiled and blew her a kiss as he went and had a seat on the recliner. Kalitha turned to the stove thinking hard. *Okay, this might be easier than thought.* She walked his beer over to him and set it on his right side the way he always liked it. He noticed it and smiled as she pranced away.

Trevor was the type who liked routine in his life. He lived on a schedule. He liked his dinner by seven, his house clean and tidy, beer set to the right, and his wife sexy. Kalitha was good at doing all the things he liked. The fact that she was a gorgeous brown with all the makings of a ghetto dimes body kept him right at home where he wanted to be.

Her curly short hair and precious brown eyes were all he needed to be content. Her heart, and the love she gave him, kept him happy and satisfied. Plus, she couldn't get enough of his dick and he loved to keep her running.

As he flicked through the channels, an overwhelming urge to laugh overtook him. He could always tell when his wife was up to something. With her rocking that fishnet suit and them heels, he knew she was definitely up to something tonight. With her curly pussy hairs, perky tits, and juicy ass cheeks exposed for all the licking and sticking he could give her, she had already breached the 50% chance mark of getting what she wanted from him. He tore his eyes away from her never realizing that he was staring in the first place. He looked down at the print of his slowly throbbing and rising manhood through his shorts. He sipped his beer as a cooling agent. Kalitha had managed to heat his loins up in under two minutes and he was truly impressed. He stared at the television and spoke in a tender voice.

"Kalitha?"

"Hmm?" she moaned her response.

"What are you buttering me up for?"

"Nothing, daddy," she quipped. "Just relax and watch T.V. until dinner is ready."

He smiled and continued on without a word. She watched him lick his lips in anticipation. She had a treat for him that night and she planned to be his little trick too. Trevor turned on the six o'clock news just as the newscaster spoke:

"And the local story about Ms. Sara Coli White has been the big news in Wilmington and the surrounding area. The funeral of the recently deceased Delmark J. Harten will be held on Friday at 11am on Shipyard and 17th Street."

A photo of Sara Coli appeared on the screen and Trevor leaned forward unknowingly to take in how attractive she was. *There's no way she's 51 years old,* he thought as the reporter spoke. To him she looked no older than forty, even more around late 30s. The screen showed several aerial views of her mansion and estate as the reporter continued to speak, saying she was burying her 5th husband in 20 years. He was awed by the fact that each one had only survived a few months at a time before passing away. Trevor didn't realize that he was locked in on Sara Coli's photo until he had to blink away the watering of his eyes.

"Babe?"

"Yeah?" Kalitha answered, walking in.

"Isn't that the lady from the paper this morning?" he asked with a humongous amount of curiosity in his tone.

"Yeah," she replied, turning to the television. "Isn't she gorgeous," she asked facetiously.

"She's very beautiful for a 51 year old woman," he said more to answer her question than anything else.

She turned and headed back to her simmering pots. "It's sad how her husbands keep dying on her."

"Yeah, that is sad," he spoke, leaning back finally.

The next scene was of Sara Coli walking surrounded by people. Her shape was visual through her dress as she moved gracefully. She resembled a much younger woman than he would have imagined. The camera captured her full on from the back as she climbed into her limo. Trevor sprang forward to see how round her ass was. His thoughts were instantaneous. *WOW. That's a phat ass.* He sipped his beer and gulped hard as they played her entrance into the limo back again. His eyes popped the second time around at how toned and round her ass truly was. *She must be an animal in bed to keep cracking their blood pumpers.*

He didn't know what had pulled him to the older grieving widow, but he knew she was gorgeous in an angelic way. He also didn't know that he was rubbing his dick through his shorts until Kalitha walked in and cut the T.V. off. She looked down at his dick print in his hand and commented knowingly. "Hmm, we shouldn't let that go to waste."

She sashayed over to him and dropped down in between his

legs. He rubbed her curly hair as she tugged at his shorts signalling for him to help by lifting his butt off of the recliner. He did, allowing Kalitha to clear his thighs and knees, then down to his ankles. He pulled one leg free and spread his legs wide.

She grabbed his swelling by the second dick and stroked it lovingly before she took the fat tip into her mouth. She stuffed him into the back of her throat and moaned, loving the taste of her husband's sweet meat stick. She pulled him out of her mouth and began to jerk his dick to its full 10 inches. She sucked the head hard and cuffed his nuts the way she knew he liked it.

Trevor closed his eyes and threw his head back in ecstasy. He didn't need his eyes to feel her soft titties that were ready to be caressed. He cuffed them as she moaned while sucking him with all of her might. He leaned up and grabbed her soft ass cheeks and parted them. He opened his eyes to watch his fingers slide between her cheeks and tickled her asshole.

Kalitha jiggled her ass nearly causing him to erupt from the excitement of it all. She knew her husband's body, so she jumped up and without a word of warning, threw her right leg above his left shoulder to give him a taste of her wet sweet pussy.

Trevor pulled her to his mouth and suckled her wet lips before stuffing his hot hungry tongue inside of her. The feel of his tongue probing her vaginal canal while his fingers tickled her anus, caused her to scream out in pleasure and pull her legs back to the seat of the recliner. She pulled herself up by his shoulders and cried out as she impaled herself with his swollen hardness.

She groaned deeply as he buried his meat deep inside of her wet and ready cavern. She clenched her eyes shut as his thickness filled her up. Her eyes tightly sealed, she gasped as he pulled her down on him bruising her back wall. Kalitha's womb threatened to split open as he used her hips to rotate her, lift her to the tip, and then slide her back down, seemingly further down than before. She clawed the thick, strong muscles of his shoulders as her legs began to tremble from the squatting position in the recliner.

Trevor licked his wife's neck and trailed down to her nipples. He sucked them both equally as she rode him cautiously, with passionate intent. The more he pulled her downward the more her body attempted to retreat. He closed his eyes and began to steady himself, stroking her in a loving, yet firm pace. She cried out softly at every stroke.

The strangest thing happened while Trevor's eyes were closed. He began to envision the face of Sara Coli. He imagined it was her riding him. Her round ass and perfect curves in his hands under his full control. He imagined her full sultry body taking all of his 10 inches into her hot multi-million dollar hole. How wet, warm and seasoned she had to be. How soft. How passionate.

He pumped harder and harder, causing Kalitha to scream out in pain filled pleasure as Trevor dug her all the way out. She stared into his closed eyes as he pounded her to the brink of not being able to take any more. She felt her orgasm rising, rushing to the edge of her pussy, threatening to shatter her spine. She was there.

Kalitha cried out and began to orgasm all over his hard slab of meat. Her hot, milky juices were running out of her and oozing onto his steady driving dick. He felt Sara Coli cumming and that pushed him over the edge. He grunted and growled as he let off a super heavy load into Sara Coli's hungry pussy. He pulled her down harder, nearly causing her to cringe from the force. He felt her fall forward leaning on his chest and shoulder. He reached up to rub her flowing silver white hair and the feel of Kalitha's short curly hair jolted his mind back to reality.

It startled him, but he didn't show it. He couldn't believe the zone he had allowed himself to fall into. A zone so deep that he totally forgot that he was making love to his own wife and not the gorgeous stranger he'd learned of today. Instantly guilt set in his bones as he silently begged Kalitha for forgiveness by kissing her sweaty forehead.

She loved the hugs and kisses. They were a bonus after such a strong orgasm. It made her feel like she had indeed accomplished the mission of pleasuring her well endowed husband. Sometimes she thought it was a job in itself. Tonight she felt good about her love making. So good that she would wait until they were snug in bed before she began to question him.

She hopped up with a tender womanhood and went to clean herself up. Trevor watched her go trying hard to get a grip on what had happened. He stood and followed her at a slower pace. Kalitha was coming out of the bathroom as he was entering. She smiled and rubbed his chest on the way to the kitchen. He walked in and leaned against the sink, staring at his reflection in the mirror. For some reason he couldn't shake Sara Coli from his mind.

They both ate dinner while enjoying small conversation. He noticed that the paper was still open to the Sara Coli article and he was amazed that he still felt shaken. Kalitha followed his gaze from the paper back to his plate.

"She's all over the news," he said just to have a reason to talk about Sara Coli and to look at her picture again.

"Yeah," she replied easily. "She's so beautiful. I honestly think that she is the sexiest older lady I've ever seen," she pitched to him. She paused as he ate seeming unconcerned. Strike one, she thought. "Well, what do you think Trevor?"

"I think that she's pretty," he said zeroing in on his plate and nothing else.

Strike two. Girl you got to do better than that. "How pretty?" she asked, chewing. "A lot or just a little?"

He looked up to see if she was baiting him towards an explosive disagreement. He saw that she wasn't showing any signs of jealousy.

Okay, maybe she got a bone to pick. He went back to eating deciding to avoid all of the nonsense, whether it be worth it or not.

She went back to eating, thinking he was being really cautious. Just give it minute girl.

They glanced at each other, then back to their plates.

God, I hope that I didn't call her Sara Coli or something, thought Trevor.

"Oh come on, Trev," Kalitha burst out saying as she dropped her fork causing it to clang and clatter off of the plate.

Startled, Trevor looked up. "Come on, what?"

"You can tell me, daddy. How does she really look to you," she persisted?

Trevor shot her an even shorter response. "She's a good looking woman."

"Is she sexy to you?"

"She's appealing."

"But is she sexy to you, Trev?" Kalitha persisted relentlessly. "I mean would you sleep with her if you had the chance?"

Her smile made him really cautious and he was grabbing up his shield and turning all systems on defense mode. It felt too much like a set up for him to ignore it.

"No, I would never cheat."

"Trev," she cut in exasperated. "Not like that. I'm saying if we weren't together. Would you fuck her?" She smiled, but Trevor's facial expression was that of pure curiosity and confusion. "I just want to know."

Sometimes silence was the best option. Trevor knew that from experience and this felt like one of those times to him when a man exercised his right to shut the hell up. No words meant no problems.

"If we were single," she added to push him for an answer.

"If we weren't together?" he repeated with distaste in his tone.

Kalitha let out a deep breath. "I'm not about to turn this into a childish argument or anything," she said in a reassuring manner. "I'm really curious to know baby."

He leaned back in his chair. "No tricks?" he asked, still being cautious.

"No tricks, daddy. I promise."

He continued to give her a doctor's examinatory glare and she gave him a trustworthy nod.

"Yes," he said calmly.

"So how do you think she looks?"

"Well," he said, stuffing some cubed steak in his mouth. "She's gorgeous for 51."

She paused for emphasis then continued. "Well, would you

fuck her if I asked you to?"

The question caught him fully off guard, and if not for his strong chin, would have knocked him out cold. "Babe, this is getting uncomfortable."

"I'm asking for a reason, Trev," she announced in a reassuring tone. "I'm not starting any BS, bay. I'm asking you a real question. Would you do it for me? For us?"

He looked deep into her eyes and everything that he'd ever said to her came to mind. He had told her that there wasn't anything he would not do to please her. That she was his whole world and he would swim the ocean for her. That he would build a bridge to the moon for her. That he would, without a question, lay down his life for her. Her eyes reminded him of all the things he said he would do and he gave her a small smile.

"Kalitha Gabrielle Mason, I would do anything to make you happy. I would do almost anything to make you smile. I love you, babe."

She blushed hard and let him go back to his dinner, and she went back to her own. They both ate in a satisfied silence with Kalitha more satisfied than him.

Chapter 3

The next month started the dreaded slow season for Trevor, so he was at home a lot more. Kalitha had been constantly studying Sara Coli's moves. There were almost detective properties in the way she analyzed the older woman. She monitored her moves, the places she frequented on a daily basis, where she ate, where she shopped, and her salons of choice. Kalitha had even driven out to find her plush estate out in Odgen.

She couldn't miss it. It was the biggest house she'd ever laid eyes on. Her being a fairly inquisitive woman, couldn't help but wonder what it looked like on the inside. Regal and grandeur were amongst the many words that came to mind as she rode past it. It was a beautiful white castle like structure, but more modern day than medieval by all standards. Kalitha thought it had way too much front lawn, but what else could you do with acres to spare.

It looked to be going up an inclined driveway making it seem up on a hill of manicured grass and fancy shrubbery. If she had to guess, she would say that it ended in a circular driveway. Homes of this magnitude were known for boasting such intricate designs. She took it all in as she inconspicuously rode past. She could dream of such a high end lifestyle as the one Sara Coli possessed. *I bet she could have anything she wanted, old diva. Even a little of what's mine*, she thought with a smile.

Kalitha began to track her own personal progress at home. She had been planting the thought of Trevor trying to get to know the old sugar momma, but he was no easy push over. He was reluctant to budge and stood his ground as firm as a mountain made of steel surrounded by reinforced titanium. It was going to be hard work and she was never opposed to breaking a sweat. She had been pouring the information in Trevor's head little by little. At every possible opportunity she had brought Sara Coli up in their dinner conversations and continuously in their sexual ones. Her every word nearly dealt with, or intentionally focused, on Sara Coli White in some way or another.

She could sense that Trevor was beginning to warm up and even semi accept the idea of him becoming her sugar baby. His compliant interest excited Kalitha. Just the fact that he was even entertaining it seriously made her get moist with desire for him. She knew that the largest obstacle to ever come up was his loyalty to her and the vows of their marriage. His southern upbringing taught him to view the union under God with the utmost respect and reverence. He was no Bible Thumper, but he believed. Kalitha also believed in a higher power, but she believed that he could bring them to a higher state of living before God did. Trevor was the one with all that good stuff hanging between his legs. The way she looked at it, that was the blessing that was sent her way.

She smiled as she turned onto the road leading to their trailer park. She had assured and reassured Trevor that no matter the outcome, she would always love him. She professed her trust to him constantly. She knew that he loved her and was only being compliant to please her. It was in his nature to do so. After all of her hard work she was rewarded by his agreeing to at least try it. She was ecstatic about it and finally gave him some peace, and by that time, it was much needed. Kalitha was sated by the thought of preparing him to go out and meet Ms. Sara Coli. She could see it all coming together perfectly.

She got out of the car and headed inside, ignoring Frankenstein as he pawed her feet playfully. She walked inside the trailer to see a relaxed Trevor. He looked up at her and smiled. "Hey babe. So what did it look like?"

She smiled back, setting her purse down. "You could not even imagine."

He reached up and pulled her by her arm down into his lap on the recliner. She giggled as he snuggled her and kissed her lightly. That led to some really hot kissing, which in turn, led to some flaming hot sex. It had been a few days, so she was due.

As the weeks sped by Kalitha began to notice how the sex got hotter, more steamy, and definitely more aggressive. Trevor sexed her with reckless abandon, and at times, she felt like he wasn't seeing her beneath him as they made love. It was as if he was trying to turn her inside out with the impact of his thrusts.

A specific time came to mind when he had hurt her much more than normal. She didn't complain, instead she aimed his sexual aggression at Sara Coli. Though she enjoyed their love making sessions, she, more times than not, found herself grateful that the episode was over with for that night.

When she was totally convinced that Trevor was ready, she encouraged him out on his mission. She knew from her notes that Sara Coli would be at the Olive Garden on Market Street that night at 5pm sharp where she always met her business and property managers. A business dinner was the routine and that is where they would start. She sat her notepad to the side and called sweetly. "Trev honey, you like the Olive Garden?"

****

Trevor sat close enough to be seen by Sara Coli, but not quite close enough to seem overly interested. He looked across the restaurant to Kalitha who sat watching him intently. She nodded her approval and then leaned her head towards Sara Coli's table. He sipped his water and took a deep breath. *Okay, man, it's your show now.*

He looked to Kalitha once more off in the distance, then back to Sara Coli, who was just now slipping out of her fur shawl. That fur made Trevor realize what a vast expanse of space separated a multi- millionaire like Sara Coli from a shit plant working, trailer home living, and regular man like himself. He wasn't working with much money, but he was dressed to impress in his best Sunday suit.

Sara Coli sat upright. Proud. Rich. Her silver white hair was in a neat ponytail neatly braided to one side. She was stunning in an elegant emerald green flowing dress with her legs crossed sexily at the knees. He couldn't help but to stare. In that brief moment, he was able to take in all of her supernatural beauty, and she was beyond stunning. She was a beautiful, exotic, and timeless vintage painting of a white haired goddess. She was the definition of radiant picturesqueness. She was simply breathtaking which reminded Trevor that he ought to take a breath or pass out.

He took a deep breath and to his complete surprise, Sara Coli was looking at him. His heart thundered in his chest, threatening to crack his rib cage. She just stared at him for what seemed an eternity as she spoke softly with an associate at her table. Her eye contact made his blood boil in his loins. She gave him a small but significant smile, then looked away.

Trevor looked back over to Kalitha who sat there giving him a silent shove. He sipped from his glass again, quenching the thirst that had begun to build from the eye contact alone. He looked back to Sara Coli's table to find they were all indulged in their meeting. He decided to wait a while and his patience paid off. He locked eyes with her again, then once more a few moments later. He glanced back over at Kalitha and nodded once more. He then stood and began to walk to where Sara Coli's party sat talking over their finished plates.

He took long, powerful strides towards her, then stopped at her side. She cut her sentence off and looked up at him admiring his sexy black details. He was in fact a fine African American man by her standards, and once she gave him a once over, she found it desirable to speak.

"Well," she crooned. "Hello there." Her voice was velvety soft and warm like the milk for a newborn baby. Her eyes were dreamy hazel orbs set in an ageless face, her neck was sleek, and her cheekbones high. She was beyond attractive for any age. "May I help you?"

Trevor had never been one who couldn't say what was on his mind, but in the case of the missing tongue, he was surely the victim. She radiated so much sensuality that he stammered on his words. His tongue would not follow the commands his brain was giving. The only word that came out was. "WOW." He immediately felt foolish and tried desperately to redeem himself to no avail. "I mean…"

"Young man," her buttery voice crooned. "Did you mean to say something?"

He looked deep into her shimmering eyes, and the golden skin of her angelic face, and felt that he had blown a golden opportunity by not being able to at least say hello. He couldn't allow that to be the truth. A truth that he would regret in the wake of his dying days. A truth that would forever challenge the man in him, his ego, and his self esteem. He pushed the words out slowly, but with confidence. "You are the most beautiful woman that I have ever…" He paused for emphasis. "Laid eyes on."

The women in her party blushed and the men nodded their approval because they knew it took real courage to approach Sara Coli. She had that humbling effect on some, but on most, there was an almost instant attraction coupled with carnal desire.

She smiled brightly at him as her party began to talk low amongst themselves. She responded almost immediately. "I do thank you very much for the compliment." She waved slowly sporting a dainty, but extremely sparkling pink diamond Tennis Bracelet. "But I'm having a business meeting here at the moment."

She took a long intentional pause knocking Trevor way off balance and off his game plan. He never planned on being met with such strength and ultimately, calculated seduction. Everything about her invited him inward, but her response was pushing him outward. The tone of the encounter had been set by her from the moment he approached her, to the second where he spoke curtly.

"I apologize, sincerely," he said, turning away with a curt smile, ready to accept his defeat. Her buttery smooth voice cut into him all the way down in the deepest part of his desire.

"Ummm, young man."

He turned as the words floated out of her mouth, caressing his eardrums.

"It won't take but a few minutes to wrap this up." She paused and waved to an empty seat. "If you'd like to join us, you're more than welcome."

He thought that declining the offer and walking away would strengthen his position in the situation, but on the other hand, he wanted to sit in the presence of Sara Coli and soak up her regal beauty.

"I really don't want to intrude on your meeting," he modestly said, though he felt more nerve wrecked than anything else. He just hoped that it didn't show.

Sara Coli's laugh was throaty and sincere. It was real laughter from a very real woman. "Excuse me," she dabbed her curvy lips with her napkin. "So you think that barging in on my meeting and speaking out of the blue wasn't in fact, interrupting?" Looking to her party, she asked, "That was interrupting, wasn't it?"

They began to agree putting Trevor on the spot and in the hot seat. He began to flush with embarrassment. "Well, I..."

"Please," she cut him off abruptly. "Do have a seat. I am truly interested in knowing why you say I am the most beautiful woman that you have ever..." She paused, nibbling on her manicured nail sexily then finished. "Ever laid eyes on." She really had him on a string, but smiled to ease his tension.

Embarrassed, he smiled and found a seat. He wasn't quite across from her, but could keep his eyes on her pretty much undetected. The meeting continued around him and he sat quiet through most of the business jargon being tossed across the table. He only joined in the conversation when directly questioned about his opinion on one thing or another. Sara Coli initiated most of the interactment with Trevor. She admired his poise and honest eyes. She was a sucker for a clean cut man with a golden smile.

He admired her sweetness and vigor when it came to dealing with her subordinates. Her throaty laugh was real. Her limbs sleek, but strong. Her skin beautiful and luminous. Trevor tried hard not to stare, but it seemed as if a light shone down on her from out of the Olive Garden's ceiling. He glanced up to make sure it wasn't a trick of the lighting. She kept making eye contact until the meeting was adjourned.

The people around them left with quick goodbyes and friendly wishes of good nights. They were now at the table alone and Sara sat with her slender fingers bridged. That's when he really noticed the high priced jewelry on her hands and neck.

She spoke softly. "My name is Sara Arania Coli White. And you are?"

"Trevor. Trevor Randale Mason," he answered getting up to close the space between them. She held her hand out to him as he reached her. He bent down, keeping his eyes on her, and kissed her hand softly. She was like satin in his rough hands. Sara Coli blushed at his sudden, surprising act of chivalry.

"Well, my close associates call me Sara Coli," she said, pulling her hand back slowly. "You can call me Sara Coli also." The sound of her voice, feel of her hand, and smell of her sweet exotic perfume, made Trevor's pulse quicken. She was arousing by nature and he was beyond that point. She lit a fire lit inside of him.

"I like Randale. May I call you that?"

"Sure,'" he replied softly, seating himself closer to her. Trevor gave her a devilish smile and continued. "Or, you could call me whatever you like."

She smiled and signaled the waiter. "You should not subject yourself to so many options?" The waiter came over and began to clear their table as another brought over the bill and Sara began to sign it. "Because, what if I wanted to call you an idiot or simpleton? Would you not mind being called such degrading things?"

He smiled and leaned back in his chair. "I guess you're right. I imagine that wouldn't sit well with me."

She gave him a sidelong glance. "You have a beautiful smile. I love a man with a beautiful smile."

She leaned over slightly and touched his face. "Such strong

features. You are very handsome Randale. How old are you?"

"Uh," he said, feeling uncomfortable. "Does it really matter?" His smile wavered with her solemn facial expression and her disposition was as serious as a terminal illness.

"Why would it not matter if I asked you your age Randale? Are you afraid that I might dismiss you on age alone?"

"It's not that, really."

"Really Randale, all we're here doing is talking. I don't know you from Adam, and aside from a bit of decent conversation, which could turn out to be utterly meaningless in the end, what did you think this was?" She looked at him inquisitively. "Did you think this was a date?"

He was jammed up again. She was way out of his league and he knew it. He was a down home southern boy. A hard working married man. She was a million dollar diva. They were never meant to be.

"Uh, no," he stammered again. "I didn't mean to offend—"

She cut him off politely. "You know what? It's okay Randale." She stood up without warning and he followed suit feeling one step behind her. "It was nice talking with you, but I really have to be going." She smiled faintly.

Trevor took in her 5'5" height and felt a warm rush as he towered over her. He figured she had to be about 130 lbs and her body distributed her weight with an air of perfection. She had an amazing body.

"I have lots of important stuff to do this evening." She reached out and shook his big hand softly. "I thank you for coming to sit in on my business dinner. I do hope to see you around sometime."

"Uh," he rubbed the back of his low cut head. "Okay."

Sara Coli knew that she had this young man off balance and unsure of himself. It surprised her given all his confidence and raw sex appeal. She actually thought he was gorgeous. A hunk of man meat that she'd love to sink her pretty straight teeth into. She had learned to always keep the upper hand. He had a strong, enticing build and she wondered delicious things about it. His big hands smothered hers, which was a huge turn on for her. She gazed up into his deep brown eyes searching for him behind his mask of uncertainty and liked what she saw there.

"But," she led him on. "If you'd like, you could walk me out to my car."

"I would," he replied honestly. "I would like that very much."

She reached for her fur, but Trevor double stepped to reach it first, and picked it up. It was the softest thing he had ever felt, next to her hands. He began to place it softly around her shoulders. Sara Coli turned with the intention of rubbing her round soft ass against him and succeeded. Feeling his crotch brush tenderly across her curvaceous asset sent a raw hot chill through her. He felt the blood rush to his crotch immediately. She turned to gauge his reaction which was cool and desirable. She was a strong minded woman and preferred that in her man. It was an attribute he had to possess. She was used to getting whatever she wanted and as she looked up at Trevor, she decided that in time, after learning a bit more about him, she would have him too. He looked like a tasty treat to her.

She took the lead and walked out of the restaurant where a stretched Bentley limousine awaited her arrival. The chauffeur stood outside with the door already opened. She turned to Trevor and smiled. "Thank you, Randale." She touched his arm. "You are such a gentleman." She searched his eyes for more, but found nothing.

"You're welcome," Trevor said as she turned and got in without another word.

The driver closed the door between them as if Trevor wasn't there. He looked at his reflection in the long vehicle's tinted glass, then looked up the street to the rows of red tail lights and white headlights. He rubbed the back of his head again as she watched him from the secluded comfort of the Bentley limousine.

Her chauffeur got in and she quickly spoke. "Tony, hold on a minute."

She wrote on a card, then tapped a button on the door, sending the window sliding down smoothly. She reached her arm out to him. "I want you to take my card," she said, flipping the card in her manicured fingers. She cast him an enticing smile.

He returned a smile of his own as he pulled the card from her fingers.

"My personal cellular number is on the back. Use it."

He nodded as she raised the window up. He turned to walk away as the window raised, but stopped at the call of his name.

"Randale."

He turned back towards Sara Coli.

"Darling, you never did answer my question."

"Your question?" he said, his confidence now bursting from the seams. "What question was that?"

"I asked you your age," she replied, knowing that he did remember, and was giving her a tiny dose of her own medicine. She decided she liked the taste of it. "Well, what is it?"

Trevor smiled defiantly. With a triumphant stride as he walked away, he glanced back over his shoulder. "Take a guess."

Sara Coli raised the window back up and sat back before signaling Tony to pull off. She smiled to herself as she pulled on her braided ponytail. She loved a little mystery and Randale was a fine young specimen of a puzzle that she intended to figure out. She didn't worry because she was Sara Coli. What Sara Coli wanted, Sara Coli got?

Chapter 4

Trevor found that he had the hardest time focusing on little things, let alone Kalitha and keeping his mind off of Sara Coli. She had an irrepressible addictive quality about her that would not allow him to deny his desire to experience her in ways that a devoted husband should not consider or even be interested in. There was no way that she could be 51. There was something in the way her body was sculpted and the way her amazing face held its youth. It was hypnotic how her eyes seemed to peer through him into his soul.

Here he was making love to his wife and all he could think about was Sara Coli. He imagined that she was underneath him crying out for more, forcing him to pump harder and deeper with each powerful thrust. He drifted away from reality, digging deeper and deeper into Kalitha.

Kalitha's face wrinkled and contorted in pain as he slammed his hard dick into the shallowness of her pussy.

"Trevor. Baby, take it down a notch," she said in a scolding tone.

His mind was too far gone. With the next few deep thrusts she cried out disapprovingly. "OUCH. SHIT." She punched his chest and used her strength to shove him off of her.

He snapped back to reality as she cooed scoldingly. "Baby, damn. What the fuck?" She stared up at him angrily. "You're gonna kill me, Trev."

Trevor set to the side of her as she sat up, rubbing her belly softly. He looked at her with apologetic eyes and a tongue heavy with the truth. There was no justifying it, but he felt like he needed to.

She rubbed his back as he spoke. "I'm sorry babe." He took a deep breath and continued. "I'm Just a little horny."

"I'm horny too, but I can't take that much." She leaned over and kissed his shoulder. "Pull back two or three inches baby."

He looked at her with sadness in his eyes for causing his wife pain and discomfort. She smiled at him, pulling him back on top of her. "I still want you."

Trevor positioned himself above her again, looking down at his beautiful wife, and for the moment seeing only her. He kissed her softly and slid his hardness back inside of her wet hot cavern. She arched her back receiving him with her mind poised on their past conversation. She wanted him and she wanted to enjoy it too. She had to admit that she liked it a little rough, but she didn't want to feel like she was going to throw up. He got deep at times and she hated the thought of her insides being damaged. She wanted to have his children one day.

She moaned aloud as his thrust drove her towards her orgasm. She looked up at his handsome face, wondering how their children would look. Their features together would produce some very beautiful children. She clawed the bed beside them as his stroke deepened. She watched him close his eyes as the pressure increased and the warm thoughts of children began to fade rapidly as he started to drill her again. Kalitha began to scoot up away from him as his strokes caused pain to shoot out to her limbs. She gritted her teeth and groaned out in pain. She was near her climax, but at the rate he was driving his dick into her, she would never reach it before she tapped out.

"OOOH!" she cried out. "Trev, baby."

He had zoned out again and Kalitha was clawing the sides of the bed in pain. She had scooted up so far that the headboard was pressing against the top of her head.

Trevor drove his dick into her with programmed purpose and she cried out louder, begging for him to stop. She was being punished without cause.

"Trevor, please!"

His mind didn't register any of her pleas. He pressed on toward his ultimate goal with Sara Coli at the forefront of his thoughts. The cries were music to his ears as he reached the point of no return. He felt his cum explode out of him and flood Sara Coli s tight womb. He gasped as the waves of the orgasm rippled through his muscular body. Kalitha's face displayed so much discomfort that a tear slid down the side of her face towards her ear.

She watched as he rolled off of her never opening his eyes. She folded up instantly as his long meat popped out of her pussy and held her stomach.

He swung his legs over the side of the bed, breathing hard. Her whimpers caught his attention and he looked back to see her folded up. Trevor stood up in alarm and hurried around the bed to her aid.

She slapped his hand away as he reached for her. "Don't touch me!" she yelled."

"I'm sorry Kalitha," he pleaded. "Babe—"

"No," she said, walking to the bathroom stooped over in pain. "What's wrong with you today?"

He began to follow her, but the bathroom door slammed in his face shutting him out. He sat down on the edge of the bed as guilt tore at his insides like a pride of lions.

"Kalitha, baby, I'm so sorry. I— " He began to apologize, but she cut him off as she came out.

"It's okay," she said, forcing a smile and climbed onto the bed beside him. "I'm okay."

He turned towards her, admiring all of her sexy curves. Her ass was super round and bubbly. Her breast were full and plump, with pretty brown Hershey Kisses for nipples. She lay on her belly with her arms around the pillow under her head and her feet up in the air.

He rubbed her lower back and her soft ass that he called her juicy cheeks. "I'm really sorry, baby," he said again in a warm and honest tone.

Kalitha turned her head towards him and gave him a small smile. "It's alright, Trevor. I just need you to be a little easier on me," she said simply.

He nodded his understanding. She rolled over and spread her arms for a hug. He hugged her and planted kisses on her shoulder and neck, then her chin. She always giggled when he kissed her on the chin. He smiled and held her close to him. She rubbed his short hair thinking this would be the perfect time to discus Sara Coli. She sighed, then spoke sweetly.

"So," she said delaying her words to make sure she had his full attention. "When are you going to call her?"

"I don't know yet," he replied in an easy manner.

"You don't know yet?" she asked, tracing the outlines or his mustache down to his chin. "She was eyeing you like she really wanted you. I can tell when a woman has the hots for a man."

It was awkward for Trevor to hear or talk with his wife like that, especially about another woman. It was a necessary evil he agreed.

"Soon I guess," he replied nonchalantly.

"You guess?" She whined more than asked it. "You need to stop guessing and get the ball rolling so we can start spending some of that money. She got plenty, and I know she could spare a million or two." She rubbed her swollen pussy lips. "Shit, we don't have any at all. I could see it if we were strapped, then you could bullshit."

He hated to hear her rant because whenever she did, it seemed to never end. She was like a waterfall at times, running endlessly with a bunch of foam bubbles at the bottom. When she thought she had ground to stand on, she had a never ending story to tell. At those times he really wished he was someplace else.

Her words were beginning to become a monotonic stretch of unintelligible gibberish, so he cut her off. "Babe. I know we could use some extra money, but we aren't that far under the board. We're making it."

"Oh yeah?" She hopped up naked and waved to the bedroom. "Well, what do you call this, Trevor?" She placed her hands on her hips and he admired how wide and defined they were. "This ain't the Embassy Suite or the Trump Plaza Hotel." She walked over to the raggedy blinds hanging on the rickety window fixture. "Look at this shit Trev." Her tone was condescending. "Do you ever really look at the shit we live in?"

He let out an exasperated breath to let her know that he was fed up with the conversation, but she didn't relent. She crossed her arms over her plump titties and turned her bare foot outward. "When are you going to make that call?"

"Soon, babe."

"How soon?" she persisted.

"Soon."

She marched over and straddled him and he looked up at her determined facial expression. She popped him on his muscular chest. "It's gotta be sooner than later." The pop on his bare flesh stung fiercely. "You need to give her some of this super dick you got and let her take care of us."

She tugged on his flaccid dick then rubbed it up and down her slit. "This is our meal ticket," she said, feeling him grow in her hands. She hurried to let it go because she was not subjecting herself to what he called lovemaking, but was really the destruction of her vagina.

He noticed her reaction. "You got it swelling, so you might as well do something with it," he said smiling.

She hopped off of him and fled, leaving three words lingering in the air. "Not a chance."

He shook his head, then placed his hands behind the base of his neck and thought about what she had said. He did want to give her much better than what they had and he knew what he had to do.

There was no promise of victory anywhere in sight, but for Kalitha, he would at least try. "Babe," he called out to her.

"I am off limits," she yelled back. "I am now a restricted area," she said with a giggle.

Frankenstein hopped up on the bed unexpectedly as always. Trevor patted him thinking about the next move he would make.

Frankenstein's purr was a soothing rumble that always helped Trevor think more clearly. He knew what needed to be done. All he had to do now was make the call.

As Kalitha sang and floated to and fro, back and forth through the house doing little odds and ins, he stared at the phone. It took all of his will power and all of his reserve to stall out the inevitable. He was going to call her. He wanted and needed to.

He waited until Kalitha bent the corner out of sight, then pulled out the card. He flipped it over and examined her personal cell number. He then picked up the phone and dialed. It rang twice, then a soft, smooth voice spoke in his ear. "Hello, Sara Coli speaking."

Trevor's pulse quickened by those four simple words. "Hi Sara Coli, it's Randale."

"Randale?"

"Yes," he said not able to conceal his happiness over the fact that she did in fact remember him.

"Great," she said quickly. "I will call you back some other time, okay?" He began to reply, but she cut him off. "Bye now."

After that, the line went dead as the detached side of an amputated limb. She had hung up without even a shadow of a fair warning. Without giving him a chance to breath on the phone once more. Within a flash, the conversation was terminated.

Trevor felt stupid. Actually, there was a level beyond stupid, one that transcended foolish, and bordered on idiotic and retarded. He felt like he was one of those.

Kalitha walked in at that instant and the look on his face told it all. She immediately questioned him. "Why do you have such a dumb look on your face?" She sat down facing him. "What did you do? What happened?"

"Nothing." He tried desperately to shade his embarrassment. "She was busy and said she'd call me back."

He leaned back seeming to relax. She searched his body language for signs of unease, but found none.

He looked up at her. "What woman?"

"I don't know what you're hiding, but you better tell me," she warned.

"Whatever," he said, rolling over and getting comfortable. "I'm going to sleep."

She watched him with curious eyes and he seemed normal enough. She grabbed her jacket and headed towards the front door. "I'm going to check the mail."

"Okay," he replied from the bedroom.

She opened the door to leave and Frankenstein darted out pass her, then back inside the house almost making her lose her balance. She shrieked in anger. "This damn cat's gonna make me kill myself."

She watched as he beelined for their bedroom knowing that he would be on their bed any second now. "I just cleaned up in there. Don't let him on our bed Trevor."

Trevor felt Frankenstein land on the bed at that very moment. He rubbed his fat furry body. "Don't listen to her, Frank." The cat purred his affection. "She's a mean mama."

Kalitha marched out and down to the mailboxes pulling her jacket closed against the cool afternoon. She reached the mailboxes just as the owner, Mr. Collins, pulled in. He stopped and made a show of speaking.

"Hello there, Kalitha."

She looked at him and mustered enough self control to speak nicely. "Hi, Mr. Collins."

"Do me a favor will ya." He spoke with a bitter and commanding tone. "Tell that husband of yours that the grass around here needs a bit of trimming." He spoke condescendingly, as if to a child just beyond infancy. "It's getting a little out of control. Can you handle that for me, gal?"

Kalitha could spit. She hated when he spoke to her like some slave who should be grateful for a dick in her mouth after supper time. She couldn't stand when he spoke of Trevor as if he never possessed a name worth remembering. *How would you like it if called you a perverted old white landlord instead of Mr. Collins, you old bag of shit shavings?*

Sucking it up, she said, "Sure thing, Mr. Collins."

"Thanks honey. You're some kind of sweet."

He pulled in past her and she turned to the mailboxes and opened theirs. She didn't want to look to see him watching her. She knew he was staring, desiring something his stale ass tongue would never taste. Something his old rusted ass dick could never handle or begin to satisfy. She shivered in disgust at the thoughts alone. *Ewwwe.*

The mailbox was filled with the regular junk mail; Publishers Clearing House Sweepstakes, credit card this, free trip that. If Trevor wasn't responsible for keeping the grounds clean, she would have thrown it all on the ground. She flipped through the endless stack of bills and to her surprise, found a card from her best friend Anastasia.

She was her long time high school and college buddy. At least until Kalitha dropped out because she couldn't afford to attend anymore. Her major was to be in the medical field as a medical technician or an anesthetist, but it was all a dream now filled with smoke and mirrors.

She opened the beautiful card with flowers on the front and a short note on the inside read:

Dear Kalitha,

Hey Kali! Times are good, and Dwayne and I are doing fine. I hope all is well with you guys too. Here is $200. It's not a handout. It's because I love you so much. Call me ASAP...

Love always, Anastasia.

The gesture brought a tear to Kalitha's eyes. Receiving $200 out of the blue felt like a gift from God when you had nothing. She began making plans on how she would use the money. She would spend $140 on groceries, $20 for the *'just-in-case'* jar, and $40 for gas. The Bronco guzzled it like she drank water. She had learned to budget even the most insignificant amounts of money. Even a blessing like some money out of the blue rarely changed the way she felt about their living circumstances.

As she walked back to the trailer she began to have all kinds of thoughts. *I wish I knew an old man worth some money. Shit, I'd have one leg on the east coast and one on the west with his face buried in the center to change our lives. I'd bet you that much.* She just hoped that Trevor would somehow start to feel the same.

She reached the trailer and hurried in out of the breezy cold day. She walked in the room to the sight of Trevor relaxing with Frankenstein perched comfortably on top of his broad chest and it infuriated her.

She became drastically possessive and pushed the big ugly cat off him. "This my man. Getcha own!" The cat scurried out quickly.

"Awww leave him alone," Trevor teased with a knowing smile as she claimed the vacant spot on his chest. "You know I love you baby."

"I know you do, but that cat still has to find its own husband," she joked.

"My cat's not gay."

"You never know," she teased.

He popped her on her round ass and she giggled, then snuggled in closer. He loved their show of affection. It always revealed just how tight of a bond they had. He loved Kalitha deeply, but he was deeply infatuated with Sara Coli and the idea of having her play him. He turned his energy to his wife and began to kiss her passionately. Their tongues danced around for a few heated kisses before Trevor began to strike. He began to tickle her out of the blue and she tickled him back. They laughed and fooled around before settling down to a peaceful cuddle.

Chapter 5

While relaxing, Trevor began to think about Sara Coli again. It was going to be a grueling wait for her to return his call. He was hoping that it would be soon. Kalitha was hoping it would be that night. Patience would always be the key, but with poverty knocking at the door, even patience couldn't wait. Kalitha needed things to begin the day before and tomorrow seemed a day too late.

Sara Coli sashayed through her incredibly large mansion in a satin robe. She displayed constant elegance and grace. Her style was reputable and viewed by the media as regal, bordering on goddess. She was like a vampire in a sense. Everything drew men towards her with carnal desires in their hearts. She felt it as she walked through her own home. The longing stares of her male, and sometimes female staff, often flattered her. Her smiles were genuine and never filled with satire. She remained authentic in that regard.

She loved her Friday nights. It was the night she yearned most to be entertained and admired by someone. She did miss her deceased husband, but the temptation of having Randale's young powerful body around all weekend was overwhelming. She decided that she would call him. She smiled to herself anticipating what was to come. *And if you're a good boy I will give you a taste of my world.*

A maid's soft octave broke her train of thought. "Good evening Ms. White." She smiled respectfully.

Sara Coli came to a smooth stop admiring the expensive

portraits and vases perched atop of her vintage $12,000 credenza.

"Please," she smiled back. "Call me Sara Coli."

"Okay, ma'am," she replied sheepishly.

Sara smiled and continued down the heated marble floor towards the vestibule. She stopped and spun in the foyer to just to appreciate all of the grand things that populated the area.

She turned to one of her living rooms and entered it. It was the perfect place to make her call. She felt like she was going to do something nice for someone that weekend. She often did nice things for random people wherever she went. It made her feel like she was doing even more than her regular donations to charity. Randale would not be a charity case, though he would probably be the one to get the gifts.

She sat down on her plush white leather sofa which wrapped around the huge expanse of the living room. It was very comfortable. A mammoth fireplace sat across from it. A remote controlled the height, width, and temperature of the flames. It had been her home for over 20 years and it boasted all of the amenities. Her mansion was delightful to say the least and attempting to state its overall appearance would be an understatement at the most.

Sara Coli enjoyed being catered to in every possible way. It was befitting of her lifestyle. She was a business owner of great magnitude and owned a vast multitude of a wide variety of ventures. Her industries ranged from massage parlors, spas, a couple of theatres, construction companies, hotels, and a YMCA, amongst many other things. Her investment firm left by her first husband was her bread and butter. She ran an airtight ship and at her rate of growth, she would probably own an ocean one day. The only thing she could not keep was a husband. They never seemed to be able to handle what she gave them.

Absently, she rubbed the tattoo of the albino black widow spider in between her breast. It brought back the memory of the day she had gotten it, along with two of her closest friends. That was 30 years ago and now 30 years later, her friends were having the same thing happening to them. Mirah had recently lost her

3rd husband and Janey had lost her 4th last year. She led the pack with 5 and had no real desire to bury a 6th. She only wanted a sex, a hang out buddy, and a spoil toy to spend her ever growing millions on.

Sara liked the thought of having Randale around. She had intentionally allotted for two weeks to accumulate before she decided to call. Though it hadn't seemed that long since he had called, she wanted, no needed, to build the anticipation up, then call him to her. It was the way she operated for it pleased her greatly to hurt her quarry in that manner. She liked to pull her men in slowly, and once they were in, she never allowed them to escape.

Her thoughts had her feeling frisky, so she picked up her home phone and pressed a number for the presets. It came up and an automated voice asked, "Name or number please."

"Randale," she stated in a sexy voice.

The phone automatically dialed the number he'd called her from and it rang twice. To her surprise a female's voice answered.

"Hello," Kalitha chimed.

"Yes, may I speak with Randale?"

Kalitha's eyebrows raised to her curly hairline. She hadn't heard anyone call Trevor by that name and not with so much emphasis on the end. She made it sound like a whole new name. Ran-Dale. From just the pronunciation alone, she knew it had to be Sara Coli. If it wasn't, then whoever it was had a voice as smooth as buttermilk.

"Hold on a moment, please."

"Sure," Sara said sweetly as she examined her newly manicured nails. She loved her manicurist. She was an Asian with the most immense imagination, but this time she'd settled for a simple French manicure, opting for a classier look over creativity.

"Hello?" His voice was even and mellow.

"Randale," she purred. "I'm so sorry darling about the other day on the phone. I was being assailed on all sides by things that required my immediate and complete attention," she lied to test his continence. "I do hope you'll forgive me."

Trevor looked down at Kalitha who lay there with her head nestled safely in his lap. His response was smooth and reserved. "It's quite okay. I'm a big boy."

Sara Coli smiled at his response. "I was thinking that you and I should have dinner tonight. That is if you're not too busy."

"Dinner?" he asked, causing Kalitha to sit up and watch him intensely.

"Yes, dinner," she said matter of factly. "I could arrange for you to join me at my home and I will have whatever you want prepared." She paused smiling. "Think of it as sort of a peace offering for the abrupt phone call."

"So you say dinner?" he asked, looking to Kalitha who instantly nodded her agreement. "Sure, that would be wonderful."

"Great," she said, kicking her feet up on the white leather sofa and folding them beside her. "All I need is your address and I will have my driver pick you up."

"How about I get your address and I drive to you," he inquired. "Heavens no, Randale," she emphasized on the no. "I'll send my private limousine and have you transported in luxury. You won't ever have to spend a dime."

Her words were mesmerizing, her tone so full of hope and excitement. He had to push the envelope. "Well—"

"I insist, Randale," she cut him off intending to stop all of his reluctance. "Let me cater to you, then if I'm a good host, you can return the favor." Her words were filled with suggestions.

He held his facial expression in check in front of Kalitha. "Well, if you insist."

"I do insist, Randale," she said, fingering her diamond necklace. "You will love to ride. I know I do."

He took a deep breath to quell his rising manhood. "My address is 414 Lot-I, Masonboro Loop Road."

"Lot-I?" she asked curiously. "You live in a trailer?"

Her question held no sympathy, nor ridicule. He didn't get offended at all, so his answer was with confidence and filled with undisguised dignity.

"Yes, I do."

"Well, darling," she began with an air of continuity. "I live in Odgen and my driver will be coming from here." She looked at her watch. "It's 6pm now. I will see you around seven."

He smiled at her cute accent when she spoke. He glanced to Kalitha then away. "I'll be waiting."

"So will I," Sara Coli said smiling.

They disconnected and Kalitha looked expectantly to Trevor. He spoke matter of factly. "Dinner at 7:30."

Kalitha hopped up clapping her hands in excitement. "That's what I'm talking about. Go and work that old bitch and bring me back a bank roll."

He stood up and shook his head while she did her happy dance. She looked at him. "What?"

"Nothing," he said, turning towards the bathroom. "Nothing at all."

"Don't be like that, Trev," she said as he shut the door behind him.

****

Sara Coli hung up thinking about what Randale and where he lived. *A trailer? Masonboro Loop area? That's interesting.* She fingered her bottom lip as she reflected on the information. She was very well aware of the area because she had a community of condominiums built there a few years ago. A quaint little subdivision called Vista Village. She decided that if he was as good companion this weekend, that she would upgrade him from his current residence to something much more suitable.

It would be considered minute to give him a condo in Vista Village. A small gift he could keep even if they parted ways eternally at the end of the night. She could afford to do hundreds of things for Trevor expecting nothing in return and not feel as much as a baby's touch to her financial standing. She loved spending money she never had to earn. Even more, she loved the fact that squandering away her fortune was never an option. In her case, it came in way faster than she could make it go out.

She stood and began her trek towards her large, gourmet kitchen. Entering it through a fancy set of swinging doors, she commanded the attention of the chef and kitchen hands alike.

"I want you to be prepared to cook whatever my guest wants tonight." She looked directly at her chef, a Spanish man named Chavez, whom she called Taco. "Taco."

"Si senora," he responded in his strong accent.

"I want my guest to be comfortable and totally satisfied with what's served," she stated.

He smiled. "As always," he replied in English.

She turned and headed out with a graceful wave of her hand. Sara Coli was all elegance. A movement such as walking seemed fluid coming from her. She seemed to glide up the winding staircase towards her master suite. Inside was a plush canopy bed with 12 pillows sat to the right. The large fluffy pillows sat atop a California king sized bed with a $8,000 mattress and box spring. She padded across the one inch thick carpet to her enormous walk in closet. Slowly walking down the isles, she looked right and left at all of the expensive fabrics of her wardrobe. She wanted something sassy, but sexy. Skimpy, but classy. Stopping in front of her Prada collection she thought Prada would do nicely.

Prada equalled perfection when the intention was to keep a man's attention solely on her. She opted for something sheer, a body dress that would accentuate her oh so feminine curves. She was stacked in that department and she knew how to flaunt it. She didn't want to be just hot, she wanted to appear in a state near scorching. She wanted Trevor to melt at the sight of her.

The splits on the sides of her dress, the open back, and swooping neckline, which didn't stop until below her navel, topped off with 6" red bottom heel, would be the perfect ensemble. She refused to wear any panties and secretly hoped that she wouldn't need them. She would be showing off her sexy midsection, the soft crease in her back, and the juicy swells of her breast. What did she need panties for?

Trevor would not be able to keep his eyes off of the tattoo in the middle of her breast. No man could. She actually wanted him to look. It turned her on.

She dressed quickly in front of the three-way body length

mirror, spinning to give herself a critical once over. She was pleased. It fit flawlessly as she knew it would. She let her long braided silver white hair out of its bun and began to brush it. It fell down to the middle of her back. She sat down at her vanity and began to fix it up with a series of brushes and simply letting it hang. Her hazel eyes stared back at her, intently observant. She loved what she saw in the reflection and was confident that Trevor would too.

After tending to her long flowing hair, she walked over to the intercom system that was positioned in the middle of the coffee table that matched the sofa set in the bedroom. She dialed the limo's number and the driver answered. "Hello, Sara Coli."

"Hello, Tony," she said softly. "I would like for him to answer the next call."

"Yes, ma'am."

She hung up, dialed right back, and waited a second. The phone answered after one ring.

"Hello."

"Hello, Randale," she cooed sexily. "What would you like to have for dinner?"

"You," he replied, catching her by surprise. He couldn't imagine how much boldness turned her on. "Are you on the menu for tonight?"

She smiled wickedly liking the way the exchange was headed. "I make the menu or better stated," she paused, then breathed out. "I am the menu."

He liked that thought.

She repeated her question. "Now what would you like to eat? By that I mean sustenance. What would you like, darling?"

"I'm open to your suggestion. Surprise me," he replied, placing the ball back in her court.

"So you like to relinquish control, huh?"

"Sometimes," Trevor said, leaning back into the plush seats of the limo.

"You don't mind if the woman leads," she teased?

"I encourage it," he kept his game flowing.

"I think that a certain level of subservience in a man is a real turn on at times," she teased back. "But nothing compares to the dominance of a powerful man."

His next statement caused her to clench the muscles in her womb. His words were provocatively spoken. "When it's time for me to take control Sara Coli," he paused for emphasis. "I am very, very well equipped, and more than capable of delivering the highest desired results." He chuckled a little. "I'm extremely well balanced."

Sara Coli ate that up. She blushed and cleared her throat. "Oh, how I do love balance." She let a brief silence pass between them. "I'll have something delightful prepared for you. I will see you soon, Randale."

The line went dead and Trevor hung up the phone, and ran his sweaty palms down his pant legs. He was amazed by the effect she had on him. He was, above all, anxious to get to her. Her voice echoing in his ear made him think she was naked in a tub filled with warm honey, milk or at the least covered in some fruity body oil. His vivid imagination gave him a lift down below and he had to force himself to relax. He was in the back of her plush Bentley limo alone and she was still at least 20 minutes away.

He rubbed his face, then smoothed the front of his suit. He looked down at his slightly shaking hands. *This is not good,* he thought. *It's only one woman man.* He mentally chastised himself. *Have a little self control man.* Trevor was trying hard to get his body under control. *Think about Kalitha. Remember, you're doing this for your wife.* The moment he tried to think about her, Sara Coli s voice bombarded his mental space, pushing Kalitha to the dark recesses of his mind. He knew without a shadow of a doubt that it was not a good sign.

He and Kalitha had been married for four years and he met Sara Coli only four months ago. He told himself that he had to remember what he was there to do and not do the complete opposite. He was a sensible thinker, so it wasn't hard to admit that he wanted Sara Coli in the worst way. But more than that, he wanted to make a better life for his wife. He needed to accomplish what he had set out to do. The problem lay in the unfortunates, which was he could end up falling for Sara Coli. Though he was a faithful man physically, he realized that a certain degree of strength was needed inside as well as out. Sara Coli was a phenomenal creature and he was just a man.

He looked out the tinted glass window and took a deep breath. How good could the sex really be? She's 51 for Christs sake. He chuckled again realizing that he was having a debatable conversation with himself.

"Relax man," he muttered. "She's only an older woman. Pull yourself together."

He stopped and mentally laughed at himself. Not only was he debating in his mind, but he was talking to himself loudly. He finally relaxed and just waited the ride out. He would be there soon. Once he found a zone where he was comfortable, he realized that the limo was making a slow incline. It came to a smooth halt and a moment later the driver opened the door.

"I hope your ride was smooth, sir."

"It was, thank you," he got out saying.

He looked up and took in the palace like structure. It looked even more extraordinary up close. His eyes settled on a male servant at the front door holding it open for him as the limo driver smiled and nodded in the direction of the house.

They began to climb the five large, wide steps towards the porch with its biblical pillars shooting up towards the overhang. Trevor was in awe. The male servant gave a curt bow to them both. His tuxedo was pressed and clean.

"Tony. Mr. Mason. Ms. Sara Coli awaits you."

Trevor was blown away by the sheer beauty of the home. The size of it was huge and mysterious, an enigma. It didn't look half as big on the television behind the reporter. As he crossed the threshold, amazement overtook him like a gigantic wave of water. A tsunami of sights, sounds, and smells greeted him in the large foyer. The pure and untainted design of the double winding staircase was impeccably done.

He was led through to a massive living room with a beautiful dining room off to the side. Beautifully sculpted chandeliers hung gracefully from cathedral ceilings. Oversized windows with semi-stained glass sprinkled the portrait spewed walls. He was truly in awe.

He was led into an even larger living room with the grandfather of all fireplaces and the whitest elongated leather wrap around sofa he had ever seen. It was a picture of splendor and calculated comfort. There was even a polar bear rug in front of the fireplace looking dwarfed in comparison.

The man servant spoke. "Make yourself at home, sir."

Trevor turned to him and spoke honestly. "Now, that would be impossible."

The servant smiled knowingly. "Yes. I understand very well what you mean, sir." He leaned in closer to Trevor. "I work here and still it's hard to believe." He straightened back up and curtly bowed his head, then disappeared out of the living room leaving Trevor to himself.

Trevor turned in a circle. *Wow. This is incredible.* He walked over to the fireplace avoiding the bear skin rug all together. He looked up to admire and take in all the beautiful paintings on the walls. Paintings of the house itself, a waterfall, a mountain ravine, and a fabulously accurate portrait of Sara Coli herself. He stared at it for a long moment, then forced himself to look away. He smoothed the front of his suit down again, hoping like hell that she wouldn't notice how cheap it was. It was a $100 suit and he had only bought it because it was on sale at an unbeatable 60% off. It was one of two for him; one for church, the other for funerals.

He continued to walk the large room looking at all the expensive works of art. He imagined that one of them cost more than he had ever earned. Try as he may, he could not help but make his way back to the portrait of her. He rubbed his short brushed hair and continued to examine her on the wall. He never heard her walk in.

Sara Coli watched him for a moment. He was visually absorbing her portrait and she liked the way he looked at it with such intense admiration. She smiled and made her presence known.

"Randale."

Trevor turned, his eyes lighting up at the mere sight of her.

He could see through her dress right to the swells of her breast, the fleshy nub prints of her nipples, and down to the trimmed hair of her very private part. The dress hugged her hips splitting at the sides with the neckline swooping in a sharp V to below her belly button, but still managing to hug her curvaceous body.

She walked gracefully and provocatively at the same time. He could not pull his eyes away from her angelic face with its long flowing white, silver hair cascading down her back. Her tattoo was demanding to be seen between the swells of her plump breast.

She reached him swiftly, and standing on her tiptoes, she pecked him lovingly on the cheek. His heart slammed hard in his chest, pounding violently from the smell of her perfume and the feel of her hands perched on top of his shoulders.

He pushed his words out, thankfully without a croak. "Hello," he said, her moist lips leaving his flesh seared. "You look ravishing."

She spun to show him that she was completely naked underneath what she wore. He took in her lovely back and plump ass through the sheer dress. As she completed her turn, he had the urge to lick her on her spider tattoo.

She spoke enticingly. "I hope you like Oysters Rockefeller because it's absolutely my favorite."

All he could do was nod as he looked her up and down, stopping at her perky nipple prints. She noticed and flirted by jiggling them in his face a bit as she spoke. "Would you like to eat in the dining room or in the heated indoor pool?"

Trevor couldn't concentrate with her there nearly naked in front of him. His blood was rushing to the wrong part of his body. He missed her question completely. "Excuse me?"

Sara Coli smiled, grabbing his hand. "Don't worry honey." She led him out into the hall and guided him down the long marble floor hallway. "I will make all of the decisions this weekend. You just enjoy yourself."

As he followed her, he locked in on her phat round ass cheeks bouncing juicily in front of him with each step she took. Her ass was causing him to miss every single word she said. He could only see her shoulders, slender back, her golden flawless skin, and her ass.

Sara Coli loved to be admired and Trevor was putting in overtime. She looked back over her shoulder to find him keyed in on her luscious bubble butt. She watched him watching her and she wanted him to enjoy the view. She had so much more to show him that night. She kept on talking. "I was really thinking a trip this weekend would be nice. Some place not too far. Would you like to go with me, Randale?"

"Huh?" He snapped back to reality. "Uh, sure," he stammered, not knowing what she had asked. He didn't care what she was saying as long as she bounced that lovely booty in front of him like that.

She didn't care whether he was paying attention or not. She had it in her mind to show him possibly the best 72 hours of his life.

They reached the indoor pool outer area. She turned and backed inside of the area holding his hand. "This is where I come to relax."

The door opened to a gorgeous pool with stunning decor and statues lining the walls. A large cherry oak wood cabinet sat at the back side near the shallowest water. A wet bar sat at the far end of the pool. The water in the pool was tinted a champagne color instead of the normal blue he was used to. He could see the strategic lighting playing a major part in the water's intriguing hue.

She smiled and waved towards the pool. "Our food will be brought to us."

She turned and headed towards the large cabinet where the heated towels and robes were kept warm and ready for use. She stopped at a control panel on the wall near the cabinet and began to press the keypad. He walked slowly towards her as she spoke.

"I'm changing the pool's temperature to something warmer."

He looked up as the lights got partially dimmer. "This is really nice, Sara Coli," he commented, taking it all in. He'd never seen such amenities.

"Mere material things, darling," she said as she turned to the large cabinet. Once opened, it revealed the heated towels and robes. "They could never measure up to intangible things such as love, desire, and lust." She smiled. "Those are the things we need. This..." She pointed to the pool with a flourishing wave. "Is only a tool, bringing two people who have the intangibles closer."

Trevor could not wrap his mind around all of the details about Sara Coli that made her stand out. She was unearthly and a seemed unreal, almost like an angel to him. He half expected to wake up next to Kalitha at home any minute now.

He smiled warmly. "You are so intricately webbed Sara Coli. How does a man find his way into the center of your world?"

She visually deliberated on that. "First, he would have to get into the pool with me. The second thing will be revealed later."

"You're being very mysterious."

"And you're very handsome," she wistfully returned. "But I'm sure you already knew that."

"I thought flattering was my job."

"Darling, it's the new millennium. Things have changed." She padded over to the steps leading into the pool.

Trevor followed her slowly. "Is there something I should change into?"

"No," she said, stepping out of her heels. "You can get in the way you're dressed. It's not wet darling. It isn't really water." He smiled her sarcasm off and she continued. "Me?" she cooed slipping out of her dress, letting it fall to the floor. "I'm wearing my skin."

She stepped out of her dress showing off her bare flesh. He watched as she walked the steps down into the warm water. She was beautiful under the dim lights. Her breast bounced with every step as he took her in, memorizing every feminine detail. His eyes stopped at her silvery white patch of pubic hairs and his dick began to fill quickly as she waded over in the waist high water.

She wasn't a bit ashamed of her body and wanted him to enjoy all of it. Her wet hair clung to her lower back. "Are you coming in? The water feels warm and refreshing. Don't tell me that you're afraid or ashamed of your body, Randale," she teased.

His mind snapped back from its daze with her words. "No," he said, as he began removing his clothes. "Of course not."

He walked over to the steps and took everything off, but his boxers. She turned from the wet bar and smiled. "Ah, ah, ah, Randale. Come as you were born," she encouraged.

He felt like a child in the presence of a grown woman who was asking to see his stuff. He had been with lots of women in his life, but here he was being punked by Sara Coli. He wasn't shy by a long shot and he was most certainly not ashamed of his size. So what was the problem, he wondered. She was. Sara Coli was a big, enormous problem. She was too sexy to be too old for him, and too rich to be into him. She was the embodiment of unrelenting intimidation and he hated to be intimidated with a passion.

His moment of courage rose like a mighty river and flooded the banks of his mind. He reacted with a rush of confidence and pulled his boxers down to his ankles and stepped out of them. "As you wish."

The water was warm as a baby's bath. Instantly, Sara Coli's eyes took in his muscular sculpted body, then lingered at his half flaccid penis. She slowly licked her lips. *Wow!* Raising her eyebrows, she watched him until the lavender water covered him at his toned waist. She turned back to the bar heavy in thought. *My goodness. The Lord sure knows how to piece them together.*

She began to mix them up a drink as he waded over to her. "Uh, Randale?"

"Yes?" he responded from beside her.

"Um," she said, looking at him from the waist up. She admired his washboard abs to his brawny shoulders, chest, and arms. She lost her train of thought and giggled girlishly.

"What?" he smiled curiously.

"Wow," she returned. "You are blessed."

Trevor blushed a little, embarrassed.

"Have you ever had a White Widow?"

The question sent him reeling off balance. She was a widow and her last name was White, or was she asking him if he had been with a white woman whose husband had died? Was she talking about that special high grade weed? He was confused.

"Excuse me," he said simply. "I don't grasp your question."

She gave him a serious look. "It's a drink, Randale. I don't believe you've ever had someone make you a White Widow before," she crooned in a sexual tone.

She turned to the bar showing him her back and long flowing white hair. He had the urge to kiss her on her shoulder, but fought against it. He wanted to do much more than that to her.

"No, I don't believe that I ever have. I'm willing to try anything once."

Glancing over her shoulder she asked, "Adventurous or experimental?"

"I don't know," he smiled. "Maybe a little bit of both."

"Great," she spun around holding two glasses of a milky white liquid.

Trevor took his glass, then shot a cursory glance at the wet bar to see what in the selection could have turned it that color. He found nothing and thought it strange.

"You'll love it. I know I do."

He looked down at her perky wet breast and almost forgot his question. "Uh, what exactly turned it white?"

"Spider venom," she said, sipping it.

He looked into his glass curiously. "Did I just hear you say spider venom?"

"Um hmm," she hummed. "Siberian White Widow venom with a few herbs mixed in to counteract the poison. It's extremely potent, darling."

He watched her sip hers again. "Siberian White Widow?"

"Yes," she encouraged. "Taste it. It's delicious."

He smiled with defiance in his eyes. He really didn't believe that she was telling the truth. He had to at least keep the joke going. He spoke his mind. "There is no such thing as a White Widow Spider. And Siberia, isn't that Russia?"

"Yes, that's in Russia," she sipped it again. "And yes, there is a such thing as a White Widow Spider."

Trevor smiled and sipped the drink. It was sweet with a bitter bite at the end. He took a bigger gulp this time and Sara Coli smiled wide. He could taste the liquor behind the strange tasting drink. It really did taste good.

She touched his chest. "Isn't it delectable?"

He nodded his agreement and sipped it again as he watched her watching him. She reached for a little silver bell on the bar and rang it. "Dinner will be here in just a moment."

She turned back to him with her glass. "You're going to love that too." She held her glass up. "Toast."

He smiled and let his glass clink lightly off hers.

****

Kalitha sat at the dinner table picking over her plate. She didn't know why she was in such a mopey mood. She was getting what she asked for. She looked over to the photo of her and Trevor on the fridge. It was of them at the beach on a beautiful summer day. She wished every day could be as good as that one was. At the feel of something brushing her feet, she snatched her knees upward banging them painfully on the bottom of the table. She screamed bending to look under the table. Pain shot through her legs as she saw Frankenstein watching her sinisterly.

"Ughh!" she yelled. "You little monster!"

The cat darted away seeking sanctuary from her wrath. She hopped up to chase it, but stopped short. She couldn't hurt Trevor's cat. To hurt it would be to hurt Trevor. She folded her arms and pouted in defeat. She would pay it back for the pain and trouble it caused, but today wouldn't be that day. She leaned against the counter wondering what Trevor and the old hag was doing. She'd bet he was rubbing Bengay on her swollen joints right now or doing a 5000 word puzzle. Or something boring like that. She laughed at her thoughts. He would be home soon enough.

****

Sara Coli smiled when she looked up to see the wait staff bringing in their meals. They were on large silver platters with covers on them. Trevor thought it was crazy how the shiny dinner wear reflected the staff and the pool. It was a weird visual contrast.

They sat them down at the bar and not one of them seemed to notice their nakedness. The food was exposed and revealed 5 star restaurant styled dishes. The staff turned and disappeared without a word or a glance in their direction.

Trevor smiled about it. "Wow, it must be really expensive to find help like that nowadays."

"No," she replied, picking up an Oyster Rockefeller. "You just have to pick the right pools to hire from."

She slurped the contents out of the shell and gave a show of how delicious it was. She sat the shell back on the tray. "Ummm," she hummed licking her thumb and forefinger.

Trevor followed suit. He had never eaten anything so expensive. He didn't know if shrimp counted, but he didn't think so. He slurped out the contents and it tasted wonderful. It was soft, creamy, cheesy, and wrapped in a tiny strip of bacon.

"Mmmm," he moaned. "This is delicious, Sara Coli."

"I know isn't it?"

They enjoyed a few more Oyster Rockefellers over light conversation. Trevor couldn't get past how beautiful she was. How she kept him on edge and sexually charged with her words and movements. He also couldn't let go of the thought about the mystical spiders she had introduced him to.

He watched as she took a dip under the water and came back up with her hair lying against her head and cascading down her back and plump ass. Water ran down her golden skin in small little streams. She opened her eyes and looked up at him.

A weakness set in his bones and inflamed his loins with carnal desire. He had to say something or risk irritating her in a way that could earn him a tragic rejection. He steered his thoughts back to the spiders, but his mind would not allow him to not tell her how she looked.

"Sara Coli," he said, causing her to give him her full attention. "You are the most beautiful woman that I have ever laid eyes on."

She smiled. "I remember you saying that not long ago," she teased.

"It's completely true. You're... You're amazing."

She blushed, something she didn't do often. There weren't many men who could make her smooth high cheeks flush red. Her attraction to him was solid. She looked back up to him. His smile was one of true luster.

"So," he continued. "You were telling me that there are white Black Widow Spiders in Siberia?"

"No, Randale," she said, correcting him. "I'm telling you that there are White Widow Spiders in Siberia. Their venom is 100 times more potent and powerful than a normal Black Widow Spider. And, they're also about 100 times bigger."

His laugh came from deep down, rumbling up from the seat of his disbelief. She smiled at the doubting tone of it.

"Fine," she said plainly. "One day, I'll show you and you can see them with your own eyes."

"You do have a weird sense of humor Sara Coli."

She ate another oyster concoction as he spoke. "100 times bigger would make it what, about 12 inches or so?" he asked smiling.

"Closer to 8 inches, darling."

He sipped the drink again. "So I'm drinking the venom of a White Widow Spider that's 100 times more powerful?"

His humoring her did not offend her at all. Her patience alone was one of her mightiest virtues.

"Yes, darling. Remember, I said the herbs counteract the poison." She sipped her glass again. "For the most part," she concluded.

"For the most part?" he echoed her response.

He swallowed another oyster concoction. "How much of this, venom, would be needed to kill a man?"

"A tear drop would kill a bear and its bite emits about a

tablespoon and a half."

His facial expression tightened into a mask of worry. "Are you serious?"

Sara Coli's whole way of living was serious. She wiped her wet hair behind her cute little ears. "Do you like chocolate?"

They took the conversation from the pool to another grand room. This one had furniture low to the floor and a beautiful fireplace with expensive Persian rugs in front of it. They sat in fine Terry cloth robes and shared a banana split smothered in chocolate syrup. Their verbal exchanges were effortless, their interchanges fluid, and their interest mirrored each other's often.

He could see that she had really lived in her 51 years. She had been there, seen that, purchased those, and spoken with them. She was as captivating a creation and as smart as she was lovely.

Sara Coli liked Trevor. He was a strong and intelligent man with strong working hands and a very complete body. A real treat for the eyes. Sexy in more than 10 ways. She was seriously contemplating the fact that she hadn't been intimate with anyone in months. She was looking at him in a desirous manner. Seeing how well endowed he was had her thirsting for his body even more. She imagined that he would fill her up and trigger her multi-orgasmic nature quickly.

She had an insatiable sex drive at times due to the White Widow constantly running through her body. She was anxious to see what the White Widow would do to Trevor.

It had been in his system for over an hour now and would undoubtedly begin to show effectual signs which lead to the exiting symptoms. She loved what it used to do to her late husbands. It made them raging bulls in the bedroom. It also sped up their heart rates tremendously, leading to the massive heart attacks that made them drop off one after another. It was not her fault she knew. They had all accepted the White Widow of their own volition and began to crave it more and more no matter the risk. They were substantially older than Trevor though.

The poison made orgasms much more intense for both male and female. A drawback was that it seemed to have the exact same addictive qualities as the drug heroin on a man. The man became weaker in a sense, slaves to the White Widow. But the woman seemed to become more youthful, activating their sexual prowess. Sara Coli had seen the two contrasting effects. She hoped that Trevor's younger body would produce better results.

The first time for all of them was a rapid build up of uncontrolled desire that led to a nearly simultaneous orgasm. The more they drank, the slower the build up. The slower the build up, the more intense the climax. Trevor had drank a half dosage. She always came too many times to count. She couldn't wait to see how he performed. She watched him wipe his head and knew that the effects were being felt.

"Wow, it's really warm in here." He looked over to the fireplace. "Did you turn that up?"

"No, darling," she laughed. "It's the White Widow. That's what you're feeling."

"Are we on that again," he smiled, tugging at the top of his robe?

"You can take the robe off if you'd like. I won't bite hard," she teased him.

He smiled and untied the robe, slipping his arms out of the sleeves revealing his bare flesh. There was a light sheen all over his body. She knew the signs well. He laid back on the robe without warning and she bit her bottom lip, watching as the flames danced off of his rapidly swelling dick.

She touched his chest, causing him to flinch hard. The venom had him in the middle of the 'sensitive touch' phase. She touched his rock hard abs and he flinched again, releasing a loud groan of pleasure.

"God, what's happening to me?" he asked in a low choppy voice. "What's going on?"

Trevor felt like her touch had stabbed him, but the pain felt so good. It was a prickly sensation that he wanted more of. He closed his eyes at the feel of thousands of little things crawling on and all through his body. He was in the throes of something he had never felt before. He was paralyzed by the need to orgasm. Something stabbed him again and he moaned out much louder than he had ever done before.

Sara Coli's voice reached out to him. "Randale, how do you feel?" He heard the question, but the words made no sense. "I'm going to touch you," she said, staring at his rock hard 10 inches standing at full attention. "I need to help you release okay?"

She knelt beside his sweaty body and grabbed his long shaft with both hands. She knew what he needed. She used the sweat from his dick to stroke him up and down with her hands. She slipped up to the head, then down to the base, licking her lips the whole time.

She wanted to see him spray cum all over her hands. Her wish came true with two more strokes. He yelled out as his body released a load of hot white sperm into the air. It pumped out and ran down Sara Coli's hands and the base of his long shaft. He gasped for air as the waves of orgasmic bliss receded.

She smiled down at him. "Sleep, darling. You will feel so much better in the morning."

Trevor's mind couldn't distinguish whether it was in a dream or if he was really feeling what he was feeling. He laid on the robe closing his eyes to quell the dizziness. *What's happening to me?* He wasn't sure. He heard a voice. Sara Coli s voice he thought, but his mind wouldn't let him understand the words. They were words alright, but they held no meaning to him.

He felt a surge of energy run through his dick and nuts as they began to get caressed. He was so sensitive that he was about to cum and didn't even know why. He felt a warm, softness ride up and down his long hard dick, once, twice, three times, and then a fourth. On the fifth time a back breaking orgasm erupted from within him. He felt himself yell as his cum shot, what he imagined to be sky high, out and onto his belly and dick.

His heart pounded against his ribcage as he squeezed his eyes tight enough to cause an ache in his head. He felt his body release a gasp of air that he didn't know he was holding in. Then, as if it hadn't ever happened, the sensations, the paralysis, and the sensitivity, all ended and he was floating off into a post orgasmic stupor. He heard more words, but they made no sense either. He would have to wait until he regained all of his faculties to put the whole experience into proper perspective. For right now, he had only one choice... Sleep.

Chapter 6

Trevor opened his eyes and looked up at the high ceiling. Instantly, he knew that the place that he lay in was not his home. The night before was extremely fuzzy in his head. He sat up and looked around, it was a really nice bedroom. His clothes lay draped over the back of a chair off in the corner. He rubbed his face with both hands, quickly noticing that his robe laid across the bottom of a huge bed. He lifted the covers and realized that he was stark naked.

He hurried out of the bed looking at the clock which read 7:15am. He got dressed, slipped his boxers on, then hurried into his pants. *Oh man, oh man, this was a screw up,* he thought. He sat back on the edge of the bed to pull his socks on. The door opened at that moment and Sara Coli walked in the room looking as refreshed as ever.

"Randale," she crooned. "I'm so glad you're awake. Did you sleep well?"

She donned a lavender, two piece business suit with her hair ponytail again. She was completely and utterly gorgeous to him. He stared up into her hazel orbs, caught by the sheer beauty of her sculpted features. She touched him lightly on the chest as he answered her.

"Yeah... I think."

She smiled and stepped in extra close to him and he could smell her sweet body spray. It lit his fire. She rested her soft hands on his shoulders, massaging them gently. "I want to take you out today."

"Okay," he responded, looking deep into her eyes.

She had him sitting completely still in her presence, as if he was entranced. She reached out and traced a line from his hairline down to the side of his face to his chin and spoke softly. "You're a very beautiful man. I have such a treat for you," she said, turning to walk out. "If you need to shower, please be my guest. I will be waiting for you in the main room."

She disappeared out through the door with Trevor watching her. He took a deep breath and lay back on the bed with his hands on his face. *Okay, man. Stick to the script.*

****

Trevor never imagined his Saturday would go the way it was going. A Saturday for him was more like a few games of football or basketball, a decent meal, and some good sex with Kalitha. What he was experiencing was a far cry from the norm.

He had been taken to a nice restaurant out in Wrightsville Beach for breakfast, then to the mall. There, Sara Coli had easily spent an amount on him he would have never been able to afford. He could never have dreamed about such nice things for himself. She purchased a $1,400 suit, a $700 pair of shoes, and a $300 durbey to match it. He felt awkwardly uncomfortable and showed reluctance when it came to accepting it all, but she all but forced the gifts on him.

She then took him to a private jeweler and without any questions, purchased him an $18,000 watch with diamonds lined down the middle of the band. Trevor was shocked. She sternly demanded him to put it on. It was worth more than his Ford Bronco and he couldn't drive it back and forth to work. She wouldn't even allow him to thank her. She had waved it off as simple friendship gifts.

They exited the private jeweler's shop, her holding on possessively to his big strong arm in his new suit. The material of the clothes felt so good on his skin. The smell of the new fabrics tickled his nose. The weight of the icy watch spoke to his wrist, which sent a message to his mind. *If I could keep Sara Coli happy then I will have hit the jackpot. Me and Kalitha,* he quickly corrected.

It was not even lunch time yet and she had already showed him what she would do for him when it pleased her to. He was delighted to have her on his arm as they headed to the limo. Tony got out and opened the door for them.

She got in first, and as Trevor began to enter, Tony spoke. "Nice suit my man."

"Thanks," Trevor said with a cool nod. He got in and the door closed behind him.

"You do look good in Armani, darling," she commented. He sat beside her and she smiled. "I think Kavali would be an even better fit for you. It would compliment your style."

"My style?" he asked, smiling.

She nodded. "Yes. All sexy black men look good in Kavali."

The ride was brief and soon they were pulling to a stop. Tony opened the door and too a step back. "We've arrived."

Sara Coli looked out at Tony, then to Trevor. "Let's have lunch in another state darling."

He didn't think her words were a joke, so he nodded and stepped out of the limo. "If it pleases you Sara Coli, it pleases me." He looked around as she stepped out and reality hit him hard. They were at the airport.

She smiled. "I like to fly to Louisiana for lunch. They have some of the finest jazz clubs I know of."

He took in all of the private jets noticing that all of the planes were on different runways, and he knew that they were in a private part of the airport. She grabbed his hand and led him to a private jet. They boarded and were in the air in minutes.

Trevor sat in his seat awed by the beauty of the aerial view. He had never flown in a jet before. He had been on one commercial flight and that was coach. He only saw this kind of indulgence in Robb Report luxury-lifestyle magazines. And now he was on a lear jet with an $860 million dollar wet dream.

It was truly exhilarating. The view was breathtaking outside of the aircraft and inside as he looked admiringly at Sara Coli. She smiled at him with satisfaction, then looked back out of the window.

They had landed and were eating lunch to live jazz being played by a local band by 2:00pm. The place was down home for New Orleans. The food was delicious, the music was melodic and filled with livelihood. It was all he imagined a live jazz band would be like since he had never imagined it at all.

Trevor was a man who liked to take the lead. He liked to be the one in control, but it wasn't the case with someone like Sara Coli. It all felt backwards to him, but since it was happening, he figured he might as well enjoy it.

Sara Coli sipped her papaya juice and leaned over to speak over the music. "Would you like to go out with me tonight, Randale?"

"Are you asking me out on a date," he teased?

She wiggled her eyebrows sexily. "Yes, I do believe that I am."

He leaned up even closer. "Let me think about it."

She bit back a huge smile feigning disappointment. "Why darling, I don't believe you'd do me like that. Especially after all we've been through," she joked.

He smiled widely staring into her eyes, causing them to have a moment. She leaned in closer, giving him the impression that she wanted a kiss and his pulse quickened. Her desire to feel his lips burned through her, threatening to bubble over. Their moment had arrived and neither one of them wanted to miss it. He was going to take his chance. Reaching out, he tilted her soft chin up a little, and leaned in slowly for a tender kiss. Her lips were warm and soft. The kiss was swift, stolen with unsung permission. She yearned for more, much more after it was over.

They each leaned back unhurriedly, heat showing in their gaze. Trevor began to nervously drum his fingers on the table to the music, while Sara Coli touched her lips in reverence. She smiled, wondering if he had even given any thought to what she meant by 'let's go out'? He had no earthly idea of what she had planned. She looked at him enjoying the music, then to the band, hoping that there would be plenty of those kisses involved. Kissing was good for her soul.

They were back in the air shortly after their lunch ended. He listened as Sara Coli spoke about the many different clubs she had been to. He hadn't done the club thing much in his day, so he was pretty much a virgin to it. Still, it excited him to hear her rant and rave about it. The club scene seemed to bring her to life.

"I like a place where they step. I love to step," she smiled radiantly. "What do you like to do Randale?"

"Well, I'm really not that much of a clubber. I do like to step though. It's a grown and sexy kind of environment."

"You fit the criteria for both darling," she said, reaching over to tap the keypad on the wall. R. Kelly's *'Step In The Name of Love'* blared out of the speakers around them.

Trevor smiled at her as she rocked and snapped her fingers to the beat. She was full of vigor and he liked that about her. He felt her vibe and began to snap along to the song with her. The system pumped out all kinds of music as they talked and sang along. They talked about his job and the dreaded off season. She asked about his trailer and he kept the details about it vague and short. She took mental notes of it all.

She liked Trevor and really wanted to do more for him, but she needed to know more about who he was. She didn't hesitate to ask whatever questions came to her mind. She asked about his financial state and whether or not he had children. She dug in hard and to her surprise, he answered all of her inquiries to the highest level of satisfaction.

She leaned back in the soft leather of her seat, ready to ask one more question. "So, if I had your name ran through my database, it wouldn't tell me that you were married or something like that?" She gave him a serious look. "Would it?"

He froze up for a brief second. The words shot out of his mouth with an erroneous edge on them. "The report wouldn't tell you about our separation." He pulled himself together mentally. "It might only state married, but it would never tell of the wrenching separation that I'm being dragged through." He let his eyes fall towards the floor for effect.

Regret instantly showed on her face. She looked at his

downcast position and spoke softly and apologetically. "I'm so sorry. I didn't mean to make you uncomfortable." She reached out and touched his hand.

He looked up at her with pain in his eyes.

"I know a break up can be painful and messy, Randale. I've had more than my fair share."

"Really," he asked somberly?

"Yes, really. Darling, I'm not immune. I am a veteran to loss. I just pray that God doesn't let me lose another?"

"Who could possibly walk away from a woman as mesmerizing as you?"

"You'd be surprised."

He rubbed her hand on top of his. She smiled as they comforted one another. He knew what sort of damage was being done and even though he loved Kalitha, deep down a part of him wished that what they were building was real. To Sara Coli, all of it was real and she loved every moment of it. He looked to her then sat back looking out of the window. She liked to just watch him in thought.

For some reason he thought about when they first met and she asked him how old he was. He hadn't wanted to tell her because he figured she would think he was too young for her. But not any more. The words floated off of his tongue softly. "Thirty-three," he said, without looking her way.

She smiled, knowing what his statement meant and took it in. They began their descent and they both quietly stared out of the window at the wings as they sliced through the clouds.

****

Kalitha walked out onto their half screened in back porch. She didn't like to smoke her weed in the house. Trevor didn't indulge because his job gave random test and was very strict on drug use. She sat on a black fold up chair and lit the small joint she'd rolled. She inhaled deeply and blew out the potent smoke. It would only take a few more pulls to have her as high as a hot air balloon. She leaned back closing her eyes as the weed high settled all the way into her system. A sudden movement on her far left caught her attention. Quickly she looked over and found Frankenstein watching her as if he understood what was going on. He was as still as a statue and she didn't like when he watched her with an unnatural stillness like that.

It irked her so she yelled at him. "GO AWAY!"

Frankenstein continued to watch her so she picked up one of Trevor's old boots and flung it at him. He darted away from the crashing sound of the loose planks of nailed down wood they called a porch.

As it scurried away, she spoke to him evilly. "That's right, run you old scaredy cat."

She leaned back in her seat satisfied that she was able to take her anger out on something. *Where the hell are you Trevor?*

****

The leer jet landed and as Trevor stepped out, the first thing he noticed was that they were not at the I.M.L. Airport in Wilmington, N.C. This airport was much bigger. He descended the steps looking around curiously. "Okay, this is not home."

"Of course it's not," she said, smiling up at him. "Ever been to Chicago? They do have the best steppers clubs."

He looked around then back to her. "Chicago?"

"Yeah, Chi-Town," she teased him mockingly. "You know, like the *Windy City*. She began to walk away, her hips moving provocatively. "We need to get you something to wear tonight for dinner and the club."

He followed her watching her every move. "You are really something else, Sara Coli," he said, trying to keep his excitement down.

They were chauffeured to a clothing store in the shopping district where they picked up a few things to wear. He settled for a black Giani suit with white trim and a pair of albino gators trimmed in black. She selected a sexy white Prada dress, with black trim and a pair of pumps to go with it. There whole ensemble was fly. He never knew what the attire cost, because she never asked the price. She merely swiped her black card and walked away without a second thought.

She led him to another store for a hat. Trevor carried the bags as she walked in and gestured to the slick hats on the shelves. "Pick one." She smiled enthusiastically. "Or two. I'll get you whatever you choose." She turned around and walked up to him. "Do you like bracelets and rings?"

"I don't know," he replied truthfully. "I've never owned anything worth having."

She smiled, then looked away in deep thought.

As they reached the rental, the driver opened their door and took the bags from Trevor. "Where to, ma'am?"

"The jewelry district, please," she said before sliding into the limo. "Then I would like you to pick a wonderful place where we can enjoy dinner."

"Yes, ma'am. I think I know just the place," the driver responded.

Trevor followed her into the back seat and the door closed behind him. The driver placed their bags in the trunk, got in behind the wheel, and pulled off.

Trevor looked at Sara Coli. She seemed to be getting more beautiful by the second. "You must really like jewelry?"

"Not as much as I like to see other people wearing it."

"Anybody," he asked curiously?

"No, Randale. Just you right now."

He smiled and looked forward smoothly. It wasn't long before they were pulling up to a humongous jewelry store. They exited and went inside. He was surprised by how large it was and the huge selection they had on display. They floated from display case to display case, gazing at all of the icy jewelry.

She watched him closely to see what pieces made his eyes sparkle and what didn't. His reaction to the white and canary yellow diamonds showed his interest. His interest really piqued at a bracelet and ring set in the white and yellow section. She asked for it to pulled out. The lady behind the counter showed a hint of reluctance and concern. After all, it was Chicago.

Sara Coli noticed and instantly dug her black card out of her purse and set it on the glass top counter. It made a crisp 'pop' sound on the glass. The girl's facial expression relaxed and she keyed open the display case pulling out the set and more. Trevor tried it on and wanted it immediately.

She smiled at him. "Do you like it?"

"Yes." He smiled brightly. "It's incredible."

The girl behind the counter smiled as well. "It makes your skin tone stand out." She was about to divvy up a shit storm of compliments to earn her commission.

The bracelet and ring set cost $26,000 and she told the sales woman to set it to the side for purchasing. Sara Coli, then decided to upgrade his watch and add a nice chain as well. She pointed out a diamond encrusted Cartier and a yellow and white invisible set diamond chain to match. She liked it all.

Trevor was ecstatic on the inside and not far from that on the outside. She looked into the next case over and saw a stunning yellow diamond bezel. She pointed to it and tapped the glass with her finely manicured finger. "I must have that placed on the Cartier."

Trevor stared at the bezel and his eyes widened. "WHOA."

His eyes popped at how fly it was. Sara Coli wanted it rung up and worn out by Trevor. They stood at the front counter as the cashier tallied their purchases up. He watched in awe as the screen flipped from $26,000 to $137,000, not including the $5,000 tip she gave to the girl behind the counter. Sara Coli had balled out on Trevor with ease having spent over $160,000 on him in less than 24 hours. He had wanted to tell her to put it all back, but she had assured him that if they never spoke another word to one another that he could keep it all. She made it clear that his time was priceless to her.

As they left, he noticed how the jewelry felt heavy, chunky, and cold around his pinky, wrists, and neck. She smiled at him with adoration. "You look like money now, Randale."

Trevor couldn't help but be a little nervous as they strolled out to the rental. He hadn't ever dreamed of that much ice, and at that moment he was looking like an igloo.

"You look like you fresh out of a B-Rap video, like P-Diddy or somebody," she joked as they entered the rental.

He was speechless and still trying to figure out whether he was still unconscious from the White Widow, or at his broke down trailer home dreaming.

"Randale," Sara Coli spoke teasingly. "Did all that ice freeze your tongue darling?"

"No," he replied, snapping back to reality with a smile. He casually examined his wrists and pinky. "I'm sorry. It's just that—"

"Feeling like the roles should be reversed?"

"Well—"

"Feeling like you should be doing these things for me?" she cut in again. "Randale, darling, it's the 21st century. Things are so very different now."

"I know that, but—"

She placed a finger over his lips. "I did what I wanted to do for you. I often do what I want to do. I wanted you to have the gifts or else I wouldn't have given them to you."

Her words were strong, nurtured, and honest. She pulled her finger away and he remained silent.

"I have over 860 million dollars. That is actual cash, not including my assets, angel investments, and other things that are pouring money into my accounts. There is no telling how much my companies will accumulate by the end of the next fiscal period, or by tomorrow for that matter. Simply put, I can't spend enough to waste it because of the things I already own. I've been extremely comfortable for a very long time darling." She snaked her fingers in-between his. "Let me do nice things for you. It makes me happy." She lifted his hand and kissed it appreciatively. She paused, then looked up to him. "Now if you want to return the favor, make love to me tonight, long and hard. I haven't had any in months and my body desperately needs the release."

She'd caught him off guard. He wanted to skip dinner and the club and go to wherever he could be alone with her and do her some justice right then and there. He kept his cool, but his mind ate at him.

"Can I say something?" he asked on the verge of telling her his thoughts. Sara Coli did not deserve to be played on. She was a great person and the knowledge of that was pulling at his morale and ethical mind. "I really need to tell you something."

"Don't say it, please," she pleaded. "Just enjoy the night okay."

He was thinking about how soft her skin felt against his, then Kalitha flashed into his mind. He was doing this for her. He didn't want to lie to Sara Coli or hurt her, but his first duty was ultimately to his wife. He really did like Sara Coli, but he loved Kalitha. He had to set his own feelings to the side and keep up the facade. He could feel the stains burning in on the fabrics of his moral self, but he was already in, and really had no other choice.

They pulled into the fancy restaurant parking lot only moments later. They were out and seated quickly, courtesy of the driver's calling and making reservations. They each ordered and had a glass of wine as they waited. Dinner was magnificently grilled t-bone steaks marinated in a Jack Daniels sauce with succulent lobster tails and a clarified butter sauce to dip them in. On the side sat steamed brown rice, artichoke, and spinach bisque with five cheese bread sticks.

They laughed and joked while enjoying their meals, all the while noticing the heated currents zapping between them in anticipation of what was to come later. After their palates had been satisfied, they paid the tab, and left a $200 tip for the nice male waiter.

Again, they entered the rental, and Sara Coli spoke to the driver. "To my penthouse suite, please."

"Yes, ma'am."

She held Trevors' hand and snuggled up against him the whole ride. He was past blown away, because Sara Coli was like a dream come true with all of the trimmings. She looked up at her young prince with eagerness. *You would make a great king, darling. I can't wait to crown you.*

Soon they had arrived at the penthouse and were riding the elevator up to the top floor in what seemed like a blink of an eye. She hurried off to shower and told him to do the same. He stood in the shower thinking as the hot water sprayed onto his body. He couldn't believe that it all was real. He was awake in Chicago, in a penthouse suite, and in a huge shower with 3 heads spraying him at once. He could think of nothing more than the sensual and sultry older lady in another shower elsewhere in the suite. He wanted her badly, but opted to wait.

He exited the shower and dried off with a heated towel, then dressed in front of a large mirror. *I look sharper than a razor made out of lasers*, he thought, then struck a pose. He shook his head, laughing at his own joke. After slipping his jewelry on, he gave himself a once over. Satisfied, he began looking for his hat, but didn't see it on the bed anymore. He decided to leave it and walked out into the large living room. He stood in front of the large bay windows to appreciate the Chicago skyline and city lights.

He'd never asked the name of the building that they were in, but he knew the famous Sear's Tower when he saw it. It was all still hard to believe, but as he stared out at all of the twinkling lights, he had no other logical explanation. It was all very real and he was having the night of his life.

Sara Coli could be quiet and stealthy at times, and when she appeared suddenly behind him, he was startled a bit. She hugged him tightly around his waist. "There's something about being in front of this window that makes me want to hug someone."

He thought about Kalitha, then turned around and hugged her back. As he looked down at her, she looked even younger than she did earlier that day. She seemed to get more intriguingly gorgeous as well. She looked up and kissed him fully on his lips. It was only their second kiss and her lips were even softer than the first time.

She smiled coyly and cleared her throat. "Ummm, as soon as I tidy up my hair we can be off."

"Alright," he said, watching her strut provocatively off towards the back.

He turned to face the window once more and saw his image reflected back at him. Trevor carefully examined himself. He looked like a rich man and no one would know the truth, but he and Sara Coli. He was nothing more than a rustic raised, Bronco driving, manure plant worker that lived in a trailer home with his wife and cat. He saw past all of the jewelry and fancy clothes, leaving behind a man that he didn't know anymore. A man that was willingly going against all that he believed in for the all mighty dollar. He felt disgusted, but the world he lived in, his world, was disgusting. He wanted change and needed it even more. *Live in the moment man*, he thought to himself. *It may not last for long.*

Sara Coli was finally satisfied with her bun and its strategically placed curly strands. Her silvery white hair appeared to glow under the vanity mirror lighting. Her White Widow tattoo glinted in between her cleavage, her breast plump and full. She stood and walked over to her second closets and opened it. The light came on automatically and revealed a slew of furs hanging up. She looked them over, then reached in and pulled out a white chinchilla. She slipped it on, then walked over to another closet.

Inside hung several larger chinchilla coats. She selected a white one off the hanger and laid it on the bed. She grabbed Trevor's hat and walked over to her dresser with it. Upon opening a drawer, she found several money clips clutching crisp $100 bills. She grabbed one and delicately placed it into his hat. Grasping the fur she headed out to where he stood at the bay windows.

"Here, darling," she said, causing him to turn. "Put this on."

She handed him the chinchilla and the hat. He accepted the hat, but hesitated to take the coat. He looked into the hat and noticed the money clip, then looked back to her.

"Come on darling," she pushed the fur towards him. "It used to my husband's."

He quickly pulled away from it. She noticed his withdrawal and sighed. "He never wore it." She held up the price tag still attached to it. "See, it still has the tag on it."

Trevor finally reached out and accepted it, but still was a little hesitant.

"I swear, darling," she purred, reassuring him.

He smiled, then slid it on. Now he looked, felt, and smelled like money. She adjusted her coat as she stared at him heatedly. "You look awfully sexy, Mr. Mason."

"As do you, Ms. White."

"Please, do call me Sara Coli," she teased.

He pulled the wad of money out of his hat and held it up. He thumbed through the money and showed it to her. It had to be a full inch thick. "Is this supposed to make me feel better?" he asked, waiting for her response.

She looked at the money, then at her watch, then back to him. "I don't know where that came from Randale," she replied, turning towards the elevator. "Our ride should be outside by now," she added smiling.

"You are something else."

"I have no idea what you're talking about."

They rode through the city in the new rental, a 600 series Benz SL, and arrived at the club in real style. It was packed outside and people were lined up to get in. Faint traces of music leaked outside creating anticipation in the waiting patrons. The driver parked out front and turned in his seat to face Sara Coli.

"At what hour should I return?" he asked politely.

She looked down at her dainty little watch, then to Trevor. "Midnight?"

He looked from her to the driver who was waiting patiently for an answer. "Midnight," Trevor said, taking control for the first time that night. "Midnight will be just fine."

"Midnight it is, sir."

The driver got out to open their door. They walked past all the people waiting in line and was admitted in at the front. Sara Coli looked to Trevor to pay and he hurriedly pulled out the money clip. He handed the doorman a crisp $100 bill as she walked past them.

He nodded to the doorman feeling confident. "Keep the change."

"There is no change," he shot back.

"Well, in that case—" Trevor handed him another bill. "What about now?"

"I appreciate it man. You have a great time, sir."

They went inside, found a table, and ordered drinks. Within twenty minutes, Sara Coli had Trevor out on the dance floor. He was glad that Kalitha had forced him to learn how to 'step' for their special dance at their reception. He never thought he'd use the moves again, but there he was doing it and making it count.

He fell swiftly into step with the young players and their sexy counterparts. He and Sara Coli looked so in step that the dancers around them parted and created a circle just to watch them. It appeared like a scene out of a love story. Their moves were fluid and their bodies telling a story of the lives they lived. Their sweat soaked bodies intertwined, nearly becoming one creature possessed by the music, driven by the instruments, and controlled by the melodic hypnotic rhythm of the drums.

Their dance, which was only a dance, but seemed like an ancient ritual of sexual rite, ended with a huge round of whistles and applause. They hurried back to their table eager to escape the attention. Sara Coli was highly impressed by how smooth and debonair Trevor was out on the dance floor. In her experience, a man that could groove on the floor could also groove in the bedroom. She was thirsting to find out whether the saying would hold true with Trevor or not.

"Wow, Randale," she chided. "You're really good on your toes."

"I'm not the one they were cheering for," he shifted the blame. "You're a crowd pleaser, Sara Coli."

"Don't even try it," she smiled. "Don't even-"

"You are," he said, cutting her off. "I'm Just stating the obvious."

She slapped his hand playfully. He looked at the crowd filling the floor again. She watched him with desire in her eyes. "Would you like a White Widow," she asked loud enough for him to hear over the pounding music?

Trevor was feeling bolder and more confident than ever. "If it'll make me step like you, then hell yeah," he answered giving her a sexy smile.

She called a waitress over to their table and ordered two Cask and Creams. Trevor didn't mind because he liked the sweet taste of it. The drinks arrived and Sara Coli reached into her purse and pulled out two little clear vials with white spider stickers on the side. They were filled with a creamy white liquid. He watched as she emptied the two vials into their glasses. She stirred each drink with her finger.

He watched her carefully. "Is that really venom?"

She licked one finger, turning him on beyond explanation. She lifted her wet finger and slipped it into his mouth. He gently sucked on it in the most erotic way, causing a surge of sexual energy to flow down her spine. She pulled her hand away, fanning herself. He smiled and winked his eye at her. He hadn't seen many strong reactions from her, so he enjoyed this new one.

"So is it," he asked again?

She disregarded the question and lifted her glass to toast. He did the same. "To questions and well kept secrets," she teased.

He gave her a nod and they both drank their sweet White Widow spiked drinks. Only she knew just how sweet they were.

The night floated by with them stepping more and more. In the middle of a dance her phone vibrated and she stopped to answer it. Glancing up at Trevor, she smiled seductively. "Our ride is here."

"Great," he replied, taking her by the hand. "Let's get out of here."

Sara Coli liked the way the words came out with so much promise. She wanted the promise to be as real as her heartbeat thudding in her chest. She wanted, no needed, to be ravished. She craved it. Her womb cried out to be conquered and pleased well into the night.

Their departure was made a spectacle by the D.J. who turned the spotlight on them. "Ladies and gentlemen, the million dollar couple is leaving the building."

Trevor looked up with a big grin on his face as he lead Sara Coli of the dance floor. The crowd cheered them all the way out the door. Outside Trevor searched for the Benz, but couldn't locate it.

Sara Coli took him by the arm. "Our car is over there."

He looked at the stretched Lincoln Town Car just as the driver stepped out and opened the door. "You're always one step ahead of me."

"Always, darling."

The ride to the penthouse was smooth and uneventful. The cold air was brisk when they got out. When it hit Trevor full on, the heat from the White Widow welled up inside him. It felt as if his veins were filled with streams of molten lava and it felt good rushing throughout his entire body.

Sara Coli noticed the change in his posture as they stepped out the car. She quickly led them directly to the elevator which took them straight up to the lavish suite. Once the door opened Trevor was already pulling at his tie and shirt. He began to peel out of his clothes as he walked dizzily through the penthouse.

She observed him from a short distance away. His undressing resembled a strip tease except he was anxious to take everything off with no entertaining show involved. The White Widow's venom was dispensing inside of him. She followed him to the bedroom where he laid on the bed completely nude. His body was toned and oh so sexy. She was turned on by all of his manly features. He rolled over onto his back and she instantly knew the reason, his dick was rock hard. She licked her lips eager to taste him.

"I'm so dizzy," he whispered, breathing heavily. "Too much spinning. Too fast."

Sara Coli's body was also hot from the White Widow. She stood at the foot of the bed and began to undress, her eyes never leaving him. She climbed onto the bed beside him and whispered back to him.

"The dizziness will fade after you release, darling. Then you will have more control, Randale."

He groaned loudly hating the spinning sensation. She leaned in and kissed his lips and his chin, before licking his neck, He moaned aloud with pleasure as she trailed sensual kisses down his chest, to his firm abs, and down to his hairy manhood. She knew that the venom would have him seized in a petrified state until he released.

She like the pure control she felt as she took his fat dick in her tiny hands and squeezed gently. She admired the shape and texture of it. The darkness of its skin against the butterscotch tone of hers. She slowly licked from the bottom of his shaft up to the head in a swirl motion. He tasted so delicious and she was eager to take him fully inside of her mouth. She needed to feel him filling her mouth, pressing against the roof, and slowly sliding down the back of her throat. He groaned from deep within as she stuffed all that she could manage between her wet lips.

She stroked him with her hands as she sucked him slowly and deliberately. Trevor's body flinched hard each time she let her wet tongue and juicy lips make the journey from the tip to the base. She rubbed his strong thighs and lifted his heavy meat to suckle gently on his balls. Hungrily she went back to his dick and concentrated on the head. Using her hands and sucking on the head with increased pressure was all he could stand.

Trevor's body tightened completely and without warning, he screamed out and exploded inside of Sara Coli's mouth. She moaned as the hot milky eruption filled her mouth, coating the back of her throat. She swallowed every bit of his cum and lapped away greedily at what might have possibly gotten away. He spasmed and jerked wildly as she massaged all of his love juice from him and into her willing mouth. She wiped her lips and sat back against the headboard waiting on him to come around. After a moment, his breathing evened out and he sat up slowly. His eyes scanned her body from her toes to her head when he realized that she was as naked as he was.

She rubbed the side of his face. "Make love to me, Randale."

Trevor all but pounced on her. He pulled her away from the headboard as if she was trying to get away. She moaned out at his raw power as he positioned her down beneath him. He devoured her supple breast one by one, taking time to lick each taunt nipple before kissing her tattoo. She moaned aloud and pulled at his lower back anxious for his touch. Her pussy walls were clenching and unclenching in anticipation. Her vaginal fluids were gushing out and sliding down between her juicy ass cheeks. He was so hard that he thought his dick would break if he didn't get it inside her soon.

Sara Coli cried out to him in need. "Oh please, Randale. Fuck me now," she begged.

He didn't hesitate to oblige her. He aimed into her wet and ready cavern and plunged in deeply. She gasped as pleasurable pain overwhelmed her body. Her womb was being stretched to its limits from the size of him and she felt fully packed beyond belief. Her scream was silently caught in her throat as her mouth gaped open, and her eyes squeezed tightly closed. She felt like heaven to Trevor. He couldn't control his urge to plow into her the way he had often fantasized about doing, so he did. He slammed his 10 inches of rock hardness into her tight hole over and over, grinding with each plunge.

She cried out as he crashed into her back wall repetitively. He looked down at the pained love faces she made, which only caused him to drive his hips harder. The tattoo between her bouncing titties caught his attention and lured him to go faster. The bed rocked and squeaked as the headboard collided with the wall in rapid succession.

Sara Coli had never in her life been so dominated. She clawed at the sheets beside her as he pumped at a hard and steady pace. Her first orgasm seemed to materialize out of thin air and came down on her so hard that all she could do was yell out his name. She wailed like a siren as her pussy walls contracted and gripped Trevor's steady long strokes.

Deciding to change it up, he stopped and pulled her legs onto his shoulders. She didn't stop him because she wanted him to have her any way he wanted. He pinned her slender legs back with his arms and began to drill her. She allowed him to fuck her as hard as he wanted, something he was denied at home.

His long, powerful thrusts were crashing deep inside of her building another orgasm, pushing her towards a spine shattering climax. She groaned and cooed as her fluids squirted and splashed his hard dick. The orgasm was powerful and nearly made her legs go numb.

This was a new experience for Trevor. He'd never before had sex with a squirter. He continued to drill Sara Coli as her hot fluids seemed to wet him all the way down to his balls. She moaned out his name and he loved the way she said it. Her throbbing hole was taking Trevor to another plateau, for she was squirting on him for a second time. The hot wetness felt amazing and was a pure turn on.

After several slower strokes, she splashed him once again. He knew seeing her cum this way would become addictive and he couldn't wait to have her do it again. He grunted with pleasure with each and every stroke. The sweat began to pour from him and his shoulders glistened with dampness. His arms were muscular and tight, his back sweaty, and tiny beads of moisture rolled down to his ass. The sweat dripped off his chin and landed on Sara Coli's jiggling breast. The force of his stroke picked up momentum causing her to release another wet orgasm, splashing him with her love juices again. She cried out his name as she surrendered full control of her body to him.

Trevor's chunky jewelry shined against his sweat soaked body, making him look even more alluring to her. She held on to his arms and lifted her pelvis upward to meet his strokes. The slapping sound of their colliding skin reverberated throughout the suite. Their bodies were trapped in a push and pull frenzy, clashing erotically. Sara Coli had never been sexed quite like this. She was being shown a whole new side of intercourse and she was being transformed into a being of pure sexual light. Her eyes began to roll back as yet another orgasm built up inside of her.

"Good Lordddddd," she whined in amazement.

Trevor was in a frenzy. His body was threatening to spill all of his cum inside her. He was seconds from bursting and giving up his entire soul. She gritted her teeth and began to cum again and her spasming pussy walls pushed him completely over the edge. He grabbed the headboard with his left hand and moaned loudly as he came. His body became stiff as an iron pole as the first load burst free. He choked on his own saliva as he sprayed all of his hot cum into Sara Coli's wet soaking love's nest. She cooed into his chest as she felt his sperm quickly decorate the walls of her womb.

Trevor fell to the side gasping for air and Sara Coli did something that she'd never ever done before. She came again as he was pulling out of her. Her body experienced millions of tiny quivers as she lay trembling beside him. His heart pounded harder than it ever had as the venom bled out of his body in his sweat.

That last unexpected orgasm sent Sara Coli over the edge. "Oh my God, yes! Please, Randale," she cried out. "Fuck me some more. Give me more of that big dick," she begged, reaching out and pulling him towards her.

Although he was exhausted, he was drawn back to her like a magnet to metal. He rolled over and pushed her on her side where he entered her from the back in a semi-spooning position. He rammed his long shaft deep inside her and began to power drive her as he held onto her right hip. She steadied herself with the headboard and begged him for more and he complied by sexing her relentlessly. While they were lost in lust, she kept begging for more, and he gave her all she could endure. The White Widow placed him in a zone that had Sara Coli clawing at the sheets and thanking him for every stroke.

****

Trevor opened his eyes to the sunlight streaming in through the large bedroom's window. He stretched his arms immediately noticing the weight of Sara Coli's body pressed against him. Looking down, he saw that their bodies were half covered by the expensive sheets and comforter. He had no earthly idea when it ended or how it ended. He only knew one thing for certain. The night before was the best he'd ever had.

He rubbed her ponytailed hair, causing her to look up at him. She smiled and a comfortable warmth passed over him. *It has to be impossible for her to be this beautiful after the wild and intense night we had last night?* He smiled back and her grin widened.

"Good morning, darling," she cooed.

"Good morning to you," he said softly. "What time is it?"

She smiled sexily. "You have a very expensive watch on,

Randale. You tell me."

He felt a hint of foolishness because he wasn't used to having a watch, let alone one so luxurious. He looked at it and saw that it was 10:12am.

"Wow," he said, shocked. "Uh, how long did we—?"

"Oh, Randale," she said, grabbing his left hand and kissing the palm. "You made love to me until five in the morning." She rubbed her inner thigh against his hip. "I feel so swollen."

He looked down at her half exposed naked flesh. Instantly a thought crossed his mind. *Holy shit? I didn't use a condom. Ah, damn. I fucked up.* He scolded himself mentally knowing that he wouldn't have used one if he had been given a choice in the first place.

He slid his body to a sitting position, placing his back against the headboard. He wiped his face with both hands, realizing the extent of how much ice he had on. He looked at it all as if he hadn't seen it before, awed by its magnificence.

Sara Coli rolled over onto her belly watching him. "Breakfast is on the way."

The comforter slid down, revealing her gorgeous creamy skin and the voluptuous curves of her ass cheeks. He looked and found his dick still covered in her silky pussy juice residue. He leaned his head back in deep thought.

"Don't do that, please," she said concerned. "There's no reason to be dismal, Randale."

He thought about Kalitha and tried hard to conceal his real thoughts. "I don't know," he began. "I didn't want to rush into things and ruin something good." He swung his legs over the side of the bed, walked over to the large bay windows, and looked out into the cloudy skyline of Chicago.

Sara Coli sat up, pulling the covers up around her breast, instantly wanting to dispel any inkling of regret he might have thought she had. She was pleased beyond her wildest dreams and didn't want the energy between them to dissipate. She watched him as he stared out of the window, her eyes admiring the back side of him as well as the front.

"Randale," she said softly. "Last night was the best night of my life. I feel pleased to have shared it with you. You are truly blessed." She waited for him to turn around, and when he didn't, she got off the bed with the comforter still wrapped loosely around her, dragging it across the soft carpeted floor.

"Please don't think anything that isn't true." She nuzzled his back with her face. "I wanted you last night. Maybe even more than you wanted me. Hell, I want you now."

Trevor listened to her soft, meaningful words. The ones she chose were calculated and careful. He still couldn't shake Kalitha from his mind though. However, the feel of Sara Coli's skin against his was helping him push his wife to the side by the second. Softly, she planted a luscious kiss on his back.

He turned to her, gazing down at her upturned face. "I just don't want it to seem like I wouldn't have waited if it was necessary."

She looked up into his sexy, brown, honest eyes. Their sincerity was a weapon in itself, never mind the sword he had below. "I couldn't wait, darling," she moaned out. "Not for another moment."

His head descended and their lips met in a passionate kissed. Trevor slid his arms slowly around her loving the feel of her pressed against him. *God, she is so soft.* As they kissed, he peeked out of one eye to see her eyes still closed. *If I just make it home with the money clip. God, let me at least make it home with that.*

Sara Coli broke the kiss and began backing up to the bed, staring at him with lust filled eyes. "Ummm, mmm, mmm," she hummed. He smiled and walked slowly towards her.

All he had to do is return with the money in his pocket and the jewelry he wore, and he would have accomplished what he'd come there to do. Even though he had been gone since Friday, and it was now Sunday, he would have still made it count. He reached Sara Coli, towering over her and staring down into her angelic face. She looked up to him in reverence, as if he was a God, immortalized in her eyes. Her very own sexual Hercules. Her passionate Atlas. Her cock Conan.

He on the other hand, wished he could get away to call Kalitha. She had to be tripping right now, but she'd have no choice but to believe him if the gifts were present. He tilted her head upward by her chin and passionately kissed her full on her lips. She leaned into it without any rejections. She fell away from him and landed on the soft bed. He smiled down at her rubbing her smooth hair back.

"I've never been sexed like that, Randale. That was a million dollar lay darling." She began to nibble on her pointer finger nail. "I think I owe you."

"I think that I'd like to keep you in debt."

A sudden burst of excited sexual energy burst forward from her as she shouted erotically. "Yes! Keep me in debt, baby!" She rolled over comically. "Oh, yes!"

Trevor laughed as he watched her act out. He couldn't wait for their breakfast to arrive because he was famished. They ate, showered, dressed, and were back on their way to N.C. in record time. Sara Coli was happy and her actions and words radiated it. He did his best not to ravish her on the flight back home and it was a substantial struggle.

As they descended to land she thought about her last minute decision. *One more gift for you darling. You deserve it.* They landed, unboarded, and walked slowly to the limo. She turned to him ready to offer him her last gift.

"I have some business to attend to, so—" She paused to look up into his eyes. "I will call you later."

"Sure," he replied. "I'm already looking forward to that call."

They stood in awkward silence as their drivers loaded his things into his ride, and hers into the limo.

"Well," he said, leaning in to kiss her.

She graced him with a simple peck on the cheek. He smiled, then looked over at the new SUV.

"Talk to you later."

With that, she disappeared into the limo with Tony closing the door behind her. The limousine glided off smoothly with Trevor watching it go.

"C'mon, bro. I gotcha ride over here."

"Cool," Trevor responded while fingering the wad of $100 bills in his pocket as he walked towards a tan Lincoln Navigator. The ride home sped by with small talk from Tony. Trevor found out that Tony had been around for a while to be so young. He was Sara Coli's personal driver. "Yeah, it's cool to work for such a beautiful creature," he said smoothly. "The financial benefits are the shit too."

"I can imagine," Trevor returned with a smile. "Your lady friend has to love it."

"Nah, I don't got one," Tony replied.

"That's hard to believe."

Tony wiped his suit sleeves down, pretended to floss. "You would think so, right. But as soon as they see who I drive around, their self confidence goes all the way down the drain."

They shared a laugh. As they pulled into the trailer park, Tony made a mental note of exactly what he had seen. Sara Coli had told him to be honest and he honestly thought that Trevor didn't deserve to live in such a run down environment. He was totally sure when he pulled into his lot in the broad daylight. That evening when he had initially collected him, the darkness hid its true dreariness.

He pulled up a little ahead of the driveway and hopped out.

"Thanks man," Trevor said, getting out. He opened the back door and reached in for the bags.

Tony followed him out. "I'll get those bags for you."

"I can get it."

"It's my job man," Tony added as he began to remove the bags from the back seat. "And I get paid extremely well to do it."

Trevor threw his hands up in surrender with a chuckle. "I'm not trying to get you fired, bro."

"Good, because my bank account wouldn't like that one bit," Tony quipped back. He handed the bags over to Trevor. "Oh, and one more thing, bro." He looked over to the Bronco. "I'm gonna need the keys to that, uh, precious little piece of junk you got over there." He smiled heartily.

"Wait a minute man. No talking about my baby," said Trevor, laughing. What Tony said about the Bronco hadn't fully registered.

Tony followed suit with a laugh. "Cool. I understand, but seriously," he said, holding his hand out. "I need the keys to the Bronco. The title to the Navigator is in the truck. Now how about handing over those keys?" he said, with his hand out.

Trevor smiled, looked to the Navigator, then back to Tony. "You're kidding, right?"

"Wouldn't dream of it." He stared at Trevor with a serious face. "Hey bro, I don't mean to be rude, but I have things to do. So if you can move a bit faster that will be cool."

Trevor looked back to the new SUV, then turned towards the driveway. Barely able to maintain his composure, he calmly carried his bags to the door and opened it. Kalitha saw him from the bedroom and became instantly ecstatic at the mere sight of him.

"TREV! Oh my God. I thought that something happened to you."

He cut her off with a quick raise of his hand. "Wait." He walked in and slowly sat the bags on the sofa.

She eyed the jewelry and the fur coat in amazement. "I need the keys to the Bronco."

"Where are you going?" she asked quickly?

"Nowhere," he said. "I just need the keys."

She hurried back to the bedroom and grabbed the keys to the truck. She slid them off of the key ring, then handed them to him.

"Stay inside," he ordered softly. He stepped out with the keys and opened the Bronco's door. After removing all of his important papers, he eased away from the old truck still slightly in shock.

Tony walked up, took the keys, and hopped in the truck. "See you soon, bro."

Trevor saluted him as he backed the Bronco out the driveway and drove away. He turned to the Navigator and muttered to himself. "In-fucking-credible. Just incredible."

He walked back in the trailer to find Kalitha jumping and

wrapping her arms and legs around him. "I'm so glad you're home." She kissed him softly and passionately. "Oh my God! I was worried to fucking death," she said in between kisses.

"I'm fine, babe," he said, putting her back on the floor.

She eyed the jewelry. "Is this shit real?"

"Yep," he replied as he pulled the money clip out. "And so is this."

She snatched it out of his hands and ran in place screaming in excitement. "Oh my goodness, baby! You did it. You really did it!" she exclaimed, hugging the money to her heart. He nodded with a smile and she pulled the clip off and began to flip through the money. "It's gotta be $5,000 or more, huh."

"Yeah, yeah," he teased. "Put these papers away."

She eyed them, confused. "They were in the Bronco. Why'd you take them out?"

"Just go on outside and put them back."

She snatched them up, tossed the money on the end table, and walked sassily out the door. He smiled when he heard her scream outside. She ran back inside, hugging him hard.

"Holy shit! When did you get that?"

"Today, I think," he answered, happy to see her happy.

She began to dance around. "Hell, yeah." She strutted off to the bedroom. "Let's go out, Trevor," she yelled back. "Can we baby?"

He would have given anything to keep her this happy. He smiled brightly and shrugged his shoulders. "What the hell. Let's do it."

She walked out rubbing his fur. As she got to the door, she turned and struck a pose with the fur. "Let's do it then."

Trevor smiled, happy to finally be back where he belonged.

CHAPTER 7

The next few weeks were a huge change for Kalitha and Trevor. Sara Coli only called for Trevor's company on the weekends and that left the whole week to Kalitha, and she surmised that she could deal with that. She figured that she could let him be with her on the weekends as long as she had him all week to herself. Every Friday Trevor left and would return on Sunday with a slew of gifts ranging from new colored diamond jewelry, expensive designer shoes, and matching suits of the finest linens.

Just this past weekend he had returned driving a fully loaded Escalade that was much better than the Navigator. It sat on 28 inch chrome rims made by Lexani with all chromed out accessories. Sara Coli had it customized to the max. It shined and flossed like it was ready to be featured in a DUB or RIDES magazine. Compared to the Escalade, the Navigator looked like the Bronco to Kalitha.

In just five weeks Kalitha had put $25,000 in their bank accounts. It felt good to have a little something and not be in need for a change. She was so accustomed to being broke and not having, that now that she actually had money, it felt alien to her. But it was an alien feeling she welcomed with open arms. She felt confident that her penny pinching days were over. Though she knew that their method was not right, she had to keep doing it. Soon she hoped they would have enough to stop the con and go on living.

All of the gifts were in Trevor's name so they couldn't be snatched away. Not legally anyway. Kalitha loved that Sara Coli didn't seem like the type to take back the gifts she's been dishing out. With $860 million, why would she? She could afford to give donations to the needy, even if she didn't know that she was giving.

She and Trevor had decided to play it extra safe, so she had gone out and gotten a nice used car instead of driving the Navigator. She had purchased herself a decent looking Acura Legend. She wanted badly to drive the SUV, but she knew it was pertinent to play her role. Her desire to drive in real style made Kalitha gravitate towards disobeying Trevor and driving on the weekend, at least while he was away. However, she fought the urge and stuck with the plan.

The decision to split their bank accounts so they would look as separated as he said they were, was all Trevor's idea. Kalitha didn't like it, but submitted to it. She didn't want to blow their cover before the mission was accomplished. The last thing she needed was for the old hag to find out that they were accomplices in a diabolical scheme to ultimately swindle her out of a duffle bag full of cash. That would fuck everything up.

Besides, she hadn't felt any form of a threat since she began leasing her husband out to Sara Coli, but at times he did make love to her much more intensely than she liked. It often made her ponder on how hard did Sara Coli like to be sexed. At times Trevor seemed to be trying to give her the whole 10 inches, something she had never taken, nor asked for. This had her wondering just how much he was enjoying sexing her.

Kalitha drove her Legend from place to place in Wilmington until she ended up where Trevor and Sara Coli spent their 'in town' time together. It only bothered her slightly seeing them together. Nevertheless, seeing them kiss out in public kind of pinched a part deep inside of her and she had to partition her feelings well to deal with it. She knew that it would be over with soon and was confident that Trevor would be able to work at least a half million dollars out of her before it was all over with. She would certainly wait it out and see. She sipped her drink and looked over to Sara Coli and Trevor.

Goodness, you are pretty, she thought as she watched Sara Coli light up because of something Trevor had said. *Okay, you're fucking gorgeous! So what, big damned deal!* Kalitha continued to watch Sara Coli, again thinking she looked much younger than 51. To her she looked more like she was in her mid thirties.

She pulled out her P.D.A. and tapped on the camera. Once the camera opened, she pointed it towards the unsuspecting couple so she could get a closer look at them. She zoomed in on Trevor and his counterfeit happiness as he interacted with her. *Was it counterfeit*, she questioned, watching him, eyes narrowed. It looked too real. An outsider wouldn't be able to discern the truth of his intentions. From where she sat watching, a stupor settled down on her, because neither could she. The truth was more than evident when they were together, but at that moment, she seriously questioned it herself.

Kalitha scolded herself mentally. *Bitch, don't you dare do that to yourself. He belongs to you. You know it and he knows it. The only person who doesn't know it is that old bitch. There is absolutely nothing to worry about.* In her eyes, Trevor was her husband who loved her very much, and that old bitch was nothing more than a glorified sugar momma who made their lives sweeter by the weekend. She sipped her wine again and kept right on watching.

Sara Coli leaned over and kissed Trevor and Kalitha looked away. *I hate that bitch.* She couldn't keep her gaze adverted though. She felt drawn to watch.

Sara Coli laughed a throaty sound. "I'd want to see that. I think you'd do great on the slopes of Aspen."

"I don't know about all that," Trevor said, taking a sip of wine. "I don't think sliding down a mountain of snow is for everyone."

She rubbed his hands. "Oh, you'd love it, darling. It's such a thrill."

"I'd rather watch other people do it," he said, smiling at her affectionately.

She looked splendid as usual in her Dolce and Gabbana gown. Her tattoo was visual, as with most of her attire, and made him want to have a White Widow. Since they've been seeing each other, they would have one every night that they were together, and it was slowly becoming something that he wanted. No, more like needed, to have every night, whether with Sara Coli or not. When they had their fixes, they made passionate love like two creatures made out of pure erotic energy. Often they challenged the sunrise and won.

They had extraordinary synergy, and he loved it. Sara Coli was talented in so many ways. Her body could bend effortlessly in the most creative positions. He could pound all of his length inside of her and all she would do was cry out for more. Her hunger for pleasure filled pain was animalistic in nature and obviously captivating to him. He looked at her, then glanced over to Kalitha.

Her facial expression was that of a jealous woman bordering hatred. Her gaze was menacing, as cold as an ice shard, and as deadly as a spike hanging from the ceiling of an unstable cave. Trevor berated himself thinking about how he hadn't told Kalitha that he had been cumming in Sara Coli constantly. That he hadn't ever used protection with her. Therefore, he, she, and Sara Coli were all sharing bodily fluids. He could never mention the places they'd been and made love in.

He shot her a small smile, then turned back to Sara Coli reflecting on their time together. He thought about New York, where they had made love in the rush hour traffic. California, where they had sex on the deck of her 145 ft. yacht in broad daylight, 100 yards off of the Shire. Then there were the Florida Keys, where they had fucked recklessly, with complete abandon, on the balcony of a beach side Presidential Suite. And he couldn't forget Colorado Springs, where she rode him to completion while they floated along the calmer parts of the rapids. Even Austin, Texas, where they had gone bareback horse riding on her ranch and made love in the middle of a grassy plain. Missouri, Kentucky, Tennessee, Georgia... The list goes on.

He could never tell his wife any of those details. The truth was, it was becoming increasingly difficult not to fall for Sara Coli. She naturally flaunted all of the elements of the perfect woman. Her attraction was otherworldly, almost eerie in nature. Her aura enveloped him in something he'd never felt before.

He hated the devilment he was being pushed to use on Sara Coli and with every kiss he experienced a deeply rooted disdain. He found that telling himself the he was devoted to Kalitha often eased the guilt, but it never remained gone. What he was doing was heartless and cruel for someone like Sara Coli. But it was all for Kalitha. At least he'd convinced himself that he was doing it all for her. He smiled and fell right back in stride on their conversation.

Sara Coli smiled back. Down in her heart, she was inconceivably filled with joy. Hopeful thoughts for a future with the young 33 year old Randale who had her as open as the plains of Africa, and twice as hot for him, bubbled up from the depths of her soul. She liked to end their sexcapades with her womb swollen and tender. It reminded her thoroughly that a real man had been inside of her.

She loved that on Thursday she could still feel his lovemaking from Sunday night. He had even licked her sweet pussy until she begged him to relent. He then rubbed her flesh in slow rhythmic circles until she fell asleep under the spell of his touch.

She was falling rather hard for him and hoped that she would soon hit the bottom to be shattered to pieces on the stones of love. He was a machine made of flesh and blood, and he was handling the White Widow like no other lover she'd ever had. She was prepared to increase the dosage, thereby increasing the risk. And though the risk rose, so did her confidence in Randale. She wanted more too. She wanted him deep inside her mouth and tight pussy tonight. She would have him amply in both before the sun rose, and she was sure of it.

Kalitha had had enough for one night. Instinct had told her to flee from the suffering long ago, but her curiosity and criticizing eyes wouldn't allow her. She decided to stop worrying since he would be back home Sunday night and got up to leave. She tried hard not to see Sara Coli licking his ear as she left out. Her head turned in aggreeance, but her eyes remained trained on them in defiance. The mixture of possessiveness and defeat caused a slight throb to pulsate in her head. She exited quickly without looking back.

Kalitha got in her Acura and headed home. As she drove she tried to occupy her mind with other things. *It's time to start looking for a better place to live. Yeah, that's what I'll do. At least it will give me something to do to keep my mind from wandering.* She turned on South College and headed home. She would start the following day.

****

Sara Coli sucked on Trevor's ear lobe. "I want you to fuck me right now," she said in a sexy enticing tone. She licked his ear again. "So let's go."

Trevor watched her get up without him. She looked over her shoulder and wiggled her eyebrows at him. His eyes dropped to her plump round ass in anticipation and he quickly pulled out a wad of cash. He threw a $100 bill on the table, then followed her out. The Bentley limo waited out front for them and the Carrabas parking lot looked dwarfed compared to the Bentley's size. Tony stood with the back door open.

"Ms. White. Mr. Mason," he greeted.

"Don't you dare do that Tony," she swatted playfully at him. "Don't you dare make me feel old."

"My apologies," he said with a smile.

After she got in he looked to Trevor. "Bro."

"Bro," Trevor returned and slid in beside her.

As soon as he was seated and the door closed behind him, Sara Coli lifted her skirt and climbed into his lap. She reached up and caressed the back of his head with a gentle massage. She then kissed him, playfully biting his bottom lip. He loved when she did that.

Trevor watched as she leaned back showing she held two vials of White Widow. He smiled and took one. They both swallowed the liquid straight from the vials like they had been doing for weeks. It absorbed into their systems faster without an agent like liquor to weaken it.

She tossed her vial behind her and began to tug at his belt. She fished out his thick dick and rubbed her already bare pussy up and down against him. He stiffened up almost instantly. She wasted no time raising up and impaling herself with his hardness. She moaned aloud as her head swivelled on her neck in pleasure until she used the ceiling of the limo for leverage. Trevor gripped her hips and rocked her back and forth, and within minutes she was creaming all over his hypnotizing dick. The ride to the house was just enough for Sara Coli to orgasm three magnificent times before the car came to a stop in front of the mansion.

Tony got out to open the door, but the rocking of the limo was a solid indication that he shouldn't disturb them. He smiled, tossed the keys up, and caught them as he made his way into the mansion. The doorman looked at the rocking limo and turned back inside without a word.

Sara Coli cried into Trevor's shoulder and climaxed for the fourth time as he thrust up into her hot soaking pussy with a sledgehammer's power. He gripped her shoulders and pulled her down forcefully, while lifting his hips, shoving his full length into her. The impact was overwhelming, causing him to yell out as he came deep inside her. Her throbbing pussy milked him for all his cum leaving him shaking in the aftershock.

Trevor gasped at the dynamism of his release and held her against his chest in awe. Sara Coli felt something change between them and hugged him tighter than she ever had. She had been won over at that very moment and vowed that she would be his if he wanted her. There was nothing on God's green earth that would make her give *her* Randale up. She inwardly swore it.

Gradually, she eased off him and pulled her skirt down. Gently, she stuffed his glistening member back into his slacks and carefully zipped them. She couldn't wait to get inside because she needed more and the White Widow was beginning to kick in.

She took a deep breath and let it out slowly trying to gain control of her senses. "Come, let's hurry in. I need you inside of me again, right now."

She nearly fled the limo with him in tow. They rushed through the mansion up to the master bedroom where they hungrily and hastily tore one another's clothes off. Trevor lifted her up effortlessly and carried her over to the bed. She felt so dominated and small in his arms which turned her on all the more. He laid her on the bed, and without warning, flipped her over into the doggystyle position. She obliged by lifting her ass high up in the air and lowering her head down to a silk covered pillow. She couldn't wait for him to bury himself deep inside her hot ready pussy.

She muffled a loud squeal into the pillow as he dug in from behind in one strong thrust. She closed her eyes and accepted all he could give her. Trevor held her in place by her smooth hips and began giving her several deep teeth grinding strokes. Sara Coli clawed at the thick grey fur covering the bed trying her best to keep up with him. Truth be told, he was fucking her in ways that shook her to her very core. It didn't matter how well he fucked her, she only wanted more and more. She craved and fiend for him. She only wanted him.

Trevor was doing what he knew she wanted him to do and drove her to near insanity. She wanted to be fucked long and hard and that is exactly how he gave it to her. Yet, every stroke, bite, caress, and moan, filled him with such power that he never wanted to give it up. Or was it that he never wanted to give her up?

****

Later that night, Trevor lay staring up at the ceiling, exhausted. He didn't know how he would ever be able to end what he and Sara Coli had, but he knew he had to. Not wanting to dwell on such negative thoughts, he wrapped his arms around her supple body and nodded off.

CHAPTER 8

Sara Coli sat at her desk in one of her favorite power suits. She twirled a pen thoughtlessly between her fingers as she spoke to Mirah and Janey on her conference phone.

"I am truly blown away," she enthused reflecting on Trevor's sexual power.

"You should be," Janey offered.

"Must be better than nice," said Mirah.

"Oh, it is," purred Sara Coli. "He lasted through a significantly larger dose of the venom."

Janey sucked her teeth and sighed with jealousy. "I would love to find a young lover to share my venom with. I thirst for similar treatment. Don't you Mirah?"

"Trust me, I've been thinking of nothing else," Mirah answered with a giggle.

Sara Coli knew that Mirah and Janey often shared almost everything, but not as often as they shared one another. Unfortunately, Sara Coli wasn't one for sharing her man. She left that to her two extra freaky extremely wealthy friends. Exclusivity was valued highly by Sara Coli and she was going to keep her prize winning dick for herself. She shared only the most minor details with them about Randale and they always ate it all up. She loved them, but in the same breath, hated the level of competition they presented. They were extremely beautiful and very capable of catching Randales' eyes with ease.

This mostly comes from their similar features. There is a chemical agent in the White Widow's venom that has somehow turned all of their hair silvery white. She never understood how it managed to bleach all of their heads, pubic areas, and underarms. Nonetheless, she figured that if she stayed on her game, Randale would never get to see their privates unless she allowed it. Then again, as possessive as she feels about him, she doesn't see that ever happening. Still, she loved to hear her friends envious rants and quips.

Sara Coli always thought that Mirah and Janey were fairly smart, but not smart enough to fly back to Siberia, and procure some of the rare spiders before they became extinct. Twenty-one years ago, they had been introduced to the spider's exceptional venom. Long before MDMA or Ecstasy came on the scene, they had been experiencing the near parallel effects of the White Widow's essence. She always smiled when people assumed that they were talking about Cannabis Sativa. It tickled her at times.

Their elite circle is what brought them in contact with the unique spiders. The venom is a fountain of youth for a woman, albeit potentially fatal if not used correctly and continuously. So twenty-one years back, Sara Coli had them shipped to the U.S. and has been cultivating the White Widow venom ever since. She had nurtured and bred the deadly spiders for decades.

Mirah and Janey realized that they couldn't get the venom from anywhere else on the planet and needed her to provide them with it or watch maliciously as their bodies rapidly deteriorated. Without the constant intake of the venom, the residual poison in their body tissue would eat them alive. Sara Coli had never fully seen what it would do, but she did see three of the twelve stages that the withdrawal would take their bodies through. She was very certain that stage five would cause the bone to turn basically into mush. She never knew why the symptoms differed between women and men.

"Don't be so stingy, Sara Coli," Janey teased.

"Yeah, we're your sisters. Caring is sharing," added Mirah.

"No, and double no," Sara Coli said, laughing, yet, sounding final.

"Oh, Arania," said Mirah. "You're always so possessive."

"It's better to be possessive, than lonely," Sara Coli said dismissively. "Sorry to end it today girls, but I have a prior verbal engagement. So, ciao."

"Bye love," Janey chimed.

"Tah tah," Mirah crooned. "Love you."

"Muah!" Sara Coli blew a kiss into the phone, disconnected, then dialed her realtor.

He answered after two rings. "Good afternoon, Ms. White."

"Is what I asked for prepared?" she asked. She leaned back in her chair and spun around to look out her office window.

"Absolutely. Three fully furnished rooms and everything state of the art," he responded. "Just as you requested ma'am."

"Great, Thomas. You're one of a kind."

"Thank you, Ms. White."

She hung up and smiled to herself. Randale would love the penthouse suite downtown Wilmington that she had just purchased for him. It was a luxurious $800,000 suite in the tallest building in Port City and he would absolutely love it. She'd sent Tony to go fetch the keys, pack up the trailer, then deliver him to his new home. Afterwards, he was to call her as soon as he dropped Randale off. For now she had nothing to do but wait on the call. She was already excited and couldn't wait to hear his voice. Until her phone rang, she would just sit back and wait.

****

Kalitha sat on the sofa with her legs folded beneath her looking at the selection of homes for rent in the newspaper when a noise outside grabbed her attention. She looked up and listened intently. It sounded like a large truck, but she wasn't sure. Tossing the paper aside, she got up and moved hastily over to the window and peeped out. Confused, she saw a black van and a moving truck pulling right up to the Navigator and Escalade. She watched as a few guys jumped out and began to open the SUV's.

"Uh, Trevor," she said as she watched them pointing at the SUV's, then to the trailer. "Trevor. TREVOR!" she screamed louder when he didn't respond.

"Yeah, babe," he said coming out of the bathroom. "What is

it?" he asked walking up behind her.

"Outside," she said in a panic stricken voice.

The men were laughing at an unheard joke as they began walking towards their door.

"What in the hell is going on?" she asked nervously.

Trevor peeked out of the window and frowned. "I don't know," he replied calmly.

"Are they about to try and take our shit baby?"

"No," he replied. "I mean, I don't know," he corrected, sounding unsure.

"They're taking our shit Trevor," she yelled. "Do something." She pushed him towards the front door.

He grabbed her by the arm. "We don't know what's going, now calm your ass down," he gritted out.

"Okay," she whined, then snatched away from his strong grip. "Fine." She rubbed her arm where it ached at.

He narrowed his eyes, giving her a reprimanding look. She walked back into the kitchen feeling put in her place. She had never been grabbed like that by him and it kind of left her a little concerned. Trevor opened the door and instantly recognized Tony. When he stepped outside his face quickly changed into one of relief.

"Tony. What's happening, bro?"

"I've come to move you," he answered, giving Trevor a light pound. "Sara Coli told me to come, have you packed up, and moved out."

"Move?"

"Yeah," he pulled a yellow envelope out and held it out to Trevor. "She sent this just in case you had a lease to pay up or something."

Trevor opened it, revealing a wad of crisp $100 bills.

Tony continued in with a smile. "You're to pay your bills off with it. You now own a penthouse suite downtown."

Trevor shook his head in disbelief. This could not be real. Just three weeks ago, she had dramatically increased his bank account by $250,000, making it just over 300K with what Kalitha had in hers.

Tony snapped him out of his trance like state. "Uh, we're here to move you, bro," he said, continuing to smile.

"Yeah, okay," Trevor said, stepping to the side. The other men moved into the house past them and he and Tony followed.

"Just tell us what you're keeping and what's trash, and we will do the rest," said Tony. When he saw Kalitha, he gave her one of his winning smiles. *Wow. Hello sexy, Chica.*

Kalithas' smile was gigantic as she looked around at all of the worn down furniture. "Leave all of this shit Trev and let's just take our clothes," she blurted out with her premature response."

All of the men looked to Kalitha. Trevor shot her a look trying to calm her. "Excuse my, uh, sister. She gets a little over excited at times."

After Trevor cleaned up her outburst, she immediately calmed down realizing that she had just made a huge mistake. She didn't want to jeopardize what they had going on, but her lack of self control said something completely different. She began pointing out things that should be taken and what should be left behind. Once she got the men busy up front, she hurried back to the bedroom to put away their wedding photos.

Trevor looked at the guys who had begun to snatch stuff up quickly, transfer it to the waiting truck.

"I gotta call the landlord." He paused, then looked at Tony. "As a matter of fact, take a walk with me, bro." Trevor and Tony left out to take the short walk to Mr. Collin's house at the very back of the trailer park.

"Some of these trailers are nice," commented Tony "

"Yeah," Trevor agreed. "Your's looked like shit though," Tony joked.

Trevor laughed it off. "I know man. But a man can only afford what a man can afford."

"That's all over with now man," Tony said reassuringly.

"Sara Coli really likes you, bro."

An awkward silence settled between them. Trevor looked to Tony and his face was warning him to say the right shit. Trevor could sense that Tony felt as if Sara Coli was family, and although Trevor was the bigger of the two, Tony didn't look like he was a slouch. He could also tell that Tony had questions in his eyes about Kalitha. He smiled and finally responded.

"I like her too, Tony. A lot."

"Yeah," he said, straightening his hat. "You'd better."

Trevor smiled it off. When they reached Mr. Collin's door, he knocked and was met by his old wife Marsha.

She looked down her nose at him. "Did we call you to our home?"

"No, ma'am," Trevor answered respectfully.

She looked over to Tony, then back to Trevor disdainfully. Her stringy brunette hair hung loosely down her shriveled neck. Her old veiny skin seemed to drape off of her bones. Trevor felt sorry for her in a way, but on the other hand, he felt like slapping her old wrinkled face with the yellow envelope filled with money.

She sniffed loudly with a snort. "Well, what in the hell do you want?"

Tony looked away to conceal his laughter. "I just came to pay the lease up because I'm moving."

"Well, good," she retorted. "Good riddance to you and that little nappy headed gal."

Not bothering to respond, Trevor handed her the envelope. She snatched it out of his hand and Tony struggled to conceal his lauger even more. Trevor fought hard to keep his cool.

"That gal with that big ole butt of hers is always flirting with my Tom. I'm glad she's leaving."

Trevor hurried to turn away before Marsha said the wrong thing. "Okay," he said, waving for Tony to follow. "Thanks Mrs. Collins."

"She thinks I don't know it, but Tom has been telling me. I know she wants my husband." Trevor and Tony hurried away hearing her jabbering fade away in the distance.

Tony laughed at her now that they had left and Trevor followed suit. He had to get Tony away before Marsha unknowingly incriminated him and Kalitha.

"I take it she means your sister?"

"Yeah," Trevor replied quickly.

"She is pretty, bro," Tony commented. "Really pretty."

Trevor kept looking straight ahead, but didn't respond. Tony let it go and they finished the walk back in silence. It didn't take long for them to get packed up and be led to their new home. The building was in the middle of downtown Wilmington and had a huge inside parking deck attached to it. It was perfect for the Navigator, Escalade, and Acura.

Tony led them into the lobby and Kalitha was shocked that there were places like this in Wilmington. She would have never guessed. There was a clerk at the front desk and a number pad by the elevator. It was high class and it was either numeric entry, or be buzzed up from the console upstairs. They stopped at the desk and the older white man greeted them with a nod.

"Good afternoon. How may I assist you?"

Tony stepped forward. "New penthouse residents. They need to set their codes."

The clerk smiled and began to click away at his computer. "Identical or separate entry codes?"

Trevor and Kalitha looked at one another, then stated their answer in unison. "Separate."

Everyone smiled and Kalitha caught Tony eyeing her with desire in his eyes. She brushed it off and turned away. That didn't bother him. He continued to enjoy the view of her juicy plump ass in her skin tight jeans. There was no denying that he was developing a severe case of the hots for her.

They turned to the elevator's keypad and programmed their entry codes one by one. The elevator opened once, closed, then opened once more signifying a successful load. They boarded and took the smooth ride up to the penthouse. Kalitha was all smiles and Trevor loved to see her like that. Tony just admired her from the side deeming that she was something truly luscious, but held his thoughts in check.

When the doors opened, they were met with an abundance of style and elegance. Kalitha instantly began floating throughout the suite with an air of astonishment. She spun slowly taking in all of the beautiful decor. All the modern furniture, colors, and style patterns blended so well. She could not believe her eyes.

Trevor entered in total admiration, almost subdued by the whole layout. A professional had to have decorated it for them and he knew that it had to be the work of Sara Coli by the amount of precision and detail of the home's design. It was expensive in every since of the word.

"Okay, bro," said Tony. "This is much more like what you deserve."

Trevor smiled and nodded. The elevator opened and the movers began to bring in their personal belongings and chosen items. Kalitha kicked off her sneakers and began to direct traffic as they came in. Trevor and Tony backed out of the way and took a look out of the big bay window where they could see clear across the Cape Fear River. The view of the famous battleship was grand. They could see straight to the Leland Bridge. Trevor imagined that at night the view of Old Wilmington would be spectacular.

Tony slid open the balcony door and motioned for Trevor to join him. Once he stepped out, Tony slid the door closed behind them.

"Beautiful, isn't it?" Tony asked.

"You hit it right on the head," Trevor answered, taking a deep breath of fresh air. "Ahhh," he breathed out.

Tony leaned against the rail and caught a glimpse of Kalitha walking back through the suite. "That is truly a wonderful sight," he said in a deep lust filled drawl.

Trevor turned to see Kalitha on her tiptoes trying to measure where to put a picture. Her arms were outstretched and her back was arched, showing off the complete shape of her bubble ass. Her shirt lifted a little and displayed the top of her pink panties. Trevor could barely contain his anger and looked away clutching the rail with a fierce intensity.

Tony continued, unaware of Trevor's change in body language. "Bro," he said, tapping Trevor on the left arm lightly. "Your sister,

Vicky." He paused to rub his hair back.

"What about her?" Trevor all but gritted out.

"She's beautiful, man," Tony said with a smile. "She's really hot, bruh."

Trevor looked to the right at the battleship steaming with anger.

Tony continued, unaware. "Maybe she'd like to hang out with us sometime."

Trevor faced Tony, who was still focused on Kalitha smiling and pointing to something for the movers. She laughed a beautiful sound and walked away. That was enough time to damper his emotions and get his face, contorted with anger, back under control. He had to remain cool at all cost.

"I don't know man," Trevor said with a lot less bite. "She does her own thing."

"I don't see anything wrong with us doing our thing together."

Trevor turned and grabbed Tony by his neck. He squeezed with all of his might as Tony choked and leaned back over the rail fighting to free himself.

"That's my fucking wife," Trevor yelled just before he pushed him over.

Tony screamed as he plummeted towards the concrete below. His body made a loud 'splat' sound causing Trevor to snap out of his malicious thoughts. He glanced at Tony with a forced smile.

"I'm just saying, bro," Tony continued. "You know me. I'm a straight up guy. Just put a tiny word in for me, that's all," Tony pleaded, sincerely.

"Alright, bro. I'll do that," Trevor lied.

"Thanks man," Tony said, looking into the suite, seeing Kalitha curiously watching them as they talked. He smiled and turned back to Trevor again, patting him on the back. He looked back at Kalitha hungrily. "If it's not too much to ask could you make it sooner than later." He gave Trevor another pat on the back, then stepped back inside.

Trevor struggled to keep his composure as he heard them leaving. "Thank you fellas," Kalitha chirped. "And have a nice day."

The men bid their farewells as they entered the elevator. Tony's voice struck a chord in Trevor when he spoke. "Bye, Vicky. I hope to see you soon."

"Bye, Tony," she returned in a sweet voice.

Trevor walked in from the balcony and gave her an ice cold stare filled with anger. She felt the chill of it and giggled. "What? I was just being nice."

His stare made her move hastily and she walked into their bedroom and sat down on the bed. She looked down at her folded hands, then back out to where Trevor stood angrily. He sat on the sofa and looked around slowly, taking it all in. It was grand. One inch carpeting all of the way through the suite. There were three master sized bedrooms with huge bathtubs, separate showers, and Jacuzzi in the middle of the floor that could easily seat five or even six people.

Kalitha got up and floated throughout the house again in awe. She saw Trevor seated on the sofa with his head laid back and didn't want to disturb him. She figured she'd leave him alone with his thinking for the time being. Her eyes took in his tense shoulders and balled fist, and had an idea. *Oh, I know what you need*. Sexily, she sashayed back into the bedroom.

Trevor's phone rang next to him on the couch. He saw that it was Tony and reluctantly answered it. "What's up, Tony?"

"I forgot to tell you that Sara Coli wants you to call her from the house phone. Cool?"

"Cool," he lied. "I will."

When the line went dead, he leaned forward and dialed her cell phone on the intercom phone. She answered on the second ring.

"Hello, darling," she crooned.

"This is amazing, Sara Coli. You always manage to outdo yourself every time."

"Well, you are an amazing man," she said, leaning back in her plush office chair. "I wanted you out of that God awful trailer and into something that more suits you," she droned in her usual buttery smooth voice.

Trevor looked up as Kalitha pranced into the living room stark naked with nothing on but heels. She sashayed over to the big bay window and leaned against it poking her big round ass out towards him. He was transfixed on the alluring sight. She spread her legs then bent over touching the floor, causing her ass cheeks to spread, and her hairy snatch to poke out. He could see how wet she was and it made his dick swell and press against his slacks begging for freedom.

"I had to place you where you truly belonged, Randale."

"Where I belong?" he asked, watching intently as Kalitha reached between her legs and parted her lips displaying her wet pinkness to him. She jammed two fingers in and began to fuck herself slowly. His heart began to pound and his dick throbbed profoundly. Kalitha was doing her thing.

"You deserve to be placed high above the city where I hold you in my eyes."

Kalitha stood, then walked a sexy cat walk over to him. She kneeled between his legs and began to massage her plump titties. While pinching her nipples she emitted a silent breathy moan.

"Really?" Trevor said to both women.

Kalitha smiled and fished his dick out of his zipper and stuffed the tip deep in her mouth. She licked him like a kitten from the base to the tip, stopping only to focus on the underside of the head where the most sensitive skin was.

"Yes, really, darling. You're stellar to me and I hope that you are really enjoying yourself right now," said Sara Coli.

"I am," he replied softly. "This is great."

Kalitha licked the base where his balls hung with tiny swirls. She then began stuffing his ball sack into her mouth while suckling softly. She let them slide out her mouth slowly, smiled, then tugged at his pants sliding them down over his hips. When she heard Sara Colis' voice again through the speaker, she began to go even harder.

"I thought you'd love it. Are we still on for Friday?"

"Oh, yesss," he said smoothly. "Yes, yes, yes."

Sara Coli smiled brightly at his enthusiasm. "Mmm, you sound really eager."

"I am," he replied in a husky voice. "I'm so eager for you."

Kalitha stared up into his eyes, knowing that he was talking to her and not that old bitch. It made her pussy clench up and produce even more slick juices.

"Oh great," said Sara Coli, blushing hard. "I will see you then, my love. Bye."

"Um hmmm," he said as the line went dead.

He pushed the button making sure the call had ended. Without warning, he reached down and pulled Kalitha up to him. She screeched in surprise at his fast movement. He gripped her curly hair with one hand, and with the other, her lower back, and flung her to the side. She loved it. He stood up and slid the rest of his clothes off in swift tugs. She watched with anticipation, licking her lips as his thick tool bounced inches from her face.

He lifted his leg and set it on the back of the sofa behind her head, then dipped down as he aimed his rod directly into her mouth. She took him in without hesitation and began to suck with pressure and passion. He reached back and fingered her juicy pussy hole making a squishing sound in the once quiet room.

She moaned around his long pole as it glided down into the back of her throat. She gagged slightly which only seemed to make her push it further in. She was hot for his dick and needed to feel it erupt in her mouth. She moaned, slurped, and begged him for his honey nectar. She pulled his heavy pole from her mouth and jerked his spit coated dick with slow strokes.

"Cum in my mouth, Trev. Please, I need to taste you." She moaned as his fingers popped her hairy wet slit. "Oooh, I need to feel it sliding down my throat, Trevor."

She began to suck with a determined and desperate purpose. He felt the power of her sucking and knew he was coming fast. Her intensity pushed him over the edge and he gripped the back of the sofa tightly. He dipped low as his orgasm sprayed hot white globs of cum down her throat, spilling from the corner of her lips.

Kalitha gagged and swallowed, almost choking on his large wad, but never pulled back. It turned her all of the way on and she continued to put in work. When he snatched his dick from her throat trap, she gasped for air. He panted heavily as he stared down at her in wonder. Calling out his name over and over, she began to finger pop herself with both hands. One massaging circles around her clit, the other jabbing her two manicured fingers deep into her sweet peach. The show she was putting on had Trevor's slowly deflating member swelling up seemingly larger than before.

She spread her legs wide, inviting him in. "Please, Trevor. Please fuck me, baby."

He pulled her up and lifted her under her arms and she wrapped her legs around his waist as he plunged deep inside her. He held her securely and bounced her up and down on his stiff dick. She cried out in ecstasy with every thrust. Gripping her ass tightly, Trevor dug into her hard and fast. She was almost at her peek yelling out in a frenzy as she held on with all her might while he drilled it home. The pain felt like passion, the ache felt like love, and his dick sliding in and out of her felt like heaven.

Trevor closed his eyes and imagined that Kalitha was Sara Coli. He imagined her silvery white pussy hair tickling the sides of his pelvic bone. Her juicy breasts bouncing in a steady rhythm. Her long white hair flowing down her back and over the front of her shoulders, sticking to her sweat soaked skin. He began to fall back onto the sofa, suddenly needing to plunge deeper.

Kalitha's pussy pulsated with every powerful thrust her husband presented her. He was way past her pussy, way past her stomach, reaching all the way up into her soul with every stroke he delivered. Her body began to tremble as the orgasm rose up from her pussy and to her ass, then spread out evenly all over her body. It traveled over her breast, making her nipples tingle before shooting out in her arms and leg. It was so extreme it made her feel weak and her body turn to putty.

Just when she thought that she would let go and fall backwards out of his arms, she felt her body falling forward. He was the one falling backwards. Her climax was on the edge, her orgasm screaming for that one final touch, as they floated through the air towards the sofa. The pressure of her body slamming down on Trevor's full 10 inches with that much force made her nature explode and gush with cum. It shot out of her with so much intensity that it threatened to rip her into pieces. She cried out, tears building within her eyes, as she came fiercely. Her pussy muscles were clenching and relaxing extending her orgasm even longer. She buried her head into Trevor's shoulder and couldn't stop the flash flood of tears which led to her sobbing.

Trevor held her gently rubbing her hair, shoulders, and back. She sniffled softly as her body slowly descended from the clouds and her tremors began to subside.

"I can't ever lose you, Trev. I swear I can't."

He looked towards the ceiling, breathing heavily, unable to respond.

CHAPTER 9

Two months had flown by in the blink of an eye, but for Kalitha, the routine remained the same. Trevor would be with her for the week, but gone on Friday to return on Monday. She couldn't deny that she missed him during the time he spent with Sara Coli. She had even gone back the day after they'd moved into the penthouse and picked up Frankenstein. Trevor had left the decision up to her and chose to keep him, thus making her husband an even happier man. Her bank account was now at $120,000, but she didn't know how much was in Trevor's account anymore. She made a mental to ask.

Her thoughts returned back to their plans for the future. She figured that they would be okay with a million dollars between the both of them. With that, they could open up their own business. She figured they would do something in maintenance since Trevor was good at fixing things and she could be the receptionist or something. *Hello? Mason and Mason. If it's broken, we can replace it.* She smiled to herself pretending to answer phone calls at their 'somewhere in the future' business.

She knew they could survive off of a million dollars. They had done so on much less. She admitted to herself that she was feeling the repercussions of her husband sleeping with another woman. His attitude often flared up unexpectedly and he was much rougher on her than her body could stand. At other times he seemed withdrawn and a bit distracted, uninterested, and sometimes even repulsed by her advances. On top of that, he had told her that he would be leaving on Thursday this week instead of Friday, and she wasn't feeling that at all.

She crossed her arms and sat up rigidly in her seat. Sara Coli was starting to cut in on her time with Trevor, and if that continued, she would end up getting three days to her four. *That shit is not about to happen, you old bitch. No! You're not about to do that. That's my fucking husband.* She peered over at her unsuspecting husband, her blood nearly scalding her veins.

Kalitha glared out the window once more. Seeing the sign for Monkey Junction reminded her that they were headed to check on her old beat up car. That's what she'd agreed to drive, but it still bothered her that she wasn't allowed to drive the Navigator or the Escalade. She understood the reason why, but she didn't want to ride around in that old piece of shit while he whipped around town in the fully customized Escalade they were riding in now.

Why do I have to drive a used hunk of trash? She cut him a glaring look and rolled her eyes. *That's why I've been dogging that piece of shit out. I hope that muthafucka can't be fixed.* She crossed her legs. *I don't even remember when I last put oil in that raggedy shit.*

She turned back to look out her window as they pulled into Blacks Auto Repairs. He parked, then looked at her curiously.

"I'm going to see what they said about the car." Kalitha continued to stare out of the window without responding. He laughed it off and got out to go do what he came to do.

She watched him go silently seething. She was tired of complaining about the Acura anyway. He rode around in style in a $75,000 SUV. Why couldn't she drive the Navigator? It just didn't make any sense. He also wouldn't allow her to use the money she had saved in her account. To her it was beginning to feel like he was controlling what she did and he'd never been that way with her. She was his wife and she deserved to buy something nice to drive, or at least push the $50,000 Navigator. She was ready to fuss and fight about it for the rest of the day if she had to. As he walked back to the SUV and got in, she turned the music down.

He spoke evenly not wanting to cause an argument. "Well

baby, you killed it."

"It was a piece of shit anyway," she mumbled under her breath. "So what now?" she asked, sarcastically.

"It means we have to get you another used car."

"Another used car?" she snapped in a nasty tone. "What in the fuck is wrong with the Navi?!"

Trevor was taken aback by her raising her voice. "First of all, calm your ass down Kalitha and relax."

"No, Trevor," she yelled, her words filled with feminine attitude. "I don't want another used car. I want something new."

"Whatever," he said starting the SUV. She reached over and turned the ignition back off and snatched the keys out. They jingled loudly as they landed somewhere in the back of the SUV.

"What is your fucking problem?" a frustrated Trevor demanded.

"I don't have a fucking problem. You're the one with the fucking problem."

"Kalitha, I don't know why you have your panties up in a bunch today, but—"

She cut him off fire shooting from her eyes. "My panties are as far up my ass as your head is up that old bitches ass."

He rubbed his face downward. "So this is about Sara Coli, huh?"

She went silent for a moment. She couldn't admit that it was because she had started it all and she couldn't request that he terminate it. She looked away, but he pulled her face back towards him by her chin.

"Is it? Is this about Sara Coli?"

"No," she yelled and snatched away from his grasp. "It's about me wanting a nice car. That's it."

Trevor looked over to his wife knowing that it was more behind her little tantrum, but he didn't want to hear anymore about this shit. He just wanted her calm and quiet until he left on Thursday so he could ride the *White Widow Coaster*, as he like to call it. He needed a fix more than he needed to hear her groan, bitch, and gripe. Besides, what could it hurt to let her drive the Navigator?

He took a deep breath and let out a long sigh. "Okay, babe. You can drive the Navi," he said, rubbing her curly hair. "Your wilding out over nothing. It's just a truck sweety."

She gave him a quick glance, looked back towards the keys, then back to him. He nodded towards them. "You threw 'em, you gotta go and get 'em."

Kalitha hurried out the truck and quickly found the keys lying on the floor. She got back in, put the keys back in the ignition, and cranked the SUV. Trevor shook his head as he pulled out of Black's Auto Repairs and hopped onto Carolina Beach Road heading back towards the penthouse.

"Oh yeah, about the bank accounts. Sooo..." She dragged it out causing Trevor to look over at her uneasily. "How much do we have? I mean collectively. Are we at $500,000 yet?"

"I don't think so," he said, glancing over his shades at her. "How much do you have?"

"100K or so." She started scratching her head. "What's in yours?"

"I don't know exactly, but I'll check it though."

You lying mutha— "Okay, just let me know."

He nodded and kept on driving. She watched him accusingly, but managed to conceal it. He reached and turned the music back up. She leaned back, eyeing him enviously. His jewelry selection today was off of the chain. He wore a black diamond Rolex, black diamond rings, and a platinum Cuban link with a black diamond cross.

She didn't have anything other than her wedding band and a tiny diamond ring that he had bought her. She didn't want to seem like she was whining, so she said nothing about it. She would just put on his canary and white invisible set diamond chain and wear it. He wouldn't mind. She could not wait to get to the Navigator because she had already been making plans to change it into her personal girl mobile. She wanted to ride on rims too, and she felt that she deserved it.

They arrived at the penthouse shortly after 12:30 pm and Kalitha hurried to the bedroom and grabbed the invisible set chain and put it on. She then snatched the Navigator's keys off of the dresser, stuffed a few thousand dollars into her purse, and headed out again.

Trevor sat back on the love seat watching her whiz out. "Babe, where are you going?"

"Out. I'll be back," she yelled over her shoulder and kept it moving.

The elevator closed as he stared at her. He shrugged, then kicked his feet up to watch some television. He rarely ever hounded her about her whereabouts because he never had any reason to. Besides, he wasn't the type to keep tabs on his woman. He trusted her, though she was stubborn, bullheaded, and unscrupulous at times.

Actually, those were some of the reasons he loved her so much. She was no white tailed deer, but she was no jackal either. He smiled when a big brown and black blur landed on his lap. He patted Frankenstein gently on the head.

"Hey, boy. You missed me?"

****

Kalitha hurried towards the tan Navigator, each of her strides filled with anticipation and liveliness. She could already see the changes she wanted to make to the SUV. She knew the perfect rim shop. *Twenty-four inch blades would look hot*, she thought. That would be a quick $4,000 she was more than willing to pay. She aimed the alarm, pressed the unlock button, and it chirped to life. After opening the door, she climbed in and looked around the interior with approval. She rubbed her fingertips across the dash and steering wheel lovingly before starting it.

"Girl, I'm about to turn you into the baddest bitch for real." She grabbed her cell phone and dialed 12th and Castle Auto Paint Shop. After a brief session of sweet talking, she convinced them to strip and paint it the next day. She was going to have it painted a light pink, almost peach. The job would cost $2,000 plus $500 more for the rush job, but it was well worth it. It would be a gift to herself since Trevor was getting all the gifts lately.

As she drove on, she thought about their earlier conversation.

His answer regarding the bank question was nonchalant and standoffish. He had made her feel as if her inquiry was not important at all. She would give him a few days to get his shit together.

She pulled up to the rim shop ready to begin the truck makeover. The staff began to work on her SUV as soon as she pointed out the blades and paid for them. She sat on the bench in the waiting area thinking about the Sara Coli situation, her mind reeling out of control. She was starting to think that she should insure herself against the worst, because Trevor seemed to only have his best interest in mind.

She decided from that day on that she would ask him for money for things, and she would instead put it away for a rainy day. She crossed her legs and held her purse tightly against her lap. *I'm gonna ask for shit every single chance I get,* she thought smugly. Her eyes lit up as the Navigator pulled back out floating on 24 inch blades. She stood as the driver got out.

"How do you like 'em, yo?" the young guy asked.

Kalitha nodded her approval. "One down, one to go."

****

A week had gone by and Kalitha was finally happy. Her light pink Navigator sat on 24 inch blades next to Trevor's white Escalade. She sat at the table in nothing but a long t-shirt and slippers. The cool breeze coming in through the sliding door caressed her pussy and she liked it. Trevor was in the shower when the lobby intercom buzzed. She nibbled on a piece of cheese and looked over to it. It buzzed again so she got up and pressed it.

"Randale," a smooth feminine voice cooed. "It's me. Surprise! Buzz me up, darling?"

Panic set in immediately as Kalitha paused for a brief second. She glanced back towards the room, then to the button. She pushed it, then dashed through the suite to their bedroom to put on some jeans and a shirt. Next, she darted to the bathroom.

"Trev, she's here," she yelled.

"What?"

"She's here! She's on her way up," she yelled again over the shower water.

Trevor leaned against the shower wall thinking that all hell was about to break loose. Kalitha looked back toward the front area as an idea popped in her head.

"Stay in the shower."

"What? Why?" Trevor asked, but she was already gone. He rubbed his forehead and face. *This is not going to be good.*

Kalitha reached the bar and sat down just as the elevator door opened. Sara Coli walked in looking even younger than she previously had. Hell, she was even sexier up close. Kalitha noticed and she instantly regretted being in her presence. They locked gazes.

"Hi, Ms. White," Kalitha said, extending her hand while walking to meet her.

Sara Coli examined her from head to toe adamantly. Kalitha could feel the microscopic once over in which she was being met with.

She finally reached out and accepted her hand. "Hello. And you are?" Sara Coli asked, still looking her over.

"Oh, wow," Kalitha feigned disappointment. "I'm Vicky? My brother didn't tell you about me?"

"No," Sara Coli said plainly. "He did not?"

"Gosh. I hope I'm not that much of an embarrassment in his eyes," she said, trying to make a light joke on herself.

Sara Coli's wall visually broke and she smiled radiantly at Kalitha. "Well, hello, Vicky. I'm Sara Coli Arania White. You can call me Sara Coli."

"It's nice to finally meet you, Sara Coli." Kalitha put her hand on her hip. "Well, he's in the shower right now, but he should be out soon."

Sara Coli's facial expression hid her thoughts well, but she was still examining the young curly haired woman. She was thick and Sara Coli could tell from the way her hips flared out that she had something round back there. She admitted to herself that the young lady was exceedingly pretty, but not Trevor's type.

Kalitha smiled. "You can have a seat if you like."

"I'm fine," she responded, still taking her in. "Don't I know you from somewhere?" she asked, smiling brightly. "You look very familiar."

Kalitha looked at her with curious confusion. "No, I don't think so and I'm pretty sure we don't hang out in the same place," she said with a chuckle. "But, you know the world isn't but so big," she added jokingly with a wave of her hand.

"Oh, I do know, honey. I've been around it a few times."

Kalitha gave her a fake smile. *And fuck you very much for that unwanted bit of information, darling.*

Kalitha watched as her eyes settled on the yellow and white diamond chain she was wearing. She reached up and touched it absently. "Oh," she laughed nervously. "My brother lets me wear this. I think that it's too fly."

Sara Coli smiled at her. "I like jewelry. I like to give it as gifts."

"I love me some colorful ice too, girl," Kalitha added slickly. "They're a girl's best friend."

"Yes. Yes, indeed...girl," Sara Coli said with a hint of sarcasm.

When Sara Coli turned to look around the place, Kalitha raised her hands up in front of her face in a clawing motion. Sara Coli didn't see anything that would suggest foul play, so she let the festering notion go. She turned back to a smiling Kalitha.

"How about I just tell him that you're here."

"That would be kind of you."

Kalitha hurried off to the bathroom in the master bedroom and knocked on the door. Trevor opened it and peeked out.

"That old bitch is out there waiting for you," Kalitha said through clenched teeth. "Sara Coli is here, Trev," she gritted out.

"Tell her I'll be out in a minute," he snapped back.

"My name is Vicky," she whispered tightly reminding him.

"I know your damn name," he grumbled back.

She pointed her finger in his face as a warning, then spun away, whizzing back out to Sara Coli. She pasted on her fake smile as she entered the room.

"He's getting out right now."

"Thank you," Sara Coli said, eyeing her with even more curiosity. Again she detected nothing peculiar and decided to let it go.

Sara Coli sat down, crossing her legs professionally. Kalitha headed towards the cheese on the bar admiring Sara Cali's smooth legs. *$800 million would keep my legs looking like that too*, she thought sarcasticly. She watched as the blonde beauty sat staring straight ahead ignoring her. *What she thinks having a conversation with me is beneath her? So sitting here in silence is a better option?*

Kalitha put the cheese away, then rinsed her hands off. She grabbed the keys and her purse. "I'm outta here, bro."

Trevor walked out at that moment and Kalitha noticed the way Sara Coli's eyes lit up at his sculptured wet chest and abs. The towel was wrapped loosely around him and his feet were bare and wet. Trevor was a fucking Greek God and a gentleman, which made him even more appealing. Kalitha nearly exploded at Sara Coli's desirous and near ravenous look.

Sara Coli stood up slowly, her eyes riveted on the tasty specimen standing before her. "Oh, Randale. You look like a big ole melting bar of chocolate."

"Hey, beautiful," Trevor said, looking past her to a seething Kalitha. "I didn't expect to see you here. Where's Tony?"

"Busy," she smiled and closed the distance between them. She touched his wet chest possessively. "Today you have me. Why? Am I not enough for you, sir?" she chided.

"Don't be ridiculous," he responded as she rose on her toes to kiss him.

Kalitha didn't realize that she was frozen stiff until the keys dropped from her hands to the floor. They broke their kiss and Kalitha nervously picked them up. She tried to think of something fast to change the vibe.

"Yuck, put some clothes on," she said wrinkling her nose.

Trevor saw that she was trying to play it off, but he could also see the rage and resentment bubbling beneath the surface that she was trying to keep in check.

"I thought you were leaving?" he said with a light chuckle.

She returned his smile and pressed the button for the elevator. "I'm going, boy." She waved to Sara Coli. "See you later."

Sara Coli gave her a faint smile as Kalitha stepped onto the elevator with one last wave. When the doors closed them out of her sight she furiously punched the elevator wall. It began to hurt instantly and her fist began to throb. "Ouch," she squeaked looking down at it. Feeling the pain shoot up her wrist only fueled her fury.

Sara Coli looked from the elevator to Trevor. She smiled, then pulled the towel from around him. She looked him up and down and licked her lips. "Um, mmm, mmm. So tasty."

He rubbed her hair back and eyed her with a sexy grin.

"Later," she panted, fanning herself. "Hurry and dress, darling. I want to show you something."

"I want to show you something too," he teased as he pressed his meat up against her.

"Go on," she giggled, pushing him away.

"Alright," he turned slowly and walked back into the master bedroom.

She watched his bare ass walking away. "Nice," she whispered.

It didn't take them long to get from the penthouse to her mansion in Ogden while relaxing in her Phantom. Since they took Market Street it was a clear shot with hardly any traffic. She was ready to show him what she believed he was ready to see. She wanted to plunge him deeper into her life, much deeper than he'd ever gotten inside her womb. She smiled at that thought because Randale really went deep in that manner. He was her blessing and she wanted to take him down to her chambers where her most prized possessions resided. She wanted him to see for himself all that she held dear.

She smiled as she rubbed his hand lightly across the knuckles. He looked over to her and she looked great as usual. He gave her a wink, which made her smile widen. His thoughts had settled on the White Widow fix he knew would be coming later on. He couldn't explain how addicted he had become to the venom. He felt as if the white milky substance was flowing through his veins, intermingling with his blood cells. It had such a residual attachment to him that it affected his thinking even when he wasn't under its powerful influence.

He glanced at her as she reached inside her purse, secretly hoping it was a vial for him. He didn't show how let down he was when he saw that it was only her phone instead of his fix. He just smiled and looked out the window. He paid no attention to her on the phone, but subconsciously realized that she was describing some kind of creation to a jeweler that she wanted specially made. His mind flashed back to a time when they were coming from the firing range.

She was great with a gun, and since he had come up in the hood, he was familiar with firearms. He had never shot anyone and probably never would. But at the range he was somewhat of a natural. He thought back on that day with a far off look on his face. He remembered they were let into the limo by Tony and once inside, he and Sara Coli sat across from one another for a change. He watched as she pulled out a wide golden box and handed it to him. He opened it to reveal a gold plated pistol inside. He examined the craftsmanship of the weapon, loving the engraved design on the handle. He thanked her profoundly before closing the case, making sure it was secure.

Afterwards, Sara Coli sat back against the seat in a sexy pose and he couldn't help but to eye her body. He scanned her from her beautiful face down to her sleek and slender legs. She twirled a pump on the tip of her toe, caught him watching, and kicked it off. She then spreads her legs wide, hiking up her skirt. Trevor licked his lips waiting to get a peek at her plump pussy. She slid down towards him and pointed to her silvery white patch of pubes with her slit open.

"Come taste me, Randale."

Trevor crawled over and licked and sucked her wet pussy until she came all over his tongue and chin, wetting his shirt. He remembered how her sweet nectar flowed out all over him, sending his mind reeling. Since that day, Trevor has been eating her pussy religiously.

He snapped out of his state of remembrance when Sara Coli spoke to him.

"Earth to Randale."

He glanced at her and smiled, but he was still thinking of how wet his silk shirt had gotten that day.

"I'm with you," he teased.

"Now you are."

When the car door opened, they got out and entered the mansion quickly. Sara Coli pulled him by his hand down the marble floor hall and down to her secret chamber. He realized they had gone into a wing of the mansion he'd never been in. They traveled down a long flight of stairs to an even longer hallway. The hallway led to a door with a hand print recognition screen on it.

She observed Trevor, who stood there in awe. Never had he seen such opulence. He'd heard of them, but until then, a hand recognition screen may as well have been something made up for the movies.

"This is my private chamber where I keep my precious babies," she said, touching the soft synthetic material that resembled some form of silicon. Her fingers eased inside it nearly to the back of her hand.

"Your babies?" he asked curiously.

Sara Coli smiled and proceeded with her tour. "I keep it pitch black in here because it keeps them calm."

The door slid open, revealing a large space. It was really too dark to determine how large it was. The light from out in the hallway gave Trevor some indication. Sara Coli walked in and a path lit up as she made her way towards the middle of the room. He entered cautiously unsure of what was inside. From the way her voice echoed, he could tell that it was a sizable room. He saw that there was something big in the middle, some sort of glass case.

"As I said, I keep it pitch dark in here because the region in Siberia they're from is cave like. They are very sensitive to light."

She touched the panel in front of the box and the door slid closed behind Trevor leaving it pitch black again. He spun to look at the door, then back to where she stood at the dimly lit panel.

He took a few steps forward. "You think we can get some light?"

"They're very docile under dark conditions and quite volatile in the light. I keep them as stress free and as comfortable as possible. Hence, why it's cool in here," she said, her voice echoing mysteriously.

"Cool?" Trevor responded quickly. "It's freaking cold." His voice bounced off the walls.

"They are from Siberia, Randale. I have to mimic their environment."

He began to chuckle as he closed the distance between them and touched her lower back. "You really expect me to believe that you have—"

She touched the panel again and raised the lighting causing Trevor to jump a full four feet back from her and the tank.

"Holy shit," he all but yelled. "What in the fuck are those things Sara Coli?" He took in the three large white spiders. "It's three of them!"

"Yes, darling. I do believe there are."

He viewed the spiders noticing that they were almost exact replicas of Black Widows, but extremely larger. They were gigantic and as white as freshly fallen snow. They moved across the case with lightning fast movements pausing only for a second before they returned. The large case had to be at least four feet tall, six feet wide, and eight feet long.

Sara Coli walked around the case tapping the glass lightly and the spiders launched themselves at her taps. The glass encasement was filled with clusters of shiny black webs. He'd never seen, nor known, of spiders producing such dark colored webs.

She looked at Trevor, who was locked in on the White Widows in awe. "Their webs are peculiar aren't they? They're exceedingly fast, and true to the nature of Black Widows. The female kills the male after they copulate and he impregnates her."

"Are those real?" he asked, taking slow steps forward towards the glass encasement. "White Widows?"

The question was rhetorical, but Sara Coli couldn't help but to answer. She eyed him closely, humor in her voice. "You see that slot over there?"

He looked and nodded. "Yes, I see it."

"Stick your arm in there and see."

He gave her a weird look and she released a throaty laugh. She rounded the case back to where he stood and rubbed his arm affectionately.

"The one off in the corner by itself is the female. I call her Charlotte. You know, like Charlotte's Web."

"Charlotte's Web doesn't come to mind when I look at them, Sara Coli," Trevor said shaking his head.

"Oh, don't be such a pooh butt," she smirked up at him. "Anyway, as for the males, I call them Samson and Goliath. They won't even go near her until it's time to mate."

He inched all of the way up to the tank so he could see them clearly. "Why are there no babies?"

She waved it off. "I've learned a lot since I've had them. I will be more prepared for the next time the babies come."

"What happened to them?"

"Let's just say that there were three males at first and one of them enjoyed eating the babies before they hatched. He was a rare kind of male. I called him an egg eater. One day I came in to find Charlotte eating him and she hasn't bred well since then."

Trevor could sense the disappointment in her tone. He felt a need to console her, but then it hit him. She was grieving over deadly spiders. That shit was crazy, so he decided to let it go.

"So what do they eat?"

Sara Coli glanced at the spiders, then up to him. "Small things," she answered simply. She turned and began to dim the lights. Grabbing his arm, she led him to the door.

"Small things," he repeated smoothly. "You mean like rats, mice, or hamsters?"

She shrugged as she reached up and opened the door through the hand recognizing screen. "More like ferrets, guinea pigs, hares, ermine... You know, small things."

He followed her out tossing his erratic thoughts back and forth. He was speechless about the spiders diets. As soon as he stepped into the hallway, he noticed the temperature change immediately. She hooked her arm through his, walking closely against him back up the hallway.

"I can't believe you have those deadly spiders in your home, Sara Coli," he said, looking down at her. "What would happen if they got loose?"

"A lot of people would die. They would probably wipe out the U.S. population in a matter of weeks," she said plainly. "It would literally be like a horror movie."

"Then why in the hell would you—"

"Oh relax, Randale," she said, tugging on his arm playfully. "I'm only joking. The climate alone would kill them," she teased, leaning her head on his shoulder. Seconds later they were standing in a huge living room decked out in white and different shades of yellow.

"I need to go and freshen up. We have a flight to catch."

He tilted his head and smiled. "And where would that be taking us?"

She took a step back from him and began to dance sexily singing Alicia Keys song. "New York. Concrete jungle where dreams are made of. There's nothing you can't do. Now you're in New Yorkkkk..." She turned and sashayed away while singing Alicia Keys part in the popular song, and he watched enjoying the seductive view.

Chapter 10

Kalitha inhaled her joint hard and blew out the potent smoke slow and easy. She looked over from the sofa at the Chinese Fan clock above the entertainment center and saw that it was a little after 1pm. She didn't like shit Trevor was trying to pull. She had waited for his return on Thursday, but here it was Monday, and he still hadn't returned.

She took another pull, then exhaled a large plume of smoke. Frankenstein watched her closely, but she didn't care. All she cared about was her husband returning home to her. The buzzing sound of the intercom startled her, causing her to drop the joint. The embers quickly burned a small black hole in the cream carpet. She picked it up and tried her best to pat it out before it got any worse. The intercom buzzed again.

She pressed the button with annoyance. "What is it?"

"Delivery for a Miss Vicky Mason."

She leaned back wondering if it was Trevor playing a trick on her or was it really a gift. "I'm on my way down."

She placed the joint in the sink, then hurried down on the elevator. When the door opened, she was met with an American Express delivery man. He was holding a small package and an electronic signing apparatus. He was tall, maybe about thirty, and had a nice smile.

"Miss Mason?"

"Yes, I'm Vicky Mason," she said as she approached him.

"Sign here please, ma'am."

She smiled and signed for the package. It was the size of an urban novel. She shook it, but it made no sound. She looked up at him and smiled.

"Thank you."

"You are most certainly welcome."

She keyed her pass code in and rode the elevator back up to their suite. She gave the package a careful once over then opened it cautiously. She peeled all of the paper away and saw that it was mailed directly from Jacob's in New York. She instantly got excited and nearly fell out of the bar stool when she opened it.

Inside was a beautiful pink, yellow, red, blue, and green, diamond necklace with not one, but two matching bracelets. They gleamed with luster reflecting the kitchen lights. She held them up to examine the precious stones. "Oh damn," she whispered as she walked over to the bay window to see how they would look when they caught the sunlight. A radiant prism of rainbow colored rays was cast onto the walls and the entertainment system. It looked like fruity pebbles and Kalitha was awestruck.

She walked back to the box and found some Christian Dior shades with fruity diamonds around the lenses. She pulled out the little card and read it. *Here's a little something for a special sister.* Kalitha smiled hard and immediately put the bracelets and necklace on. She hurried over to the full body mirror to check her image.

"Um hmm. He won't tell me how much he has in his account, but he can afford to buy this type of shit." She turned to examine the shades next. "Humph, he must feel guilty."

She couldn't help but to love them though. He'd sent her the best gift ever and she had to get out and floss her new jewelry at the mall. She was going to push her pink Navigator and slay her Fruity Pebble diamonds in style. *Shit. I deserve this. Fuck it. I'm going shopping.* She walked to her closet and searched through her meager outfits for something worthwhile to wear. She wanted to have people watching her, because she was aiming to turn heads today big time.

She pulled out her skin tight spandex set with a pair of black open heel clogs. Since Trevor was out doing him, she would be doing her, and she'd start by flaunting her goods around the mall a little. She smiled to herself. "You go girl. Have you some fun today."

****

Sara Coli sat across from Trevor in a coffee house smiling brightly at him. She was on her iPad looking at Trevor's marriage certificate that she had found with ease. She looked at the name Kalitha G. Mason, and played it back in her head over and over, making sure to remember it. She intended on running it through a database search engine that would produce her photo or at least a driver's license. On the other hand, the thought of going behind Trevor's back wouldn't allow her to do it. He hadn't given her any reason not to trust him or the things he had told her.

Trevor paid no attention to what Sara Coli was looking up. He was still thrilled with going to see his first live play. He had never even considered whether or not he would like a play, because it was never an option for him to go and see one. It amazed him how similar the play last night was to their situation.

Sara Coli pulled up the date of the marriage certificate and learned that it was 5 years old. She smiled and closed the iPad as she listened to him speak.

"I would love to see another one," he said before sipping his coffee. "It really was a fantastic and heart warming experience."

"I always catch plays whenever possible."

"I think that you have turned me on to yet another thing that I never imagined myself doing."

She smiled brightly, She wanted him to like the things that she liked because she wanted him to stay in her life. She had become tremendously attached to him and loved the feelings he gave her.

"I love the essence that is engulfed in theatrics," she said.

He smiled and took a deep breath as he looked out to the streets of Soho, NY. People were hustling and bustling, going about their business. He felt out of place for only a moment when they first arrived. He was a down home southern boy in the big city of all big cities, with his multi-million dollar girlfriend, and he had a wife at home that knew nothing about it. Life couldn't possibly get any better. *This has to be the life*, he thought, enjoying the moment.

Sara Coli reached over and rubbed his hand. Every so often she needed to feel their skin touch. She was into him that much. It was a drawback that she recognized, but couldn't seem to do anything about it. She was afraid of crowding his personal space or demanding all of his time, so she gave him the few days a week she thought would be necessary for him to miss her company and desire her more. She wanted for his friends, if he had any, to admire and even envy him the way her friends did.

She leaned back in her chair, relaxed and content. "Next month is your birthday, darling."

"Yes, it is. Thirty four wonderful years," he said, taking another sip of coffee.

"What do you say we go to Paris?" She winked at him sexily. "It's for lovers you know."

Trevor's shock was evident on his face. The thought was hard to grasp. He wiped his mouth with a napkin and leaned back. "Wow."

She looked on in anticipation. To see him going through that kind of emotion because of something that she had said drove her crazy. It turned her on when he showed awe and excitement.

"Paris? I don't know what to say. I mean, I've never even dreamed of going to Paris."

She touched his hand softly. "I can make every dream that you've ever had come to be. I want to make them a reality for you, Randale. Just say yes, darling. Let me do this for you."

Trevor leaned up and kissed her softly, but passionately. He broke the kiss and nuzzled her ear. "Yes, Sara Coli. I would love to go to Paris with you," he whispered, staring admirably into her hazel eyes.

She leaned back in a daze from the sweetness of his kiss, blushed, then looked coyly away from him. It was at that moment she realized what had happened. She was totally and irrevocably head over heals for her young lover. It felt so good to own up to her feeling and she knew that she would do anything to lock him in for good.

A thought came to her mind. "Maybe Vicky would like to come. I will treat her and a friend," she happily offered. "We could all have so much fun together."

He looked away thinking how disastrous that would be. It would definitely be the wrong thing to do. He, Kalitha, and Sara Coli in Paris. Now that would most definitely destroy their relationship. Kalitha would go crazy if she learned that he and Sara Coli made love off the White Widow. He couldn't risk that.

"I don't know," he said slowly.

"Oh come now, darling. We're all adults. She would absolutely adore Paris. Don't be such a brother."

"Tell you what. I'll ask her if she has plans," he lied.

"Great," she chimed excitedly.

****

Kalitha spun around looking at her phat ass in her black and white Prada outfit. She gave her sparkling jewelry a once over, then slid on her Christian Dior shades. She was a diva in that moment. Her curly hair was all shined up, her purse was stuffed full of money, and her heart was full of desire. She was planning to hit the mall, turn a few heads, and act like a whole donkey. Today she was the rich bitch with no worries and cash to burn.

With one last sexy look over her shoulder at the mirror, she headed towards the elevator door. Frankenstein meowed as she stepped over him, pissed that he was stuck inside. He had food, milk, water, and a clean litter box. She looked to the balcony door. *Okay, I'll give you some fresh air, but that's all you got coming.*

She walked over to the door and opened it. Frankenstein dashed out immediately. She shook her head smiling, then made her way downstairs on the elevator. She was glad that Frankenstein chose the porch over the elevator, because if he took the ride down with her, he would have more than likely gotten lost. She knew that there were droves of hungry gators in Greenfield Lake that would love his fat furry ass. She left him alone out of love for Trevor, but if she had her way, she would have been kicked his ass out.

She smiled as the door slid open to the lobby. The desk clerk looked up and immediately began to admire her. She gave him a flirty wink.

"Good afternoon."

"Good afternoon, Miss Mason," he replied kindly.

She gave a wave and walked out, the clerk watching her bubble butt bounce with each step. Her Prada spandex pants and shirt was tight enough to nearly give him an erection, especially with her perfume smelling like a sexual invite. *She had to know what she was doing to me*, he thought eyeing her fat ass. He watched as she stopped at the door and looked back over her shoulder, grinning knowingly. He couldn't peel his eyes away from her as she waved, then walked over to the parking deck.

"Hell yeah she knows," he mumbled, smiling.

Kalitha hurried to her light pink Navigator parked directly next to Trevor's white Escalade, and as of last week, a powder blue Audi A-8. She got in the Navigator and looked over at his two vehicles. *Used car my ass.*

"Humph, I wish you would tell me no to anything," she said maliciously.

The Navigator purred to life and eased down through the parking deck towards the exit. As she reached the exit arm barrier, the sunlight bathed the inside of the SUV, causing her jewelry to throw a rainbow of light across the interior. It was fascinating.

The arm raised and Kalitha eased out and down to the street. She looked both ways, but the colorful light kept grabbing her attention. She couldn't believe all that shine was coming from her alone. Pulling into traffic when she found a safe opening, she was still mesmerized by the colorful array of sparkle that looked like Fruity Pebbles made of light. She rotated her wrist, causing it to twinkle on the windshield. She was all caught by how beautiful the diamonds were. The colors overlapped and danced off one other looking enchanting. She almost forgot that she was in traffic, but that actual fact became apparent in the next moment.

Kalitha looked up to see that the car in front of her had

stopped, but she was still going. She slammed on the brakes, but at the speed she was going, it only made her skid. Her tires screeched and screamed against the hot pavement and the SUV came to a jolting stop at the rear end of the police cruiser. She could see the police officer's eyes in the rearview mirror and held her breath while praying that the lights atop of the cruiser didn't turn on. Before she could finish her prayer, the lights flashed blue and white, competing persistently with the daylight.

Two officers exited their vehicle and calmly sauntered back to look at the cruiser's rear bumper. After accessing the damage, the driver headed straight to her driver's side window. The other stayed at the bumper. He was trying to rub the scrape mark it with his hand. With no luck, he looked at Kalitha with a look that screamed, *'you dumb broad.'*

She let her window down as the officer approached. "Ma'am, you hit my cruiser"

"Are you guys okay?" she asked apologetically."

"Yes, we're fine. But I'll need to see your license and registration, please."

She dug out the proper documents and handed them over.

"I'm going to run these through my system. Please stay right here, ma'am."

"Yes, officer."

He walked back to the cruiser and ran her papers. She laid her head back and cursed herself softly. "So stupid. So fucking stupid. I can't tell him about this. I just can't."

A few minutes later, the officer came back with three tickets for her. He passed them to her looking down at her truck. "Mrs. Mason, you do realize that this truck is the wrong color? Its in our database as tan, ma'am."

"I just had it repainted about three days ago." She smiled. "I was about to—"

"You're in violation of not registering that also. It says here that a Trevor Mason—"

She cut in quickly. "That's my husband."

"Let me finish speaking, ma'am," he said in a reprimanding

tone. "Are you intoxicated or under the influence of any illegal substance or narcotic?"

"No. I'm not—"

"Ma'am," he said aggressively. "I said not to cut me off."

She remained silent as he finished.

"Are you currently under any strong medications that would prohibit you from operating a motor vehicle?"

"No, sir," she answered softly.

"I'm as sober as a baby," she lied.

"Then why did you slam into the back of my cruiser?" His question was stern and straight-faced.

Shame flooded her features and her skin began to flush red. "The light from my jewelry temporarily blinded me, sir."

The officer shot a cursory look into the SUV, then back to her. "Your court date is at the bottom of the citation." He handed her her license back. "Try and be more careful, ma'am."

"Thank you officer. And I will."

He tipped his hat before walking back to his cruiser. He and his partner got in, killed the lights, then pulled away. She pulled off as well, this time more mindful of the road. She couldn't believe that she had actually rear ended a police car. She had lied too, because she was as high as a punted football. That lie was a minor thing to the secret she would have to keep from Trevor. If he found out, he would curse her from the soles of her feet, to the tips of her curls.

The accident was something that she could handle on her own. She could take care of it and he would never have to know. After all, it wasn't that serious. Nobody got hurt. *Really, what's the worse that happen? A fine? A few points on my license?* The points wouldn't mean jack shit to her and she could pay any fine that she ends up with. She figured either way she could resolve the issue without Trevor ever knowing. With that plan in motion, she decided to enjoy the rest of her day.

As she drove, she couldn't help the foolish feeling that tugged at her mind. *My jewelry blinded me officer. I'm such a blond,* she thought, laughing at herself. Why didn't she think to re-register the new color of the truck with the D.M.V.? She would handle all of those issues in the next few days. She would be a big girl and fix it all without his help. She was confident that she could at least do that.

She turned onto Oleander Drive heading towards the mall. *Nothing like some good ole shopping to get rid of the problems.* She planned to shop until she dropped.

****

Kalitha entered the elevator with two hands filled with bags. She felt so much better, almost refreshed after the incident earlier that day. She was going to spend the rest of the evening trying on her new things and hiding them in the closet out of Trevor's sight. He didn't like for her to spend so recklessly and $23,000 worth of clothes would surely land her a trip to the gallows. She had purchased Fendi, Gucci, and Versace galore. *What a great day*, she thought beaming.

The elevator door opened and she crossed the threshold directly into Trevor's surprising presence. He was looking directly at the television with his feet comfortably perched on the footstool of the recliner.

"Hey, babe."

Kalitha drew back from his words with a scowl. She sat the bags down and stepped directly in front of him. She crossed her arms and turned her foot outward, her stance filled with attitude.

He looked up to her. "I said hey, babe."

"Nice to see you finally fucking decided to bring your ass home," she spat out, her tone pregnant with malice and jealousy.

"Please," he waved for her to stop blocking the television. "Don't start with the bullshit."

"Don't start with the bullshit!" She planted herself firmly in front of the screen. "How in the fuck is it that she's getting more time than me now?"

He released an exasperated breath.

"You've been gone since Thursday and I ain't heard a peep out of you. It's Monday and your ass is going to sit there like it's all cool and shit."

Trevor exploded. "Kill all that whining and complaining bullshit!" He leapt up and shouted. "I'm doing my part, Kalitha."

"Doing your part?"

"Yeah," he responded. "I'm doing my fucking part. Why don't you start doing yours?"

Her words were snotty and challenging. "And what the fuck is my part Trev?"

He stood towering over her taking a menacing step towards her with each word he spoke. "Staying off my fucking back and allowing me to get this fucking money."

She backed up hard into the T.V. with him breathing down on her like an angry dragon. She drew back from him, frightened by his words and actions.

Trevor's muscles tensed up, and his nose flared, as he backed away from his frightened wife. He had never spoken to her with that much aggression before and I made him sick to his stomach. The lucidity of the situation washed over him like a gentle rain. *It had to be the White Widow.* The elixir was changing him rapidly and seemed to be lingering in his system, creating a hungry desire for more. He backed up to the sofa and slowly sat down.

Kalitha watched him, her fear gradually dissipating. She couldn't believe that he had talked to her that way. His manner was every bit of terrifying, not to mention downright disrespectful and degrading. She believed that the money was changing him into a harder and uncontrolled person. Maybe it was being with Sara Coli that was doing it. She had to blame herself because it was her complacency, which was at an all time low, that had led them into their current argument.

Timidly, she walked over to the sofa and sat beside him. He sat with his hands placed on each side of his head. His treatment of her was alien and foreign, but in a strange way it turned her on more than she wanted to admit. His verbally manhandling her had her feeling racy and hot, almost raunchy. She pushed his hands away from his head and in one smooth motion straddled his lap.

"I'm sorry, baby," she said, kissing his chin and cheeks. "I know that you are doing what you're supposed to be doing." She kissed his forehead and hugged him tightly. "I don't mean to stress you out."

"It's not as easy as you think it is Kalitha. Not nearly as fun as it might seem neither. I didn't want this in the first place," he said, rubbing her lower back.

"I know, baby," she whispered into his ear, then kissed his neck. "Please forgive me."

He watched as she sat up and looked deep into his eyes. He knew what looking into her sexy brown eyes would do. She was gorgeous with her baby face and cute little curls atop of her head. She was his first real love and he had married her in the worst of circumstances.

He trailed a finger down the side of her face, causing her to smile. "Now you know that I can't stay mad at you."

She gyrated her hips on his lap making sure her pussy print created friction on his dick. "Good, because I want that big thang right now baby."

They began to kiss passionately, which led to them wildly pulling off each other's clothing. They went into an erotic feeding frenzy squeezing and touching as they were starving for each other. Trevor stood hard and ready as he bent her over the sofa and entered her sweet wet pussy from behind.

Kalitha cried out and held onto the soft cushions of the sofa for support. He pumped her with enough force to make her moan, but not enough to hurt her. She arched her back and got on the balls of her feet as he slapped her ass playfully. Her pussy felt extra good to him. She was tight, slick and hot, and he loved the feeling for it was molded to fit him perfectly.

He rubbed her sweaty back and noticed the fruity jewelry on her neck. He noticed her wrists as well and wondered when and where she had gotten that kind of jewelry. Mostly he wondered what in the world did she spend on it.

"Oooh shit, daddy!" she moaned, panting and gripping the sofa. "I'm about to cum!"

"Cum for me then," he motivated her with a low growl.

Kalitha shook violently as the orgasm took control of her. Her pussy muscles clenched around the girth of his dick as she felt the orgasm rock her soul. Her juices gushed from her plump lips and slid down his rod creating their own passion lube. She screamed and cooed as her pussy pulsated with every wave of orgasmic bliss. She looked back at him and licked her lips, and pressed her ass back for more.

An hour and a half later, Kalitha had cum 3 times, yet he hadn't cum once. That concerned her a little, but she held on to hope when he turned her over and began to fuck her missionary style. Her legs wrapped lovingly round his waist as he carefully fed his long shaft to her greedy slit.

That went on for another half hour and still nothing. That really made her worry because he would usually cum from the missionary position rather quickly. It was his favorite way to have her and now nothing. She looked up at his sweat drenched body as he stroked her passionately. She watched as he closed his eyes and threw his head back. His intensity increased and so did the force of his thrust. The way he began to drill into her made her bite back her words to stop him.

She wanted him to get off, because the more he turned it up, the more it hurt. She fought diligently against the urge to beg him to stop. She bit her bottom lip, and clenched her fist, her manicured nails digging into the soft flesh of her palms. She let out a loud hiss as he hit her back wall with spine shattering force and had to beg her mind not to allow her mouth to say 'stop'. She needed him to climax inside of her, so she dealt with the pain until his last stroke.

Trevor closed his eyes and envisioned Sara Coli beneath him, but even that wouldn't push him over the edge. He needed her there with him in the flesh, not in his mind. Nothing was working. Sadly, Kalitha wasn't enough. He stopped all of a sudden and slid his rock hard dick out of her.

Kalitha thanked the heavens for the relief, but at the same time, a tremendous feeling of failure crashed down on her. She covered her plump breast in shame as she watched him get up and simply walk back to the master bedroom without uttering a single word. She sat there panting as she watched him leave, feeling useless and downhearted.

She got up and followed him down the hall as quiet as a church mouse. She entered the bedroom to see him getting under the covers and he didn't look back at her at all. He just laid down and breathed evenly.

She climbed into the bed with him and drew her body close to his. He turned and hugged her tightly, his hardness pressing into her, reminding her of her uselessness. She buried her head in his chest and began to cry silently with her tears being the only indication. Her heart was filled with an inexcusable feeling of inadequacy and ineptness.

Trevor had fallen into a pit of exhaustion like slumber, but she couldn't get her teary eyes to close but for a minute at a time. Her mind reeled and replayed their love making session from earlier nearly making her tear up again. The fact that she couldn't make her husband cum haunted and tormented her.

She glanced at the clock and it read 2:12am. Looking over at Trevor sleeping, a cloud of anger passed over her. Her anger wasn't directed at him, but at herself. He was her husband and she was not about to let that old bitch take him from her. At that moment she decided that she would give satisfying him another try. She slid under the covers and began to massage him erect. She took him into her hot mouth and began to suck him firmly as he slept.

Trevor felt her hot mouth cover his dick and he moaned deep in his throat. He began rubbing her shoulders, encouraging her to take him deeper. Kalitha kept at it until he was rock hard and throbbing in her mouth. She used both hands twisting in opposite directions as her mouth licked, flicked and sucked his dick. His hips were lifting and rocking, enjoying the mouth massage she was inflicting upon him.

The tension began to build and her hands tightened applying more pressure. His moaning had gotten louder, and she sucked even harder. Feeling his control slipping, he took a deep breath and rocked harder, sliding to the back of her throat. He filled her mouth with his seed calling out her name as he began to cum.

"Damn, Sara Coli. Only you can make me cum, baby. Only you."

Chapter 11

Sara Coli's business dinner was going smoothly. All of her companies were in the black and she was just about ready to issue out substantial bonuses to her business managers when her phone rang.

"Hello?"

"Hi, my name is Sheila and I'm with Nationwide Insurance Company. I'm calling to report that a Lincoln Navigator registered to one Trevor R. Mason was involved in an accident yesterday," the caller said.

"Okay," Sara Coli said listening.

"You insure that vehicle, ma'am, and it's standard procedure to alert you of any complications."

"Yes, well, did anyone get hurt?" Sara Coli asked.

"No, ma'am. But the person operating the vehicle was a Kalitha G. Mason."

The words began to fade into unintelligible noises in Sara Coli's ear. Her heart pounded loud enough to drown out all of the other sounds around her at the restaurant. A huge lump grew in her throat as she repeated the name in her mind. *Kalitha Mason? Kalitha Gabrielle Mason?*

She stared out at nothing, her mind creating an abyss of darkness around her. Everything, all of the people, the restaurant, the whole world, became complete blackness. All she could see was the curly head girl who claimed to be Trevor's sister Vicky. *Vicky? Did he even have a sister named Vicky?* She was not his sister. She was his wife! Her heart continued to pound loudly in her ears as she pictured the $140,000 dollar jewelry set she had bought for her. *Not his sister, but his wife. An $800,000 penthouse for he and his wife to live in! To make sweet love in! To fuck on 10 and 20 thousand dollar furniture!*

The darkness became crimson red and she began to snort in short bursts of air, hyperventilating. If she hadn't kept the insurance in her name, she would have never known. She saw Trevor's face. His honest eyes and beautiful smile. Randale, the man who was turning her whole world around, was not the man he said he was. He was a pretender, a fooler, a trickster, and a player.

She gritted her teeth in fury as the red all around her began to swirl violently. She was being gamed, scammed, tricked, and conned! *Played by a player and his wife.* She slammed her phone down on the table, knocking a few glasses over. The crimson swirling mass evaporated to reveal a table full of concerned onlookers and a jabbering woman on her cell phone.

She looked to them as she disconnected the call. "You all may leave."

They looked to one another curiously and she repeated with finality. "I said you all can go. We will reconvene at a later date." They all immediately got up and quietly left her table.

Sara Coli reached over and grabbed her still standing glass of wine and downed it. She set the glass down nearly crushing it in her stressful grip. She was beyond hurt in her findings and felt that only her Vera Wang dress was holding her body together. She was a shattered piece of crystal reeling in pain. She had begun to love Trevor and she felt that he was beginning to love her as well. *How could he do that? Why would he do such a thing?*

She reached up and wiped away the droplet of warm liquid that was rolling down the side of her cheekbone in shock. It hurt her more because she hadn't seen her own tears in years. At least not from heartache. She sat there examining the wetness on her fingertip as she let her anger fester and grow. *It was probably her idea. It reeks of a woman's thoughts.*

She just couldn't bring herself to pin the blame on Trevor. She had looked into his eyes and saw that he was an honest man. He had to have been pressured into it. Her anger rolled through her body slow and steady. *That conniving little bitch!* Her thoughts began to twist and turn, her feelings put on hold for the time being.

If it was a game they wanted to play, then a game will be played. She had been on this earth for 51 years and she had a few games of her own. After all, she was no lowly competitor. She knew how to do better than play, she could coach a team of players. She smiled through her pain.

"I will fix you. I will fix you both," she said, picking up her phone and scrolling down to Trevor's number. "I know how to come out on top. I've been doing it for years, darling."

She dialed Trevor's number deciding to call for him tonight and keep him busy for a while. She knew just how to do that.

"Hello, beautiful," he sang to her creating a familiar flutter in her chest.

"Hi, handsome. Can I have you today?" she cooed in the undeniable voice she reserved for him? A voice full of sexual promises to come. "I want to take you to Hot-Lanta, darling."

"I'm all yours."

"I know," she responded smoothly.

****

Sara Coli and Trevor were in Atlanta by 7pm. She had arranged a lock-in at Strokers, one of the hottest strip clubs in the area. She was going to show him the time of his life and record it. It took a few pulls, and one good tug on a string or two, but by 9pm, they were pulling up in a limo.

Sara Coli knew that no man could resist the Atlanta strippers and Trevor was no different in that sense. He was a healthy man, therefore, subject to the laws of human nature. They were escorted into the near empty club and seated dead center in front of the stage. Before he got comfortable, he had a bottle of Rose and $20,000 in ones piled up in front of him. He smiled at her with a cautious grin. "What's the occasion?"

"You're the occasion," she responded sweetly.

The music came on and the lights began to flash as 12 strippers came out and began to strip and dance. It was way too much to take in all at once. His eyes darted back and forth between all of the naked women doing pole tricks and popping their pussies at him. They came down off of the stage and pulled him out from behind their table. Sara Coli sat back and watched the action.

They took Trevor onto the stage and sat him down in a chair and took turns giving him lap dances. He flung money left and right at them, paying them well for their performance. They pulled him out of his shirt and began to rub pussy juice all on his arms, back, and chest. Trevor was having a ball, for there were naked pussies, titties, and asses everywhere.

Sara Coli observed that he favored two out of the bunch and could tell that he was really taking a liking to the pair. She got the manager's attention and he came to her. She pointed at the two women. "I'd like to speak privately to those two."

"I will set it up," he said, then walked off towards the belle's.

While Trevor painted a stripper with dollar bills, Sara Coli met with the two strippers off in the corner. "I will give the two of you $5,000 each if you will accompany us at our hotel tonight."

"Hell yeah!" they said in unison.

Sara Coli smiled. "My limo will be waiting."

Sara Coli had fun watching the strippers go crazy for the dollars with Trevor being the center of attention the whole night. She glanced up at the D.J.'s booth to see that the cameraman was doing his job. She was getting great footage. She loved every minute of the show and she was sure that someone else would too. She smiled to herself, knowing that Randale sure did.

Trevor looked back to see Sara Coli smiling lustfully and filled with sexual energy as the strippers catered to him. His dick was harder than Iron Man's costume. He was really tossing money at two in particular. They had caught and held his eyes all night. The one with a fire red hairdo named Flames had the fattest ass in America and the other one named Golden had amazingly similar curly hair like Kalitha's. She was a redbone with gorgeous blue contacts.

Watching them dance wasn't enough. He wanted to slide his dick deep inside of them until they begged him to stop. He showered them with the bulk of the 20,000 singles. He knew that if his desire for the two lingered until after they left, he was going to fuck Sara Cali's brains out of her head tonight.

Sara Coli called to him and he walked off of the stage to join her. She smiled warmly. "Have you had enough, darling?"

He looked back at all of the naked women just swaying and waiting for his return, and he noticed that Golden and Flame weren't amongst them any longer. He looked back to Sara Coli, now bored. "I believe that I have."

She pulled him by the arm towards the door. It was not even midnight yet. As they got outside Sara Coli got his attention. "I do believe that two of the girls really had your attention, Randale."

"They were all beautiful women," he said, trying to generalize them.

"Yes, they were," she agreed as the limo driver opened the door. "But not as beautiful as these two."

Trevor looked in and saw Golden and Flames smiling and drinking from a new bottle of Rose.

They waved enticing him to climb in and join them. "Hey big boy," said Golden.

"We've got room for two more," said Flames joining in the fun.

They flirted the whole ride back to the hotel suite. Once upstairs, Trevor and Sara Coli both had their White Widows, then sat back as the two shook their phat juicy asses. Trevor slapped their asses and watched gleefully as they jiggled. They hopped onto the bed with him and pulled him out of his slacks and shirt.

Sara Coli opened the balcony door and sat back out of view. She wanted them to be seen clearly and she wanted a clear shot of the bed and the action.

The two women giggled and pulled him out of his boxers. They admired his size with fear in their hungry eyes.

Sara Coli spoke softly. "Go ahead ladies. Earn your keep."

She watched as the pair took turns rolling around and popping their pussies all over him. When they began sucking Trevor's big rigid dick together, he was in heaven. Two Gold Magnums landed on Trevor's chest and belly and they all looked up.

"Put both on him and fuck him good ladies," said Sara Coli. Her voice was laced with lust.

Trevor looked down his naked body, then over at Sara Coli. She watched with approval as they strapped him up double time and began to take turns. The White Widow came down on him fast and effective.

Golden slid off of him still trembling as she came and tagged Flames, who eagerly straddled him next. Trevor waited until Flames cautiously took seven of his ten inches inside of her, then without warning, rolled her over under him and began to give her all she could stand. Her light moans became deep groans, which soon became pain filled screams with every powerful thrust he delivered.

She cried out for him to stop as he stroked her several more spine breaking times. With his last thrust, he shoved his engorged shaft all of the way to the hilt, balls deep. He pulled out of her and she began to back peddle away in pain. Golden's eyes showed extreme fear when he pulled her to him. She submitted as he put her in the doggystyle position.

One hard stroke had her lunging forward into the headboard. He was right on her, holding her hips secure and digging in deep as she screamed into the pillow and clawed at the sheets. She squealed out in pain as he increased his pace, trying hard to cum in her. Nothing happened and that only made him bang her harder and harder until she begged him to stop. Flames watched in awe from the corner of the bed. He slammed into Golden a few more times, then pulled out in frustration.

She rolled off of the bed hitting the floor with a dull thud. Holding her belly, she reached for her loose clothing sprawled all over the floor. Flames hurried around to retrieve her clothes also, but kept a safe distance between herself, and the machine of a man kneeling naked on the bed.

Sara Coli was highly impressed with the sheer power her young lover had. He made these women run from him because they lacked what he needed. Something only she could provide. She looked at the women and nodded towards the door.

"You two may go. Thank you for your services."

In anger, Trevor pulled the condoms off and flung them to the floor as the strippers scurried out. Stroking his hard dick, he looked towards Sara Coli.

She walked over and closed the balcony door. "So you want me to make you cum?"

"Yes," he growled. "Bring that sweet pussy over here right now."

She quickly stripped out of all of her clothes and climbed onto the bed. She rolled over and spread her legs wide fingering her silvery white haired slit open for him. She touched his hips with the bottom of her soft toes.

"You want to fuck me, Randale?"

"Yes." He stared down at her silvery gift, breathing heavily.

She stared right into his eyes, hard. "Say please."

Trevor's eyes narrowed. He wanted desperately to fuck her and she knew it. Her fingers steadily slid back and forth over her mound and her juices were clinging to her skin. His dick was so hard that it was painful and he needed relief from the torture.

"Please." The word came out more like a rumble with his irregular breathing.

Sara Coli continued to eye him in a strange way. Then suddenly she smiled and summoned him to her.

"Since you asked nicely. Come fuck me baby."

Trevor crawled on her like a starved man. He slammed his dick home inside of her and shuddered at the feeling of belonging. She screamed out from the impact of his dick's head colliding with her back wall with force. The strokes he delivered were strong and meticulous, and her body began to sing and thrive beneath him. Her walls gripped him tightly and drove him to near panic in his need for more.

Lifting her hips from the bed, he found a better position for control, and proceeded to climb the sweet ladder to his release. Her pussy, hot, wet, and deliciously tight, was all he needed to explode. He yelled out something unrecognizable and erupted hot milky cum inside of her. He choked and gasped as the orgasm took him to a whole other level of ecstasy. He continued to stroke her until his body weakened and relaxed, then remained still inside of her throbbing wildly.

Sara Coli rubbed his back gently and kissed his chest. She loved the feeling of him shooting his hot load inside of her. She knew from the feel of him that he would crank back up any second now and she was right. The first stroke was smooth and loving, the second more powerful and dominating, and the third set off a series of heavy duty thrusts that drove her insane. He crashed against her back wall, hitting every nerve ending inside her. The impact alone was enough to push her over the edge. She clenched up and erupted from deep within her pussy, splashing him with her searing hot orgasmic fluids.

Sweat began to pour from him, puddling up at his lower back and dripping down onto her. He drilled her as she cried out to him in pleasurable pain. She watched him move madly in the mirrors on the ceiling. Seeing him in action from above fueled her desire and she orgasmed yet again.

She gasped and called out his name as she came, sloshing his dick and nuts. She held on tightly to him as the orgasmic waves ran through her body.

"Oh yes, baby! Yes!"

Suddenly, his stroke became slow and loving, and she let his passionate energy take her. He held her tightly in his arms with every deep stroke and soon she felt herself climaxing again beneath. She came back from her ecstasy joy ride just as he blasted her with his second eruption. His load filled her up, before oozing out and soaking the bed sheets.

As they lay there catching their breaths, Sara Coli came to a decision. She wanted to keep her young lover. She knew it down in her soul that she loved him. She hadn't told him yet, but she did, and she was going to die trying to keep him. She would just have to get rid of his wife somehow. It was all coming together in her mind like a puzzle. Somehow she would win. Sara Coli is a winner and she would continue to win.

Minutes later, she felt him growing against her thigh just before he eased into her gently. Feeling him gradually gliding inside her tunnel, stretching her to accept his size, was incredible. Trevor made love to her deep and slow, allowing their fervor to build up once again. The control he possessed over her body was unnatural and the orgasm that broke free had her eyes rolling back in pleasure.

Oh, Randale. I love you, she thought. *Ummm, I love you so much, baby.*

****

Sara Coli was up early. She always beat him up in the morning, so by the time he did awaken, she had made all of the proper calls. She had a few private investigators hired to keep an eye on both of them. And she'd hired a photographer to take photos of her and Trevor as they go out and have a good time.

A long night of love making, followed by a few hours of rest, had Sara Coli recharged and thinking clearly. She had come to terms with the truth of her feelings for Trevor. She would never be ready to relinquish and release him back into the arms of his money hungry whore of a wife. She loathed the thought of the curly haired woman who had lied to her face and attempted to make a fool out of her.

She stood looking down at Trevor's sleeping body and smiled. She loved every part of his chocolate frame and vowed to make it her own. She saw him stir and reach out for her. When he came up empty, his eyes opened as he rolled over searching the room. When he saw her staring down at his naked body, he returned the favor, taking in her beautiful and remarkably youthful body.

"Good morning, beautiful," he said in a raspy, sleepy voice.

"Actually, it's a great morning," said Sara Coli as she walked over to him and climbed atop his naked body, stretching out beside him.

She was so soft and warm and he wanted to plant kisses all over her. She had a truly captivating energy around her. She was like the most beautiful supernova, with the power to destroy entire worlds with no chance of ever escaping. As he kissed her softly, he felt his existence slipping away into her. Tasting her tongue as it delicately darted in and out of his mouth caused him to easily forget that she was a 51 year old woman. She seemed younger and more rambunctious than she had on the day he had first met her. The smell of her galvanized him and called his manhood to attention. He couldn't fight the overwhelming feeling of voraciousness when he was near her.

She broke the kiss. "Did you enjoy last?"

"Yes, I did."

"Good, because we're going to do it again tonight."

She leaned up and straddled him. "Different club, different city."

Trevor looked up at her frowning. *Okay, I know I'm in trouble now.* He could no longer deny that he was falling harder than ever for her. Falling for her in every sense of the word. She and the White Widow ranked highest amongst his innermost thoughts. He would go so far as to say that it was the White Widow, then Sara Coli. And he found that it was getting increasingly easier to not think about Kalitha. She was becoming miniscule in his world. He felt like he was lost to her.

Hell, the biggest part of his day was his fix, and at that very moment, Sara Coli and her sexy hazel brown eyes were at the forefront of his life. She was the one with the ever flowing supply of White Widow. However, even without the White Widow, he felt like he was falling in love with her and out of love with his wife. He turned away from her feeling ashamed, selfish, and guilty. He was going through something that no one could help him with and he didn't have a clue how to fix it.

Sara Coli reached down and turned his face back towards her. "Don't you dare look away from me," she teased, laughing. She leaned in closer looking into his eyes. "Look into your future, darling."

****

The next two weeks were spent in pure sexual bliss. Sara Coli and Trevor hit different clubs every night in different cities, bringing up to three strippers at a time back to their hotel. He was being showered with threesomes and foursomes by Sara Coli for reasons he couldn't fathom. He was exhausted and didn't have time to do anything else but have sex, shop, party, and sleep. He felt like a groupie who had landed a big Rockstar.

Sara Coli told him that she wanted to fulfill all of his fantasies and all of his dreams. He was well beyond the limits of his dreams. He spent thousands as if they were penny tokens at a game room. He had sex with some of the most beautiful and curvaceous women in the south. At least the ones he's ever laid eyes on. She gave him whatever and whoever he asked for. The women were more than willing to please her handsome, young, and hung lover. She had what they desired, all of the money that they could earn.

She got a kick out of seeing the strippers beg for mercy at the hands of Trevor. To him, it was like a super long wet dream that had no end, all the while she was getting all of the photos she needed at the same time.

When the stripper fest ended, Sara Coli flew them out to Jamaica for a week where they had romantic dinners in exotic settings, and frequented reggae clubs. Trevor couldn't deny that he was awed beyond his wildest dreams. She treated him to rubdowns by nude women at Hedonisms, Asian massages, acupuncture, and at last, flew him out to Hawaii where he waded in the crystal clear waters.

He sat in his lawn chair under his umbrella watching Sara Coli in the ankle high waters. His straw hat kept the sun out of his eyes and concealed his features. She turned and waved to him as she spoke on her phone. He smiled and waved back. The sun sparkled off of his green diamond bracelet she had purchased him as a gift recently. He looked at it and pinched himself. The pinch hurt, so he knew it wasn't a dream. It was all real. He had different colored stones, diamond watches, necklaces, and bracelets, courtesy of Sara Coli. She'd even started to wear colorful diamond jewelry to match his. She was on a 'his and hers' everything kick as of late. She was balling out of control on Trevor.

She watched Trevor relaxing as she spoke into her phone. "Yes,

$100,000. I will have the paperwork in your hands by next week." She looked away out towards the beautiful water. "You'd better be worth it."

"Well, I could send you a picture, and you can be the judge of that," the voice on the phone said.

"As a matter of fact, you do that." Sara Coli waited a moment as the picture came in on her phone. She looked at the male escort's face. He was a handsome man with short curly hair and a full beard. She scrolled down and looked at his cut up physique. He was a gorgeous hunk of a man. His chest and arms were chiseled and when she scrolled down to his privates she smiled brightly. He was well hung. He would most definitely do. She put the phone to her ear again. "You will most certainly do." She waved to Trevor and he waved back again. "The quicker you do the job the more I'll pay."

"May I contact you at this number?"

"You may," she said. "This will be your contact number."

"No problem, Mrs. White."

"Great. Bye now."

She spun and swayed towards Trevor sexily. He tilted his shades down to watch her. Her movements in her two piece bikini were turning him on. She reached him and sat back in her lawn chair. He scanned her body down from her breast, to her toned and smoothly shaved legs, all the way down to her pedicured toes in her thong slippers.

She tilted her hat up giving him a questioning look. "Are you sure that Vicky doesn't want to go?"

"I..." He leaned back and looked out at the water. "I don't think so."

Sara Coli smiled knowingly and looked out over the water again. *Oh, this is going to be easy. Like taking candy from a baby,* she thought to herself. She reached over and touched his hand and he threaded his fingers into hers. She looked over to him pondering. *I wonder if you love me?*

Trevor held her hand feeling her eyes on him. He didn't want to look at her knowing that he was lying with every omission of the truth. It ate at him deep down in the recesses of his mind. He was not that type of man, yet, he was living that role to a 'T'. He looked the other way feeling trapped. God, *what I wouldn't give to tell her the truth.* He knew he couldn't do that. He had to see it through. He could at least give Kalitha that. The thought that he'd never be able to get Sara Coli out of his system became more real every day. Her or the White Widow.

He looked over to her silently pleading with his thoughts. *I need a fix.* She smiled at him, then looked away, gazing at the clear water.

Chapter 12

Karen Cox was good at what she did. Some would go as far as to say she was great. What she did was investigate people for others privately. She was being paid top dollar for her subject, but she didn't know why. However, she understood that it was not her job to know why. She didn't get paid to know why. She got paid to do what she was doing now, watching Kalitha G. Mason.

Kalitha never had company over to the house. She left alone, stayed alone, and ate alone, except for the woman she met to have lunch with a week ago whom Karen found out to be a friend of hers. No foul play there. She was bored because Kalitha was a boring subject for the most part.

Karen looked down at her watch. The black band against her pale white skin was a weird contrast. She mostly wore dark colors because it made her feel as if she was invisible and could do her job better. She just hoped she'd see something worthwhile seeing today. *I'm bored as fuck.*

Suddenly, Kalitha exited the building, and Karen turned her attention to her. She watched as Kalitha disappeared into the parking deck and emerged walking towards city center. Karen hopped out and followed her on foot. She felt a little spark of adrenaline and expected that today would be the day it all changed.

Careful not to be seen, she followed as Kalitha leisurely walked down to Market and Second Street, and made a left. As Karen turned the corner, she saw Kalitha walking straight for the courthouse building. *Okay. This is the perfect place to meet someone. Good choice.* She hurried across the street and into the courthouse, tracking Kalitha all of the way to traffic court where she was ordered to pay $1,000 to the Wilmington Police Department. Other than that, nothing. Karen disappointedly trailed Kalitha back to the penthouse building. She watched her go inside, then returned back to the driver seat of her car. *What a waste of time*, she thought.

Kalitha had walked from the penthouse to the parking deck and decided she would just walk down to the court building. Her shoulders were slumped as she walked. She hadn't seen, nor heard, from Trevor in five complete weeks. On top of that, Frankenstein had gotten the stupid notion to jump onto the slippery banister of the balcony and plunged to his death on the sidewalk below. It was a sad situation. Whatever he was trying to catch had gotten him caught up. She only felt half bad about it.

She eased into traffic court and listened to judge chew her ear off about a whole lot of bullshit, then fined her $1,000. She also had to pay for the imaginary damages she inflicted on the police cruiser. After taking care of her business, she walked back to the penthouse building and went inside. As as she entered, she ran into a super sexy black man standing in the waiting area. She gave him a once over. *Mmm, mmm, mmm. I could sure go for a slice of you.* But she was married and feeling saddened about her husband's unexcused absence.

"That's Mrs. Mason," the clerk said in a low voice.

The sexy man looked up from the desk clerk over to Kalitha. "Um, Mrs. Mason?"

"Yes?" She turned to him. "Are you talking to me?" *Damn, you are fine,* she thought.

"If you're Kalitha G. Mason, then yes. I have something that I think you might want to see," he said firmly. She gave him an interrogating once over trying to pick up on who he might be. She looked to the desk clerk for help. He merely shrugged, then turned away to mind his own business.

"Why? Is everything alright? Are you the FED's?"

"No. No, of course not."

"Are you I.R.S.," she quickly asked.

"No." His smile was breathtaking. "I'm William Victor Longe, Private Investigator."

"A private investigator?" she repeated, looking him up and down.

"What? I don't look like one?" he asked with a smooth smile. She smiled back ad he could see the ice visibly breaking.

"No, I didn't mean it like that. I mean, you look, um..." She looked away, then back to him unsure of what to say. "So what can I help you with, Mr. Longe?"

"Please, call me Willie. Uh, do you have a moment. Can you spare an hour or so for lunch? On me, of course." His words were warm and innocent.

She looked around absently seeing nothing out of the ordinary. *What the hell. Its only lunch.* Plus a little attention wouldn't hurt. It would be more than what she was getting from Trevor.

"Just for an hour," he encouraged her.

"If it's on you then, alright."

Willie smiled and nodded. She turned and led the way out to the street. Willie glanced down at her bubble of an ass and the way her hips flared and licked his lips. *My goodness. Girl you stacked like pancakes!* He couldn't help but admire the roundness of her ass and the way her walk was filled with sexual temptation. He could see that he was going to really enjoy this job. She was gorgeous to begin with and her voice was so soft that it turned him on instantly.

Kalitha stopped and turned towards him. "Should I follow you?"

"If you don't mind, you can ride with me," he said, pointing to the silver Cadillac STS sitting on 22 inch rims.

She looked at the car sideways. "You drive this and you're a private investigator?" she asked, smiling.

"What? I can't have a nice car too?" he said teasing her.

He opened the Cadillac's door and she slid and took his time admiring the view. After closing the door, he quickly moved around the car and slid in beside her.

"I ain't mean nothing by it," she said with a wide smile."

"No?" he said, bringing the car to life. "First, you said I don't look like a private investigator, now my car isn't a P.I's vehicle."

"I didn't say all that," she jokingly defended.

"You might as well," he teased.

"Oh, whatever," she grinned, showing bright white teeth.

He loved a woman with a great smile. William checked the traffic before pulling off.

Karen became excited when she saw Kalitha and an extremely handsome man come out the building together smiling and interacting with one another with a sweet banter. Quickly, she snatched up her camera and clicked away as they pulled off. She followed them out into traffic, making sure not to get too close. *Okay miss goody two shoes. The truth comes out today. Finally freaking action.*

Karen followed them to the Bonefish restaurant on New Centre and Market Street. They walked from the parking lot to the front door exchanging light conversation. Karen waited a few minutes, then followed them inside.

As they walked in, Kalitha could not help but size Willie up deliciously. She looked at him in ways that she knew were inappropriate, and her mind incessantly guessed at what he looked like nude. She felt her kitty begin to purr and knew she had to get ahold of herself, and fast.

William pulled out a chair for her to sit, then took the seat across from her. After they were seated, he sat a manila envelope on the table.

You can't seriously be that fine and a gentleman. I'll wait to see what's wrong with him. She eyed the envelope and then looked back at him.

"Soooo...," she dragged it out. "What is it that you think I might want to see?"

Willie leaned back becoming extra professional. Kalitha thought that made him appear even more desirable. His words were smooth and creamy to her ears.

"Well, first off, I was doing some private investigative work for a well-to-do and prominent client, which entailed me watching a Ms. Sara Coli White," he looked at her curiously. "Do you know her?"

"I've seen her around." Kalitha looked away, then back to him. "I've seen her in the paper before."

"Well, while investigating Ms. White, I managed to take a few shots of a Trevor Mason with her an awful lot lately."

Kalitha turned away upset. She didn't want to be reminded that she hadn't seen him in weeks.

"It was part of my job to find out who he was, so I researched him and found out that he is married to you."

Kalitha looked around as if he had told the whole place her most private business. She looked back to him, crossing her arms over her plump breast. "Okay, and?" she asked, seeming uninterested. "What if I knew that already?" Willie fiddled with the silverware as she spoke. "What is it to you?"

"I thought that you might already. And to answer your question, in all honesty, it is nothing to me." He looked away as if he was in deep thought. "See," he said, staring her in her eyes. "I don't know what's going on between Ms. White, Mr. Mason, and yourself, and it's really not my business to find out. All I know is I took some pictures that I thought you might like to see." He slowly slid the manilla envelope across the table towards her.

She looked down at it for a long moment before slowly opening it. She extracted a large stack of photos and flipped through them. Pain welled up inside of her. Her heart began to beat rapidly, threatening to crack her rib cage. Her breath shortened and her pulse raced as she took in the images of *her* Trevor with over a dozen different women, in over 35 different photos. They were all sexually explicit and in sharp detail. Her heart plummeted into the pit of her stomach when she came across the blond curly haired girl who looked like her. The photos were graphic. She could see his dick inside of the women, their mouths on him, and his mouth on them. She could even see the creamy wetness of their pussy juices on the condoms. She nearly vomited, but turned away from the photos just in time. Holding her hand over her mouth, she tried drastically to get herself under control.

Willie looked at Kalitha concerned. "I'm sorry—"

She held her hand up for a moment as her body suppressed the urge to throw up. She fought it down, but only for a minute. Kalitha jumped up from her seat rushing from the table, knocking her silverware over, and dashing to the restroom. She pushed the door open and fell into an empty stall. The bile and food from breakfast shot out of her in a sickening stream.

Tears began to pour from her eyes instantly blurring her vision. She sobbed and fought them back as her body dry heaved a few more times. She flushed the toilet and backed out of the stall, leaning on the sink heavily for support. Pain and anguish flooded her senses, making it hard for her to calm down.

She could not believe what she had seen. She turned and looked at herself in the mirror and flinched at her image. She had to fix herself up as best she could so she could return to the table. She turned on the water, leaned over, and rinsed her mouth out several times. Next, she splashed some on her face and the coolness helped to calm her. After patting her face dry, she checked her image again, noting it was the best she could do. Taking a deep breath, she returned to the table.

Willie stood up as she reached the table. "My God. Are you okay?" he asked, helping her sit again. He leaned over and pulled his chair closer to her and sat down next to her.

"I didn't know if you were going to be alright so I had the waiter bring you some cold water."

"Thank you." Kalitha sipped from her glass, then glanced down at the envelope. "When did you take these?"

"Over the past five weeks or so."

"Where? Where did you take them?"

"Georgia," he said, rubbing her back softly.

"Where in Georgia?" she spat impatiently.

"Atlanta, Decatur, Colli Park, and Savannah."

"Okay!" she cut him off. "Okay." She ran her hands through her short curly hair. "So, what are these women, like strippers or something? Are they escorts or prostitutes?"

"As far as I can tell, they're mostly strippers. I wouldn't doubt that a few are prostitutes, maybe both in some cases," he said driving it home in her head.

Kalitha picked up her glass and downed it. She called for a waiter to bring her some more water. Willie patted her hand and rubbed her back. He could feel the strap of her bra through her shirt and felt like an ass. *Real classy William to notice some shit like that right now.*

Kalitha knew that William was a stranger, but she still let him rub her back. She needed a man's touch and she would accept his, even if it was only briefly and out of pity. She was happy when the waiter finally brought her another glass of water.

"I'm sorry that you had to see those, Mrs. Mason."

She looked up at him, then back down at her glass.

He pushed his limits by lightly rubbing her hair. When she didn't reject him, he continued. "You really should eat something. You'll feel much better after you've eaten."

She looked to him with sad eyes and nodded.

"Would you like me to order for us both?" he asked her in a sweet caring voice. She nodded once more. He smiled and looked up to the waiter waving him over. He came, took their orders, and left.

Kalitha tried to hold her head up, but the golden envelope on the table was burning a hole through her mind. He noticed her staring at it and quickly removed it from her sight. "Don't do that to yourself." He smiled sympathetically at her and she flashed him a small unsure smile. It was all she could muster.

The food arrived shortly after and they ate in relative silence. When their plates had been cleared, she looked up at Willie and asked in a soft voice. "Why did you bring these to me? I didn't pay for this information."

"Mrs. Mason, I don't believe that any woman should be done that way. I have sisters. I have a mother." He tossed his handkerchief down theatrically. He leaned forward closer to her. "I'm just tired of the brothers doing our black sisters wrong." He leaned back and took on a serious tone. "It's hard for a good, honest man to find a woman as beautiful as yourself and keep her. I guess I was tired of standing by watching it happen." The compliment made Kalitha smile and blush. "Someone has to take a stand and do something," he said looking at her intently. "Why not me, right now?"

She gave him a genuine smile this time and began to truly take notice just how fine Willie was.

She cocked her head to the side slightly interested. "As fine as you are, why aren't you married?" She was genuinely curious.

Willie felt embarrassed by her compliment. "Thank you," he said quietly. "I guess I just can't seem to find that special someone. With my line of work, I meet a lot of women that I can see myself falling for, but they always seem to belong to lowdown, dirty, cheating husbands."

Kalitha blushed hearing all of the double meanings in his words. She liked that he could be so straightforward and so sublime in the same breath. It was intriguing to her. She glanced around the restaurant, then back to him.

"Yes, well, people sometimes become available again once those lowdown, dirty, cheating husband's secrets are revealed."

Karen Cox watched their whole exchange over her plate. The camera in her purse recorded their whole time together. When they got up and left, she hurried out behind them. She had to see if the cute little hunk would make it upstairs. She sure hoped so because she needed to report much more than what she had to support an adultery case. In her experience, affairs were much more than lunches in public places and a comforting back rub. She was sure that her employer would want a lot more proof than that.

It looked to Karen like it was a simple ride back to the penthouse, kissless and touchless, but she kept her camera trained on them anyway. They parked in front of the building and Karen parked across the street a few cars ahead. It wasn't an ideal parking space, but it would do.

Willie got out the car first, and like a true gentleman, came around and opened her door. He walked her to the building's entrance, waiting for her next words.

"Thank you for lunch and for..." She patted the manilla envelope. "The information, Mr. Longe."

"I thought I asked you to call me, Willie?" he smiled, teasing.

She returned his smile. "Only if you will call me Kalitha, not Mrs. Mason."

"I definitely will."

Willie could see the evident sadness in her eyes. It was seeping through her like a drop of black ink in a glass of clear water. They stood staring at each other silently until Kalitha broke eye contact and turned to go in. He touched her hand on the door handle causing her to look up at him.

"If you ever need someone to talk to, you know, just to vent or anything, my card is in the envelope," he pointed to the envelope she held tightly. "Just give me a ring and I promise that I will make time for you." That one sentence made her feel important and warmed her on the inside.

She nodded with a small smile. "Thank you for that."

"I'm serious," he said, reinforcing his words. "Anytime, Kalitha." He turned to walk away with a light wave. She waved, then entered the glass doors.

Once inside, she turned to look out the tinted window to watch him leave. He hopped in his Cadillac and drove away with one last wave. She watched him drive all of the way out of sight. When she turned, she found the desk clerk watching her with wondering eyes. She spoke to break the awkward silence.

"Beautiful day, isn't it?"

"Yes, it is Mrs. Mason."

His calling her Mrs. Mason brought reality crashing down on her again. She hastily made her way past the desk and keyed in her entry access code. She could feel her eyes begin to water. She boarded the elevator and was up to their apartment in less than a minute. She walked on unsteady legs to the bar and let the envelope drop onto it. She used the bar to help keep her standing as her head began to spin and a cool sheen of sweat coated her body.

She breathed in deeply, trying to quell the feeling of her passing out as she pulled the photos from the envelope again. She examined them with an expert eye. They were not doctored. She could see as clear as day that they were real and that it was in fact Trevor. The faces they were making as he fucked them were real. They were crying out in pain from Trevor's size and length. She knew those faces all too well.

Fury seized her as she flung the photos onto the living room's floor. She released a wail of anguish as huge sobs racked her body. She threw herself into the midst of the photos on the floor and cried out even harder. She couldn't believe that they were real. Struggling to see through her teary eyes, she tried to count all of the different women through her blurred vision. She counted eighteen women in five weeks. She wiped her eyes and runny nose as she sat back up against the wall unit. She didn't know what to do.

He hadn't been home in five weeks. She looked at all of the spread out pornographic photos and covered her mouth in horror at the truth of what was happening when he was gone away from her. She let out a heart wrenching cry, then folded over into the fetal position.

Kalitha continued to cry all through the night. Her mind, body, and soul grieving the hell that her greed had created. She wished more than ever that she had never read Sara Coli's name in the paper. She knew at that exact moment that she had made a grave mistake that was sure to cost her everything.

Chapter 13

At the end of the seventh week of Trevor's ill informed marital hiatus, Kalitha was up and motivated to do something. She had laid in their bed hopeless and pitifully, not eating and looking at the raunchy heartbreaking photos over and over. She was all cried out and wondering where Trevor was had her mind wander aimlessly around in her head. She hadn't received a single call from him. No card. Nothing. It had been seven complete weeks since she had heard her husband's voice. She hadn't received any sign that might indicate that he was dead or alive. She knew in her heart that he wasn't dead and that he was out somewhere having all of his needs met.

She folded her arms across her chest and leaned on the wall in the hallway. *I'm a grown ass woman. Shit, right now I'm a horny woman, and I have needs too. He's probably out licking and sticking every woman he rests his eyes on. Who is he to deny me my well deserved sexual gratification? As my husband, he has obligations to me,* she thought indignantly.

She sucked her teeth. "That old bitch's money is turning your ass into a real player, huh?" She nibbled on her fingernail as she walked into the kitchen and sat at the bar. "You can't tell me that I'm not justified in having a little fun now too," she discussed with herself. "I can if I choose to."

She swirled her finger around on the countertop absent-mindedly. She didn't have a clue where Trevor was or whether he was with Sara Coli or doing his own thang. *Were they even together?* Anger boiled over inside of her at her stupidity.

Muthafucka. You playing me and her, she thought, anger clouding her judgement. *Okay. Fuck it!* She hopped up and walked with determination to the bedroom. Looking in her closet, she began searching for something to wear. "Shit. If you can play, then so can I."

Kalitha began to pull out the sexiest clothing she had hidden in her closet. She decided that if he could disappear for seven weeks, then she could get lost for seven days. Myrtle Beach, South Carolina would be the perfect hiding place for her to kick back and think about her next move.

There were plenty of attractions there with the male strip clubs being the biggest one for her. She could go down there, throw a few dollars, pull on a few fat dicks, and try to pick up one or two. If Trevor could fuck out of both sides of his drawers, then she could too. She was definitely planning to stay a week or more and was sure that she could find some distracting sex to occupy her time.

She was as fine as China, as thick as peanut butter, and as horny as a porn star on ecstasy. And she had a little bit of money to play with. She was positive that she could do her for a week or so. She wanted it and she needed it. To hell with Trevor. He had given up on her, so why was she still holding on to him?

She got undressed and headed for the shower. The warm therapeutic water caressed her worrisome thoughts away. She washed herself softly, stopping to linger at her throbbing twat. She couldn't help wanting to ease the ache of need inside of her, so she gave in and surrendered to the desire.

She held onto the wall as she lifted her leg up to the edge of the shower ledge and slid her 2 slender fingers in and out of her wet slit. She closed her eyes as the water sprayed her taunt nipples, neck, belly, and inner thigh. Kalitha moaned out as the wave of an orgasm began to manifest itself with every deep thrust of her fingers.

"Ooooh," she moaned into the steam filled air. "Ahhh, yes." She clenched her pussy muscles together continuously as a picture of Willie popped into her mind. She latched onto it, imagining him rubbing her titties and finger popping her center. She cried out sexily and pumped her fingers harder as her fantasy played out in her mind.

She envisioned him pinning her against the bed and sliding his dick deep inside of her. "Oh shit, oooh yes, fuck me." She imagined him fucking her slowly while whispering in her ear how wet she felt. She tightened up and began to breath heavily.

He bound her tightly against him, grinding his thick dick into her, losing his battle with control. His body tensed up signaling that he was about to cum and that did it. Kalitha bucked harder against her hand and began to orgasm in wild abandon. Her pussy clenched and released around her fingers as she sought to ride her orgasmic wave.

Kalitha cried out in a soft panting rhythm as the orgasm took her higher, then released her back down to earth. She swung her leg down and slid down the shower wall to the little shower seat as she gasped for air. She looked at her creamy cum soaked fingers as the thought of Willie Longe lingered in her mind. The water pelted her softly as she looked away in deep thought. She wished that the handsome private investigator was there right at that moment, but he wasn't. It didn't kill her daydream about him though. She smiled and stood back up to finish her shower.

After she completed her shower, she dressed in low cut jeans, a sexy blouse, and four inch heels. She felt like being a little wild so she didn't put on any panties, which made her feel accessible. She liked that thought.

She grabbed her travel bag and packed it with a few sets to wear for the week. She snatched her keys and headed for the elevator. She looked back at the lonely apartment, then over to the manilla envelope. She quickly walked back in to grab it also. It hurt her to have them in her presence, but it would hurt even more if she lost them and lost all of her proof. She would seriously consider using it as leverage in a divorce case.

She shook the thought away as she boarded the elevator knowing that she could never let Trevor go. For her it was until death do them part and nothing less. She didn't have the strength to let him go. Maybe to go and get her groove on, then come back, but not to let go.

She rode the elevator down while considering making a call to the fine ass private investigator she had met two weeks ago. *Maybe I should hang out with him,* she thought. *Maybe he would be the lucky one to let sample this pussy.* She walked through the lobby perked up and ready for her getaway.

She reached her pink Navigator in minutes, got in, and cranked up the system. She was on a cloud and no one was going to bring her down. A trip to be wild and crazy was going to be her therapy. Something had to heal the wound that the photos had created. She pulled onto the highway heading south west, her destination, Myrtle Beach.

****

Trevor sat in the back seat of the limo with a bouquet of pink and red roses. He was relieved to be home after being gone for so long. He knew that Kalitha would be steamed at him, but he had bought her and expensive gift that he hoped would ease her anger. The limo came to a stop in front of the building and Tony got out and opened the door. Trevor exited, giving him a nod.

"Hey, did you ever put in a good word for me with Vicky?" asked Tony.

Trevor compressed his urge to put Tony in his place. "She wasn't interested man," he lied. "I'm sorry."

"It's cool, bro," Tony said, brushing his sleeves off. "There's one out there for me."

"There always is," said Trevor before heading inside the building.

Tony watched him go, frowning. *Bouquet of roses? Who buys their sister a bouquet of roses?* He shook his head and got back in the driver's seat. His phone rang and he promptly answered it.

"Hello?"

"Hi, Mr. Mason!"

"Oh, hello Ms. Cox."

"I have Mrs. Mason in my sights. I'm tracking her to Myrtle Beach."

"Okay," said Tony. "Just keep an eye on her and report back to me soon."

"Yes, sir," replied Karen as she pulled onto the Conway exit. She hung up smiling broadly. She loved her job with a passion.

Tony hung up the phone and immediately dialed Sara Coli. She waded down to the other end of the pool before she answered.

"Yes, Tony," she cooed happily. "Any good news?"

"I don't know if it's good or not, but Kalitha's on her way to Myrtle Beach, and Karen is still tracking her every move."

"Great. Call Victor and have him go to her."

She looked down at her two beautiful friends standing naked at the bar. "Do whatever you have to do to connect the dots Tony."

"Yes, ma'am. Whatever you need done, I'll do."

"I know, Tony. That's why you're my number one guy," she said before hanging up.

She waded back over to Mirah and Janey. They were down for the week and that was why she had finally released Trevor from her secret state of captivity. She trusted them, but she trusted herself to play it safe. They were sirens with the very same ability she possessed. They also had sexual appetites that matched, and even surpassed hers. The only difference is they didn't mind sexing each other. Sara Coli didn't indulge in that sort of activity, but she had been in the habit of their naked pool get together's for so long that it meant nothing to her.

They called it their time of freedom and purity amongst one another. Sara Coli loved them, that was beyond question, but she loved what was hers even more. Trevor was hers. Him and his powerful ten inches. She joined back into the conversation with a gorgeous smile plastered on her lips.

"So where did I leave off?"

****

Trevor stepped off the elevator expecting to hear Kalitha's raging anger and high pitched voice screaming and cursing him out. He was utterly shocked when he was met with complete silence. He called out to her, but received no response. He called out to Frankenstein, but even his friend hadn't hurried out to greet him like usual. It was eerie and made him feel uncomfortable. He walked through the penthouse as a heavy feeling of unease settled in the pit of his stomach.

After checking all of the rooms he returned to the living room. He sat the bouquet and gift he'd bought for her onto the bar's counter. He checked the fridge for a note. No note. He picked up the phone and called her number. No answer. "Okay," he said, opening the little leather box to reveal the black diamond female Rolex watch he had gotten for her. "So you're mad at me," he said closing the box. "I get it."

He called her once more, but still got no answer. He shrugged, rubbed his head, and turned to the clock. It was only a little after six in the evening. It was still relatively early and she would be home soon. At least he hoped that she'd be home soon.

He walked slowly to the back to take a shower. He would wait her out. She never stayed out late. Of that much he was sure.

****

Kalitha sang Beyonce and bobbed her head to the beat. Her ringer was off, so when she glanced over at her phone and saw it glowing, she answered it. She turned the loud music down first.

" Hello?"

"Hey chick," Anastasia said cheerfully. "How on earth have you been?"

"Fine girl," Kalitha lied. "And you?"

"Oh, just expecting."

It took a minute for Kalitha to catch on to what she'd said. "Oh my God! Congratulations girl," Kalitha shouted. "I'm so happy for the both of you."

"Soon to be the three of us," Anastasia said happily. "But thank you so much Kalitha."

The realization smashed into Kalitha like a head on collision. Her and Trevor's chances of having children were probably in the low five percentile. She had let greed clutter her mode of thinking causing her to literally push her husband into the arms of a rich woman. She could never tell her friend Anastasia what she had done to her marriage. She would never look at her the same way again.

"Anyway, where are you girl?"

"I'm on my way to the strip club. I'm going to see some dick and balls bounce around."

They shared a squealing girly bout of laughter. "Oooh, you are so nasty," Anastasia said then giggled.

"What's so nasty about it?" Kalitha shot back. "Niggas do it all of the time."

"You go ahead then. Don't let me hold you up."

"I'll call you tomorrow, Okay?" Kalitha asked right before she pulled over at a corner store.

"That's cool. I love you girl."

"I love you too girl," Kalitha returned.

They disconnected and Kalitha leaned her head against the headrest. Her mind was being pulled in one thousand different ways. She looked to her phone to examine the missed calls, but chose to ignore them. Trevor didn't deserve to hear from her now that he had called. She sat the phone in her lap and looked out at the busy North Kings Highway, then over to the envelope. *Girl, you here to get down and dirty, so why not?*

She picked up the envelope and traced the open flap with her fingers thinking about how sexy Willie was and how she had came so hard by fantasizing about him earlier that day. *You know you wanna call him girl. Be a bad bitch for once. Do it. Do it.*

Kalitha fingered the manilla envelope open and dug around the inside until her fingers located the card that he'd placed there for her. She pulled it out and studied the embroidered letters and number. Holding it down in her lap, she stared at it for a long moment. She looked to her phone and back to the card.

Settling on a decision, she picked up the phone and programmed his number into it before she changed her mind. She sat there holding the phone while staring at the new entry. Her heart pumped in her throat as her thumb lingered over the dial button. She knew that she didn't want to be alone anymore and could really benefit from his company. She really wanted to hang out with him. She desired it. She took a deep breath, then dialed his number.

His smooth voice answered. "Hello?"

Her whole body reacted in a radical way to that one word and it made her nervous.

"Hi, Willie," she said, hesitating briefly. "This is Kalitha Mason."

"Wow! Hello Ms. Beautiful," he said, causing her to get a warm and fuzzy feeling inside. "I'm glad you called. I've been thinking about you a lot lately."

"Really?" she asked quietly.

"Yes. I was hoping that you would call me. I would like to—" he cut himself off intentionally.

"What?" she pursued. "What would you like?"

"I was going to ask if you would like to meet me somewhere?"

"Umm, I don't know. I mean, I do know." She became nervous and got caught up in her words. "I would like to see you, but I'm kind of in Myrtle Beach right now."

"Are you serious?" he asked excitedly.

"Yes," she replied unhappily.

"What a coincidence! So am I. I'm on N. Kings Highway headed towards Conway."

"Wow! You're kidding," she giggled flirtatiously. "I'm just off of the Conway Exit next to Benjamin's."

"Hell, I could be there in fifteen minutes. Do you want to meet up?"

She looked at her dash clock, it was now seven. She could hang out with him for a while and still go to the strip club later on.

She smiled. "Sure. I'm parked at the Citgo across from Taco Bell in a Pink Navigator."

"Cool. I'll be there shortly. And please don't leave. I really want to see you," he said in his deep voice.

Kalitha blushed profusely. "I'll be right here waiting."

When the call ended, she released a nervous breath. There were butterflies in her belly the size of the Liberty Bell. She was hot, horny, sex deprived, and overly excited to be meeting a sexy black man like Willie. Shoot, she was just happy that someone would be showing her some attention.

She glanced over to the Citgo, got out, and walked in. As soon a she stepped in her eyes went straight to the condom section. She looked over a few varieties until she realized what she was doing. Feeling embarrassed, she left out deciding to sit in the SUV and wait for Willie.

Karen Cox watched Kalitha as she went into the store and seemed to be studying something. Karen thought it looked like condoms, but couldn't tell for sure. She would return later and have a better look. At the moment she had more action to record. She watched patiently as a chromed out 760 BMW pulled up beside the Navigator. *Okay, let's get this party started Ms. Mason. Karen got bills to pay!*

Kalitha looked over as a horn beeped from a fly platinum gray BMW. The windows were tinted, so she looked away from it. Willie stepped out and walked over to her driver's side window. She admired his sexy stride, and the promising print in the front of his jeans. Her mouth watered at the way his body shirt fit him tight across his chest. She cocked her eyebrow approvingly and lowered her window.

"Oh, so that's yours too?" she teased.

"What can I say? The business pays good," he said smiling.

"Yeah, I bet," she said, returning his smile.

He looked into her eyes, ready to say whatever she needed to hear, so he could give her everything she wanted. "Wow. You look beautiful," he said with his mesmerizing smile.

She blushed. "Thank you. You're looking mighty good yourself," she countered.

"Well, when I'm in the presence of someone as beautiful as you..." He touched her chin gently causing a little chill to shoot down her body. "All I can do is try my best."

"Umm," she moaned, then cleared her throat, trying to regain her poise. "So what are you doing down here?"

Willie gave her a hungry look. "I'm trying to find something to get into." Her coochie lips twitched as his next two words flowed out of his mouth and into her ears. "You open?"

She wanted to tell him how badly she wanted to be open. How badly she needed to be opened up and handled with a little raunchiness. That she needed to be fucked and made to surrender. She opted to respond with much more reserve than she wanted to.

"It depends on what you want to do."

He placed his hands on her door. "Let's eat and shoot some billiards." He flashed her a sexy smile. "I love to shoot."

His subliminal innuendos turned her on. He spoke with so many double meanings, never truly saying what he wanted. He only hinted at it. She could only imagine how his mind worked and how that translated into the way his body moved. After seven weeks of vaginal neglect from Trevor, she wanted nothing more than to hold a thick stick and play with some balls.

"I don't shoot pool all that well," she stated truthfully.

"Oh, don't worry. I'm very good at what I do and have an outstanding stroke."

She raised her eyebrows.

"I'll show you how good it is. I'll get you right before the night is out."

She blushed stronger than before. He was killing her with his slick words and hidden promises. She averted her eyes as she squeezed her legs together.

"Okay," she agreed.

"Cool," he said, looking over at where Karen was parked. She quickly looked away from them as if she was looking for something. "Follow me then."

Willie led the way up the main street. They pulled into a little pool hall about a mile away from the Citgo. Whenever he visited Myrtle Beach, which wasn't that often, he shot pool there. He had banged a bartender who worked there long ago.

When they pulled into the parking lot he didn't see her car. That was a plus, because Angela didn't take him not calling her back too well and showed some aggressive tendencies when they ran into each other again. It ended with him having to punch her in the head and get his car window fixed. He did not feel like going through that again.

He exited his vehicle just as Kaltiha got out of hers. Even in the darkness of the night he could see how tight her jeans were and how her shirt hugged her tightly showing off her curvy breast and nipple prints. She was a hottie and he was ready to lay his game on thick and in layers. He wanted more than just a few photos of them flirting or being out together. He wanted a real piece of Kalitha's honey brown goodness.

He walked up to her so they could walk in together. "You look as sweet as candy Kalitha." She smiled and he continued. "Got me wondering what you taste like."

They began walking towards the door and she felt a rush of heat go through her body when she flirted back.

"Sweet ain't even the half of it."

He held the door for her and glanced down at her ass. "Yeah, I bet."

Karen clicked away as Willie studied Kalitha's switching hips and round booty bouncing as she walked in. He followed behind her rubbing his hands together and Karen liked it. It was some real action going on between them and she was going to capture it all. Waiting a few minutes, she readied herself, then joined them inside.

Karen watched as they flirted over the pool table. Willie got behind Kalitha and showed her how to hold the pool stick properly. She giggled and pressed her ass back against him. She wasn't being discreet about her behavior at all. Willie was pouring on the honey and Kalitha was eating it up by the spoonful.

Sitting at the bar, Karen was loving the footage she was getting. Her phone was recording a red handed act of adulterous behavior. First, Karen had thought that Mr. Mason was tripping, but now her beliefs of his assumption and accusations were being manifested right before her eyes. *She's a patient little cheater though. Oh well, keep it up honey and I'll have all that I need by tonight.* She sipped her beer and continued to watch.

Kalitha truly liked how witty and smooth Willie was. He had a wonderful personality with the physique to match. At least the prints in his clothes told her so. She had been rubbing against him to try and see what he was working with and it felt awfully promising to her.

She gazed into his dark, serious eyes and at his curly hair with a full beard. It was so much different from Trevor's clean cut face. *More manly,* she thought. Watching him lean over and shoot, she held onto her stick tightly, knowing that she was leaning towards letting him have a piece of her tonight. She was tight and needed a good opening up, and he looked like he would do it right. His big hands at the ends of his strong, sculpted arms made her think he was more than capable.

She was hungry for a black banana to ride up and down on and invade her sugar walls, so she kept her smiles bright and her touching heavy. She wanted him to read the signs and she had put them in neon against a black background.

Willie reads her intentions swiftly and accurately. Her advances were as clear as a fish bowl. He was having only one small problem. He needed a place where the private investigator sitting at the bar would be able to get great footage. He knew what needed to be done. Now he had to find the perfect place to do it. That was the best part of his job to him. Being paid to do something that he wanted to do for free.

Sometimes he needed the date rape drug in his pocket to get the right photos taken, but he didn't think that he would need it for Kalitha. She was hot for him and showing all of the necessary signs. He was confident that their attraction was real and that he could get her goodies of her own volition. She was willing and he was ready to take full advantage of it.

As she leaned in to shoot, he poked her in her side. Her shot was sloppy as she giggled playfully. She tapped him on the arm. "Hey, you're cheating. That's not fair man."

He poked her again. "You're a beginner. There are no rules."

She smiled up at him invitingly, giving such an aura of sexuality that he got a strong wave of pulsating energy in his groin area.

"You can't be taking advantage of me like that," Kalitha teased. "I'm still learning."

"Aww, that's too bad," he said as he touched her chin. "And here I am, ready to show you my advanced stroke."

Kalitha swallowed hard as she touched her neck absently.

He smiled knowingly. "Go ahead now. It's your shot."

She batted her eyes and turned to shoot again. Willie observed her curvy ass as she bent over and decided to step it up. He was ready to give the private investigator a real show. As Kalitha went to shoot, he grabbed the back of the stick, stopping it in place. Kalitha spun around quickly pretending that she was upset, only to be caught by surprise by his closeness. His lips brushed against hers, causing fire to explode inside of her. The feel of his lips and the soft hairs of his mustache lit her world up, but she couldn't allow it to be too obvious. She leaned back and looked around the bar guiltily.

She looked back to Willie. "You kissed me," she said in a half question, half statement.

Willie feigned worry. "I'm sorry," he said, backing up a step. "I guess I got caught up in my desire for you. I didn't mean to offend you Kalitha."

Suddenly, she became the aggressor by closing the distance between them. "You didn't." She leaned up and kissed him again fully on the lips.

Willie slid an arm around her lower back and pulled her tightly to him. The kiss deepened and became more passionate with their tongues dancing around in each other's mouths. The taste of her fruity drink sweetened the kiss even more.

Kalitha broke the kiss and licked her lips slowly. She looked up into his dark brown eyes and told him what was on her mind. "You just made my pussy so wet." She couldn't believe she had just said that. It had to be the two shots of liquor talking.

Willie leaned in close to her ear. "I don't believe you. I need some proof," he whispered. Trying his hand, he added, "show me."

She held his gaze as she began to undo her tight jeans. He looked down to see her unzipping them. She lifted her shirt and showed him that she wasn't wearing any panties. He looked into her eyes, surprised that she'd taken him up on his challenge. "Stick your fingers in it and feel for yourself."

Willie couldn't believe his eyes or his ears. He'd met women who turned him on, but Kalitha was by far the most sexiest and fascinating of them all. Stepping closer, he slipped his hand into the front of her opened jeans and slid down her soft hairs to her clit. She bit her bottom lip in arousal as he folded his pointer and middle fingers up and eased inside her. She released a soft moan as he pushed them in further, only to pull them out gradually. He lifted his fingers up to see the creamy wetness coating them, before sliding them into his mouth. He sucked her juices from his two fingers making sure nothing was left.

She whispered in a husky voice. "That's a good boy. Now let's go to my truck."

He nodded and she took his hand, pulling him behind her. He sat his beer down and followed her out of the door. He saw Karen cutting her eyes to watch them and he smiled deviously.

Once outside, she unlocked her SUV's door with the push of a button on the keyless entry from a few yards away. She pulled him to the SUV and pressed against him for a long sensual kiss that made her even wetter. She could feel his dick pressing into her and it made her pussy muscles clench with desire and anticipation.

Reaching around him, she opened the back door to the Navigator. He let her get in, then he followed. As soon as the door closed, she hungrily tugged at his belt and jeans. She pulled the fly of his jeans wide and fished his semi-erect member out of his boxers and held it in her hands. He was thick and at least eight inches long. He wasn't as big as Trevor, but in her tiny hands, he looked massive.

She stroked his dick a few times whispering more to herself than to him. "Ooh, it's so fat, daddy. Mmm, just let me suck it." She looked into his eyes, then back at his dick in her hands.

Willie spread his arms across the top of the seat and spread his legs more. He looked towards the door of the pool hall and saw Karen exiting conspicuously. He hoped that she could see them from where she stood. Before he could think another thought, Kalitha leaned down and took him deep into her hot wet mouth. He groaned and placed his hand on top of her soft curly hair pushing her down further.

Kalitha went down on him with a vengeance, sucking him deep into her mouth, then back up to the tip. She pulled back and licked the base of the head, flicking her tongue slowly with pressure. Her tongue didn't recognize his taste and it jolted her back to reality. Her mind screamed for her to stop.

She sprang back up to a sitting position looking over to him in the dark truck as if she was just now comprehending that he was not her husband. The revelation hit her hard. It was not her husband's dick she'd just had in her mouth. Her facial expression was that of pure shock and shame. She looked back down at his fat hard dick that she still held on to and quickly let it go.

"Holy shit," she said hastily. "I'm sorry Willie. Oh my God, I didn't mean to." She looked away as he stuffed his hard dick back into his boxers and jeans.

"It's cool. It's cool," he said, trying to ease the weird tension in the air. "It's alright, baby."

"No," she said still looking away. "I didn't mean to... and it was the liquor... and I..." She began to stammer. "I don't know," she finished buttoning her jeans and got out the truck. She hurried around the SUV and got in the driver's seat.

He got out and walked up to her window. "Hey."

She turned to look at him, her eyes bright from holding in her tears.

"Don't trip, Kalitha. It was a heat of the moment thing."

"Yeah, but I'm married, Willie. I know better."

"Don't do that to yourself. He doesn't deserve a woman as special as you," he said sternly. She looked away disappointed in herself. Willie knew that he needed to ease that feeling in her and create another opening. "I do." He let the words hang in the air for a moment.

She looked back to him, then dropped her gaze.

"Hey, listen," he said, tilting her chin back upward so he could see her eyes. "I still want to hang out sometime."

She shook her head, still reeling about what she'd almost done. Then she thought about all the bullshit Trevor had been doing and remembered why she was there. She started the SUV and glanced up at him standing there looking at her. Although she had some thinking to do, she couldn't just pull off and leave him standing there like that.

"All things considered, I had a really great time with you tonight," she said giving him an approving once over. "And I do hope that we can do it again soon."

He placed his hand in the windows opening. "Just give me a call, beautiful. I'll always have time for you."

She nodded and smiled, thankful that she hadn't totally ruined everything. They locked eyes, and Willie leaned in and gave her a soft kiss on the lips.

She watched as he backed up from the vehicle. "Call me Kalitha. Please." She gave him a small smile and pulled off.

He watched her drive out of the parking lot and turn left on the main street. He looked back over to Karen, who stood in front of the pool hall smoking a cigarette, and smiled. He watched her hurry to her car and pull out after Kalitha.

Okay, I'll just follow you. He got into his car and pulled out after her. He picked up his phone and dialed.

"Hello, Sara Coli speaking."

"Hello, Ms. White. This is Victor," he said searching for Karens car. "I might need a place to hold up here. I'm confident that I can do exceedingly more if I had one."

Sara Coli reached up to grab her tea cup. "I believe I can accommodate you. Meet me tomorrow and I will hand you the keys to my beach front. It has a lot of windows."

"Tomorrow it is," he said and ended the call.

Sara Coli sipped her tea. She had never stayed at her beach front property and it would be a great fit for Victor. It suited him well. She smiled, thinking about the drama that was about to unfold. *This is how the real games are played.*

****

Kalitha was driving with her pussy pulsating with need. She faulted herself for folding under pressure. She wanted to be fucked and she knew it. She wanted to fuck Willie, but had lied to herself saying that she hadn't wanted it like that. *Not in the back of your SUV girl! Right?* Wrong. The way her pussy was jumping right now she'd take it all night if he was willing to do it. She was lying to herself, knowing she'd literally take it whenever, however, and wherever she could get it.

She popped herself on the forehead with the palm of her hand three quick times. "Stupid, stupid, stupid." She could have at least gotten her pussy ate before she'd backed up off the situation. Now she wished she was back at the pool hall in the back seat with Willie and his fat dick was still in her mouth.

Glancing at the clock on the dash, she figured that she had wasted two hours at least. She still felt the buzz from the liquor and didn't think that she should be driving. But then again, she still wanted to see what she had driven down there to see, which was an array of naked men shaking their packages in her face. She wanted to feel on some dicks and inhale the scent of sweaty dancing men. That was all blown for now as she found herself turning into a motel's parking lot.

She turned her SUV off and stared up at the motel sign. She released an exasperated breath as the size and feel of Willie's hard dick in her hands shot back across her mind. She slapped her forehead one last time a little harder than intended. "Ouch," she said rubbing it softly.

She laughed at herself for her slip up and figured it was nothing she could do to bring back the past. She decided to call it a night. She had a whole week to cut up and act a fool at the strip clubs. Kalitha got out and walked in the office to get a room.

Karen pulled up just as Kalitha was going into the office. She parked far away from her truck and cut out her lights. A light shining inside her car caught her attention and she noticed that it was the 760.

He pulled in and to her great surprise parked right beside her car. She tried to scoot down in her seat, but he could still see her. It was really no use. She tried to act like she didn't notice him, but he was right beside her in a flashy vehicle. Who could not notice it? She imagined that he was looking right at her through the tinted glass. It was nothing she could do anyway, so she kept looking towards the office.

Kalitha soon emerged and walked about eleven doors down to a room and entered it. Karen pulled out her recorder and spoke into it stating the hotel's name, the time, room number, and the fact that the guy from the pool hall was parked right beside her car. She glanced over as something glowed in his car. It had to be a phone.

She pressed record on the recorder. "It's 10:28 pm, the subject's potential lover is making a phone call."

As soon as Kalitha walked into the room, she kicked off her heels, pulled her shirt and bra off, and unfastened her jeans again. She lay back on the bed, slid her hand down and felt her soft pussy hairs. Her thoughts returned to Willie and how his hand felt down there. It had her closing her eyes, envisioning his plump dick, and how it felt so hard and fat in her tiny hands.

She pulled her knees up together and rolled over onto her side. She wanted to call him badly. She wanted him to come through the room door like and apparition and take her body to the promised land. She wanted him to stuff his fat erection inside of her tight wet pussy and fuck her until she exploded.

She didn't know why she was deciding against it. She thought about the photos in the manilla envelope again. The ones that proved that her supposedly faithful husband was really a player and a liar. He had completely forgotten that she existed.

She sat up with a jolt. *I should have done it*, she thought. *I should have fucked him right there at the pool hall in my damn truck.* She laid back down on the bed with a flop. *I'm so stupid.* She rolled over, staring at the door. *And his ass is probably balls deep in pussy right now.*

Kalitha attempted to shake her thoughts away, but it was

impossible. She loved Trevor and she was devastated by his betrayal. However, his cheating and being gone for over a month was something unforgivable. Yet, she felt that everything that had transpired from her idea was all her fault. She had to blame herself as much, or even more, for the turns her scam had taken. She was a big girl and she'd own that shit. But his actions would forever leave deep lacerations in the flesh of their trust.

A heavy sadness settled into her bones and she'd never felt so alone. Her marriage was in disarray and her heart invaded by pain. Her thoughts were interrupted by the ringing of her cell. She reached over and answered it without checking to see who was calling.

"Hello?"

"Kalitha," Willie's voice whispered. "Kalitha."

She sat up listening quietly.

He continued speaking softly. "I tasted my fingers and now I want to taste you."

OH SHIT! She grabbed her aching twat through her jeans. She merely breathed into the phone as a response. "I can come wherever you are sexy," he said in a husky baritone voice. "I can make you cum wherever you are."

Kalitha moaned sliding her fingers inside her moist folds. If she let him continue to talk, she would be having an orgasm to the sound of his voice.

"Tell me," he growled lowly. "How long has it been?"

"Seven weeks," she whimpered out her only answer.

"Let me make you cum seven times."

Her pussy walls throbbed nonstop, causing her to moan and end the call. She tossed the phone on the bed beside her. Her heart pounded as she imagined his thick meat inside her wetness, drilling continuously into her.

She pushed her jeans down, kicked them off of her legs, and watched them fall to the floor. She caressed her titties and gently pinched her erect nipples, before slipping the same two fingers Willie had sucked inside her soaked slit. She surprised herself when she pulled her fingers out and sucked her own juices. She was locked and loaded in freak mode tonight and she began to please herself to the memory of his words.

Willie smiled when the call ended. The private investigator had led him right to where Kalitha was. It was like the planets had lined up and pointed to her tonight. He was concocting the perfect way to use it to his advantage. He already had her going sexually. Now all he had to do was seal the deal. He decided to keep on teasing her until she broke and he would be there to catch all of the delicious pieces as she fell apart. He was as determined as a cheetah to catch this fine piece of pussy prey. Smiling, he picked up the phone to call her again.

Kalitha picked up on the second ring. She lay sprawled out on the bed with her fingers snugly placed in her hot womb listening.

"Are you still soaking wet?"

"Yes," she whispered.

"Ahhh damn, baby. Let me find you. You know I'm a private investigator. Let me find you so I can come taste all of your most private places."

She cooed softly and continued to listen.

"I can find you if you want me to," he paused to breathe into the phone hungrily.

She was eating up every sound he made up. She rubbed her clit gently, then slid down to tickle her ass. She lifted her legs off of the bed, pulling them towards her breast.

"Do you want me to find you?" he asked in a deep, pleading voice. "Do you, baby? Tell me."

She moaned as she neared her orgasm. "If you find me, you can have me," she whispered, giving in to her desire.

"All of you?"

"All of me, Daddy," she moaned.

That was all he needed to hear. He got out of the Beamer and began to speak softly with his instructions.

"Take off your clothes sexy, because I'm going to find you. Dim the lights and pull back the sheets." She moaned as his voice made her wetter by the second. "Are you ready for me, baby?"

"Yes, Daddy," she answered without hesitation.

Walking up to the door, he took a long pause. "Good. Now guess what?"

"What?"

"I found you."

The phone went dead in her ear just as a knock came at the door. If it was a coincidence, it was timed perfectly. She pulled the blanket off of the bed and walked to the door with it draped around her. She looked through the peephole and nearly fainted. He was there, right at her room's threshold. She opened the door and he stepped inside, grabbing her up, and tonguing her deeply.

Kalitha went crazy trying to pull his clothes off him. She dropped the blanket and wrapped her arms around his waist. He licked her ears and neck as she tugged at his jeans. When they cleared his hips, his fat dick popped out and grazed across her plump pussy lips. Willie stepped out of his shoes and jeans, and spun Kalitha around to the door where he hoisted her up. Instantly, she wrapped her legs around his hips and her arms around his neck. He leaned down and began kissing her softly.

She closed her eyes as he licked her neck and he took that moment to discreetly slide the curtain open a little. While cupping her round ass, he turned and headed towards the bed. She loved how it felt to be up in the air with his fat dick at the split of her ass cheeks. A low moan escaped her as he laid her on the bed with a light bounce. She looked up at him admiringly. His body was spectacular. His chest was sculpted with smooth hair, and his skin almost glowing golden. She pulled her legs back, exposing all of her womanhood to him.

"You ready for another taste?" she purred.

Willie licked his lips and hurriedly dove between her legs. He shoved his tongue deep inside of her pussy and she cried out his name in pleasure. "Oh, Willie"

He sucked and tickled her lips and clit, pushing her beyond her limitations. The fullness of his beard brushed her clit and caused her to explode in an earth shattering orgasm. "Oh my God!" she yelled and grabbed a handful of his curly hair. "Oooh shit," she cried as she came all on his tongue.

Willie kept the focus on her clit, causing her to do something that she'd never done before, have multiple orgasms. She squeezed her eyes shut as she was hit with a strong spasm of shutters as another orgasm rushed through her like wildfire. She nearly choked as the waves of climatic pressure rippled from deep within her pussy over and over. She gasped for breath as her body quaked under the pressure of her cumming. He hadn't been licking her for five minutes and she had already coated his beard with her glistening dew.

Wanting to return the favor, she pulled herself to a sitting position and buried his dick inside her hungry mouth. She sucked and slurped on his stick until he was rock hard and murmuring unintelligible phrases. She loved the way he filled her mouth with his manly goodness and she became unrelenting as she jerked and suck on his dick. Her hands were sliding easily over his dick because it was saturated with her saliva.

Loving the feel of her mouth, Willie cupped both sides of her face and shoved his dick deeper until his it slid down the tight canal of her throat. Kalitha gagged hard, her stomach tightening, but it only turned her on more seeing how he wasn't afraid to gag her to show his dominance. She looked up at him with burning eyes, feeling hungrier than she'd ever had for Trevor.

Willie had brought out her wild side. She gripped his firm ass cheeks and pulled him in for another gag sensation. She gagged again, then did it once more. That set him on go. He pushed her back on the bed, pulled her legs up, and pushed them back to her shoulders. Without hesitating, he drove his hardness home, deep inside her pulsating tunnel.

Kalitha arched her back and groaned in pleasure as his girth stretched her out further than she'd ever felt it go. When his pelvic bone hit hers, she was filled to capacity. She gripped the sheets on either side of her as he kept his wood pressed snugly against her back wall and kissed her neck. He was noticeably thicker than Trevor, but shorter, and was the perfect fit for her. Her pussy clenched up tightly around him threatening to release another orgasm. He began an easy, powerful stroke that translated into the perfect mixture of thickness and length for Kalitha. He was her dream dick.

Every thrust seemed to be right at the places inside her that triggered orgasm after orgasm. He caused her to cream in less than four minutes and her belly tightened as she came for a third time from his great penetration. He bent to lick her breast seemingly exactly the way she liked it.

Kalitha's toes curled and her eyes rolled back. Willie picked up the momentum and rammed his thick rod inside her a few times, then slowed down switching it to powerful grinding thrust. His teeth were clenched, and his breath hot against her neck, as he fucked her with sturdy strokes. Nothing could be heard, but their breathing and sex talk. Their love making had their bodies sweating and the bed rocking.

Willie felt his world tilt as the first onslaught of his orgasm rocked him hard. Quickly, he pulled out and gushed hot white cum all over her flat belly, calling her name with every drop. "Kalitha! Oh damn!"

Kalitha leaned up and massaged the rest of his milky sperm into her mouth. He leaned back and rubbed her hair, lifting his hips to feed her more. She held his dick, still half rigid, and licked him lovingly.

She had never been so perfectly fitted during any other sexual encounter in her whole entire life. At full penetration, Willie hurt just enough to feel wonderful. He was better than Trevor in that area because he hurt her the way she needed it. It made her hungrier for him.

She worked his manhood back to a full erection and nearly begged him to hit her from the back. Willie obliged his curly haired vixen with a smile. He slid inside her from behind all the way to the hilt. When he felt how she constricted around him, the tightness almost made him pull his dick back out. He had to admit, she had that certified snap back.

Willie held her hips and admired how her back arched. Her ass cheeks spread enticingly and her pussy lips gripped him as he slid in and out. She had that firebomb pussy and he pressed in deeper loving her slickness. He got creative with his thrusts, causing her to cry out and cum on his dick again. What she said to him next pushed him into overdrive.

"Hurt me, Daddy. Fuck me hard."

He turned up his dick game to the max. Willie slapped her ass cheeks and began to power drive his dick deeply into her cavern. The loud clapping sound of their bodies colliding told the story of how forceful he was being and Kalitha loved everything about it. She began tossing her ass back meeting his assault and tightening her pussy when he withdrew.

Soon he couldn't hold back any longer. He couldn't handle the grip of her pussy working his muscle and he began to shake violently. The tingling rush to his nuts caught him off guard and he yanked his dick out shooting cum all over her round ass cheeks.

"Fuuuuucccckkk! Ahhh fuck!" He gripped his dick loosely in his hand as he jerked out the last of his load.

Kalitha fell forward, panting with exhaustion. He fell forward onto the back of her legs, glancing back at the parted curtain where he knew Karen was. He had seen her shadow by the window and smiled, knowing that he had gotten his and her job done. He rubbed Kalitha's round ass, causing her to flinch and giggle.

"Sensitive, huh?" he asked smiling.

"Umm hmm," she moaned.

He wanted to give a good show for Karen, so he parted Kalitha's ass cheeks and took a long slow lick. She shuddered in pleasure. He hoped Karen got a good look at that.

Karen hurried to the window, trying to get a good angle, but the curtain was closed. She jumped back, startled, as the curtain suddenly opened just enough for her to see the entire bed. She felt like her job couldn't be easier. She recorded everything from the moment they started, until the second it ended. She'd captured Kalitha's lover fucking her senseless with his hard fat tool. Fatter than any she'd ever seen. She even recorded when he seemed to look right at her and licked between Kalitha's cheeks.

She had seen more than enough to convict her in front of a

blind jury. Plus, Karen's panties were dripping wet, and she kind of wished that she could have been part of the action. She had been watching Kalitha Mason for so long that she had been neglecting her own boyfriend. She needed her instrument tuned up. Her job was now complete, she was confident of that.

She walked to her car with intentions of calling Mr. Mason tomorrow and bringing the case to a close. She got back into her car and pulled out her tape recorder. "Near 12 am, the subject Kalitha Mason, was caught on video involved in extramarital sex with an unknown male, not Mr. Mason." She stopped for a second and looked back over to the motel room. Feeling her twat soaking wet, she set the recorder down and undid her slacks. She felt a rush of excitement at the dirty thoughts, she was having.

She pulled out the video camera and began to play it back. Karen wiggled out of her pants and lifted her right leg over onto the console. Her blonde pussy hairs were exposed, and she began to finger herself slowly making little circles around her clit. She watched the playback as the man fucked Kalitha, making her shiver and cry out over and over.

Karen felt her pussy tightening up as she watched the recording. Her orgasm began to build up inside her, and before she knew it, she was squirming and cumming all over her slender fingers. She laid her seat back and stared at the ceiling of her car. She breathed hard as she watched the recording play. She felt relieved, but not satisfied. *I need my mans dick.* She watched as the man began to hit Kalitha from the back and bit her lip. *Hell, one more can't hurt.* She began to rubbed her swollen clit until she exploded again.

Chapter 14

Kalitha woke up the next morning feeling like a brand new woman. Even the sunlight streaming through the cracked curtains seemed brighter than usual. She rolled over and swallowed up the vision of her one night stand trophy dick and decided to have it for breakfast.

She looked him up and down slowly, admiring his body. He was a work of art. Handsome as ever, chiseled like a sculpture, and hanging all fat and limp. She couldn't contain her prowess and rolled over onto him, causing him to open his eyes and look at her. He stretched beneath her enjoying the feel of her pressed up against him.

"Good morning, beautiful."

"Mmm," she said, sitting up and rubbing his chest down to his tight abs. "I gotta have some more of this good dick this morning." She rubbed her flat belly, then cuffed her titties, pinching her nipples as she gyrated on his limp dick. "You gonna give it to me?"

His answer was a sexy smile.

Willie looked up at her sexy face and beautifully toned body, and smiled. Just the feel of her hot pussy on his dick was making him rise. She bent over to massage him until he was firm and ready. She slipped him inside her wetness, registering just how swollen and tender she was. She ignored it in her attempts to get one more episode with him.

Kalitha rode him passionately with her hands planted firmly on his chest. He fondled her breast as she rocked and ground small circles on his stiff member. She felt her orgasm building and kept her pace steady. It began to rush down when he parted her cheeks and fingered her ass. It made her cum harder than ever and she felt like her body would come apart at the seams. The orgasm was of extraordinary proportions and took her entire body in its possession. It was in her ass, pussy, inner thighs, and her belly. She nearly shed a tear when it came to its sweet end.

Willie wasn't done and he continued to rock into her. His strokes were deep and thorough as he gripped her hips controlling the tempo. Suddenly, the feel of her pussy muscles clenching and pulsating around him caused him to lose the battle of making it last. He pulled out of her quickly ready to spill his load.

Instantly, Kalitha slid down his body and took him deep in her mouth, allowing him to shoot warm cum down her throat. She licked his opening and suckled his head gently as he shuddered and rubbed her curly hair. She was pleased with his performance and lapped the remaining drops up with long, hot licks.

He gazed down at her smiling. "Somebody's hungry," he teased.

"Whatever. I'm about to shower," she said, heading to the bathroom. "You gonna join me?"

"Give me a minute sexy," he replied, eyeing her fat ass.

She smiled brightly and got in the shower. The water began to run and he heard her singing. *She had a beautiful voice*, he thought listening. Sluggishly, he sat up and looked for his jeans to get his phone. He retrieved it and dialed Sara Coli's number.

"Hello?"

"Ms. White, you should have the shots you need by this afternoon," he said, then listened for a moment.

"You want more?" He glanced back towards the shower door.

"Yes, more. I want it to be unbeatable in court, Victor.

"It would be really hard to deny with the shots I gave."

"Let me make it a little simpler for you. I want to destroy her," Sara Coli stated with conviction.

"Alright," he said, wondering what Kalitha had done to make Sara Coli hate her so much.

"Oh, and I have the keys for the Beach House," she said evenly as if she wasn't making plans to ruin someones life.

"Okay," said Victor, listening without any interruptions.

"I have something that I want you to give to her," she said then laughed her throaty way. "I also want those photos back, if you can manage that."

"I think I can," he said confidently.

"Great, then I will have someone meet you with the keys and the vials later.

"Vials?" he asked curiously.

"No questions, remember?"

"You do pay well, Ms. White."

"Indeed I do," she replied arrogantly. "I hope you like the beach because I'm putting you up in my beach side estate. Enjoy!"

The phone went dead in his ear and he smiled. He loved how powerful Sara Coli was. It was a complete turn on to him. He stood up and walked to the shower. She washed his back leisurely as he thought about how he would take her to Sara Coli's beach front estate and show her a great time. He was really a Virginia resident, but would be holding up at the estate for now. He would get Kalitha to come there just as Sara Coli wished.

He was getting paid handsomely and loved the perks. He turned to wash her back, knowing she needed that kind of attention. He couldn't help but to admire how pieced together Kalitha was from head to toe. He kissed the back of her neck and began to butter her up.

"God you're so sexy Kalitha."

"Thank you," she blushed.

They finished their shower, and after Willie got dressed, he went to retrieve her luggage from the SUV. Spotting the envelope in the passenger seat, he made a mental note to remember to take it. He knew that he could get it soon. Right then would not have been the best time. He walked back into the room to see Kaltiha wrapped in a towel. She smiled at him.

"Thank you. I meant to bring it in last night."

"It's nothing, baby."

Kalitha began to dig through her baggage for a pair of sexy underwear and a nice tight fitting outfit. He admired her and thought that it was as good a time as any to begin to lay the groundwork. His statement stilled her.

"I wish that you were mine."

She blushed hard. "No you don't."

"I do Kalitha. Ever since I first met you I've been feeling that way." He took a deep breath and looked up at the ceiling then continued. "I would make sweet love to you every day and spend every night holding close to my heart."

The words were music to Kalitha's ears. Like harps and violins playing softly in her thoughts. She didn't want to speak. All she wanted was to hear more about how he desired to be with her. His words were the comfort that her betrayed heart needed. As he spoke, she hung on to every syllable.

"I just wish I could spend today with you." He looked deep into her eyes. "I want one day of you being mine."

She hastened to speak. "You... I'm..." she stammered. "We can... I mean, if you really want to," she cooed. "I want to, Willie."

He knew that he had her hooked then. He only needed to reel her in. "I want to. Trust me," he smiled. "But I have some work to do."

He watched as her facial expression went from hopeful to disappointment.

"But," he continued as he stood and closed the distance between them. "I should be free by three."

Kalitha jumped on that. "I can be available at three. Hell, I can be available at two-fifty-nine," she said excitedly.

"Great," he said, rubbing the curly hair of his full beard. "You could come out to my place if you like?"

She smiled and nodded her agreement.

He smiled back. "Then I'll call you around three, sweetie."

"Or I'll call you," she stated, looking up into his handsome face. He leaned down and kissed her softly.

His kiss was so sensuous and tender that she grew moist again. She got lost in the kiss and leaned into it. She felt on fire just from his touch and never felt that kind of power over her before. Even Trevor didn't make her body react like that. They broke their kiss with them both breathing fast. After settling down, they prepped for their departure. She watched him as he walked towards the door. Just watching him turned her on. He carried her baggage out and she followed him.

"You won't need to get another room," he said, opening her back door and placing her bag inside. "You can just stay with me."

"That's fine with me," she said, stepping into his arms.

He smiled and hugged her close. This sudden show of affection caught him off guard and surprised him. He knew that he had her open after receiving some good dick. The tell tale signs were there. He held glanced down and looked into her light brown eyes, rubbing her shoulders down to her arms.

"I guess I will see you a little later," he said softly. She smiled and nodded. He touched her on the tip of her nose, then turned to walk to his Beamer. Willie got in his car and pulled out, beeping as he drove past her. She gave him a wave as he rode past, headed the way they had come.

Kalitha looked at her watch; 1:35 in the afternoon. She was glad that it would only be about three hours before she would get to see him again. She felt really good about the night she shared with Willie, and about everything he said or done.

She got into her SUV and pulled off deciding to buy something to wear to his house tonight. She wanted to impress him. At least she would have someone to look nice for. Trevor hadn't been home to dress up for. He probably wouldn't notice anyway. But Willie on the other hand had asked to see her again. He wanted to spend the day with her. It was his self proclaimed idea and she dove at the chance to do so. He was the one who alerted her and made her fully aware of Trevor's double crossing, two timing, and cheating ass.

She stopped at the light and looked all around at the different places she could go for a few hours. The sun was bright and she was full of ideas. She just needed to kill some time, then shop, and meet back up with him later. He had proven himself worthy of at least a few more nights of fun., *I need to find something really sexy.*

She glanced down at the manilla envelope in her passenger seat, then swore to herself that Willie would receive the royal treatment if he kept making her feel the way she did. She couldn't help but to think about Trevor for a brief moment. Instead of dragging her heart through the turmoil of wondering what he was doing or where he was, she quickly dismissed him. He was on his own time and now so was she. *My goal is to have the time of my life for a week. So fuck him!*

****

Karen captured the entire exchange from a parking space far away from them. She felt more comfortable that way. She continued to trail Kalitha per Mr. Mason's request. Personally, she thought that she had sufficient evidence to prove beyond a shadow of a doubt, that Kalitha Mason was having an affair. She had taped her and her lover red handed and in the act. The only reason she hadn't closed the case yet was the other job required more proof. So she would be at it for another day. Mr. Mason was paying top dollar, plus all expenses, so she couldn't lose anyway. She combed through her hair with her fingers and kept hot on Kalitha's trail.

****

Trevor sat on the side of the bed stressing. He looked at the clock which read eleven minutes after twelve and reached for his phone and dialed his wife's number.

"Come on, babe. Answer the phone," he said, sounding anxious.

After receiving no answer, he flopped back on the bed. Worry plagued Trevor's body. He knew that she wasn't answering out of anger and couldn't blame her at all. It was his inconsideration that had her freezing him out.

In between the vials of White Widow, and the jet lag from flying through the black skies in a Lear Jet, he had lost track of the days and weeks. He dialed her number again, no answer. He squeezed the phone tightly in frustration. *You know that I'm calling, babe.*

He got up and paced around the apartment. He knew that she would be home soon because she knew that he was calling, and when she did come home, they would sit down and have a long talk. The scam was beginning to weigh down on their marriage and he didn't want to lose his wife.

He was more than prepared to admit to his addiction to the White Widow and comprise a solution that would allow him and Kalitha to escape with the spoils they had already pilfered from Sara Coli. Then, they could find somewhere where they could continue on with their lives. To push the con any further would not be sensible at all. They would be showing a total lack of discipline if they continued on.

He laughed at himself. He was hooked on the White Widow, bordering on the dependence of its rush and erotic affects. The thought of going without the drink was horrifying to him and nearly made him vomit at the mere consideration.

He sat at the bar and laid his head on his hands closing his eyes for a moment. When he opened them again, the house was dark, and his back and neck was stiff from lying in the same position.

He dialed Kalitha's number over and over with no answer. He tossed his phone on the sofa as he walked to the patio porch door. He opened it and stepped out into the warm night's air. He looked over at the lit up Old Wilmington, then over to the battleship, which sat across the river.

It was crazy how he had watched them go from the slums of a broken down trailer home, to the penthouse suite of the tallest building in their city. It was a true to life, from nothing to something, and better than anything they had ever known, tale. Yet, right now, the one thing he wanted was his wife.

He wished that Kalitha would have answered and that she was there with him. He gazed up at the star filled night sky and wished that he could stop wishing for things he wanted, and just have them. He wished that things were back right with his wife. But more than that, he wished that he had a White Widow elixir to set his night off.

Trevor lowered his head in defeat. Here he was wishing for his wife, but yearning for the White Widow. He wished he was with Sara Coli because she had the fix he yearned for. And with her, he could live in that sex zone haze he had gotten used to. The sex zone haze he knew he needed. He started wishing that he could somehow obtain his own supply. He liked it tremendously while he was with Sara Coli because she could take all of him with no problem. She loved to be hurt and had confessed to being addicted to the pain he gave her.

He envisioned her beautiful youthful body with her seasoned, sweet pussy. He shook his head, realizing how quickly Kalitha had slipped from the forefront of his mind. He figured that he couldn't make her return any quicker, so he went inside and made himself some food to eat, and kicked back to watch T.V.

He somehow knew that she would waltz in any minute now and he would be ready to apologize. Until then, he would watch sports and leave the wishing game to the genie in the lamp.

****

Kalitha stared out of the large bay window in the dining room of the huge beach front home. She absently watched the quickly dimming sky as it casts an orange glow on the large boat off in the distance. His home was lovely and she was happy he'd invited her.

Willie watched her, admiring all of her feminine curves, as he prepared their dinners. He carried their plates over to the bar and sat them down so they could face the window as they ate. He knew his way around the kitchen and had prepared a Tomato Basil Pasta with seasoned chicken strips, and a chilled white wine. He began to pour them both a glass as Kalitha walked over.

"Wow," she looked at him. "That really does smell great."

"Thank you." He sat the bottle of wine back into the ice bucket. "I do my thing here and there."

She smiled and looked back out to the lights on the water. "That's so beautiful out there on that pitch black water," Kalitha commented. "You ever been on a yacht?"

"A yacht?" he asked, sitting down. "Sure. A friend of mine had a little get together. Nothing big though."

"I've never been on a yacht. I would like to see what it's like to be on one," Kalitha said, turning and walking to the bar to have a seat.

Willie took notice of her Baby Phat dress which hugged her hips tightly, then flared out at the bottom. Her nails matched the dress and her heels were long and screamed, *'come fuck me'*. Her walk was confident and sexy.

She sat down and smelled the food. "This really smells good, Willie."

"Just wait until you taste it," he said, reaching over to take her hand. "Let's pray."

She was caught by surprise by that, and smiled. As he bowed his head to pray, she watched him. *How will ever let this man go. God, look at him*. She squeezed her legs together tightly. *What a man.*

Willie lifted his head after completing the prayer. "Amen."

"Amen," she repeated, staring at him hungrily.

He noticed and smiled. "Eat your food woman."

"Yes, Daddy," she mocked him and laughed.

They ate over light conversation. She was in rare form and flirting nonstop. He fed her advances with witty responses and a lot of touching. She used her foot to rub his leg as they sipped their wine. His phone rang and he excused himself to answer it.

"Hurry back, Mr Longe," Kalitha teased.

He smiled and clicked the phone to answer it. "Hello?"

"Hi, Victor," Sara Coli crooned.

Kalitha picked a piece of sun dried tomato off of her plate and began to tease it with her tongue. She began to fantasize about how she would use her tongue on Willie's fat meat tonight and it made her get hot. She sipped her wine in an attempt to cool off, but it didn't help. In fact, the intoxicating liquid only served to make her feel racier.

Willie walked back into the room and caught her tickling the sun-dried tomato and gave her a knowing look. She smiled guiltily. "What?"

He sat down and sipped his wine. "I was wondering if you'd like to go with me to a yacht party on Friday?"

Kalitha lit up in excitement. "Oh my God, are you serious?"

"I am," he answered smiling.

"Hell, yeah," she shouted, causing him to laugh. "I would love to go."

"Sweet. Then it's a date."

"Yes it is," she said as a rush of desire flooded her body.

She felt overwhelmingly horny all of a sudden. She wanted to prepay Willie for the experience that was to come on Friday. He was the only thing in her life giving her a reason to not feel like her world was caving in. She stood and walked in between his legs, rubbed his chest, and kissed him passionately. It seemed to her that Trevor had chosen something else, so maybe it was time for her to do the same thing.

She stared into Willie's dreamy eyes, and though he was the epitome of perfection to her, she could only dream that it would be that easy to walk away from her husband. Trevor was her life. *He will always be in my life, but not tonight,* she thought mischievously. Tonight she would let Willie be her everything.

Their passionate kiss led to them making love. She took notice of how soft and tender he was with her. How his every touch displayed confidence. As he lay her down on the king sized bed he paused.

"Kalitha, would you like to try something new?"

She agreed, wondering what crazy sex position he wanted to put her in. When he pulled out a small vial of white liquid, she raised her eyebrows. *What the hell!*

"What is it, drugs? I don't do drugs Willie."

"No, baby, it's not drugs," he said chuckling. "And I don't do drugs either. Its an enhancer. It sensitizes your skin to heighten your sexual experience."

She eyed the vial unsure.

"Do you trust me, baby?" He leaned in closer, his eyes steady and focused.

"Yes."

"Then try this with me. If you don't like it, we won't ever do it again. I promise."

She thought about it for another moment, then nodded. "Okay."

Willie smiled and gave her the vial of milky liquid that Sara Coli wanted him to. She drank it with a shot of white liquor to make it go down smoothly. Out of curiosity, he let the remaining drops slide out of the vial onto his tongue. *It tastes good*, he thought.

Once the contents of the vial were consumed, they fell back into each others arms ready to put his enhancer to the test. The curiosity to see what the liquid could do drove him wild. He started to lick all over her body, stopping to nip and suck here and there. The small amount of venom he ingested began to create a yearning he was itching to fulfill.

Kalitha seemed normal until the venom came down on her. When it did, she went sexually ballistic on him. He'd never seen ecstasy do what the vial of liquid did to her, or to anyone, in his life. She oozed vaginal juices and came many more times than the night before that Willie was astonished. She literally cried out for him to hurt her. He drove his dick inside her to the hilt until it began to hurt him, but she screamed for more. He listened to her shout, pleading for him not to stop.

"Please, don't stop. Fuck me harder. Please go deeper. Deeper baby. Hurt me, oh please hurt me?"

She yelled out his name loud as she orgasmed once again. Willie had never seen any woman so crazed for sex. She pulled at him and begged for more. He had climaxed twice and was totally spent, but she continued to masturbate and finger herself to orgasm after orgasm. He watched her in amazement, as she came one last time, then fell limply onto the bed panting and rubbing her throbbing pussy.

When he touched her, he saw her whole body flinched and spasm uncontrollably. She rolled over onto her stomach and fell into a coma-like slumber. He was concerned at first, but his worries eased as her breathing became even. Her body was soaked in sweat and her skin glistened.

Willie stood up and grabbed his phone on the way out, then

dialed Sara Coli's number.

"Hello?"

"I've done what you asked."

"Great!" she said. "Now come get some more tomorrow?"

"Alright, but..." he looked back at Kalitha's sexy, but sweaty body lying there unconscious. "What the hell was that stuff?"

"If I told you, you wouldn't believe me," she said smiling. "Let's just say that it's powerful."

Willie listened to the phone go dead in his ear.

Chapter 15

Trevor woke up to the phone ringing. He sat up with a jolt and looked over at the clock. It was one in the afternoon. He had stayed up to after three in the morning waiting on Kalitha to come home, but she hadn't. The sickness was nestled down deep in his stomach with the thought that something was terribly wrong with her.

He picked up the ringing phone and answered it.

"Hello?" His voice was groggy.

"Randale," Sara Coli said in a firm voice. "We need to talk. Are you home?"

"Yeah," he rubbed his forehead with his left hand. "I'm home. What's wrong Sara Co—?"

"Stay there," she cut him off for impact. "I'll be there momentarily." She hung the phone up without further words.

He laid back and wiped his face, wondering what was happening now. With the way his life was going, he believed that anything was possible. He pulled himself up out of bed and got cleaned up. He needed to desperately get his mind right before Sara Coli arrived.

She was there in 20 minutes and he buzzed her up. As she exited the elevator, she looked from him to the bouquet of decaying roses suspiciously. He glanced at the flowers and chose to ignore them as he watched her walk in with an air of negativity around her. He could feel that something had happened, and it was bad by the look on her face.

He broke the uncomfortable silence. "What is it?" he asked,

eyeing the manilla envelope in her hands as she sat down.

She sat with her knees closed firmly, hands close together atop of the envelope, and staring out into nothing. Trevor instantly sensed that everything was about to come crumbling down around him. From the way she looked, it was even worse than that. He stood looking at her waiting for her to drop the bomb.

Her voice was distant. "This came to my home today. It arrived without a return address." She patted the envelope. "It's from your wife."

Trevor's heart pounded as she let the words linger in the air. Beads of sweat began to form almost instantaneously on his forehead. This was it, he thought. Sara Coli watched him go from cool to sweating from being in the hot seat. She was getting a real kick out of seeing him like that. He had crossed her and she wanted him to suffer a little bit. In her heart she knew that she would forgive him and they could go on. If he lied, she would punish him more, but she would still go on with him. Sara Coli accepted the fact that she was in love with him. She just had to know.

"I think that you ought to look at it."

She held it out to him. He gave the envelope a disdainful look before walking over and collecting it from her hand. He checked the postal markings, then looked over to Sara Coli, who had gotten up and walked over to the large bay window. Cautiously he pulled out the contents revealing explicit photos. He gasped in horror, his chest constricted, and his throat became as dry as dirt. He stared down at the photos unblinking. The faces of the women were of the many strippers he had been with and they were graphic. Very graphic. In the midst of all of the sex photos, he found a little note typed neatly and folded in fours. He unfolded it.

My dearest Trevor, I see you are really doing your thang. Now, I guess I can do mine's too. I thought we were a team, but now I see the truth. Maybe I should tell Ms. White and end your happiness the way you've ended mine. Maybe you should tell her to have a look at these. I just did.

Sincerely yours, Double Crossed

Trevor swallowed hard while folding the note back up neatly. Sara Coli turned to him with a serious face.

"What on earth could she be talking about, Randale?" she asked, walking slowly and deliberately towards him. "Tell me what?"

Trevor's spit got caught up in his throat as he looked down at the pictures again. He dropped them carelessly onto the coffee table and sat heavily on the soft cushion of the sofa. He didn't want to hurt Sara Coli, but by the looks of the computer generated letter from Kalitha, she was half aware.

He looked up to her standing over him, his tongue heavy with a lie, his heart dying to be truthful, and his soul irreparably soiled by the use of so much deception.

Sara Coli could see the turmoil in his eyes and conflict shone evident in his posture. He was trapped in his own mind. She knew that she had obtained full control over the situation and he was exactly where she wanted him. He was in the place that she somehow kept all of the men in her life. She could force him to lie or lead him into the realms of honesty. She didn't desire neither of the two extremes, so she took her diamond clad index finger and tilted his entire world.

"Personally, I think that she wants something out of the divorce case. I'd bet you that somehow she has found out that you have come into some..." She paused for emphasis. "Some things."

Trevor finally breathed. He didn't even know that he was holding his breath and chalked the light headedness up to the situation. Oxygen flooded his lungs as she continued to lead the conversation.

"Darling, I have lawyers who would eat her alive in civil court."

He looked away from her.

"They would tear her flesh from the bone like hungry carnivores."

His mind zoned out while he was thinking frantically. *Divorce Kalitha? What?* Sara Coli was talking about helping him divorce her. He wondered how in the hell did he get this deep in? How did they get that deep? What did they do to their marriage and where on God's earth was Kalitha? The game needed to come to an end, and soon, before they were beyond repair. He had to first locate Kalitha. It was pertinent that they speak urgently. He needed to know what was really on his wife's mind and in her heart.

Sara Coli sat down beside him. He looked to her only to see how radiant and gorgeous she was. He couldn't deny that under any circumstances, but at the moment he didn't care.

Her words were aimed to soothe him. "Don't worry my darling. I will do everything in my power to help you get away from that sneaky little bitch." The maliciousness at the end of her sentence caused him extreme concern. She smiled a bit, but it was the phoniest smile he had ever seen her muster. She leaned in and kissed him softly. "I'll take care of it for you my love," she said reassuringly.

That's what he was inevitably afraid of.

****

Kalitha woke up to Willie dressed and about to leave out. She stretched and sat up. He looked over to her taking in her plump breast, then looked into her eyes.

"There you are beautiful," he said smiling.

"Yes," she said, blushing. "Here I am."

"Mmm," he said, eyeing her juicy breast. "I think that you'd better cover up before I get an animal urge to attack you."

Kalitha smiled and pulled the blanket up around herself. "So you're running out on me?"

"Of course not beautiful. I have some business to attend to. So..." He slipped on his shades. "If you'd like, you could hang out here."

Kalitha rubbed her eyes, still trying to clear her head.

"But, if you decide to leave, make it a point to call me later. I want to take you out for dinner, maybe even a movie."

She nodded her answer, smiling. She felt at a lost for words and sat there staring at all his sexiness. He walked over to her and rubbed her curly hair, down to her neck.

"Okay?" he asked, making sure they were on the same page, then kissed her softly?

She bit her bottom lip and nodded again.

With that, he headed out of the room to the front door. She hopped up, wrapping the blanket around her, hurrying to catch up with him.

"Willie, hold on."

He opened the front door and stopped when she called out to him. He turned to watch her sashay up to him sexily. She rubbed his chest through his smooth silk shirt. "Just one more kiss, please. Before you go."

He smiled and pulled her into him and kissed her passionately, their tongues doing the tango. He broke the kiss by sucking softly on her bottom lip. She leaned in for more and he pulled away.

He touched her face, then the tip of her nose. She smiled like a little girl as he turned to walk to his car. She stood in the doorway captivated by his sexy body walking away. He got in his car and backed out with a wave. She waved and watched him pull out onto the main road. She closed the door, disappearing from Karen's watchful lenses.

She had observed the whole exchange as they kissed in broad daylight as if they were a happy couple. She was ending her investigation with the photos of the doorway kiss and the ones she had taken the night before. Kalitha had turned into a sex crazed whore and she had the pleasure of watching her make Willie tap out. She had more than enough sufficient evidence to win the divorce case to the 10th power. Mr. Mason wouldn't need any more than what she had.

She pulled out and headed to her office to build the case files with the photos and video feeds to match. She was ready to close the case. Watching them fuck in that manner had Karen thirsting to see her boyfriend. She was down right horny and knew he could satisfy her in the deepest of ways. She smiled, knowing that the $35,000 overpaid price for this investigation would be collected that evening. She had all of her receipts to be reimbursed also.

She was looking to profit at least $38,000, and she was very happy and satisfied with her work. She picked up her phone and dialed the office.

"Hello. Special Investigative Services."

"Hi baby, it's Karen," she cooed.

"Hey. I'm kinda in the middle of interviewing a new client," said Mathew.

"My pussy is gushing wet and I need you to fill it with that big cock of yours."

"Okay," he said smoothly. "How about you get here and we can fix that problem."

"I'm on my way," she said sexily. She hung the phone up just in time to see the 760 Beamer go back past her the other way. She peeped at it in her side view mirror. *Couldn't enough of her, huh?* She continued to drive to her office.

****

Victor pulled back into the street where Sara Coli's beach side estate was. He parked the car and cautiously walked the forty yards to Kalitha's SUV. He hoped that she didn't re-lock it after he left. He reached it and after surveying the area, reached to open the door. It opened with no protest. He reached inside, grabbed the manila envelope, and closed the door.

He turned to leave, but caught the house door opening at that moment and ducked behind her SUV praying that she didn't see him. Peeking around the SUV, he saw Kalitha with her hands on her hips, looking up at the beautiful blue sky. She couldn't see him and he could tell. He stayed low as she pointed her keys at the SUV. It beeped and flashed its lights, locking itself again. She turned and walked back inside.

He took a deep breath of relief, stood, and with urgent steps, hurried down the street to his Beamer. Seconds later, he made a U-turn and headed back the way he had come from, and drove on. He figured that she wouldn't have had them duplicated, because she didn't seem that sharp to him. *Why would she be riding around with them?* He glanced at the manila envelope in his passenger seat. *Who does that to themselves?*

He looked back to the road banking on her not being that swift on her toes. Retrieving it was not much of a challenge. If they were in fact the originals, and no other copies existed, he would benefit from them much more than she could. They say a picture is worth a thousand words. Well, these were worth $10,000. All he had to do was deliver them to Sara Coli, and he was guaranteed the money.

He liked the sound of adding $10,000 on top of the handsome $100,000 Sara Coli was paying him. Kalitha was the most lucrative screw he had ever had. Everything seemed to be rolling well, except for the tiny fact that he liked her. A lot. These feelings of attraction made him wonder if when it was all said and done, she'd be available for him to be with. Being a paid male escort, he could deal with a few lies and inconsistencies between them.

He turned onto North Kings Highway and headed back to Wilmington to report to his sexpot of an employer. He didn't mind meeting her face to face. She was gorgeous and he would be a fool to deny the attraction. He'd chosen not to act on it in the interest of good business.

She was rich and powerful and pulled a lust filled reaction out of him whenever he was in her presence. He smiled, thinking to himself. *Shit. Leave well enough alone, Victor.* He popped a stick of gum into his mouth. *All I gotta do is fuck her on the yacht Friday night.* He tossed the wrapper out of the window. "After that," he said talking to himself. "It's back to Virginia or maybe I'll stick around and enjoy Kalitha for a while." He would make his decision based on what happened Friday. *How bad could a yacht party be?* He refocused on the business at hand.

****

Trevor's mind was far from his body as he and Sara Coli rode to her mansion hugged up in the back of her Bentley Limo. She talked happily about spending Thursday through Saturday on her yacht with her two friends and their beaus. Trevor nodded and feigned interest with a small smile as his thoughts continued to circle Kalitha like a vulture to wounded prey.

How could she blow their cover and then go missing? Why

would she have them followed and watched? Why would she go through all of the trouble of making him do it, just to turn on him when he did what had to be done? She wanted this, not him. He wanted a normal life. She wanted all of what was happening now.

His mind began to create all kinds of scenarios where Kalitha was made to be the villain, Sara Coli the victim, ending with him being the catalyst. He could see this resulting in a situation that would leave him withdrawing from White Widow deficiency. The thought alone of not having the elixir made him lurch away from Sara Coli with a lurid feeling built up inside of his stomach.

Her voice called him from his trance like state to join her in her revealing. "Darling! Come back to me. Did you hear what I just said?" she asked, smiling.

"Forgive me," he replied smoothly. "I was deep in thought, my love." He managed a convincing phony smile. "Tell me again."

"I want to introduce you to Mirah and Janey. They're my two best friends in the world. They'll love you darling."

He smiled hard, but still struggled to pay attention. It was going to be a task for him and he couldn't be sure that he was up to it. She rubbed his hands when she realized that he was slipping out of it again.

"I know just what you need my love."

He looked at her and touched her soft chin. "You always do my love."

They spent the rest of the day being pampered at the mansion. After the massage and rub down with scented oil, his body relaxed, but his mind remained tense and enveloped in a tumultuous state.

It all seemed to fade into oblivion as he stood at the edge of the pool and downed his White Widow. It rushed down his throat and into his belly, bringing him an instant calm. His body seemed to practically absorb it. He thought that he could feel it flowing through his veins, cascading throughout his body, and pushing him towards paradise. He felt all of this and it hadn't even come down yet.

He dived into the pool of champagne colored water and swam

to Sara Coli where he surfaced in the perfect position to penetrate her. He lifted her and pinned her against the wet bar, and she held onto him as she wrapped her toned legs around his waist.

She loved that he was able to control it now. He was a lion when he wanted to be and a gentle giant when he needed to be. He was sexual perfection to her, manifested in dark brown living flesh. He entered her tenderly, lovingly, and she cried into his muscular shoulder while motivating him to sex her the way she needed him to. It wasn't long before Sara Coli was being slowly, but intensely driven to spine shattering orgasm after earth quaking orgasm. Trevor exploded inside of her with volcanic force. The orgasms took longer for him, but were a world of difference in intensity.

He loved to make love to her because she could take him in a way that no other woman could. He gained full satisfaction from intercourse with Sara Coli, and she, on the other hand, was addicted to his lovemaking. Her addiction gave her more of a reason to do what she planned to do. She was devising a plan to keep him to herself forever.

She closed her eyes and met each thrust he gave as her mind thought about what she knew to be true. Every single element was in place, according to Tony. All she needed was the right moment to reveal what she had on Kalitha. That, she believed, would make him hers for sure. She more than wanted it, she needed it. Her body needed Trevor. Her heart needed Trevor. Her world needed Trevor. She gasped for air and clenched her pussy muscles as she came again.

He will be mine. He is mine.

CHAPTER 16

Friday was finally there and Kalitha felt like the Queen of England. She was convinced that Willie felt like she was the most important thing in the world. At least in his world. She had seen Trevor calls, but as far as she was concerned, he wasn't worth her conversation. She had actually thrown her phone in the ocean Tuesday night after she and Willie had made sweet love on the patio porch.

Only a small part of her regretted what she had done. The other part of her felt liberated and free. Until the false sense of freedom faded like an old pair of jeans, she would bask in it. She would enjoy it as if it was angelic iridescence. She no longer needed Trevor to care, or desire to hear what she had to say. She was gone. Lost. And Willie Longe had found her. Now she was his, as long as he wanted her to be.

Every time he made her the milky drink, she came more times than ever. It was unreal to her. The drink made her feel as if she had more stamina and vigor than she'd ever had. It was a rush so potent that she orgasmed the night before from kissing alone. The thought propelled her out of her daydream.

She looked around the department store to see that no one was watching her. She smiled to herself. *Girl, you better wake the hell up!* She didn't want to wake up though. She was ready for the yacht party. She had plans to really let go and be Kalitha Gabrielle Simpson, the woman she was before Mrs. Mason came in and stole her identity.

Silently, to her Mrs Mason was fading away. She looked over to a nice dress and caught her reflection in a mirror. *Mrs. Kalitha Longe.* She could only wonder, wish, and hope. She tossed the thought to the back of her mind and focused on getting the perfect outfit.

A fresh low cut Dolce and Gabbana dress caught her attention. She pulled it off of the rack and examined it lovingly. This is the one right here. She pressed it against her body, looked down it to her feet, and smiles naughtily. *Nope! No drawers!* She decided that no panties would be the best option just in case an opportunity arose where she and Willie could do their thing. She purchased the dress and headed to buy some heels. Afterwards, she drove back to the beach house and spent the rest of the day getting ready.

Willie arrived at a little after six and took care of his toiletries also. He had somehow found a cream suit that matched her cream dress. Her fruity pebble jewelry glistened against the lights in the kitchen and he looked as handsome as ever in his cream set and cream shades. He looked over and caught her admiring him.

Kalitha blushed under his sexy gaze, and looked away. She knew that it was going to be a great night. He escorted her out to the 760 Beamer and helped her in. He got in and looked at her with honest appreciation.

"I don't even have to tell you how stunning you look tonight Kalitha, but..." He smiled, then touched her face gently. "I think you get the point though."

She gave him a dazzling smile. *He always said and did the right things.*

Willie let her speechless response tell it all. They pulled off with soft jazz music playing out of the speakers.

****

As they pulled up to the dock, Kalitha's eyes lit up with excitement. She could see all of the yachts off of the coast. Willie smiled down at her, feeling her excitement. "You should see your eyes, baby."

She smiled and hurried out of the car. She took a few steps towards the wooden dock area and was instantly awed. There was a steady stream of speed boats taking people to and from the yachts. Willie walked up behind her. She was mesmerized by the eight large yachts anchored out in the water. She had never seen anything quite like it. It was like a small lit up city on the water.

"It's like Atlantis or something," she breathed out softly.

Willie kissed her neck gently. "It is Atlantis."

She smiled back at him. "And what do you call those?" She pointed to the speed boats.

"The speed boat express."

They laughed together at his silly joke.

They walked hand and hand down towards the loading and unloading area for the speed boats. The salt water stung her skin on the soft breeze. She took in the spectacle as the speed boats traveled from yacht to yacht. Watching the action made her even more anxious to get to the huge boats.

"Oh my God, Willie. This is amazing."

"It doesn't become amazing until you get out there," he said pointing to the boats.

She watched in anticipation until their time came. They were speeding out to one of the large boats and boarded within minutes. Once on the yacht, Kalitha found herself surrounded by big wigs and professional types. Willie seemed to know lots of people whom all called him Victor. She preferred to call him Willie.

They got their drinks and were on to the next yacht. She was dumbfounded at all that was taking place on the boats. She noticed that on one of them, the passengers were nude, and on another, there was gambling of all sorts. She got to play a few gambling games, danced, and was on to the next yacht to get something to eat.

Even the salt water making her curls drop couldn't spoil her wondrous experience. Kalitha was blown away. She found herself leaning against the rail looking out at a yacht that was out further than all of the others. She tapped Willies' arm to get his attention. He smiled as he fumbled around almost dropping his steak and shrimp kabob. "What woman?"

"Why is that one so far out," she asked nodding to it?

He turned to look at it. "Private party I guess." He turned back to her. "Maybe invites only."

"Really?" she asked, picking at her kabob as she continued to stare out at it? He looked from her to the far away yacht. "There's always a way."

Willie walked off, his stride powerful and marked by determination. She looked back out to the distant boat. He surprised her when he returned a few moments later with two wristbands.

"Voila," he said, smiling.

She hugged him excitedly. "Let's alert the express man."

They were on their way to the distant yacht in no time. Kalitha smiled all of the way across the water. Sara Coli held her phone in her lap. She stood up staring out at the approaching boat. *There's always room for two more!* She walked down to the lower chamber master bedroom and opened the door to the beautiful Asian woman massaging Trevor.

She watched from the doorway as she needed the stiffness out of his back. *He was tense and needed it,* Sara Coli thought. He had been up there with their guests long enough and was hers for the rest of the night.

To no surprise, Mirah and Janey had reacted the way she had expected them to. They begged to have a piece of her Randale. She disagreed to their cunning and blustering advances, but did agree to give them a free show. A very private show. They wanted to see him perform and she was going to give them front row seats. That was the extent of their agreement and she decreed that they had to find their own.

The passengers on her yacht consisted only of her friends and her personal staff. Mirah, and Janey had brought their newest boy toy along. He was a gorgeous Mongolian man of large stature. At 6'7", he was too much man for Sara Coli. She liked her men with Trevor's dimensions. She decided to make her presence known to him.

"Darling, how do you feel?"

"I feel wonderful," he replied in a low tone. "Did you make my fix yet?"

"I'll do it right away," she said as submissively as she could.

Tonight she decided to up the dosage. She hurried away to prepare it. She was going to give the whole yacht a show in an hour or so. She fixed his drink and brought it back to him, then dismissed the masseuse. She handed him his drink and toasted to a beautiful night. She could not wait to start the show.

As Kalitha and Willie pulled up to the yacht, she instantly realized that it was massive in comparison to the others she had been on. It was luxurious and spacious to no end. She thought it odd to be nearly empty as they boarded it. They walked past waiters and staff hands, but not many people.

She looked up at Willie. "Where are all of the people? The other yachts were filled."

"I would guess that everyone's in the main room below," he replied smoothly.

She figured it was cool because she really hadn't gotten any alone time with him all night. She wasn't in a rush to find company when she had him all to herself. Actually, it was much more privacy up top. She snatched two champagne flutes off of a waiter's tray as he came out to them. She handed one to him and grabbed his arm to lead him over to the rail.

There they stood talking and had a few more glasses of champagne. She led the conversation talking about her future plans. She wondered if she was dreaming when from Willie's mouth, she heard him ask where did he fit in? That was everything she ever wanted to hear. She was completely sold on the idea of starting fresh and new with William Longe and he sealed the deal with a sensuous kiss.

Forty-five minutes had gone by in what seemed like a few seconds. His phone rang in the middle of their moment. Reluctantly, he answered it.

"Hello? Yes. Alright. Yes," he said and hung up. He looked at his watch, then back to her. "Let's at least see who's on this baby before we split."

"I'm with you," she said, snaking her arm through his.

Willie led her down into the bows of the boat to the main room. Kalitha took in the regal furnishing with fabulous decorations all over. In the corner of the main room sat a calm crown of people watching what looked to be a huge wide screen T.V.

She looked over to see a very handsome light skinned man with a wavy black ponytailed. From his sitting position she could tell that he was a tower of a human being. He sat in between two breathtakingly beautiful women with silvery white hair. They bore a striking resemblance to Sara Coli which caused Kalitha to feel apprehensive all of a sudden. Her intuition shot a red flag up in her mind. *Why do they look like her?*

A few other people sat all around, spread out. She walked in noticing how splendid and expensive everything was. There was a flat screen monitor above the lounge area. Willie's touch startled her and she looked up at him.

"I'm going to the restroom." He kissed her on the cheek and vanished back the way they had come.

She stepped further into the main room, sat her glass down on the bar, and walked aimlessly towards the paintings on the wall. The artworks were the picture of splendor. The two women with the silvery hair began to point and comment, and it made Kalitha curious as to what they were watching. She eased over, but maintained her silence because she didn't want to disturb them and ruin what had them totally captivated. Mirah and Janey looked up to Kalitha at the same time. She felt awkward and chose to speak.

"Hello."

"Hi honey. Have a seat," Janey said softly. "Enjoy the live show."

Kalitha gave a small smile and sat down. As she looked up at the screen, her heart plunged through the floor of the boat, threatening to drown them all. She saw Trevor naked and mounted securely above Sara Coli. She watched as he pulled out to the tip of his dick and slid his long fat ten inches into her tight silver haired pussy.

The feed was in slow motion causing it to seem like he was making the sweetest and most passionate love to her. Kalitha was stuck and couldn't pull her eyes away from the television screen. The camera feed bounced from all angles allowing Kalitha to see his face and his body, giving all of his love to her. She got to see them from at least eight different camera angles. The aerial hit Kalitha the hardest because it seemed as though Sara Coli was looking directly at her. She stood up clumsily knocking her chair over on its back. Mirah and Janey stared at her in confusion.

"Are you okay," Mirah asked?

Kalitha looked to her, then back up at the screen where Trevor was banging Sara Coli as hard as he could. She watched in horror as he pulled his dick out and shot white sperm all over Sara Coli's belly. She turned and ran from the room colliding with a waiter and making him drop his tray.

"Hey! Watch where you're going," he yelled as food and bowls clanged loudly off of the glossy wooden floor.

She ran up the stairs that led to the top deck and crashed into Willie. He caught her and wrapped his arms around her. "What happened? What's wrong?"

Tears cascaded from her eyes. "Please. Get me out of here," she cried.

"Kalitha, what happened?" he asked with concern.

Kalitha became unbalanced and desperate. "Get me off of this fucking yacht." She pushed away from him as the sobs broke free and took control of her.

"Okay," he said, rushing to locate a speed boat driver. They hurried from the yacht and headed for the dock.

She couldn't keep her tears from falling. In her mind, she knew that was something she'd never wanted to see! Trevor was making love to Sara Coli like he had never been able to do with her. It made Kalitha feel less than a woman and inferior to all women. She couldn't get the images of tat bitch and *her* Trevor out of her head.

She had thought that she was done with him. She'd thought

she had successfully suppressed her love for him, but seeing that brought her back to reality. She couldn't imagine such an insufferable reality as the one where she would no longer have Trevor. The revelation struck her like a billion volts of electricity. She loved Trevor and wanted her husband back. No circumstances, nor consequences mattered to her. She was through with her affair and with Willie. She had to get her husband back and prayed that it wasn't too late.

Once back at the shore she asked to be taken to her SUV so she could get her clothes and go home. Willie obliged her without any hindrance. He didn't know what had happened, but he wished he knew how to comfort her. Her body language in the passenger seat was withdrawn. He hated to see her that way, but didn't know what to say to soothe her. Victor rarely ever felt regret when he worked, but this time was one of the few and far inbetween.

As they pulled up to the beach house, Kalitha began to become livid. She nearly got out before he stopped his car. The Navigator was gone. She screamed out furiously as he tried to calm her.

"NO! NO!" She shoved him away, "Don't you dare fucking touch me!" She pulled her hair spinning around to look for her SUV. "My truck. Somebody stole my truck."

"Kalitha!" he yelled, trying to get her to snap out of her fit of rage. "It's alright." He spoke softly, trying to comfort her, but she refused to be comforted. He didn't know what had happened, but he could see that everything was going sour.

Fuck this! His decision had just been made final. He was off to Virginia as soon as he could. First, he wanted to see her home safely. He watched her standing away from him crying. "I'll take you home." She wiped her snotty nose and headed inside to gather her clothes. Willie rubbed his hand down his face and followed her in.

****

Sara Coli looked up into the camera and smiled deviously. If her plan had worked, Kalitha would have gotten an eyeful of her and Trevor. She imagined that the commotion she had heard stemmed from that. She liked that the truck would have been gone by the time Kaltiha got back to the beach house. She couldn't wait for her confirmations.

She cried out as Trevor slammed against her back wall with enough force to bring a tear from her eyes. She cried out, came hard, flooding his dick with her juices, and loved every second of it. It turned her on knowing that everyone's eyes were glued to the screen and imagined what they were saying. Mirah and Janey sent their boy toy away so they could talk.

"He is truly amazing," said Janey.

"Oh, I do agree," Mirah concurred.

"We have to get her to share the wealth."

"What's a little competition between friends?" Janey laughed, causing Mirah to laugh as well.

From that moment on they were in on a collaborated effort to share Trevor with Sara Coli. They stared back at the screen intently. Trevor exploded his hot white load on Sara Coli's belly the way she had asked him to. He was back inside of her in less than a minute. He knew it was the White Widow that made him perform like that, but he no longer cared. Sara Coli and the White Widow venom was all he'd ever need.

****

Kalitha hurried out of the Beamer and grabbed her bags from the back seat. She hurried to the front door of the building and Willie got out calling out to her.

"Kalitha. Kalitha!" he yelled as she entered the building with no further words.

The door closed him out and she was gone for good. He shook his head feeling a little guilty about the whole ordeal, but she was a job that he hated to admit he liked doing. He looked up at the tall building, then got back into his car. As far as he was concerned, his job was complete. He pulled out into the street and headed back towards the beach house.

He would pack his things, collect his money, and be gone the next day. He couldn't help wanting to pursue Kalitha, but it had ended badly. He would always remember her, though. She was one sexy woman with one hell of a secret and story to tell. *Maybe one day Kalitha. Maybe one day.* He turned onto the highway and punched it. *Just not today.*

****

Kalitha dragged her bags onto the elevator, rode upstairs, and dropped them on the floor as she came in crying. Her tears blurred her vision. She instantly became drawn to the bouquet of dead molded roses and the opened box next to it. She turned it towards her to see the black diamond Rolex. She opened the little card and read it.

KALITHA, NO AMOUNT OF TIME CAN TAKE ME AWAY FROM YOU. I LOVE YOU. TREVOR MASON.

Kalitha's body went limp as she broke down to the floor in a pitiful pile of pain and regret. She called out to him in a wailing voice filled with hopelessness and agony. She called his name again and again. She knew where he was and he couldn't hear, nor answer her. She curled up into the fetal position on the kitchen floor. Her cries stifled by her loneliness.

Chapter 17

Kalitha called Trevor's phone repeatedly. She just needed to hear his voice and tell him that everything would be alright. They could get through anything together. It was Monday and after a weekend of unanswered phone calls, she was defeated.

The Escalade was still in the parking deck so she knew he hadn't taken it. She had the keys, but was afraid to leave because she didn't want to miss his call. She sat on the sofa staring out into the void as the phone rang. Her heart raced as she rushed to answer it and nearly knocked it over when she did.

"Hello?" She fumbled with it, caught it, and put it back to her ear. "Hello?"

"Hello," Sara Coli's buttery smooth voice purred into the receiver. "I believe you know who this is."

"Oh yes, this is—"

Sara Coli cut her off abruptly. "Look, I'm going to be brief and straightforward with you girl. We need to meet and have a woman to woman talk."

Girl? Kalitha thought as fury ran hot and heavy through her. "I am not your girl you old bitch!"

"See, you have something that I think should be mine, and likewise, I think that I have something that you probably desperately want."

This bitch calling desperate? Kalitha maintained her composure. "Excuse me?"

"Kalitha," she paused. "There is no acceptable excuse for you.

So let's just be ready in say an hour or so."

Kalitha caught an instant attitude. She held the phone away looking at it with disgust. She finally answered her, ready to get shit poppin'.

"An hour will be fine." The phone went dead in her ear.

She sat the phone back on the receiver still finding it hard to believe that she had called her by her real name. It was all bad. She recognized that from the tone in Sara Coli's voice. She thrummed her fingers on the counter. She had to see what Sara Coli knew so she would know exactly how to play it. The way she had addressed her didn't give her a good feeling about any of it. She ran her hands through her curly hair thinking. *Okay, let's see what this old bitch knows.*

Kalitha dressed and waited. The buzz came in over the intercom. She headed down on the elevator and was met by Tony who gave her a straight faced look.

"I'm here to transport you to Mrs. White's whereabouts."

"Oh, hi Tony," she said, trying to ease her own tension. His response was nearly non-existent.

"Good afternoon, Mrs. Mason."

His words seemed to put her in her place so she followed him quietly. He held the door for her and she got in silently. He closed the door and ran his hand regretfully along the side of the door before he got in and pulled off. The ride was fairly swift for Kalitha. It was her first time in a car so luxurious. She hadn't ever seen a Bentley and now she was riding in a Bentley Limo. She was anxious to reach her destination and get it over with. The limo came to a final stop and the door opened and Tony helped her out.

She realized that she was at Arlie Seafood Restaurant, one of the places she was dying to go to. She hated that it had to be on these terms. The wait staff met her and Tony at the door. Leaving Tony behind, the waiter led her out onto the furnished deck to where Sara Coli sat. She was sitting in a corner alone.

She and Kalitha locked eyes and held each other's gaze until Kalitha reached the table. The tension between the two women was practically thick enough to cut and serve. She stood looking down at Sara Coli and couldn't come to terms with the fact that she appeared to be getting younger and younger. Sara Coli looked down at the menu and a few seconds later looked back up to Kalitha.

"So you're just going to stand there like a Roman statue?" She waved her hand. "Please, do have a seat."

Kalitha pulled her chair out and sat down. Sara Coli pushed a menu across the table to her. "Order whatever your little heart desires, on me."

Her words were condescending and held an edge of content. Kalitha's response was firm and cross. "I'm not hungry."

"I can't tell," Sara Coli mumbled, then continued. "Well, suit yourself," she said cheerfully. She sipped her wine. "Isn't it just a fabulous day."

Kalitha rolled her eyes and responded dryly. "It's absolutely wonderful."

As Sara Coli talked, Kalitha looked away disrespectfully.

Sara Coli leaned forward with serious eyes. "If my cheerful nature offends you, you can just leave. You are more than welcome to walk your little ass out of here and our business will be considered handled."

Her words cut Kalitha. *Little ass? Who is this old dusty pussy hag bitch talking to?* Kalitha held her thoughts in check. "Business? What business?"

"Oh no darling. I never discuss business on an empty stomach," Sara Coli said with a small smile as the waitress came over.

She ordered herself something to eat while Kalitha sat there cross armed and irritated beyond understanding. She didn't seem to mind her disposition and quietly waited for her food to arrive. When it was finally served, Sara Coli ate deliberately slow as she watched her guest grow more furious by the bite.

Kalitha felt insulted on a level she had never known and to say that she wanted to strangle the older woman would not have been an exaggeration. Strangle viciously was an understatement. It was clear to Kalitha that things were more than bad. Their plan had gone sour enough to smell three cities away. She was positive that nothing good could come of their meeting.

A deep seeded hatred was brewing inside of her for Sara Coli as she watched her eat as if no one sat waiting. By the time she had wiped her mouth, pushed the plate away, and took another sip of wine, Kalitha's blood was boiling in her veins. A thermometer would have read a temperature of two hundred degrees. She was so hot she thought that the marrow in her bones would begin to melt.

Sara Coli sat back and observed an angry Kalitha for a few more seconds before she decided to speak. She was on her time and no one could tell her any different. She gave her a simple look.

"Now, as I've undoubtedly told you earlier, we have things that I believe would fair better in an equal trade."

"Things?" Kalitha spat back. "Like what?"

"Well, for one, " she paused. "Trevor."

Kalitha instantly sat rigid in her chair, her body language defensive and aggressive. "Trevor?"

"Yes, Trevor. You know, that scrumptious husband of yours. You do remember your husband?"

Kalitha was ready to curse her ass out, but Sara Coli kept on strongly.

"I think he should trade up from your revolting black claws to my highly capable hands."

"Yours?" Kalitha spat in revulsion.

"You can hear can't you?"

"I can hear very well you old bitch."

Sara Coli liked that. It was a show of anger. She needed that in order to gauge how far she could push her before she broke. She smiled evilly.

"Well, the way I see it is, no husband wants a filthy lowdown sneaky two-timing loose whore for a wife."

"Two-timing?" Kalitha defended herself with a tenacious spirit. "I've never cheated on my husband."

"Add liar to the list, then," Sara Coli said, reaching over into her

Coach bag. "I know your type. I've ran across a million little skanks like you—"

Kalitha cut her off and pointed in her face. "You don't know anything about me."

"Oh, I know you're not Randale's sister. I know that you're his wife of nearly five years. No children, no job, no dreams, no aspirations."

"I got dreams—"

"No loyalty to your husband."

Kalitha gritted her teeth through her next words. "You don't know shit about me."

Sara Coli leaned forward to meet her aggressive posture. "I know that you're a money hungry, selfish, little capricious and wicked hearted bitch, who would pimp her husband out for a financial gain."

Kalitha held on tightly to the edge of the table, it being the only thing separating her and the foul mouthed woman who sat across from her.

"You don't know shit about me."

Sara Coli leaned back cockily. "I know where you were all last week." She slid the envelope across the table to Kalitha.

She looked down at the manila envelope disdainfully knowing that she didn't want to see what was in it. She knew what she had done last week and pictures of it would be too much to handle.

Sara Coli noticed her look of apprehension. "Looks like someone's scared to see the truth."

"I ain't scared of anything, nor anyone," Kalitha retorted. "And definitely not you."

"So you *ain't* scared," Sara Coli mocked her bad grammar, then waved her off. "Say whatever you need to say to make yourself feel strong, or whatever women like you feel, but... "

Kalitha felt insulted to the max and wanted to hit her with something blunt and hard more than she wanted to take her next breath.

Sara Coli smiled. "The truth of the matter is, you're a hit honey."

"Hit?" Kalitha folded her arms again.

"You might want to take a look at those," she said, then sipped her wine. "They're quite graphic."

Kalitha pulled the photos from the envelope with all of the attitude that she could muster. The first one to clear the envelope instantly made her head throb. They were graphic. They were of her, and they were very real. She swallowed hard. "Where did you get these?"

"Honey, I've been rich for far too many years. That's neither here, nor there. Actually, where I got them is of no real importance. What is of the utmost importance is what will you do to make them go away?"

Kalitha let out a forced chuckle. "You're blackmailing me?"

"No worse than what you tried to have my Randale do to me," Sara Coli gritted her teeth in anger.

They sat in uncomfortable silence for a long moment, eyes locked in a hate filled stare down match. Their eyes portrayed their true feelings for each other. The staring match was getting her nowhere so Sara Coli broke the gaze.

"Look girl—"

"My name is Kalitha," she corrected her.

Sara Coli waved it off. "Whatever. I'm prepared to buy you out of the picture. Literally." She smiled at a serious Kalitha. "I'm offering you a million tax free dollars to just, I don't know, vanish." Sara Coli nodded to the photos. "These would also vanish along with you."

Kalitha rolled her eyes and her neck in defiance. "And if I don't accept?"

"Let's just say that..." she thought tapping her chin with her diamond clad index finger. "The speed of light couldn't beat these documents into Randale's hands. Then you get nothing."

"If you take my husband, I will have nothing."

"Nothing but $1,000,000," she waved her rainbow jewelry. "The things you have now. Your dignity."

"I want to talk to Trevor."

"Go ahead," Sara Coli said, touching her pony tailed silvery hair. "Talk your whole damned head off."

"I can't reach him and you know that."

"My point exactly," she replied with a serious overlay in her tone.

Sara Coli sat back and bridged her slender fingers. Kalitha breathed furiously as she watched her cocky, yet classy way of dominating the situation. She had the upper hand and was twisting Kalitha's arm into a gnarled mess. There seemed to be no end to her reach.

"I'll tell you what, Kalitha. I will give you $2,000,000."

Kalitha sucked her teeth and folded her arms defiantly.

Sara Coli eyes narrowed. "Okay Missy. I'll make it $3,000,000."

Kalitha looked away. "You will never get my husband."

"Kalitha, darling—"

"I'm not your darling," she cut in quickly. "I'm not shit to you."

"That goes without saying, darling. I don't think that you're shit to anyone," she quipped back.

Kalitha turned towards her, looking her up and down offensively. "You know what? Fuck you!" she said loudly. "Fuck you!"

People began to look their way, but Kalitha didn't care anymore. She was beyond reason now and ready to fight to the death and beyond.

"Oh, quit the ghetto antics," Sara Coli said firmly. "I have a black belt in Karate, so don't go there because you surely can't win child."

"I'm not your child, you 50 year old bag of worms," Kalitha spat out.

"51," Sara Coli corrected her. "Besides, I'm really trying to help you," she sarcastically feigned genuine concern. "I don't want to see you come out of this with nothing and alone."

"You old ratchet ass bitch!" She struggled to calm herself as people pointed and watched. "Trevor will never ever be yours."

"I already have him," she said simply.

The reality of her words set in. She couldn't achieve anything there with her. She had to see Trevor. Kalitha's foot bounced up and down uncontrollably, something she did when she wanted to hurt someone. She looked to the steak knife, then back to Sara Coli as she spoke.

"You know what? I can't fathom what would make a real man like my Randale put up with a stubborn little thing like you."

Kalitha stared at her with ice in her eyes.

Sara Coli shook her head sadly. "You're so difficult."

"I hate you!" Kalitha growled in a near whisper.

"Don't hate the player." Sara Coli held up her fingers in quotation marks. "Hate the game. Ain't that how you young people say it?" She smiled teasingly.

"Fuck you," Kalitha said stiffly.

"How about four million?" she chirped.

"How about fuck you?" said Kalitha. She began to rise, but stopped as she felt her grab her arm.

Sara Coli spoke quickly. "Think about my last offer. Take $5,000,000 and go and enjoy a wealthy life. See the world, have children, and marry someone who really loves you."

Kalitha snatched her arm away and looked down at her with pure hatred.

Sara Coli didn't see her giving in, so she shot a low blow.

"Don't let that stinking little rundown pussy of yours that can't handle big dick, go to waste."

Kalitha was lightning quick as she grabbed the sharp steak knife off the table and with all of her might, plunged it into Sara Coli's neck. In shock, Sara Coli reached up to hold the blood spurting hole in her throat. Kalitha screamed as she pulled the knife free. Sara Coli fell to the side on the floor and Kalitha was on her. Using both hands, she stabbed her repeatedly until the blood shot up into her face, blurring her vision.

"Well, little girl? Are you going to take the $5,000,000?"

Sara Coli's voice snapped her back from her daydream. She realized that she had blacked out. Yet, it was enough incentive to spur her into action.

Kalitha grabbed the steak knife and pointed it at Sara Coli's neck. The customers began to shout and point, alerting the management. Sara Coli froze under the aim of the knife wilding Kalitha.

"You listen to me, you old bitch," Kalitha gritted out. "Trevor is mine!" she yelled, shaking with anger. "Leave us the fuck alone."

A waiter approached the situation with caution. "Ma'am, you don't want to do that. Please, put the knife down."

"She's fine," Sara Coli said confidently.

"You leave us alone," Kalitha said in tears. "Leave us alone." She threw the knife onto the table and it made a loud clanging sound as it bounced off of the plates and glasses.

She looked around embarrassed, and hurried out of the restaurant under speculating stares.

Sara Coli looked up to the waiter. "Are you okay, ma'am?"

"I'm fine young man," she replied, looking at all of the shaken up customers. "Please tell your manager that I would like to pay for everyone's tab for the inconvenience."

He nodded and walked off as Sara Coli pulled out her phone and dialed.

"Hello."

"I need you to give my Randale the package that I left for him."

She closed her phone and smiled to herself. *Simple bitch. I'd have given you 10 million for him.*

****

As Kalitha rode in the cab home, she wondered if she had made the right choice. Turning down $5,000,000 seemed down right idiotic when the old wench was right. Trevor was with her already. He surely hadn't been home to check on her and she hadn't seen him in over nine weeks. Maybe she'd made the wrong choice.

She drug herself from the cab into the building and up the elevator. Once inside, she fell onto the bed crying. She had to admit to herself that she was the queen of bad choices. She had managed to break what was God sent in their marriage and now had the audacity to wish they would somehow fix themselves She cried until unexplained darkness overpowered her and sleep took her in its midst.

She didn't realize she was asleep until her name being called stirred her. Her eyes shot open and her pulse raced. Her heart rammed against her rib cage painfully. She recognized his voice. Trevor's voice. She climbed out of bed and ran down the hall to him. He was standing at the elevator door when she saw him. It was him. She knew she wasn't dreaming and that made her run even faster.

She leapt full speed to hug him and was stopped in mid air by his powerful arms and strong hand threatening to crush her tiny throat. His massive hand constricted around her neck and windpipe. She grabbed his arm as her feet dangled several inches off of the floor. He yelled through his tear soaked face as he slammed her hard against the kitchen wall, causing a portrait to fall and shatter.

"You lying, cheating bitch." He slammed her against the wall again. "What are these?"

Through her blurry eyes she saw the photos. Her eyes protruded as the air seeped out of her body.

"What the fuck is this?" He yelled in her face.

She couldn't utter a word as she felt herself slowly losing consciousness. A vacuum of darkness was sucking her in as she pulled at his arm, thinking that he was going to kill her. Right then and there, she let go of his arm, thinking she deserved it. *Kill me, just don't leave me.*

She could see the tears streaming down his face before her eyes rolled back in her head. Trevor gasped and let go. Kalitha's body tumbled to the floor in a heap of flesh gasping and choking to get air back in her lungs. She began to cough up spit. When she was able to speak, she cried out to him.

"Please, Trevor. Please..."

"You started this shit. You Kalitha! You made me into this. You did!"

"Trevor, please," she begged and cried. "I'm so sorry. I'm sorry." She reached out to him crying pitifully as he paced the floor cursing her.

He flung the photos down at her and they landed scattered out around her. She looked down to see her and Willie in all of them. She looked up to Trevor, who stood staring down at her and the photos furiously. He dropped to his knees in the midst of all of the explicit pictures of another man and his wife, and cried uncontrollably into his palms. His sobs were heart wrenching and Kalitha wanted to touch him, but fear kept her at bay.

He spoke through his palms. "Why Kalitha? Why did we do this? Why did we do this to each other?"

She cried even harder and tried to pick up the photos to hide them from his sight. She looked to see Trevor staring at her with mixed emotions in his eyes. He stood up slowly wiping his face dry. She looked up to him in fear and confusion.

He breathed hard down on her, then shook his head in dissatisfaction. It was as if he was looking down at a mangy animal instead of his wife. She cowered under his gaze. She wanted to touch him, his feet, leg, anything, just once. She continued gathering up the photos as he turned and walked to the bedroom, slamming the door closed behind him. She flinched and stared at the door. She stopped collecting the photos and stooped over holding her belly, crying into the floor.

****

Sara Coli stood in her backyard looking down into the man made pond and watched the fish swim around beneath the lighting system she'd had installed many years ago. The world was like that pond to her. She only wanted it to remain beautiful. She turned as she heard Tony walking up behind her. "Do you think he's going to come back?" she asked softly.

He answered as truthfully as he knew how to. "Well, in my opinion, he'd be a damned fool not to." She smiled. She loved Tony like a son and a good friend. He was security, and everything wrapped in one. And at times, he was her shoulder.

"He'll be back," he said, looking at the fish.

She believed that he would.

Chapter 18

Trevor stayed secluded for three days to himself. It was the worst three days of Kalitha's marriage to him. She attempted to talk more, but he wouldn't allow her to draw him into more than single word answers. He spent his days and nights alone. She didn't know what had him so distant, but Trevor knew.

It was the deficiency coupled with his ultra high level of dependency. The elixir seemed to call to him and on the fourth day of his return, he couldn't stand it anymore. He called Sara Coli and had her send Tony, because he didn't believe that he could drive to her house. When he walked out of the master bedroom, Kalitha hopped up off of the sofa curiously. He was heading towards the elevator.

"Trev. Where are you going baby?" His response was as sharp as a knife and cut just as deep.

"None of your business." She stepped into his pathway. "Don't leave, please. Stay with me one more night."

"No," he said, attempting to sidestep her.

She continued to block his passage. "Please stay."

"I said no," he spoke firmly.

"Please, Trevor. Don't go," she begged throwing herself back into his path.

He shoved her lightly out of his way. She dove back in front of him and he shoved her even harder. She stumbled into the bar stools hitting her hip hard. She winced in pain and looked back to him in fear.

"Stay the fuck out of my way," he bellowed as he walked past her. He turned back to her. "You know, you're going to get exactly what you want."

"Trevor," she whispered in pain. "Please."

"Don't you dare try to stop me." She watched in trepidation as he boarded the elevator and the doors closed him out of sight.

She straightened up and winced from the bruise that was rapidly forming on her hip. All of a sudden her whole side began to throb. She walked over to the elevator door and slid down it not knowing what to do.

She hugged her knees to her chest and cried silently. She was alone and it felt like she was destined to remain that way. Trevor got off of the elevator and walked outside to see Tony holding the door open for him. He stopped and gave him a small smile.

"I know bro," Tony said, knowingly.

"Take me to the bank, Tony," Trevor said getting in.

"No problem, sir."

As they pulled off, he thought about the amount of money he had and decided that he would transfer it all over to Kalitha's account. She could have it all. She wanted the money and he wanted the White Widow drink. In the end, it was probably best for the both of them.

****

Kalitha lay in the spot where Trevor had slept for the past three nights and tried to absorb all of the smell he had left. She had located the keys to the Escalade and was holding them close to her as if they were the last piece of him she'd ever see. Soon, a pain stricken slumber took her until the phone ringing woke her up.

She popped up dizzy from jerking awake too fast, and reached for the phone. She answered it sounding hopeful.

"Hello? Trevor?"

"No, I'm afraid not," Sara Coli said triumphantly. "I rather like who I am."

"Where is Trevor?" Kalitha asked in voice similar to the hiss of a deadly viper?

"You're his wife," she giggled. "If you don't know, then how should I," she teased?

"Don't fuck with me—"

Sara Coli interjected. "You don't possess the power, nor the money to tell me what to do," she snapped, putting Kalitha in her place. "So let's not jump the gun honey. People get shot in the head that way."

Kalitha squeezed the phone and gritted her teeth in anger. She couldn't think of any insult that would combat the way Sara Coli was making her feel. She had come out with exactly what she said she would, nothing.

"Now, Kalitha, sweetheart. I want you to still give my offer some thought. Take the $5,000,000 for your troubles and just disappear. Never come back. That is a lot of money to have tax free, darling."

"That's my husband!" Kalitha explode. "He is my husband!"

"He used to be—"

"He still is!" she yelled. "Drink my piss and die you old bitch. You will never have him."

"You dumb heifer, you gave him to me in the first place. He was all yours, but just like a streetwalker, you couldn't see anything but the dollar signs. I never asked for Randale. But now I want to buy him and you're telling me that you can't see the dollar signs anymore. I'm wondering if your stupidity is genetically enhanced or were you born that way?"

Kalitha was fuming. She wanted to kill her and put an end to their problems. Enraged, her words came tumbling out of her trembling mouth like fire from the throat of a dragon.

"You can't have him. I will never go away."

"Oh, you will honey. That I can promise you," Sara Coli said with a real knowing edge in her voice.

"Go fuck yourself," Kalitha spat out.

"Why would I do a thing like that when I have Randale doing it for me? Ten whole inches of yummy goodness."

Kalitha let out a shrill scream and hung the phone up. She pulled on her hair, causing herself pain since she couldn't inflict it on Sara Coli. The woman was a fucking snake and she hated her with a passion.

Trevor. I need to talk to Trevor. All she could think about was talking to Trevor. She had to find a way or risk losing the one thing she needed, *her* Trevor.

****

Sara Coli allowed a devious smile to spread across her beautiful face as she hung the phone up. She didn't mind being hung up on. It just showed her that she had the control over Kalitha. She walked into the dining room where Trevor was sitting with Mirah and Janey for the first time since he had met them on the yacht. She was aware of her friends' carnal desires for her Randale and it shamed her to admit that it turned her on.

She would play keep away for a while, but she was giving their advances some serious consideration. They loved to play the flirting game and she thought that it was cute the way they fed him and touch him sneakily. He smiled his enjoyment. She stood next to him and listened as her two gorgeous friends spoke to her.

"You really shouldn't be so greedy love," Janey said pouting.

"Clearly he has more than enough to go around twice," Mirah added.

"I'm sure you can spare a little taste," Janey said while rubbing Trevor's muscular chest.

"Not a chance," Sara Coli replied in her buttery smooth voice.

She shooed them away from him playfully. They began to frolic around the table and Trevor smiled as he watched the three sexy older women play girlishly in front of him. He figured that when you had millions to burn, fun was the only thing to be had. He secretly hoped she would allow him to have the three of them at one time. It seemed to him that she was on the verge of giving in and allowing it to happen. But being true to her word, she hadn't let it happen yet. However, the night was still young.

Trevor kept his thoughts light when it came to Kalitha. He'd had all of his money transferred into her bank account. The whole $405,634.82. With what she already had, it had to be over a half million dollars for her. Maybe that would satisfy her hunger for the mighty dollar. A dollar so mighty that she had willingly given him up for it.

It was her idea that sparked it all in the first place. He never wanted any of what was happening. He only wanted to be a good husband, a provider, and hopefully a great father. Those dreams had faded away and his reality flooded back into full view.

He was watching the women around the table, each planting a juicy kiss on his face as they passed. Sara Coli reached him and whispered in his ear in a husky voice.

"Would you like some company tonight?"

He smiled as she skittered off before he could answer. She looked back over her shoulder sexily as she chased Mirah and Janey out of view. Trevor popped a grape into his mouth. *Maybe it's gonna be your night after all.*

He listened to them giggle in the next room and stood. "Don't leave me behind ladies."

****

Kalitha sat staring at the phone. Things had gotten to their worst and she wouldn't be able to reverse them. She wanted Trevor to come back home to her. She wanted to go all of the way back to when they lived in the rundown trailer. They had come from that, to the way they were now, and there was no way back. She knew that. She just couldn't understand the drastic changes in Trevor. His volatile actions frightened her. He seemed like a totally different person now.

She walked into the bathroom and as she walked past the mirror, something in her hair caught her attention. She stopped to examine it. It was a small, but noticeable patch of silvery white hair. It was as curly as the rest of her hair, but a bright blonde. She touched it in shock.

"What the fuck?" she whined.

She couldn't believe what she was seeing. She wondered if it was stress that was giving her the silvery white hair. And if so, she wondered how was it such a large patch. She touched it curiously, moving her fingers through it, thinking hard. *What an odd color for it to change to. Not grey, but pure white.*

Suddenly, Sara Coli's face came to her. Her silvery white hair and the other two women on the yacht. Their hair was the same color. Her mind churned all kinds of crazy thoughts. Did Sara Coli give her whatever sort of disease she had through Trevor? Examining the patch in fear, she massaged her temples, trying to put a time frame on it. She was so gone lately that she had no idea when it had happened.

She attempted to steady her thoughts by splashing water on her face. She set the toilet seat cover down and sat down on it with a heavy thump. She knew that she had to find Trevor to see if he was too far gone or did they still have a chance. Did their marriage still stand a chance? Would he forgive her?

Nervously she began to bite her nails. *If it's not the money. Then what the fuck did she do to him?* She had to know what the great attraction was to Sara Coli. Was he really in love with her? If he was, then why did he come home to her? Her head began to hurt badly from her thoughts and a dull thud began to make her nauseated. The tears began to roll from her eyes yet again. She realized that she didn't know where to go, nor what to do. She sat on the toilet seat and cried softly.

She had created a monster that she couldn't control. It was big, ferocious, and threatened to eat her marriage alive. She had never really known how to tame it and never even imagined that she would have needed to. She desperately needed someone to tell her what to do.

Wiping her tears she closed her eyes. "God, please help me. Please God."

The phone rang, causing her to bolt towards it. She banged her shoulder on the doorway nearly knocking herself down. She reached the phone and snatched it off of the receiver.

"Hello?"

Anastasia's voice seemed angelic. "Kalitha? What's wrong, sis?"

"How did you know I needed you?" Kalitha asked, crying.

"I heard your name loud and clear in my head. God told me to call you, sis. Now tell me what's wrong. Who I gotta fuck up?"

Kalitha flopped down on the bed and confessed the whole

situation to her best friend. She told her all that had transpired, from the beginning up to what was taking place now. Anastasia didn't sugar coat how stupid she thought it all was.

"Kalitha, I can't believe you did that. You took the best thing God ever gave you and sent it to the devil. Bitch are you crazy?"

"I know, and I wish I can take it all back," she whined.

"Well, unfortunately, life doesn't work that way."

Kalitha knew the depth of her sad situation had long been reached and admitted that she never once imagined that it would have backfired to such a degree. The situation was now catastrophic.

"Anastasia, please tell me what to do. I don't want to lose my husband."

Anastasia sighed heavily in her ear. "I wish I had an answer for you, but I ain't never been in no shit like that. Shit, I never even heard anyone go through that madness."

Kalitha was sitting on Trevor's side of the bed listening to Anastasia. She absently fingered her way through his nightstand drawer, finding a minimal amount of comfort in touching his things when she came across a key. She lifted it up and examined it. It was tiny with a gold card attached to it. She listened to Anastasia's voice while staring at the key.

"Look, I'll be here for you no matter what, but you're on your own as far as a solution is concerned. Now, if you want to kick that bitch's ass, call me back. You know I'm wit' that!"

"Thank's for that, Ana," she said in a far off voice.

Anastasia felt bad that she couldn't do more. "I'm sorry Kalitha," she said miserably. "I love you, and if you need me, just call."

"I love you too girl," Kalitha said then hung up. She couldn't expect much more than that.

She gave the key a better examination and opened the little card to see five digits on it. She looked towards the window thinking. *This key wasn't going to correct my life, so it really didn't matter what it went to.* She laid back on the bed with an exasperated sigh. Nothing could fix her problems. Only God could change what she had done and he didn't work like that.

She rolled over onto her side and looked at the darkness outside the window. She felt like the world held nothing but darkness for her. Her life was a pitch black hole and her marriage had lost all of its light. The darkness was all that she had to hold onto. She grabbed a pillow and hugged it possessively, the key clutched tightly in her palm, and closed the world out. If she was lucky, she would dream about Trevor tonight.

****

Trevor hoped the double dose of White Widow didn't give him a massive heart attack. He didn't want to feel his heart burst inside of his chest. He rolled over as Mirah flopped her beautifully toned dark chocolate, naked body on the bed beside of him. Janey's white creamy skin shone like porcelain beneath the blue light of Sara Coli's pleasure room. She suckled his toes, while he fingered her wet tight slit.

Sara Coli watched from behind the tri-pod camera. Her body was naked and tingling as she played with her own clit and wet pussy lips. She would have never considered them sharing her Trevor, but he wanted it, and whatever he wanted, he could have without dispute. She was in love with him and would do absolutely anything to please him.

She couldn't tell him no to anything. She had often shared her best parts of her life with her two friends. Why not her Randale love machine.

The lights switched colors on their automatic timers and the room instantly glowed orange. She set the camera on auto and hurried to join them on the super sized pallet. It was made of the softest materials with fluffy pillows all over it. The bed alone costed her $7,000 and was worth every penny of it.

She laid down beside them looking like three flavors of ice cream around his body. They wiggled, giggled, and touched him lovingly. Sara Coli's soft hands cupped his hairy balls as she leaned over Mirah to take his rapid swelling member into her mouth. He looked down to see her deep throating him in the orange light. As it switched to a fluorescent green, he looked up to see Mirah s chocolate ass and pussy, slowly descending on his mouth.

Her pussy tasted sweet to him. He suckled her clit and tongue fucked her until she came with a cute little cry. He watched her fall to the side giggling and Janey hopped on next.

Sara Coli licked his dick while watching as Janey rode his face until completion. She came with a throaty purr, her pussy splashing his lips. The taste of her nectar was driving Trevor crazy. The train continued as Sara Coli took her seat on his facial throne. He sucked her lips and shoved his tongue deep inside of her. He knew exactly how she liked it.

He felt Mirah and Janey hungrily taking turns licking and sucking him. He was as rigid as steel and oozing pre-cum with readiness. They savored the taste of his treat over a raunchy hot tongue kiss. Sara Coli cried out and came, her juices, hot and running down his neck.

That started off their sex fest. Trevor jumped from hole to hole, mouth to mouth, and back again, pounding them into submission. They came so much that the bed sheets were saturated with their juices. Trevor's climax was so tremendous that he feared the worst. As Mirah and Janey double sucked him, his chest began to tighten and his legs were growing stiffer. He clawed at the sheet beside him as the orgasm rushed through his body with titanic force. He gasped for air as the hot white sperm ejected out of him into the air.

The women watched lustfully, then suddenly realized that he was holding his heart. Sara Coli climbed over to him and watched in fear thinking that her curse was repeating itself with Trevor. She prayed that it wasn't. Mirah and Janey made room for his spasming body and Sara Coli placed her hands on his legs trying to still his shaking body, but couldn't.

Panic gripped her in a way that she had never known. He released a wail so blood curdling that both, Mirah and Janey, covered their ears in horror.

"Baby. Randale, please be alright," Sara Coli pled to her young trembling lover. "Please be okay?"

His trembles subsided until he lay there in a daze staring up at

WHITE WIDOW | U.E. WYNN

the yellow light above. His irises bounced around uncontrollably, then slowly focused in on Sara Coli's beautiful worry stricken face. He breathed air into his lungs deeply, then looked at all of them.

He turned back to Sara Coli. "So," he mumbled. "Who's ready for some more?"

Relief flooded her body as she laid on his chest, holding him tightly and laughing with joy. He surprised her by rolling her over and burying his rigid dick back inside of ready pussy. He began to bang her as Mirah and Janey spectated.

He gave them something to feel frightened about as he made Sara Coli cry out in pain. For the first time since they had been intimate, Sara Coli tapped out after she orgasmed, and soaked his balls and dick. Then, Trevor all but attacked Janey. She shouted as he pulled her to him, spun her around, and gave her the most solid fucking she'd ever had. With every thrust she squealed in pain and clawed the bed. She cried out as he let it ride to the hilt inside of her. She trembled as the orgasm rocked her body forward, causing her back to tighten, and her pussy walls to pulsate wildly. Janey's milky white body collapsed in front of him on the bed.

Mirah stood against the far wall looking like fear stricken prey as he hunted her down. She moaned as he lifted her off of the floor and plunged his ten fat inches up into her wet and ready world. She cried out as he held her by her plump ass cheeks and pulled her down until their pelvises met.

After a few strokes like that, she was cumming and screaming at the top of her lungs. He tossed her on the bed in a heap of spent flesh. He then went back to Sara Coli, who welcomed him with open arms and legs. It went on in that manner until the morning sunlight came shining through the window.

Sara Coli fell onto Trevor's chest as he lay there in a sexually fulfilled daze. His eyes glazed over as the sweat poured from his head. She watched him close his eyes, and then closed hers as she listened to the beat of his thrumming heart. She felt like there was no other man on earth for her. No one had ever lasted through a double dose of the venom. He was superman and no one could tell her any different. He had mastered her body and in the same token, dominated her friends until they both had passed out from exhaustion. She was proud of her lover and kissed him on the chest as a form of worship.

Trevor rubbed her soft back and then fell into a coma like sleep. He was the one she thought. After twenty years of searching, she had finally found her soulmate. Sara Coli drifted into her dreams as she rested her head on the one thing that mattered most to her. Her Randale.

Chapter 19

Trevor remained gone for two days, during which time, Kalitha hadn't left the penthouse for anything. She didn't even take the trip downstairs to check the mailbox. She was all broken up into pieces over the events that led to the circumstances that she could not change. Self blame was ripping her to shreds and forcing her to contemplate accepting Sara Coli's offer. She could take the five million dollars and create a new life for herself if she wanted to. She could start all over and could maybe even find love again. The biggest problem was that she loved Trevor too much to even want to try. She couldn't live without his love. Sara Coli would have to force her out of his life and would have to fully eliminate her in order to have peace.

She rolled over in the bed and stared at the ceiling. She had to get up and do something because laying in their bed wasn't going to fix her problems. She got up, showered, dressed, and grabbed the keys to the Escalade. As she began to walk out, the elevator door opened. *I did hear a buzz.*

Kalitha froze in her steps as she saw eight people attired in all black with scarves over their faces. She screamed and spun on her heels to run, but to no avail as she felt herself being tripped by one of her assailants. She hit the carpeted floor hard. Her wrist caught the brunt of the fall and she could instantly feel the rug burn stinging.

"Come here bitch!" It was a female. Kalitha screamed out as what felt like a knee plunge into her back.

"Where you going, bitch?" she said striking Kalitha across the back of her curly haired head with something solid.

Kalitha tried to curl up as the pain set in. Two other girls ran past her as the vibration from the blow rang in her brain. The girl on top of Kalitha pulled a blade from its sheath and pressed it to her throat. Terror resonated throughout her whole being. With a fist full of Kalitha's hair, the girl spoke into her ear menacingly.

"How does it feel to be the victim?"

Tears flowed from Kalitha's eyes as she listened.

"I like what you got here. You balling, huh? We taking all this shit bitch!"

"Please, don't."

"Shut the hell up, slut," the attacker yelled as she slapped Kalitha from the back. "Where that fruity shit at, bitch?"

"I don't know," Kalitha cried. The other girls ransacked the house, bagging up all that was valuable.

"Find all of that shit yall," the assailant yelled out. "Find that paper. Take everything!"

Kalitha covered her head with her hands. She tried to peek back at her aggressor, but was met with the tip of the knife in her flesh. Her eyes darted to the other girls stuffing all of their jewelry in their nap sacks. Trevor's green and red diamond chains. The his and hers black diamond Rolexes. She wailed out when she saw them taking her Fruity Pebbles chain.

"No... Please."

A blow landed on her head so sturdy that the whole living room began to spin. They seemed to be walking sideways and upside down, rather than right side up. They stooped over her and took turns kicking her in her stomach, ass, back, and legs. Kalitha covered her face during the whole assault. A second later they were on the elevator. She watched it close slowly. Then they were gone.

Unsteadily, Kalitha stood and stumbled into the entertainment center, getting her balance. She staggered on wobbly legs to the phone and leaned against the wall. Her entire body was aching. She picked up the phone, but the line was dead. She slid down the wall and held her stomach. She had to call the police and alert the desk man.

She looked down the hall of the ransacked apartment and thought that it couldn't have happened. It was broad daylight outside. She felt the tender spots on her head and winced in pain. *Ouch*, she thought.

How in the fuck did they get in here? How can a person get robbed in a penthouse? Where is the fucking security, she said unbelievingly. She pulled herself up again and hung up the phone. It had to be a setup. They would have never been given access without her approval to the front desk.

She turned to walk away when the phone rang. She turned to it as if a ghost was there. It couldn't be ringing if it was dead. She reached for it slowly and answered it.

"Hello?"

"Four million?" Sara Coli's voice sang on the line.

"FUCK YOU!!!"

Kalitha slammed the phone down hard enough to break the receiver. She backed away from it huffing and puffing with fury as the broken receiver and phone dangled loosely from the wall.

****

The police arrived, dusted the whole apartment for prints, but found none. There was absolutely no evidence to suggest that what Kalitha was claiming had happened, actually happened. She stood with her arms crossed as the building manager spoke.

"If anyone had been in the penthouse the way she claims, then she would have had to buzz them in."

"I didn't buzz any fucking body in!" Kalitha yelled. "You're a fucking liar. You're all a bunch of liars."

"Calm down, ma'am," the officer said. "Do you have receipts for the jewelry?"

"No," she replied, defeated. "They were gifts."

"Well, without anything to prove that they ever existed, there's really nothing we can do."

"I personally don't think there's anything to be done," the manager added.

She fumed as the police dispersed without any further words. The manager casts her a disdainful look. She rolled her eyes, then walked outside to get some fresh air.

She couldn't believe it. The police couldn't investigate it as a break-in because other than keypad entry, a visitor had to be buzzed up. Then there was no tangible proof that the jewelry ever existed except in the raunchy photos with Willie.

She most definitely didn't want to show the scandalous photos to the police or the manager. She didn't need the scrutiny of the police examining them. There was absolutely no proof that anything ever happened. She was left with no one to help her with her situation. She had even asked them to examine the phone call afterwards, but it was from an untraceable source. They would have to get back to her on that.

Fire burned hot and fierce throughout her body knowing who was behind her attack. "That old treacherous bitch!!!"

She paced in front of the building feeling like it was too dangerous to stay there right now. She needed to get away from Wilmington. A name popped in her head quickly. *Willie. He would know how to help me.*

She hurried into the parking deck, jumped into the Escalade and pulled out heading to the beach house. The building manager walked out just in time to see her driving the big white SUV. He pulled out his phone and dialed.

"Hello," Sara Coli answered.

"This is Lawrence," he said, looking down the block. "She just left ma'am."

****

Kalitha pulled up to the beach house and noticed that neither of Willie's cars were in the driveway. She parked and turned the SUV off, eyeing the home suspiciously. It looked empty for all intents and purposes. She got out and walked up to the door and knocked. No answer. She walked around to the back patio door and peeked inside. It was completely empty. No visual signs existed that would have led her to believe that anyone had been there for months.

She didn't have his number any longer and it made her curse herself. She shouldn't have turned her back on him the way that she did. Now she needed him and he was gone.

Kalitha leaned against the glass door in total defeat. She watched the waves crash against the shore as the sun began to drop in the sky. She walked down to the shore with her shoulders slumped. It took all of her strength to lift her head to look out into the nothingness of the ocean. She shook her head, feeling the tenderness of the lumps.

She couldn't come to terms with her being assaulted and robbed at knife point in the secure confines of the penthouse suite. There was no way it wasn't a set up and she couldn't prove it at all. She knew it had to be Sara Coli who orchestrated the attack. She closed her eyes, remembering the words of her attacker.

"How does it feel to be the victim?"

If she could be beaten and mugged in broad daylight in a penthouse, then she wasn't safe anywhere. A frightening chill ran down the length of her spine just from the thought of how vulnerable she actually was. She felt helpless and leery of everything. She was in a big world all alone with no Trevor to protect her.

She hurried to her feet as the feeling that she was being watched crept over her. She fearfully sprinted to the Escalade. She keyed it open looking over her shoulders in the darkening night. Frightened, she dropped them. A dog's bark caused her to crouch down as if someone had fired a pistol at her. She scrambled to get under the SUV as if she was sure that she was a target for murder.

The barks continued bringing her back to reality. She was nearly all of the way under the Escalade ready to hide in fear. *No! Don't hide! Run!* Kalitha hurried to her feet and got in the truck. She pulled out quickly and drove back to the penthouse.

As she parked in the parking deck and turned off the SUV, her mind reeled. She came to the conclusion that she was not safe there, nor any other place that Sara Coli could reach her. She pulled off and went in search of the nearest pay phone. She found one in front of a gas station and got out cautiously approaching it. She dialed Anastasia's number with shaking hands.

"Hello?"

"Anastasia, it's me, Kalitha."

"Where are you calling from?" Anastasia asked in a curious, but concerned voice.

"A pay phone."

"A pay phone?"

"Look," Kalitha scanned the convenience store's parking lot that was connected to the gas station for anything out of place. "I'm coming to you."

"Kalitha, what's wrong? What's going on?"

"Just please..." She paused to look over her shoulder. "Wait up for me."

"Okay," Anastasia said. "I'll be up waiting for you."

Kalitha pulled up to Anastasia's house in Whiteville, N.C. a little over two hours later. She was glad to be out of Port City, but hated that Whiteville had the word 'White' in it. It made her think of the old bitch who was making her life a living hell.

She got out and was met by her best friend at the door. Anastasia greeted her with a loving hug, then pulled her inside. Kalitha took a well needed deep breath and relaxed a little as she hit the softness of her friend's sofa. It felt heaven sent to be around Anastasia in the comfort and safety of her home. There she felt a love that she was sure of.

After telling Anastasia all that had happened, she received a face of total and utter disbelief. She hugged her comfortingly and gave Kalitha all the support she needed.

"You're staying the night, right?" Anastasia asked, while rubbing Kalitha's back gently. "I can make up the couch for you."

"Yeah. I mean, it's not like I got anywhere else to go," she answered miserably.

Kalitha needed the calm and familiarity of her friend's home. Anastasia left her to sleep on the sofa with a soft warm comforter. She needed a good night's rest. Her mind, as well as her battered and bruised body, needed to rest and she took advantage of the peace and stability. She slept a satisfying slumber and didn't leave her friend's home for two days.

Finally getting some rest, she felt refreshed as she got out of the Escalade and headed towards the penthouse. The desk clerk gave her an acknowledging nod as she boarded the elevator and rode it up. When the door opened, Kalitha's eyes protrude in disbelief. The living room was stark empty and the kitchen was too. She hurried to the bedrooms to see that the whole apartment was bare as a new born baby.

"What the fuck?" Her voice echoed in the room. She could see that even her clothes were gone and nothing remained in the whole entire apartment. She screamed out at the top of her lungs frustrated with the shit that was happening to her.

She quieted down when she heard the chirping of a phone and followed it to the kitchen. It chirped again. She squatted down and opened the cabinet under the sink. There sat a white cellular phone and it chirped again. She snatched it out and answered it.

"What!" she snapped agitated.

"Hello, darling," Sara Coli crooned. "I took the liberty of remodeling for you. You like?"

"You slithering snake bitch!"

"Oh, you sound so tense. Why don't you take a seat," Sara Coli teased. "Oh wait. I've taken them all."

"You... you..." Kalitha growled in anger.

"Oh come on girl. Where's your sense of humor?"

"Kiss my ass you slimy bitch," Kalitha yelled.

"Don't be naïve, Kalitha. Three million dollars is a lot of cheese. Especially for a hood rat."

"You low down bitch—"

"Ah, ah," she cut her off. "You can't afford to talk to me that way."

"Fuck you," Kalitha barked. "He's mine!" she yelled into the phone. "MINE!"

"Have it your way then!"

Sara Coli hung up the phone, then dialed the bank's number.

They answered after a few rings.

"South Trust Savings and Loans."

"Yes, this is Sara Coli White. I need a huge favor today."

****

Kalitha stomped around in anger. For the life of her she didn't understand how she could have gotten into the penthouse to take all of their shit. Trevor had to allow it, because she couldn't do it without their passcode. Suddenly she thought about the money in the bank. *Holy shit! I have to move my money,* she thought. She had to get it out of her reach, because Trevor probably told her about that too.

She ran to the elevator, rode it down, and headed straight for the bank. It was on the upper end of Market Street and the penthouse was downtown. The afternoon traffic was thick as usual. She called the directory for South Trust's number, then called them. The lines were all busy.

She glanced at the clock. It was a little after three and the bank didn't close until five. She felt pressed for time. She also felt that Sara Coli was out to destroy her world and that Trevor was helping.

Kalitha pulled up to the bank at three forty five. She hopped out, and walked in. It was packed and panic set in on her. She couldn't help but to become fidgety in the line and it seemed as if there were a hundred people ahead of her. She saw a seat come open and hurried under the partition rope to the seat, cutting the line. The customers began to complain loudly, but Kalitha ignored them.

She sat down to the teller's disdainful facial expression. "Ma'am, you cut the line"

"Save it," she rudely cut him off. She sat her card on the desk. "I want to make a withdrawal."

"Sure, Mrs. Mason," he replied, taken aback. He handed her a withdrawal form. "Just fill out one of these."

She snatched it and began to pen in her information.

"Uh, would you like a balance check?"

"Yeah, whatever," she replied being short with him.

He tapped the keys on his computer. "Okay. As of today, you have a total of five hundred dollars."

"What!" she yelled. The customers turned to her outburst.

"Five hundred dollars, ma'am," he said caught off guard.

"Unh, unh," she said boisterously. "You better check that mutherfucker again. I had over a half a million two days ago. Yall better check your computer or something."

A male manager walked over. "Ma'am, is everything alright? What seems to be the problem?"

"Your computer is off by five hundred grand." She stood up pissed off. "So, somebody needs to fix it."

The manager started clicking away at the computer keys. "Your account is correct. It was five hundred dollars two days ago."

"That's bullshit!" Kalitha yelled, fighting the urge to pummel the young male manager.

"Ma'am, I—"

"I got it, Tommy," a female manager said, walking up and dismissing Tommy and the young teller. She looked to Kalitha and began to click away on the computer. "Mrs. Mason, your account balance is correct right down to the cents."

"No, it isn't," Kalitha retorted through gritted teeth. "That's bullshit!"

"Mrs. Mason," Marsha snapped at Kalitha. "If you'd like to make a withdrawal, you are more than welcome, but one more outburst and I will be forced to call the authorities. Now make your choice."

Now that she was broke, Kalitha knew that she would need every penny she had to get by. Hanging her head, she replied sullenly. "Okay." She sat down slowly, catching a tear as it rolled from her eye.

After withdrawing the five hundred dollars, she left without any further interruptions. She slammed the door behind her in the Escalade, threw the money envelope at the windshield, and covered her face crying. She couldn't accept it. How did Sara Coli do it and why would Trevor help her do it?

She began to bang against the steering wheel with her hand,

her anger taking complete control over her. She exhausted herself emotionally crying and screaming. How would she begin to accept that over a half of a million dollars had just up and vanished into thin air? How could she wipe out her bank account? Why couldn't Sara Coli be stopped? Did she really possess infinite reach? Kalitha didn't know, but she did know that Sara Coli was slowly wiping out every chance that she had of surviving. She was losing the battle by all the scorecards.

The little white phone she'd found in the penthouse rang, but she merely wiped her face and ignored it. She knew who it was whenever the phone rang, it was her. She disregarded it and headed back to the penthouse.

When she entered the lobby that was as far as she could get. She dialed her code into the keypad and it glowed red. She looked at it confused, then turned and walked over to the lobby clerk's desk.

"Why won't my passcode work?"

"Well," he said, looking down at the information log. "It was deactivated as of four o'clock today. It's now unoccupied."

Kalitha's mouth dropped open.

The desk clerk looked towards the manager who stepped up. "Ma'am, I have to ask you to please vacate the premises." His words were said with an air of satisfaction.

Too weary and beaten to argue with him, she slowly turned and left the building. She climbed back into the Escalade and instantly the little white phone began to ring. She glanced down at it loathing the sound it made. It seemed to her that the phone was a perpetual symbol of her failures. A poisonous needle jammed underneath her fingernails.

The phone kept ringing so she picked it up and answered without speaking.

"Are you ready to make a deal?" Sara Coli asked softly.

"Why are you doing this to me?" Kalitha asked in more of a whine than anything else.

"I have done nothing. You have done it all to yourself. I tried to give you a beautiful way out. I offered you much more than you deserve, but you are intrepid and filled with muddled hypocrisies. You adamantly chose the fight that I tried to avoid."

"Please," Kaltha said sarcastically. "Slow down with all of the big fucking words."

"Well, how about this? My last call which you undoubtedly ignored was my offer of two million dollars. Now I'm only offering you one million dollars."

"I'd rather die," Kalitha spat.

"Even that can be arranged."

Sara Coli's words humbled Kalitha to the point of fear. She ducked down in the seat of the Escalade as she looked around cautiously.

Sara Coli continued with her plan. "I would much rather have you disappear of your own volition. I prefer a more subtle approach, but if you want to play hardball..." She paused for emphasis and Kalitha got the point loud and clear. "I'll tell you what, child," she said slowly. "I will give you seven days to make up your little mind. In those seven days, if you call me, I will discuss the closing of this business deal. Until then, try and stay safe darling."

Kalitha hung on her every word as the phone went dead in her ear. She had no earthly idea how she would survive this war when she couldn't see her enemy. That only made her a warrior in a battle where she couldn't fight back. She felt as if she had brought a knife to a gun fight. She wondered how far would her five hundred take her? She pictured nowhere being the place that she was headed.

As Kilitha pulled the keys to Escalade out, the little golden key fell into her lap. The little card attached to it drew her attention to it. She held it up to the light and read the digits on it. *Three two four*. She didn't recognize the numbers. They meant nothing to her.

She glanced at them once more, then looked over to the glove compartment. She inserted the SUV's key into the lock and opened it for the first time, finding a small golden box inside. She pulled it out and set it in her lap. It was a beautifully designed carved box that had a combination nozzle at the top of it. There were only six spots on the number nozzle and the card had only fve on it.

She set the numbers in the same sequence as the card, then tried to pop the latch. It didn't work. She looked at the numbers on the box and immediately noticed that a two was missing. She put the two in the last spot and it made a small click sound and popped open.

****

Sara Coli sat behind her desk with her fingers bridged. She didn't want to result to such harsh dealings, but Trevor's wife was as stubborn as a bull elephant. Her resilience was remarkable and Sara Coli admired that kind of strength and fight in a person, just not when it came to her and her happiness. She picked up the phone and dialed a number.

"Yes, this is Sara Coli. I need you guys to pick up something for me except..." She thrummed her fingers on the desk. "I don't quite know where it is."

Chapter 20

For the next three days Kalitha spent her time holed up in a cheap Travel Lodge Motel room thinking about what she would do next. Aside from examining the gold plated 380 caliber pistol with its pearl handle and diamond embedded T.M. on the side, she just stared absent-mindedly at the wall. Only someone with too much money, and not enough to spend it on, would have diamonds placed in the handle of a pistol.

She turned her nose up at the thought. It must have been a gift for Trevor. She couldn't deny the fact that it was beautiful. Beautiful, expensive, and dangerous. It came with eight flawless, shiny, silver, and copper bullets. She hadn't ever held a gun before, let alone fired one. However, with it in her possession, she felt confident that nothing else could happen to her.

She learned how to work the on and off safety, and felt that it was only right to keep it close. Especially since she could look out of the window and see drug deals being made and hookers hopping in and out of cars with buyers.

She hated to have to stay in such a lowlife infested area, but she didn't have much of a choice. Sara Coli hadn't left her with many options to choose from. She couldn't reach Trevor and Sara Coli had done as she had said and left the contacting up to Kalitha. With her five hundred dwindling down fast, she was going to have to make a decision.

She peeped out of the window at all of the illegal dealings going on and really felt the loneliness set in more than she'd ever had. She wished she would have taken the five million dollars and ran off to God knows where, and eventually become happy again.

She scratched the curly white patch of hair thinking that she really could have started over alone. Alone, with no Trevor, and with no more Sara Coli to make her life a living hell. She wouldn't have to be alone for long. She was young and beautiful and would have found someone in no time.

She just could not get her heart to agree with her mind. Her heart yearned for Trevor's love, but the circumstances told her that her husband's love was no longer her's anymore. She was more subject to believe that he had fallen for Sara Coli now more than any other time in the past. He was with her after all.

Kalitha knew that in four days she would have to take Sara Coli's offer. Maybe she could bargain for more than a million if she tried hard enough. Sara Coli was worth over 800 million. She could spare a few more.

She stuffed the pistol securely in her purse after readying herself to go out. The moment she exited the motel room, she was met by drug dealers trying to sell her anything she could think of, and foul mouthed prostitutes threatening her about moving in on their territory. She rushed to the Escalade and quickly locked all of the riff raff on the outside.

She did not like driving the fly SUV in the most rundown part of the city, but she was alone, and driving would be a thousand times safer than walking. She drove to the gas station across the street to fill up the truck. The gas for the big SUV was picking her pockets apart, but her safety was the number one priority.

Once she pulled up to the pump and got out, her heart began to beat sporadically. Her attention was drawn to the full length of the Bentley limo riding by and stopping at the light. The tinted windows becoming no factor, she craned her neck to see inside, wondering if Trevor was in it or not. It took all of her reserve not to run out into the street and attempt to snatch the door open. She watched it pull off, then got back in the Escalade, never minding the gas. She needed to track the limo down. It was her only way of finding Trevor. He was her last source of hope.

As Tony drove the Bentley limo up Market Street, he glanced to the right, and low and behold at the gas station was the white Escalade. He watched Kalitha get out, then gooseneck to see inside of the limo. He felt bad for her, but his first duty was to his employer and good friend. He pressed a button on the limo's phone.

"Quality Repo Service," a voice stated.

"This is Tony Ramirez calling for Mrs. White. I just spotted the SUV."

"Where about sir?"

"A Petro on the four hundred block of Market Street."

****

Trevor smiled as Sara Coli rubbed his leg flirtatiously. He looked out of the tinted side window just in time to see the white Escalade. He couldn't conceal his curiosity which made Sara Coli look with observing eyes. She saw Kalitha trying to see into the limo and she burst with triumph.

She snaked her fingers into Trevor's. "You know darling. I'd like to see you in a new Maybach for the new year."

He averted his gaze and replied somberly. "That sounds great."

His thoughts remained on Kalitha as they pulled off. He really missed her, but had taken some precautions to make sure that she would be alright without him. When he came all of the way clean to Sara Coli, she made him a promise to take care of her. It was a non-disputable condition of their relationship. He did not want to worry about Kalitha and Sara Coli promised to grant all of his wishes. His thoughts lightened up knowing that Kalitha would fair well without him.

"Triple black?" She smiled and gave him two thumbs up.

****

Kalitha pulled out of the Petro Station about four cars behind the limo. She had to maneuver through the heavy traffic just to get close to them. When she managed to get behind them, she tried to see inside again, but to no avail. Her mind envisioned Sara Coli in the back alone and the thought of ramming the SUV into the limo at full speed was almost seductive.

If she could destroy the whole back end of the limo with Sara Coli inside of it, she would be rid of her for good. She knew it would never work. With her luck, she'd end up paralyzed and still out of a husband. She would be better off taking the final offer. She believed that she could do it, but she just needed to see Trevor once more.

Kalitha followed the limo to the far end of Market Street just to feel closer to Trevor not knowing if he was in the limo or not. As she approached Wilmington City limits, the gas light came on. She was running on fumes and wouldn't be able to make it to Odgen.

"Uhhh," she sounded hitting the steering wheel hard. "Stupid, stupid me. Just hold on until I reach him, please," she begged the SUV.

The Escalade's only response was the jerking motion that happens when a vehicle is out of gas. She watched the limo glide on ahead towards Odgen as she pulled over into Smithfield's Chicken and BBQ. It was the only place to pull into before the wide road to Odgen began.

She parked in the parking lot feeling defeated. She wanted badly to make the drive to Sara Coli's mansion and be a welcomed visitor, but knew that would never be the case. She would have to be invited to even have a small chance of seeing Trevor.

It dawned on her that Sara Coli had won. She was broke, broken down, and beaten, battered, bruised, sore, out classed, out thought, and out of gas. She hopped out and walked back up to the sidewalk and could see the gas station a few blocks down. She figured that she could get the SUV moving, and if worse came to worst, roll into the station. She got back in and drove down behind the restaurant to make the turn. As she began to turn, a pair of headlights flashed at her. She skidded to a stop as red and blue lights flooded the inside of the SUV.

She shoved the gearshift into park. "God, what now?"

She began to reach for her license as two men rushed the driver's side door. Her heart pumped blood faster than ever as the door was flung open and pistols were jammed into her face. They began barking orders at her, confusing her, and scaring her to death.

She screamed as she felt herself being jerked from the driver's seat and slammed hard on the ground. She cringed in fear as the yelled at her.

"Get on the ground! You're under arrest!"

Kalitha lay flat on the ground crying out if fear. "Please don't shoot me!" she begged as she stretched her arms out. Her right hand still gripping her purse with the golden pistol in it.

"Face down. Hands behind your head!"

She complied as they barked orders. The two men's aggressive commotion was too much for Kalitha to deal with and seemed as if it was a lot more people screaming at her. She just knew that the gun in her purse would surely mean charges. Jail. Prison.

She felt her arms being pulled behind her and cuffed. She closed her eyes, praying that it would all go away. It was as if God had answered her prayers, because all of a sudden she heard both the SUV and the other vehicle speeding off, tires screeching. She looked up to see the Escalade bending the corner of the building. *What the fuck? I just got carjacked by the police?* She pulled at her cuffs, and to her great surprise, they popped. She pushed up to her knees seeing that they were plastic, but looked very real.

She stood up grabbing her purse, then looked around the parking lot. She began throwing a stomping tantrum which led to her sitting back on the dirty concrete. She hung her head and cried at downfall. There was nothing else to do. She had been reduced to what she had the day she got the newspaper article about Sara Coli. Nothing.

She wiped her tears in one last attempt to pull herself together. Standing up, she walked the parking lot to the entrance of Smithfields. She walked inside to a friendly cashier.

"Welcome to Smith fields"

"Save it," Kalitha rudely cut the young girl off as she turned to the restroom. She went in and looked at herself in the mirror, and found that she looked a mess. She sat her purse on the sink and wiped her face. She couldn't prevent the tears from rolling from her eyes and spent a long moment, looking at herself in the mirror. She realized that there was only one logical thing to do. She pulled the white phone from her purse and dialed Sara Coli's number. She answered after three rings.

"Hello," answered Sara Coli giggling as she, Trevor, Mirah, and Janey flirted their way down the hallway towards the pool.

"I surrender," Kalitha breathed out. "I can't fight you any longer. I'm waving my white flag."

"How wonderful of you to come to your senses, darling," she replied as they entered the pool room ahead of her. Sara Coli stopped just outside of the door. " I'm at my mansion right now. Do you think that you could make it here on your own?"

Kalitha squeezed the sink at the asinine question. It was a direct insult to injury, but she wasn't going to blow her opportunity. "No, I can't," she answered stiffly.

"Of course you can't honey," she teased. "So how about I send my driver?"

Kalitha knew that she couldn't win even verbally with the older woman, so she let it go. She had to grit her teeth, grin, and bear it all until she saw her chance. She spoke calmly and respectfully.

"I'm at Smith—"

"Field," Sara Coli finished her sentence. "Oh, I know exactly where you are. Give my driver fifteen minutes." Sara Coli walked into the pool area to see Trevor being stripped naked by Mirah and Janey. She smiled and said into her phone softly. "See you soon," and hung up.

Feeling the excitement of her victory over Kalitha, she walked over to them and began to unwrap her sari. Mirah and Janey giggled and pulled Trevor into the warm water. "Oh, wait for mama," Sara Coli cooed girlishly. She got in and waded towards them wrapping her arms around Trevor's neck for a sensuous kiss. A thrill ran down her spine. He was minutes away from being all her's. She was excited to the point of arousal and wanted to show her desire at that exact moment. Her friends touched and tickled him and she smiled when he laughed.

Trevor kissed Sara Coli passionately looking forward to the White Widow drink that they would be enjoying in a moment. He glanced over to Mirah fixing them up while Janey fed herself fruit from the wet bar. He knew that once he got his fix, he would be on top of the world, and on top of their worlds also.

He lifted Sara Coli up and spun her around in the water. She gazed into his dark brown eyes lovingly. " I love you, Randale."

He sat her on her feet in the warm champagne colored water as his mind put together the right words for her. He realized that he loved her too, and knew it was time to let her know. He looked into her beautiful hazel eyes and gently rubbed her hair. "I love you too, Sara Coli."

She jumped into his arms nearly crying tears of joy. He smiled and walked her over to the bar. Mirah and Janey clapped at their moment, causing Sara Coli to blush and hide her face against Trevor's chest.

Twenty minutes later, Tony pulled up outside of Smithfields where Kalitha stood waiting. He got out, walked to the back door, and opened it for her. He looked up to her, but remained silent. She averted her eyes as she walked to the open door and got in. The limo reeked of money to Kalitha.

She only wished that her comings and goings could be as extravagant as Sara Coli's. She clutched her purse to her, knowing that the ride in the Bentley limo could very well be her last one. She would never know such luxury. This was the life she had given to her husband. She needed to know what his heart felt and couldn't live knowing that she didn't. She would ask him to speak to him just a chance to say goodbye. Hopefully Sara Coli would give her that last chance. If he was really done with her, then it wouldn't matter. If she denied her that, she had one last option left.

They pulled up to the mansion about fifteen minutes later. It was huge and lit on all sides. It almost glowed in the night. They drove the long driveway and pulled up behind the Escalade, then Tony let her out. She instantly noticed the SUV and her temper flared through the roof of her head. She took in the mansion's humongous size. *Trevor's in there.*

The doorman led them in and Kalitha was blown away by the

size of the foyer and the height of the cathedral ceilings. The chandelier was immaculate. "Where is Mrs. White," Tony asked the doorman?

"She is currently in the indoor pool," he said simply, then turned and walked away.

Tony turned to Kalitha. "I'll take you to her."

"Where is Trevor?"

He turned and began to walk away without replying. She followed him taking in the regal décor of the mansion with its plush carpets and priceless sculptures and painting that adorned the walls. It was all breathtaking. Now she understood why he didn't want to come back home. The elegant color schemes and the flawless architectural designs demanded respect. It was a home worthy of a near billionaire. It was a creation for the high and mighty and she was just a regular woman who hadn't even dreamed of something so splendid.

They turned down a long hall and came to a stop in front of a large door. Tony looked to her. "Wait right here, Mrs. Mason." He turned to go in but stopped, spun on his heels, and touched Kalitha on the side of her face catching her by surprise. "I wish you were really Vicky." Just as quickly, he turned and went inside.

You just don't know how much I wish that I was Vicky too.

It seemed like forever, but Tony finally returned with Sara Coli in tow. He turned up the hall and left them alone. She immediately noticed that Sara Coli was wearing a satin robe that was only a few inches from the floor. It was tied in the middle and Kalitha could see the white spider tattoo inbetween her wet supple breast. She was even more beautiful in the lit up hallway. Kalitha clutched her purse tightly in her hand as Sara Coli spoke confidently.

"It's nice to see you made it here safely." She smiled deviously. "Those streets can be a dangerous place."

"So I've learned," Kalitha said, looking around to the door behind her. She could hear people laughing and splashing water. "Where is Trevor?"

Sara Coli waved for her to follow without answering her inquiry and Kalitha followed her reluctantly. "So, I was thinking that my offer of one million dollars shouldn't stand due to the fact that it is four days late."

"Three!" Kalitha corrected her sharply. "Three days!"

"Who's counting anyway," Sara Coli asked sarcastically.

"Apparently you were," Kalitha quipped.

Sara Coli turned to look back at Kalitha with disdain. "You, know what—"

"No, I don't, but I'm sure you're gonna tell me—"

"It befuddles me how you can be so far into enemy territory and still be so..." She waved her hands for emphasis. "I don't know, feisty." Kalitha folded her arms in defiance as Sara Coli spoke. "That means that you're either extremely courageous or what I find myself leaning more towards."

Kalitha couldn't help but to bite the bait. "And what's that?"

"Exceptionally stupid," Sara Coli replied intending on drilling it home.

Kalitha sucked her teeth and clutched her purse even tighter. She wouldn't be able to take much more verbal abuse from the older woman. Sara Coli already had her foot on Kalitha's neck. She refused to suck her toes as an added bonus.

"Can we just get back to business?" Kalitha hissed between gritted teeth.

"Fine. I'm prepared to offer you a half million dollars."

Kalitha's eyes bucked in disbelief. "A half million?" She laughed almost hysterically. "Shit. You might as well slap me on the ass on my way out."

"If that's what you're into," Sara Coli returned as she began to walk again. "I aim to please you know?"

Kalitha followed her, becoming angrier by the second. She wasn't going to win at all, so she decided to speak her mind. "Please," she barked. "What can your old wrinkled ass do?"

"You've seen it, haven't you?" She turned with a devious smile. "Or would you like to have a copy for your own personal use?"

Kalitha had to restrain herself from trying to claw Sara Coli's hazel eyes out of her face. She was at that point in her mind.

"So what's it going to be girl?"

That sent Kalitha into verbal attack mode. "I know that it can't possibly be you. So what did you really do to my husband?"

Sara Coli shook off the insult. "Apparently, I did what you couldn't do."

Kalitha chuckled. "Okay, seriously. What the fuck did you do to my husband?"

"If you really must know," said Sara Coli, looking back at Kalitha. "I gave my Randale a dose of a drink called White Widow. Then," she winded her hips sexily. "I fucked his brains out."

"White Widow? Fucking weed?"

"No you dense dimwitted broad. I said a drink called White Widow."

"White Widow?" she repeated.

"Yes," Sara Coli turned to lead her to a side door in the hall. "It's the venom of an eight inch Siberiari White Widow Spider. Along with a few herbs to counteract the effects of the poison."

"Wow. You really can tell a fucking lie."

Sara Coli gave Kalitha a wicked smile and touched her hair at the white patch, then touched her own. Kalitha stared at her in curious confusion.

"Really," she said leading Kalitha from one door, to another. "We both know who's the better liar out of us two, but if you don't believe me, I will show you." Sara Coli held the door open. "Follow me."

Kalitha cautiously followed her down the long corridor, listening as Sara Coli rattled off places she had been and things she had seen. Foods she had tasted and things she had collected. She ended by stating that Trevor was her greatest treasure. Kalitha wanted to refute her words, but in their current positions, she was more right than wrong about him being hers.

"My Randale has been on the venom for months now, Kalitha. And, might I add, he can't get enough of this pussy when he is," she shot the insult back.

"Whatever bitch" Kalitha mumbled.

Sara Coli stopped in front of the door that led to the private chamber. She walked in and Kalitha followed. Once inside, she placed her hand on the recognition screen and her hand slid into the silicon substance. The door slid open without any sound. Kalitha peeked into the dark room as she trailed behind Sara Coli, who walked directly down a lit path on the floor to the middle. She could see the gigantic glass case, but didn't know what it was.

Sara Coli walked up to the panel near the glass box. "They're very sensitive to light so I keep it dark in here."

"Why is it so fucking cold?"

"Siberia is in Russia, darling."

As the lights came on slowly, Kalitha's eyes nearly popped out of her head as she took in the two larger than life spiders in the glass case. It was filled with black webs and what seemed like hundreds of smaller ones. Sara Coli smiled down at the case realizing that the mating was successful. She didn't notice Kalitha fishing the golden pistol out of her purse behind her. When she heard the purse landing on the floor, she turned to see Kalitha approaching with the pistol she had bought Trevor. Sara Coli lifted her hands in surrender.

"What in the fuck are those things?" Kalitha yelled.

"Have you not been listening?" Sara Coli held her hand out and upward. "You really need to put that thing away in here."

"Shut up," Kalitha ordered, aiming at her face. "What have you done to him? You've been giving him spider poison?"

"No. He's been taking it on his own you silly, bitch. Now please put that pistol away before you hurt someone."

"Don't tell me what to do." Kalitha's tone was condescending now. "I have the control now." She stepped in closer to get a better look at the two large spiders and all of the creepy little baby ones.

"Kalitha, this is the wrong place for that gun. They're extremely dangerous. There must be—"

"No!" she cut her off yelling. "No!" She kept her eyes on the deadly spiders as they moved about agitated.

"Kalitha—"

"No," she stopped her. "You're trying to kill him the way you killed all of the others. I read about you. You're a murderer."

"You're the one in my home with a gun."

Kalitha stepped closer to get an even better look at the creatures.

"I want my husband back."

Sara Coli saw her opportunity and took full advantage of it by latching onto Kalitha's arm with the pistol in it. They began to power struggle near the glass encasement. Kalitha never imagined that Sara Coli would have been that strong at fifty one. She used all of her might to push the older woman against the glass box and accidentally pulled the trigger. The 380 exploded inside of the small metal encased room. The bullet made a metallic clang as it ricocheted around the room. She fired again as Sara Coli rolled her against the large glass case. They grunted and screamed as they tussled with the second bullet bouncing around them.

****

As Mirah rubbed Trevor's back, the first shot rang out and he turned to listen. Another shot sounded inside of the house somewhere and he bolted from the pool. He slipped into his pants without bothering to dry off. He had to see what was going on and if Sara Coli was alright. Mirah and Janey hurried to their robes with the intentions of getting as far away from the gunfire as possible.

Trevor ran out into the hallway, barefoot, bare chested, and still wet, into a group of worried staff members trying to listen to locate the source of the gunshots. He looked down the hall towards the secret chamber and headed that way. He wanted to make sure Sara Coli was alright, but a large part of him wanted to make sure the spiders were also safe. His bare feet stung on the hard floors as he ran down the long corridor towards the secret chamber. He could hear the grunts, curses, and screams.

"Sara!" he yelled as he pushed the outside door open. He ducked back when he heard the third gunshot fired. He could hear it ricocheting off of the metal surface of the chamber followed by Sara Coli's shriek of pain.

"Sara Coli!" he yelled in concern as he rushed into the chamber and instantly recognized Kalitha from the back. She was standing over Sara Coli, who lay on the floor next to the glass encasement bleeding profusely from her lower body.

"No!" he yelled, causing Kalitha to spin on him. "What have you done?" he asked, noticing the small hole in the glass encasement? "What in the fuck are you doing?"

Kalitha screamed her responses fed up with him, Sara Coli, and all of it. "You don't know what she did to me. You don't care!" She pointed the gun at him. "You don't care!"

"Kalitha, calm down babe."

"No!" she yelled out. "I can't let her take you from me. She's already taken everything else Trevor. Everything!"

He looked curiously down at Sara Coli. "You said that you'd take care of her. You said she wouldn't have to worry about money or anything."

"The bitch is crazy, Randale," Sara Coli moaned out in pain. "Look at what she's done." She showed him her bloody side.

"Shut up you old bitch!" Kalitha screamed back at her.

"She came here to take a payoff Randale. Five hundred thousand. That's all you're worth to her."

Kalitha screamed and turned on Sara Coli, shooting the control panel near her head. It sparked and began to smoke.

Trevor moved to advance on her, but she turned on him and began to cry.

"Don't you go near her! I'll kill you and that old bitch before I lose you!"

"Kalitha, babe," Trevor said, taking a step forward.

Kalitha fired a bullet past his head into the hand recognition screen, the door squealed and slid shut behind him.

"No! She can't have you. I'd rather die!"

"Kalitha," Trevor said, watching a few of the tiny spiders escape out of the big glass box. "Please, babe," he stepped forward again. "Calm down and give me the gun."

She laughed hysterically. "It's not her Trevor, it's the spiders that got you." She pointed to the spiders. "It's those fucking spiders."

"No," he said earnestly. "Please, don't do that. Don't hurt the spiders, babe."

Her mind snapped. "Hurt the spiders? The spiders? Fuck those spiders!"

She turned and shot two bullets at the case. One went wide and bounced off of the metal walls. Kalitha yelped in pain, dropped the pistol, and fell holding her leg. Trevor quickly kicked the pistol away from her, then knelt to examine her wound because it was bleeding profusely.

She looked up to him with pitiful eyes. "Come home to me Trevor, please?" She held the blood pumping hole. "I'm sorry. I'll be good."

He looked over at Sara Coli, who had a simple look on her face. He glanced up to see the spiders coming fast across the case. Lifting Kalitha out of harms way, he quickly carried her over to the far wall. As he began to head back over for Sara Coli, Kalitha grabbed him with a bloody hand. "No. Stay with me. Don't leave me Trev."

He pulled her hand away "She needs my help too."

When he snatched away to go to Sara Coli's aid, Kalitha could literally feel her world crumbling. Trevor lifted Sara Coli, carried her over to the wall, and placed her a few feet away from Kalitha. He surveyed the wound in her hip trying not to cause her pain.

"Ouch, darling. That's going to leave a mark."

"I have to get some help in here for the both of you." He stood and examined the busted silicon handprint recognition screen. "Sara Coli, how does this work? How do I get it open?"

Sara Coli's laugh was filled with pain, but was still throaty. "Your little genius wife shot the screen and the control panel. There's no way out, Randale."

"Fuck you," Kalitha yelled through her trembling lips.

"Oh, you're very much fucked us all."

Trevor turned to see the spiders coming towards them. "There's gotta be something I can do. What should I do?"

He began to panic as he saw all of the little baby spiders coming straight for them. Sara Coli looked up at him. "Get the gun, Randale."

He sprinted to the pistol shaking a spider off of it, then quickly backed away from them. Kalitha began to scream as she saw the spiders three feet away from her. She rolled her legs in and cringed in fear.

"What now?" Trevor asked fearfully.

"Shoot the light out Randale. Do it now."

He aimed up at the large bulb in the ceiling and with the last bullet, shot it, causing it to spark and shatter. The glass showered the case as the room became pitch black. Trevor stood back against wall holding the pistol. He dropped it with a loud clank and slid down to the floor.

"Now what?"

"Now nothing," Sara Coli replied softly.

"Why, did you tell him to do that then?" Kalitha asked in a fearful moan. "What is that going to do?"

"Nothing you simple, bitch!" Sara Coli released a bone chilling laugh. "Now at least we won't see them coming."

"God, help us," Trevor said.

A moment later they all began to scream.

****

Tony came running with his gun drawn. He didn't locate them until he was near the chamber. By the time he reached it, the door was sealed shut. The staff began to crowd the hallway to the secret chamber as he tried to open the door. He heard a gunshot and began to panic. Looking for the help he spotted a maid.

"Call the police. Go, get help." A moment later he heard three blood curdling screams.

"Sara Coli!" he yelled. "Sara Coli!"

Tony began to bang on the door. "Oh God." A tear formed in his eyes as he rested his forehead against the door, hearing their screams loud and clear.

Chapter 21

The media circuits had a field day with the White Estate incident. The hospital was calling it a double miracle. Two people had survived the deadliest spider attack ever recorded in North Carolina. Sara Coli was already back up and moving. After a tough fight with N.C. about the exotic species laws, she had won and kept her rights to keep her rare breed of White Widow Spiders.

Kalitha's prints were all over the weapon so it was being written up as an attempt on Sara Coli's life by the soon to be divorcee. The residue on Kalitha's hands had proven that she had fired all eight shots and Sara Coli's attorneys had it air tight. She was the victim in the end. The same way they had made her the victim in the beginning. It was all over the news about the adultress, Kalitha Mason, and how she had tried to stop her husband from leaving her for Sara Coli.

She and Trevor were the victims, simple as that. Even beyond her life and buried in the grave, Kalitha was still losing the battle with Sara Coli. She had given her a befitting burial by having her buried in a five hundred thousand dollar casket. She felt as though she had kept her end of the bargain by doing so.

Sara Coli folded the newspaper up and looked down the hall. She didn't like hospitals, but her Randale was inside of the room that she patiently sat outside of. She looked up to Tony and was warmed by his genuine smile.

"I'm going for coffee. Want some?"

"No darling. I'm fine."

He smiled again, nodded, and walked off. She saw the doctor's coming out and stood to meet him. "Mrs. White?" he asked softly.

"Yes," she responded anxiously. "Is he okay?"

He nodded and smiled brightly. "Yes, ma'am. I'm happy to report that he's doing just fine. His vital signs are strong and he's actually speaking."

She smiled and held her hands over her heart. "It's been two weeks. Is his memory okay?"

"As far as we can tell, he's doing amazingly well considering the one hundred and two spider bites."

"May I?" She nodded to the room. "May I see him?"

"I don't see why not," he said, closing his clipboard. "Oh, and one other thing," the doctor warned her. "His hair is, well, different."

Sara Coli walked in and found Trevor watching the news on the television. She sat down at his side and looked at him. He looked over at her and gave her a weak smile.

"Are you alright, my love?"

"I feel different," he replied, rubbing his silvery white hair. "How did I survive? How did we survive?"

"The venom was counteracted by the herbs, darling," she said smiling. "Weren't you ever listening?"

He looked away, then back to her and she could tell what was on his mind. "Randale, I'm sorry about Kalitha"

"Please," he cut her off. "Save it."

She touched him on the shoulder. She never wanted to bring him pain and didn't want him to be upset with her neither. She loved him and only wanted him to love her the same. The thought of anything less tormented her.

"I only have two questions."

"Yes, my love," she said, holding his hand.

"Did the White Widows survive?"

She nodded her response.

He fingered for her to come closer as he looked around suspiciously. He leaned in close and whispered near her ear.

"Then where is my fix?"

THE END.

Order Information
Wynn Publishing
P.O. Box 40411
Raleigh, N.C. 27629
www.wynnpubication.com
wynnpublications@yahoo.com
Contact: 984-220-2638

We accept Visa, MasterCard, Ammex, PayPal and Cash App.

SEND MONEY ORDER/CHECK TO:

WYNN PUBLICATIONS
P.O, Box 40411
2777 Brentwood RD.
Raleigh, NC 27604

NAME	
ADDRESS	
CITY	
STATE	ZIP
EMAIL	

BOOK TITLE	PRICE EACH	QUANTITY	TOTAL
BEHIND THE MASK	12.00		
FALSE	12.00		
MY BROTHERS KEEPER PT 1	12.00		
MY BROTHERS KEEPER PT 2	12.00		
A WHORE'S CONSCIENCE	12.00		
TAINTED	12.00		

	TOTAL	
THANK YOU FOR YOUR BUSINESS	SHIPPING & HANDLING	6.00
	FINAL TOTAL	

www.ingramcontent.com/pod-product-compliance
Lightning Source LLC
Chambersburg PA
CBHW070858180626
46817CB00003B/813